VALENTINE

VALENTINE
George Sand

TRANSLATED BY GEORGE BURNHAM IVES

———

With a Chronology
of Her Life and Work

———

Academy Chicago Publishers
1995

Published by
Academy Chicago Publishers
363 West Erie Street
Chicago, IL 60610

Chronology © Academy Chicago Publishers 1977

First Printing 1978
Second Printing 1995

Printed and bound in the USA.

Cover: Jean-Honoré Fragonard, *The Stolen Kiss*, c. 1786-89.

Library of Congress Cataloging-in-Publication Data
Sand, George, pseud. of Mme. Dudevant, 1804-1876.
        Valentine.

        Reprint of the 1902 ed. published by G. Barrie,
Philadelphia, as a volume The Masterpieces of George Sand.
        I. Title.
PZ3.S21 Vol. 1978 [PQ2411] 843'.8 77-28026
ISBN 0-915864-59-2 pbk.
ISBN 0-915864-60-6 lib. bdg.

GEORGE SAND: CHRONOLOGY

1804
July 1: Birth at 15 rue Meslée, Paris, to Maurice Dupin and Sophie-Victoire Delaborde. Christened Amantine-Lucile-Aurore. Family moves to rue de la Grande-Batelière, Paris.

1808
Aurore travels to Spain with her mother. They join her father at the Palace de Godoy in Madrid where he is serving in Napoleon's army under General Murat. The family travels to Nohant in France, the home of Maurice Dupin's mother, born Marie-Aurore de Saxe, Comtesse de Horne, daughter of the illegitimate son of King Frederick-Augustus II of Poland.
Sept 16: Death of Maurice Dupin, age 30, in a fall from a horse.

1809
Feb 3: Sophie-Victoire gives custody of Aurore to Mme Dupin de Francueil, her mother-in-law, in return for payment of Maurice's debts and a pension of 1000 francs a year.

1810-1814
Winters in Paris at rue Neuve-des-Mathurins with her grandmother. Visits from Sophie-Victoire. Summers at Nohant.

1818-1820
Educated at the English Convent des Augustines in Paris.

1820
Returns to Nohant. Studies with her father's tutor, Deschartres. Rides horseback in male clothing.

1821
Death of Mme Dupin de Francueil. Aurore inherits money, a house in Paris and the house at Nohant.

1822
Moves in with her mother at 80 rue St-Lazare, Paris.
April: Meets Casimir-François Dudevant, son of Baron Dudevant, on a visit to the Duplessis family.
September 10: Marries Dudevant. They move to Nohant in October.

1823
June 30: Maurice is born at Hôtel de Florence, 56 rue Neuve-des-Mathurins, Paris.

1824
Spring and summer at the Duplessis' at Plessis-Picard near Melun; autumn at a Parisian suburb, Ormesson; winter in an apartment at rue du Faubourg-St Honoré.

1825
Spring at Nohant. Aurore is ill in the summer. Dudevants travel to his family home in Gascony. Vacation in the Pyrenees where she meets Aurélian de Sèze and recovers her health.
Nov 5: Writes long letter to Casimir confessing attraction to de Sèze. She gives him up. Winter in Gascony.

1827
Takes Stéphane de Grandsagne as lover. They meet in Paris.

1828
Sept 13: Birth of Solange.

1829
Writes *Voyage en Auvergne*, unpublished in her lifetime. Sees de Sèze.

1830
Visit to de Sèze in Bordeaux. Their correspondence ceases. She writes a novel, *Aimée*, which she later burns. Meets new lover, Jules Sandeau.
Dec: Discovers Casimir's will, filled with antipathy toward her. Decides to separate from him, to spend half the year in Paris, leaving the children in Nohant.

1831
Jan 4: Moves to Paris, to 31 rue de Seine, to live secretly with Sandeau. Joins staff of *Le Figaro*. Writes three short stories: "La Molinara" (in *Figaro*), "La Prima Donna" (in *Revue de Paris*) and "La Fille d'Albano" (in *La Mode*).
April: Returns to Nohant for three months. Writes *Indiana*.
July: Moves to 25 Quai St-Michel, Paris.
Dec: Publishes *Rose et Blanche* in collaboration with Jules Sandeau. Book is signed Jules Sand.

1832

Travel between Paris and Nohant.
April: Brings Solange to Paris. Quarrels with Sandeau.
May: *Indiana* published.
Nov: Moves to 19 Quai Malaquais with Solange. *Valentine* published. Maurice sent by Casimir to the Lycée Henri Quatre in Paris.

1833

Breaks with Sandeau.
June: Meets Alfred de Musset.
Publishes *Lélia*.
Sept: To Fontainebleau with Musset.
Dec 10: To Italy with Musset.
Publishes novellas in various journals.

1834

Jan 19: Hotel Danieli in Venice. Musset attempts a break with Aurore, becomes ill. His physician is Pietro Pagello.
March 29: Musset returns to Paris. Aurore remains with Pagello. Publication of *André, Mattéa, Jacques, Léone Léoni* and the first *Lettres d'un Voyageur*.
July: Returns to Paris with Pagello.
Aug 24: Musset goes to Baden.
Aug 29: Aurore to Nohant.
Oct: Returns to Paris. Musset returns from Baden. Pagello returns to Venice.
Nov 25: Begins journal to de Musset.
Dec: Returns to Nohant.

1835
Jan: Returns to Paris.
Mar 6: Final break with de Musset.
Meets Michel de Bourges, her lawyer and political mentor.
Writes *Simon*.
Autumn: Returns to Nohant for Maurice's holiday.
Oct 19: Casimir threatens her physically. Begins suit for legal separation.
Dec 1: Judgment in her favor won by default.

1836
Feb 16: She wins second judgment. Casimir brings suit.
May 10, 11: Another verdict in her favor from civil court of La Chatre. Casimir appeals to a higher court.
July 25, 26: Trial in royal court of Bourges. Jury divided. Out-of-court settlement. Her fortune is divided with Casimir.
Aug: To Switzerland with Maurice and Solange, Franz Liszt and Aurore's friend Marie d'Agoult.
Autumn: Hôtel de la France, 15 rue Lafitte, Paris, with Liszt and d'Agoult. Meets Chopin.

1837
Jan: Returns to Nohant.
Publishes *Mauprat* in spring. Writes *Les Maîtres Mosaïstes*. Liszt and d'Agoult visit Nohant. Fatal illness of Sophie-Victoire in Paris. Visit to Fontainebleau. Writes *La Dernière Aldini*. Trip to Gascony to recover Solange, who has been kidnapped by Casimir.

1838

Writes *L'Orco* and *L'Uscoque*, two Venetian novels.
May: To Paris. Romance with Chopin.
Nov: Trip to Majorca with children and Chopin.
Writes *Spiridion*. *La Dernière Aldini* published.

1839

Feb: Leaves Majorca for three months in Marseilles. Then
to Nohant.
Publishes *L'Uscoque*, *Spiridion* and revised *Lélia*.
Oct: Occupies adjoining apartments with Chopin until
spring of 1841 at 16 rue Pigalle, Paris. Summer is spent at
Nohant, with Chopin as guest.

1840

Writes *Le Compagnon du Tour de France* and *Horace*. Influenced by Pierre Leroux. Publication of *Gabriel, Cosima*, a
novel based on her play.

1841

Moves from rue Pigalle to 5 and 9 rue St-Lazare, Square
d'Orléans, with Chopin. Publication of *Pauline*.

1842

Vols 1 and 2 of *Consuelo* published, and *Horace*. Chopin
and Delacroix at Nohant. Publishes *Un Hiver à Majorque*.

1843

Vols 3-4 of *Consuelo* published, along with *Fanchette* and
vols 1-2 of *La Comtesse de Rudolstadt*, the sequel to *Consuelo*.

1844

Jeanne published, first of the pastoral novels. Also the last vols of *La Comtesse de Rudolstadt.* Established liberal newspaper *L'Éclaireur.* Writes articles on *Politics and Socialism.*

1845

Publishes *Le Meunier d'Angibault.*

1846

Publishes *La Mare au Diable,* second pastoral novel, *Isidora,* and *Teverino.*

1847

Solange marries Auguste-Jean Clésinger. Estrangement from Chopin, who has sided with Solange in a family quarrel, and whose health is deteriorating. *Lucrezia Floriani, Le Péché de M. Antoine* and *Le Piccinino* published.

1848

On behalf of the Second Republic, writes government circulars, contributes to *Bulletins de la République* and publishes her newspaper *La Cause du Peuple.* Death of Solange's newborn daughter.

1849

La Petite Fadette published. Birth of Solange's daughter Jeanne-Gabriel. *François le Champi* successfully performed as a play at the Odéon theater in Paris.

1850

Begins liason with Alexandre Manceau, Maurice's friend. *François le Champi* published as both play and novel.

1851

Republic falls. Plays *Claudie* and *Le Mariage de Victorine* published.

1852

Uses her influence with Louis Napoleon to save her friends from political reprisal. Solange and her husband quarrel, leave Jeanne-Gabriel with Sand at Nohant.

1853

Death of Michel de Bourges. *Les Maîtres Sonneurs, La Filleule, Mont-Revêche* published.

1854

Clésingers officially separated. Vols 1-4 of *Histoire de Ma Vie, Adriani* and *Flaminio* published.

1855

Jan 13: Death of Jeanne-Gabriel at school. Visit to Italy with Maurice and Alexandre Manceau. Vols 5-20 of *Histoire de Ma Vie* published.

1856

Does French adaptation of *As You Like It.*

1857

Death of Musset. Manceau buys cottage at Gargilesse for himself and Sand. *Le Diable aux Champs* and *La Daniella* published.

1858
Holidays at Gargilesse on River Creuse, 30 miles from Nohant, with Monceau. *Les Beaux Messieurs de Bois-Doré* published and *Légendes Rustiques*, illustrated by Maurice.

1859
Publishes *Elle et Lui, L'Homme de Neige, Les Dames Vertes, Promenades Autour d'un Village, La Guerre* and *Garibaldi.*

1860
Writes *La Ville Noire* and *Marquis de Villemer.*
Nov: Contracts typhus or typhoid fever.

1862
Marriage of Maurice to Caroline Calametta. *Autour de la Table, Souvenirs et Impressions Littéraires* published.

1863
Marc-Antoine Dudevant born, son of Maurice and Caroline. Manceau and Maurice quarrel. *Mademoiselle La Quintinie* and *Pourquoi les Femmes à l'Académie?* published.

1864
Death of Marc-Antoine Dudevant. Play *Le Marquis de Villemer* presented. Moves from 3 rue Racine near the Odéon to 97 rue des Feuillantines. Leaves Nohant, because of difficulties with Maurice, to stay at Palaiseau with Manceau.

1865
Aug 21: Death of Manceau from tuberculosis, at Palaiseau. *La Confession d'une Jeune Fille* and *Laura* published.

xiv

1866

Birth of Aurore Dudevant to Maurice and Caroline. Visits Flaubert at Croisset, dedicates *Le Dernier Amour* to him. *Monsieur Sylvestre* published.

1867

Return to Nohant. Publishes *Le Dernier Amour*.

1868

Birth of Gabrielle Sand Dudevant.

1870

Play *L'Autre* with Sarah Bernhardt. *Pierre Qui Roule, Le Beau Laurence* and *Malgré Tout* published.

1871

Death of Casimir Dudevant. Seige of Paris. Sand protests Paris Commune. *Césarine Dietrich* and *Journal d'un Voyageur pendant la Guerre* published.

1872

Turgenev visits Nohant. *Francia* and *Nanon* published.

1873

Flaubert and Turgenev at Nohant. Travels in France. *Impressions et Souvenirs* and *Contes d'une Grand-mère* published.

1874

Ma Soeur Jeanne published.

1875
Flamande and *Les Deux Frères* published.

1876
June 8: Death of George Sand. *Le Tour de Percemont* and *Marianne Chevreuse* published.

VALENTINE

1

In the southeastern part of Berri there is a peculiarly picturesque bit of country some three or four leagues in extent. As the highroad from Paris to Clermont, which passes through it, is thickly settled on both sides, it is difficult for the traveller to suspect the beauty of the country near at hand. But he who, seeking shade and silence, should turn aside into one of the winding roads, enclosed between high banks, which branch off from the main highway at every moment, would soon see before him a cool and tranquil landscape, fields of a delicate green, melancholy streamlets, clumps of alders and ash trees—a delicious pastoral scene. In vain would he seek within a radius of several leagues a house built of stone or with a slated roof. At rare intervals a tiny thread of blue smoke, rising slowly above the foliage, would announce that a thatched roof was near at hand ; and if he should spy above the walnut trees on the hill the weather vane of a little church, a few steps farther on he would come upon a bell-tower sheathed in moss-covered tiles, a dozen scattered cottages surrounded by their orchards and their hemp-fields, a brook with its bridge formed of three pieces of timber, a cemetery a few rods square, enclosed by a quick-set hedge, five elms arranged in a quincunx and a ruined tower. This is what is called in the province a *bourg*.

There is nothing like the absolute repose of those unknown regions. Luxury has not found its way thither, nor the arts, nor the mania for scientific investigation, nor the hundred-armed monster called industry. Revolutions are hardly perceptible there, and the last war of which the soil retains a barely perceptible trace is that between Huguenots and Catholics ; and, even of that, the tradition is so uncertain and so faint that if you should question the natives, they would reply that those things took place at least two thousand years ago ; for the principal virtue of that race of tillers of the soil is heedlessness in the matter of antiquities. You can travel all over their domains, pray before their saints, drink from their wells, without ever running the risk of having to listen to the usual feudal chronicles or the indispensable miraculous legend. The grave and silent disposition of the peasant is not one of the least potent attractions of that region. Nothing surprises him, nothing attracts him. Your chance presence in his pathway will not even make him turn his head, and, if you ask him to direct you to a town or a farm, his sole response will be a condescending smile, as if to prove to you that he is not deceived by your pleasantry. The peasant of Berri cannot understand how a man can walk without knowing where he is going. His dog will hardly deign to bark after you ; his children will hide behind the hedge to evade your eyes or your questions, and the smallest of them, if he has not been able to follow his brothers in their flight, will throw himself into the ditch from fright, shrieking with all his strength. But the most impassive countenance will be that of a great white ox, the inevitable dean of every pasture, who, staring fixedly at you from among the bushes, will seem to hold in check the less solemn and less kindly disposed family of frightened bulls.

Aside from this initial coldness to the overtures of the stranger, the husbandman of that region is pleasant and hospitable, like his peaceful glades, like his aromatic meadows.

A particular tract of land between two small streams is especially remarkable for the healthy dark hues of its vegetation, which have caused it to be called the *Black Valley*. It is peopled only by scattered cottages and a few farms which yield a good revenue. The farm called *Grangeneuve* is of considerable size, but in the simplicity of its aspect there is nothing at variance with that of its surroundings. An avenue of maples leads to the house, and at the foot of the rustic buildings the Indre, in that place nothing more than a babbling brook, flows peacefully among the rushes and yellow irises of the meadow.

The first of May is a day of excitement and merrymaking for the people of the Black Valley. At its farther end, about two leagues from its centre, where Grangeneuve is situated, there is held one of those rustic fêtes which in every province bring together all the people of the neighborhood, from the sub-prefect of the department to the pretty grisette who has plaited that functionary's shirt-frill on the preceding day ; from the noble châtelaine to the little shepherd—*pâtour* is the local word—who pastures his goat and his sheep at the expense of the seignioral hedges. They all come to eat and dance on the grass, with more or less appetite, more or less enjoyment ; they all exhibit themselves in calèches or on donkey-back, in caps or Italian straw hats, in clogs of poplar-wood or slippers of Turkish satin, in silk dresses or drugget skirts. It is a red-letter day for the pretty girls, a day of retribution for beauty, when the somewhat problematical charms of the salons are summoned forth into the bright sunlight, to compete with the vigorous health and blooming youth of the village maidens ; when the masculine areopagus is made up of judges of all ranks, and the contending parties are brought face to face, amid the dust and under the blaze of keen glances, while the violins are playing. Many righteous triumphs, many well-merited reparations, many long contested judgments, make the day of the *fête champêtre* memorable in the annals of coquetry ; and the first of May was, in the Black Valley as elsewhere, a great subject of secret rivalry between the peasant women in their Sunday clothes and the ladies of the neighboring town.

But it was at Grangeneuve that the most formidable arsenal of these artless fascinations was prepared for use early in the morning. It was in a large, low room, lighted by small-paned windows ; the walls were covered with a gaudy-hued paper, which clashed with the blackened beams of the ceiling, the solid oak doors, and the common clothes-press. In that imperfectly decorated apartment, where the classic rusticity of its primitive condition was emphasized by some handsome modern furniture, a lovely girl of sixteen stood before the scalloped gilt frame of an old mirror which seemed to lean forward to admire her, giving the last touches to a costume more gorgeous than refined. But Athénaïs, the honest farmer's only heir, was so youthful, so rosy, so delicious to look upon, that she seemed graceful and natural even in her borrowed finery. While she arranged the folds of her tulle dress, madame her mother was stooping in front of the door, with her sleeves rolled up to the elbow, preparing in a huge kettle some sort of a compound of bran and water, about which a demi-brigade of ducks stood in good order, in an ecstasy of anticipation. A bright and joyous sunbeam entered through the open door, and fell upon the gayly bedecked maiden, rosy-cheeked and dainty, so different from her buxom, sun-burned, homespun-clad mother.

At the other end of the room, a young man dressed in black sat carelessly on a couch and gazed at Athénaïs without speaking. But his features did not express that effusive, childish delight which every one of the girl's movements betrayed. At times indeed a faint expression of irony and compassion seemed to raise the corners of his large, thin-lipped, mobile mouth.

Monsieur Lhéry, or Père Lhéry, as he was still called from habit by the peasants whose companion and equal he had been for many years, was placidly warming his white-stockinged shins at the fire of fagots which burned on the hearth at all seasons, as the custom is in the country. He was a most worthy man, still hale and hearty, and he wore striped short-clothes, a flowered waistcoat, a long coat and a queue. The queue is a priceless vestige of the past, which is rapidly vanishing on French soil. Berri having suffered less than any other province from the inroads of civilization, that style of head-dress still prevails there among a few loyal adherents in the class of half-bourgeois, half-rustic farmers. In their youth it was the first step toward aristocratic habits, and they would consider that they were going backward to-day, if they should deprive their heads of that social distinction. Monsieur Lhéry had protected his against the satirical assaults of his daughter, and it was perhaps the only subject upon which Athénaïs's doting father had refused to accede to her wishes during her whole life.

"Come, come, mamma!" said Athénaïs, fastening the golden clasp of her black belt, "haven't you finished feeding your ducks? Aren't you dressed yet? Why, we shall never get started!"

"Patience, patience, my girl!" said Mère Lhéry, distrib-
uting the food among her fowls with noble impartiality;
"I shall have all the time I need to fix myself while
they're hitching Mignon to the wagon. Ah! bless my
soul, my child, I don't need all the time you do! I am no
longer young; and when I was, I didn't have the time
nor the means to make myself pretty as you do. I
didn't spend two hours over my dressing, I tell you!"

"Are you reproaching me now?" said Athénaïs with a
pout.

"No, my girl, no," replied the old woman. "Enjoy
yourself, make yourself *fine*, my child; you are rich,
make the most of your father and mother's hard work.
We are too old to enjoy it now. And then, when you've
got into the habit of being poor, you can't get out of it.
I might have servants to wait on me for my money, but
it's impossible; the old habit is too strong for me, and I
must do everything in the house with my own hands.
But you play the great lady, my girl; you were
brought up for that; it's what your father intended;
you're not made for any ploughboy, and the husband
you get will be glad enough to find you with white
hands, eh?"

As Madame Lhéry finished wiping her kettle and de-
livering this affectionate rather than sensible harangue,
she made a grimace at the young man by way of a
smile. He pretended not to notice it, and Père Lhéry,
who was gazing at his shoe buckles in the state of
vacuous stupidity so sweet to the peasant in his hours of
repose, lifted his half-closed eyes to his future son-in-
law, as if to share his satisfaction. But the future son-
in-law in order to escape those mute attentions, rose,
changed his seat, and finally said to Madame Lhéry:

"Shall I go to get the carriage ready, aunt?"

"Go, my boy, go if you will. I shan't keep you waiting."

The nephew was about to leave the room when a fifth person entered, who, in manner and in costume, presented a striking contrast to the occupants of the farmhouse.

II

She was a small, slender woman, who seemed, at first glance, to be about twenty-five years of age ; but, upon a closer view, one might credit her with thirty years and not be too liberal to her. Her slight and well proportioned figure still had the grace of youth ; but her face, which was both distinguished and pretty, bore the marks of grief, which is even more blasting in its effects than the lapse of years. Her careless attire, her undressed hair, her tranquil manner, were sufficiently indicative of her purpose not to attend the fête. But, in the diminutive size of her slipper, in the modest and graceful arrangement of her gray dress, in the whiteness of her neck, in her firm and elastic step, there was more genuine aristocracy than in all Athénaïs's finery. And yet this imposing personage, at whose entrance all the others rose respectfully, bore no other name among her hosts at the farm than that of Mademoiselle Louise.

She offered her hand affectionately to Madame Lhéry, kissed her daughter on the forehead, and bestowed a friendly smile on the young man.

"Well," said Père Lhéry, "have you had a nice long walk this morning, my dear young lady ? "

"Guess where I really dared to go?" replied Mademoiselle Louise, seating herself familiarly beside him.

"Not to the château, I hope?" said the nephew, hastily.

"To the château, just so, Bénédict," she replied.

"How imprudent!" exclaimed Athénaïs, suspending for a moment the operation of crimping her curly locks, and curiously drawing near.

"Why so?" rejoined Louise; "didn't you tell me that all the servants had been changed except poor nurse? And she certainly would not have betrayed me if I had happened to meet her."

"But you might have met madame."

"At six o'clock in the morning? *Madame* stays in bed until noon."

"So you rose before dawn, did you?" said Bénédict. "Indeed, I thought that I heard you open the garden door."

"But there's *mademoiselle!*" exclaimed Madame Lhéry; "they say she's a very early riser, and very active. Suppose you had met her?"

"Ah! if I only could!" said Louise, excitedly; "I shall have no rest till I have seen her face, and heard the sound of her voice. You know her, Athénaïs; do tell me again that she is pretty and sweet and resembles her father!"

"There is someone here whom she resembles much more," replied Athénaïs, looking at Louise; "which is as much as to say that she is sweet and pretty."

Bénédict's face brightened and his eyes rested kindly on his fiancée.

"But listen," said Athénaïs to Louise, "if you're so anxious to see Mademoiselle Valentine, you should come to the fête with us; you can keep out of sight in Cousin

Simonne's house on the square, and from there you will
certainly see the ladies, for Mademoiselle Valentine assured me they would come."

"That is impossible, my dear love," Louise replied;
"I could not alight from the carriage without being recognized or suspected. Besides, there is only one person
in that family whom I want to see; the presence of the,
others would spoil the pleasure I anticipate in seeing her.
But we have talked enough about my plans; let us talk
of yours, Athénaïs. I should judge that you propose to
crush the whole province by such a display of bloom and
beauty!"

The young farmer-maid blushed with delight and kissed
Louise with a warmth which demonstrated clearly
enough the artless satisfaction she felt in being admired.

"I am going to get my hat," she said; "you'll help
me to put it on, won't you?"

And she hurriedly ascended the wooden staircase leading to her chamber.

Meanwhile Mère Lhéry left the room by another door
to go to change her dress; her husband took a pitchfork
and went to give his instructions for the day to the herds-
man.

Thereupon Bénédict, being left alone with Louise, drew
closer to her and said in a low tone:

"You spoil Athénaïs like all the rest. You are the
only one who has any right to talk to her, and you do
not condescend to do it."

"Why, what cause of reproach have you against the
poor child?" said Louise, in amazement. "O Bénédict,
you are very hard to suit!"

"That is what everybody tells me, even you, mademoiselle, who are so well able to understand what I suffer from this young woman's character and absurdities!"

"Absurdities?" repeated Louise. "Can it be that you are not in love with her?"

Bénédict did not answer, but after a moment of silent embarrassment, he said:

"You must agree that her costume is extravagant to-day. The idea of dancing in the sun and dust in a ball dress, satin slippers, a cashmere shawl and feathers! Not only is such finery out of place, but I consider it in execrable taste. At her age, a young woman ought to think first of simplicity and to know how to embellish herself at small expense."

"Is it Athénaïs's fault if she has been brought up so? How much you make of trifles! Give your attention rather to pleasing her and obtaining supreme influence over her mind and heart; then you may be sure that your wishes will be laws to her. But you think only of thwarting her and contradicting her, and she so petted, so like a queen in her family! Remember how kind and how sensitive her heart is."

"Her heart, her heart! no doubt she has a good heart; but her intellect is so limited! her kindness of heart is all native, all born of the soil, like the plants which grow well or ill without understanding the reason. How I detest her coquetry! I shall have to give her my arm, walk her about and exhibit her at this fête, listen to the idiotic admiration of some and the idiotic disparagement of others! What a bore! I wish it were over!"

"What an extraordinary disposition! Do you know, Bénédict, I can't understand you. How many men in your place would take the greatest pride in being seen in public with the prettiest girl and the richest heiress in our whole district, in arousing the envy of twenty discarded rivals, in being able to say that you are her fiancé? Instead of that, you think of nothing but indulging in bitter criticism of some trivial failings, common to all young women of her class, whose education is not in harmony with their birth. You consider it a crime on her part to submit to the consequences of her parents' vanity—a most harmless sort of vanity after all, and something of which you should be the last to complain."

"I know it," he rejoined hastily, "I know all that you are going to say. They owed me nothing and they have given me everything. They took me in, the son of their brother, a peasant like themselves, but a poor peasant—me, a penniless orphan. They gave me a home, adopted me, and instead of putting me at the plough, to which I was apparently destined by the laws of society, they sent me to Paris at their expense ; they gave me an education, they transformed me into a bourgeois, a student, a wit, and they also intend their daughter for me, their rich, lovely and vain daughter. They have reserved her for me, they offer her to me! Oh! undoubtedly they are very fond of me, these simple-hearted and generous kindred of mine! but their blind affection has gone astray, and all the good they have sought to do me has changed into evil. Cursed be the passion for aspiring to a higher place than one can reach ! "

Bénédict stamped on the floor ; Louise looked at him with a pained but stern expression.

"Is this the way you talked yesterday, when you returned from the hunt, to that ignorant, shallow-brained young nobleman, who denied the benefits of education and wanted to arrest the progress of the inferior ranks of society ? What excellent arguments you had at hand to defend the propagation of knowledge, and the theory that all men should be free to grow and succeed ! Bénédict, this fickle, irresolute, disappointed mind of yours, this mind which scrutinizes and depreciates everything, surprises me and grieves me. I am afraid that in you the good seed is changing to tares ; I am afraid that you are much below your education, or much above it, which would be no less a misfortune."

"Louise, Louise !" said Bénédict in an altered voice, seizing the young woman's hand.

He gazed at her earnestly and with moist eyes ; Louise blushed and turned her eyes away with a displeased air. Bénédict dropped her hand and began to pace the floor excitedly and angrily ; then he returned to her and made an effort to become calm once more.

"You are too indulgent," he said to her ; "you have lived longer than I, and yet I think that you are much younger. You have the experience of your sentiments, which are noble and generous, but you have not studied the hearts of others, you have no suspicion of their deformities and pettiness ; you attach no importance to the imperfections of others, perhaps you do not even see them ! Ah ! mademoiselle, mademoiselle ! you are a very indulgent and a very dangerous guide."

"These are singular reproaches," said Louise with forced gayety. "Whose mentor have I assumed to be ? Have I not always told you, on the contrary, that I was no better fitted to guide others than to guide myself ? I lack experience, you say ? Oh ! I do not complain of that, I promise you !"

Tears rolled down Louise's cheeks. There was a moment's silence, during which Bénédict again approached and stood beside her, deeply moved and trembling. Trying to conceal her melancholy, Louise continued :

"But you are right ; I have lived too much within myself to observe others thoroughly. I have wasted too much time in suffering ; my life has been ill employed."

Louise discovered that Bénédict was weeping. She

was afraid of the young man's excessive sensitiveness, and, pointing to the courtyard, she motioned to him to go to assist his uncle, who was himself harnessing a stout Poitou nag to the family conveyance. But Bénédict did not grasp her meaning.

"Louise!" he said ardently; "Louise!" he repeated in a lower tone. "It is a pretty name," he continued, "so simple and so sweet! and you bear that name, while my cousin, who is so well fitted to milk cows and watch sheep, is named Athénaïs! I have another cousin named Zoraïde, and she has just named her little brat Adhémar! The nobles are perfectly justified in despising our absurd foibles; they are shocking! don't you think so? Here's a spinning-wheel, my good aunt's spinning-wheel; who supplies it with flax? who turns it patiently in her absence? Not Athénaïs. Oh! no! she would think that she debased herself if she touched a spindle; she would be afraid of going down again into the social condition from which she came if she should learn to do any useful work. No, no; she knows how to embroider, play the guitar, paint flowers and dance; but you, mademoiselle, who were born in opulence, know how to spin; you are sweet, humble and industrious. I hear footsteps overhead. She is coming; she had forgotten herself before her mirror, I doubt not!"

"Bénédict! do go to get your hat," cried Athénaïs from the top of the staircase.

"Pray, go!" said Louise in an undertone, seeing that Bénédict did not stir.

"Curse the fête!" he replied in the same tone. "I must go, so be it; but as soon as I have deposited my fair cousin on the greensward, I shall take pains to have my foot trodden on and return to the farm. Will you be here, Mademoiselle Louise?"

"No, monsieur, I shall not be here," she replied dryly. Bénédict's faced flushed with indignation. He made ready to go. Madame Lhéry reappeared in a less gorgeous but even more absurd costume than her daughter's. The satin and lace served admirably to set off the coppery tinge of her sunburned face, her strongly accentuated features and her plebeian gait. Athénaïs passed a quarter of an hour arranging her skirts, with much ill-humor, on the back seat of the carriage, reproving her mother for rumpling her sleeves by taking up too much room beside her, and regretting in her heart that the folly of her parents had not reached a point of procuring a *calèche*.

Père Lhéry held his hat on his knees, in order not to expose it to the risk of accident from the jolting of the vehicle by keeping it on his head. Bénédict mounted the front seat, and, as he took the reins, ventured to cast a last glance at Louise; but he encountered such a cold, stern expression in her eyes, that he lowered his own, bit his lips, and angrily lashed the horse. Mignon started off at a gallop, and, as she struck the deep mud holes in the road, imparted to the vehicle a series of violent shocks, most disastrous to the hats of the two *ladies* and to Athénaïs's temper.

III

But, after a few rods, the mare, being ill adapted by nature for racing, slackened her pace ; Bénédict's irascible mood passed away, giving place to shame and remorse ; and Père Lhéry slept soundly.

They followed one of the little grass-grown roads called in village parlance *traînes;* a road so narrow that the narrow carriage touched the branches of the trees on both sides, and that Athénaïs was able to pluck a large bunch of hawthorn by passing her arm, encased in a white glove, through the side window. There are no words to describe the freshness and charm of those little tortuous paths which wind capriciously in and out under the never-failing arbors of foliage, revealing at each turn fresh depths of shadow, ever greener and more mysterious. When the noonday sun burns even to its roots the tall, dense grass of the fields, when the insects buzz noisily and the quail amorously clucks in the furrows, coolness and silence seem to take refuge in the *traînes.* You may walk an hour there without hearing other sounds than the flight of a blackbird alarmed by your approach, or the leap of a little green frog, gleaming like an emerald, who was sleeping in his cabin of interlaced rushes. Even yonder ditch contains a whole world of inhabitants, a whole forest of plants ; its limpid water flows noiselessly over the clay, casting off its impurities, and kisses gently the watercress, balsam and hepatica on the banks ; the water-moss, the long grasses called *water ribbons,* the hairy, hanging aquatic mosses, quiver incessantly in its silent little eddies ; the yellow wagtail runs along the sand with a mischievous yet timid air ; the clematis and the honeysuckle shade it with leafy arbors where the nightingale hides his nest. In spring it is all flowers and fragrance ; in autumn, purple sloes cover the twigs which turn white first of all in April ; the red haw, of which the thrushes are so fond, replaces the hawthorn flower, and the bramble bushes, all covered with bits of fleece left by the sheep in passing through, are tinged with purple by small wild berries pleasant to the taste.

Bénédict, allowing the placid steed's reins to hang loosely, fell into a profound reverie. He was a young man of a strange temperament ; those who were closest to him, in default of another of the same sort to whom to liken him, considered him as being altogether outside of the common run of mankind. The majority despised him as a man incapable of doing anything useful and substantial ; and if they did not show in what slight esteem they held him, it was because they were forced to accord him the possession of true physical courage and enduring resentment. On the other hand, the Lhéry family, simple-hearted and kindly as they were, did not hesitate to accord him a place in the very highest rank in the matter of intellect and learning. Blind to his defects, those excellent people saw in their nephew simply a young man whose imagination was too fertile and his learning too extensive to allow him to enjoy repose of mind. But Bénédict, at the age of twenty-two, had not received what is called a practical education. At Paris, being possessed by love of art and of science in turn, he had become proficient in no specialty. He had worked hard, but he had stopped when practical application of what he had learned became necessary.

He had become disgusted just at the moment when others reap the fruit of their labors. To him love of study ended where the necessity of adopting a profession began. Having once acquired the treasures of art and science, he was no longer spurred on by the selfish impulse to apply them to his own interests; and as he did not know how to be useful to himself, people said when they saw him without occupation: "What is he good for?"

His cousin had been destined for him from the beginning of time; that was the best retort which could be made to those envious persons who accused the Lhérys of allowing their hearts as well as their minds to be corrupted by wealth. It cannot be denied that their common sense, the common sense of the peasant, usually so straightforward and sure, had received a rude blow in the bosom of prosperity. They had ceased to esteem the simple and modest virtues, and, after vain efforts to destroy them in themselves, they had done their utmost to stifle the germs of those virtues in their children; but they had not ceased to love them with almost equal affection, and, while working at their ruin, they had believed that they were working for their happiness.

Such a bringing-up had proved disastrous to both. Athénaïs, like soft and flexible wax, had acquired in a boarding-school at Orléans all the faults of provincial young ladies—vanity, ambition, envy and pettiness of spirit. However, goodness of heart was in her a sort of sacred heritage transmitted by her mother, and outside influences had been unable to destroy it. Thus there was much to hope for her from the lessons of experience and the future.

The harm done was greater in the case of Bénédict. Instead of benumbing his generous impulses, education had developed them immeasurably, and had changed them into a deplorable feverish sort of irritation. That ardent temperament, that impressionable soul needed a course of tranquillizing ideas, of repressive treatment. Perhaps, too, labor in the fields and bodily fatigue would have employed to advantage the excess of force which fermented to no purpose in that vigorous organization. The enlightenment of civilization, which has developed so many precious qualities, has, perhaps, vitiated quite as many. It is a misfortune of the generations placed between those which knew nothing and those which will know just enough : they know too much.

Lhéry and his wife could not understand the misfortunes of this situation. They refused even to imagine them, and having no conception of any other felicities than those which they could confer, they boasted artlessly of having the power to put Bénédict's ennui to flight : according to them it could be done by a good farm, a pretty farmer-maid, and a dowry of two hundred thousand francs in cash with which to begin housekeeping. But Bénédict was insensible to these flattering marks of their affection. Money aroused in him profound contempt, the enthusiastic, exaggerated contempt of a generation of young men often too quick to change their principles and to bend a converted knee before the god of the universe. Bénédict felt that he was consumed by a secret ambition ; but it was not that ; it was the ambition of his age, of the things which flatter the self-esteem in a nobler way.

He did not as yet know the special object of his vague and painful expectation. He had thought several times that he recognized it in the vivid caprices of his imagination. Those caprices had vanished without bringing him any lasting enjoyment. Now, he was constantly conscious of it as of a pitiless pain confined in his breast, and it had never tortured him so cruelly as when he least knew what use to make of it. Ennui, that horrible disease which is more prevalent at the present time than at any other period in the history of society, had attacked Bénédict's destiny in its bloom ; it stretched out like a black cloud over his whole future. It had already blighted the most priceless faculty of his age—hope.

At Paris, solitude had disgusted him. Although he considered it far preferable to society, it was too dismal in his little student's chamber, too dangerous for faculties so active as his. His health had suffered, and his kind-hearted relations, in dismay, had sent for him to return. He had been at home a month, and his complexion had already recovered the ruddy coloring of health ; but his heart was more perturbed than ever. The poetic atmosphere of the fields, to which he was so susceptible, excited to delirium the intensity of the unfathomed cravings which were consuming him. His home life, always so beneficent and soothing at first, whenever he made a trial of it, had already become more tedious than ever. He felt no inclination for Athénaïs. She was too far below the chimeras of his imagination, and the idea of settling down among the extravagant or puerile habits which were conjoined and contrasted in his family was hateful to him. His heart opened, it is true, to affection and gratitude ; but those sentiments were to him a source of constant combats and remorse. He could not refrain from reflections pitiless and cruel in their irony, at sight of all the mean and trivial struggles amid which he lived, of that mixture of parsimony and extravagance which makes the ways of the parvenu so ridiculous. Monsieur and Madame Lhéry, paternal and tyrannical at the same time, gave excellent wine to their farmhands on Sunday; during the week they reproved them for putting a dash of vinegar in their water. They readily supplied their daughter with a fine piano, a lemonwood toilet set and richly-bound books; they scolded her for throwing an extra stick on the fire. At home they were poor and niggardly, in order to make their servants industrious and economical; abroad they were puffed up with pride, and would have considered the slightest doubt of their opulence an insult. Kind-hearted, charitable, easily moved to pity as they were, they had succeeded, by their folly, in making themselves detested by their neighbors, who were even more vain and foolish than they.

These were failings which Bénédict could not endure. Youth is much more bitter and intolerant to old age than old age is to youth. But in the midst of his discouragement certain vague and confused impulses had shed a ray or two of hope upon his life. Louise, Madame or Mademoiselle Louise—she was called by both names indifferently—had taken up her abode at Grangeneuve about three weeks before. At first the difference in their ages had kept their acquaintance upon a tranquil, careless footing; certain preconceived ideas unfavorable to Louise, whom Bénédict had not seen for twelve years, speedily vanished in the pure and appealing fascination of intimate intercourse with her. Their tastes, their education, their sympathetic ideas had rapidly brought them together, and Louise, by virtue of her age, her misfortunes and her qualities, had acquired complete ascendancy over her young friend's mind. But the joys of this intimacy were of short duration. Bénédict, always quick to pass the goal, always eager to deify his admirations, and to poison his pleasures by carrying them to excess, imagined that he was in love with Louise, that she was the one woman after his own heart, and that he could not live where she was not. It was the error of a day. The coldness with which Louise received his timid declarations angered more than it grieved him. In his resentment he inwardly accused her of pride and lack of heart. Then he recalled her misfortunes and admitted to himself that she was no less deserving of respect than of compassion. On two or three occasions he was conscious of a rekindling of the impetuous aspirations of a heart too passionate for friendship; but Louise was able to soothe him. She did not employ to that end the reason which goes astray while splitting hairs; her experience taught her to distrust compassion; she manifested none for him, and although her heart was by no means disposed to harshness, she resorted to it to effect the young man's cure. The emotion which Bénédict had displayed during their interview that morning had been, as it were, his last attempt at rebellion. Now he repented of his folly, and, buried in his reflections, he felt, in his ever increasing disquietude, that the time had not come for him to love anybody or anything exclusively.

Madame Lhéry broke the silence with a trivial remark.

"You'll stain your gloves with those flowers," she said to her daughter. "Pray remember that *madame* said the other day before you: 'You can always recognize a woman of the common people in the provinces by her feet and hands.' She didn't think, the dear soul, that we might take that to ourselves."

"On the contrary, I think she said it expressly for us. Poor mamma, you know Madame de Raimbault very little if you think that she would regret having insulted us."

"Insulted us!" rejoined Madame Lhéry. "She

meant to *insult* us ? I'd like to see her do it ! Yes, indeed I would ! Do you suppose I'd stand an insult from
anybody, I don't care who ? "

"Still, we shall have to put up with more than one
impertinence so long as we are her farmers. Farmers,
always farmers ! when we have an estate at least as
good as madame la comtesse's ! Papa, I won't let you
alone till you've got rid of this wretched farm. I don't
like it, I can't endure it."

Père Lhéry shook his head.

"Three thousand francs profit every year is always a
good thing to have," he replied.

"It would be better to earn three thousand francs less
and recover our liberty, enjoy our wealth, free ourselves
from the kind of tyranny that that harsh, arrogant woman
exercises over us."

"Psha ! " said Madame Lhéry, "we almost never
have dealings with her. Since that unfortunate event
she comes to the province every five or six years only.
This time she came only on account of her *demoiselle's*
wedding. Who knows that this won't be the last time ?
It's my belief that Mademoiselle Valentine will have the
château and the farm for her dowry. Then what a kind
mistress we should have ! "

"To be sure, Valentine is a dear girl," said Athénaïs,
proud to be able to speak in that familiar tone of a person
whose rank she envied. "Oh ! she's not proud ; she
hasn't forgotten that we played together when we were
little. And then she has the good sense to understand
that money is the only distinguishing mark, and that our
money's as honorable as hers."

"I should say so ! " rejoined Madame Lhéry ; "for
she has only had the trouble of being born, while we
have earned our money by hard work and at our peril.

But still there's nothing to say against her; she's a good
young lady and a pretty girl, *da!* Did you ever see her,
Bénédict?"

"Never, aunt."

"And then I'm attached to that family," continued
Madame Lhéry. "The father was such a good man!
There was a real man for you! and handsome! A general, on my word, all covered with gold and crosses, and
he asked me to dance on fête-days just as if I was a
duchess. Madame didn't like that much——"

"Nor I, either," observed Père Lhéry, ingenuously.

"That Père Lhéry," retorted his wife, "must always
have his joke. But all the same, what I mean to say is
that, except for madame, who's a little high and mighty,
it's a fine family. Can anyone find a better woman than
the grandmother?"

"Ah!" said Athénaïs, "she's the best of all. She always has something pleasant to say to you; she never
calls you anything but *my heart,* or *my beauty,* or *my
pretty puss.*"

"And that always pleases you!" said Bénédict, mockingly. "Well, well, add that to the three thousand francs
profit, which will buy a good many gewgaws——"

"Eh! that isn't to be despised, is it, my boy?" said
Père Lhéry. "Just tell her so; she'll listen to you."

"No, no, I won't listen to anything," cried the girl.
"I won't let you alone tell you've left the farm. Your
lease expires in six months; you mustn't renew it, do
you hear, papa?"

"But what shall I do?" said the old man, shaken by
the wheedling yet imperious tone adopted by his daughter. "Must I fold my arms, I'd like to know? I can't
amuse myself reading and singing, like you; ennui will
kill me."

" But, papa, haven't you your property to look out for ? "

" It all takes care of itself so nicely ! there won't be anything left for me to do. And another thing, where shall we live ? You don't want to live with the tenant farmers, do you ? "

" No, certainly not ! you must build ; we'll have a house of our own ; we'll decorate it very differently from that nasty farm-house ; you shall see how well I understand such things ! "

" Yes, no doubt, you understand all about eating up money," retorted her father.

Athénaïs began to sulk.

" All right," she said spitefully, " do as you please ; perhaps you'll be sorry you didn't listen to me ; but then it will be too late."

" What do you mean ? " queried Bénédict.

" I mean," she replied, " that, when Madame de Raimbault finds out who the person is whom we have been boarding for three weeks, she will be furious with us, and will turn us out at the end of the lease with all sorts of lawyer's tricks and spiteful treatment. Wouldn't it be better to have the honors of war on our side and retire before we are driven back ? "

This reflection seemed to produce an impression on the Lhérys. They said nothing, and Bénédict, who was more and more disgusted with Athénaïs's remarks, did not hesitate to put a bad construction on her last argument.

" That is to say," he rejoined, " you mean to blame your parents for making Madame Louise welcome ? "

Athénaïs started and glanced at Bénédict in amazement, her face inflamed by anger and chagrin. Then she turned pale and burst into tears.

Bénédict understood her and took her hand.

"Oh! this is frightful," she cried in a voice broken by sobs, "to interpret my words so! when I love Madame Louise like my own sister!"

"Come, come, it's a misunderstanding!" said Père Lhéry; "kiss and make it up."

Bénédict kissed his cousin, whose cheeks at once recovered their usual lovely color.

"Come, child, wipe away your tears," said Mère Lhéry; "we're almost there; don't let people see you with red eyes; here's somebody looking for you already."

In truth the strains of violin and bagpipe could be heard, and several young men lay in ambush on the road, awaiting the arrival of the young ladies, in order to be the first to ask them to dance.

IV

They were young men of the same class as Bénédict, but had not his superior education, which they were inclined to look upon as a cause of reproach rather than as an advantage. Several of them were not without aspirations to the hand of Athénaïs.

"A fine prize!" cried one who had mounted a hillock to watch for the carriages; "it's Mademoiselle Lhéry, the beauty of the Black Valley."

"Gently, Simonneau! she belongs to me; I have been courting her for a year. By right of priority, if you please!"

The one who spoke thus was a tall, sturdy fellow

with a black eye, copper-colored skin and broad shoulders; he was the son of the richest cattle-dealer in the province.

"That's all very well, Pierre Blutty," said the first speaker, "but her intended is with her."

"What's that! her intended?" cried all the rest.

"To be sure; Cousin Bénédict."

"Ah! Bénédict, the lawyer, the fine talker, the scholar!"

"Oh! Père Lhéry 'll give him gold crowns enough to make something good of him."

"He's going to marry her?"

"He's going to marry her."

"Oh! but he hasn't done it yet!"

"The parents are set on it, the girl's set on it; it would be devilish strange if the man should refuse."

"We mustn't stand that, you fellows," cried Georges Moret. "On my soul, we should have a fine neighbor, shouldn't we? What mighty airs the *spitter of Greek* would put on! That fellow get the prettiest girl and the prettiest dowry? No, may God strike me dumb rather!"

"The little one's a flirt; the pale gawk"—that was the name they gave Bénédict—"isn't handsome, neither is he a lady's man. It's our place to prevent this match. I say, comrades, the luckiest one of us will treat all the others on his wedding day. But first of all we must learn what to expect about Bénédict's pretensions."

As he spoke, Pierre Blutty walked into the middle of the road, seized the horse's bridle, and having forced the animal to halt, presented his respects and his invitation to the young woman. Bénédict was desirous to atone for his unjust treatment of her; moreover, although he was not anxious to dispute possession of her with numerous rivals, he was very glad to mortify them a little.

So he leaned against the front of the carriage in such a way as to conceal Athénaïs from them.

" Messieurs, my cousin thanks you with all her heart," he said to them ; " but you will allow me to have the first contra-dance. She has just promised me ; you are a little late."

And, without waiting for a second invitation, he lashed the horse and drove into the village, raising clouds of dust.

Athénaïs did not anticipate such pleasure. On the day before, and again that morning, Bénédict, as he did not wish to dance with her, had pretended that he had sprained his ankle, and could not walk without limping. When she saw him walking by her side, with a determined air, her heart leaped for joy ; for, not only would it have been humiliating to the self-esteem of so pretty a girl not to open the dance with her fiancé, but Athénaïs really loved Bénédict. She instinctively realized all his superiority to herself, and as there is always a goodly share of vanity in love, she was flattered by the thought that she was destined to belong to a man who was better educated than any of those in her circle. So that she was really dazzling with bloom and animation ; and her costume, which Bénédict had criticized so severely, seemed charming to less refined tastes. The women turned green with jealousy, and the men proclaimed Athénaïs Lhéry the queen of the ball.

But toward evening that brilliant star paled before the purer and more radiant light of Mademoiselle de Raimbault.

As he heard that name passing from mouth to mouth, Bénédict, impelled by curiosity, followed the crowds of admirers who thronged her path. In order to see her, he was compelled to mount a pedestal of unhewn stone, on which stood a cross held in great veneration in the village. That act of impiety—of thoughtlessness rather —caused everyone to look at him, and, as Mademoiselle de Raimbault's eyes followed the same direction as those of the multitude, he had an unobstructed full-face view of her. He did not like her face. He had imagined a sallow, dark, passionate, mobile, Spanish type of woman, and he was unwilling to accept any other. Mademoiselle Valentine did not realize his ideal ; she was fair, tall, rosy, placid, admirably beautiful in every respect. She had none of those defects with which Bénédict's unhealthy brain had fallen in love at sight of those works of art wherein the brush, by making ugliness poetic, has made it more attractive than beauty itself. Moreover, Mademoiselle de Raimbault had a mild but true dignity of manner which was too imposing to attract at first sight. In the curve of her profile, in the fineness of her hair, in the graceful bend of her neck, in the breadth of her wide shoulders, there were a thousand reminders of the court of Louis XIV. One felt that nothing less than a long line of ancestors could have produced that combination of pure and noble features, all those almost regal graces, which revealed themselves one by one, like those of a swan basking in the sunshine with majestic languor.

Bénédict descended from his post at the foot of the cross, and, despite the mutterings of the good women of the village, a score of other young men succeeded one another on that desirable elevation, which enabled them to see and be seen. An hour later, Bénédict found himself being led towards Mesdames de Raimbault. His uncle, who had been talking to them hat in hand, having noticed him at a little distance, had taken him by the arm and presented him to them.

Valentine was sitting on the turf, between her mother, the Comtesse de Raimbault, and her grandmother, the Marquise de Raimbault. Bénédict did not know either of the three ladies, but he had so often heard them spoken of at the farm that he was prepared for the icy and contemptuous nod of the countess and the familiar and affable greeting of the marchioness. It was as if the latter intended, by effusive demonstrations, to make up for her daughter-in-law's disdainful silence. But in that affectation of popular manners there were traces of a habit of patronizing that was truly feudal.

"What! is that Bénédict?" she cried; "is that the little fellow I saw at his mother's breast? Good-day, *my lad!* I am delighted to see you so tall and so well dressed. You look so like your mother that it's enough to frighten one. By the way, do you know we're old acquaintances? You're the godson of my poor son, the general, who was killed at Waterloo. It was I who gave you your first frock; but you can hardly remember that. How long ago was it? You must be at least eighteen?"

"I am twenty-two, madame," Bénédict replied.

"*Sangodémi!*" cried the marchioness; "twenty-two already! How time flies! I thought you were about my granddaughter's age. You dont't know my granddaughter do you? Here she is; look at her. We know how to get children too, you see! Valentine, say good-evening to Bénédict; he's honest Lhéry's nephew, and engaged to your little playmate Athénaïs. Speak to him, my child."

This apostrophe might be translated thus: "Inheritress of my name, imitate me; make yourself popular, in order to carry your head safely through future revolutions, as I was shrewd enough to do in past revolutions."
—Nevertheless, Mademoiselle de Raimbault, whether by

tact, breeding or sincerity, effaced by her glance and smile all the wrath that the marchioness's impertinent affability had aroused in Bénédict's breast. He had looked at her with bold and mocking eyes, for his wounded pride had banished for an instant the natural shyness of his years. But the expression of that lovely face was so gentle and serene, the tones of that voice so melodious and soothing, that the young man lowered his eyes and blushed like a girl.

"Ah! monsieur," she said, "I can say nothing to you more sincerely than that I love Athénaïs as if she were my sister. Have the kindness to bring her to me; I have been looking for her a long while, but cannot find her. I would like very much to embrace her."

Bénédict bowed low, and soon returned with his cousin. Athénaïs walked about amid the merry-making, arm-in-arm with the nobly-born daughter of the Comtes de Raimbault. Although she pretended to consider it a perfectly natural thing, and although Valentine so understood it, it was impossible for her to conceal the joyful triumph of her pride in the presence of those other women, who envied her while exerting themselves to disparage her. Meanwhile the viol gave the signal for the *bourrée*. Athénaïs was engaged to dance it with the young man who had stopped her on the road. She begged Mademoiselle de Raimbault to be her vis-à-vis.

"I will wait till I have an invitation," Valentine replied, with a smile.

"Well, Bénédict," cried Athénaïs, eagerly, "go and invite mademoiselle."

The awestruck Bénédict consulted Valentine's face with his eyes. He read in its sweet and innocent expression a wish to accept his invitation. Thereupon he stepped toward her. But the countess, her mother,

abruptly seized her arm, saying to her in so loud a tone
that Bénédict could hear her :

"My child, I forbid you to dance the *bourrée* with anyone but Monsieur de Lansac."

Thereupon, Bénédict noticed for the first time a tall
young man with an exceedingly handsome face, on whose
arm the countess was leaning, and he remembered that
that was the name of Mademoiselle de Raimbault's
fiancé.

He soon understood the cause of her mother's alarm.
At a certain *trill* executed by the viol before beginning
the *bourrée,* every dancer must, in accordance with im-
memorial custom, kiss his partner. The Comte de Lansac, being too well bred to take that liberty in public,
compromised with the custom of Berri by kissing Valentine's hand respectfully.

He then tried a few steps forward and back ; but realizing at once that he could not catch the rhythm of that
dance, in which no stranger to the province can ever
acquit himself with credit, he stopped and said to Valentine :

"Now I have done my duty, I have established you
here in accordance with your mother's wish ; but I will
not spoil your pleasure by my awkwardness. You had
a partner all ready just now, allow me to cede my rights
to him.—Will you kindly take my place, monsieur ? " he
said, turning to Bénédict, in a tone of the utmost courtesy. "You will act my part much better than I."

And as Bénédict, torn between shyness and pride,
hesitated to take that place, the most valuable privilege
of which had been taken from him, Monsieur de Lansac
graciously added :

"You will be sufficiently repaid for the favor I ask
you ; perhaps, indeed, it is your place to thank me."

Bénédict did not require much urging; Valentine's hand was placed with no sign of repugnance in his trembling one. The countess was satisfied with the diplomatic way in which her future son-in-law had arranged the affair. But suddenly the viol player, who was a sly, facetious fellow, like all true artists, interrupted the music of the *bourrée* and played again, with malicious emphasis, the imperative *trill*. The new dancer was thereby enjoined to kiss his partner. Bénédict turned pale and lost his self-possession. Père Lhéry, terrified by the wrath which he saw blazing in the countess's eyes, rushed to the musician and implored him to go on. But the fellow would not listen, enjoyed his triumph amid a chorus of laughter and bravos, and persisted in not resuming the air until after the indispensable formality had been complied with. The other dancers lost patience. Madame de Raimbault prepared to take her daughter away. But Monsieur de Lansac, a man of sense and spirit, realizing the utter absurdity of the scene, went to Bénédict again and said with a slightly sarcastic politeness:

"Well, monsieur, must I authorize you to assume a privilege of which I dared not take advantage? You make your triumph complete."

Bénédict pressed his trembling lips on the young countess's soft cheeks. A thrill of pride and pleasure made his pulses throb for an instant; but he noticed that Valentine, although blushing, laughed like a school-girl at the incident. He remembered that she blushed but did not laugh when Monsieur de Lansac kissed her hand. He said to himself that that handsome nobleman, so courteous, so clever, and so sensible, must have won her heart; and he took no further pleasure in dancing with her, although she danced the *bourrée* marvellously well, with all the self-possession and unconstraint of a village damsel.

But Athénaïs displayed even more charm and coquetry in that dance ; her beauty was of a type which is more generally popular. Men of mediocre education love the charms that allure, the eyes that invite, the smile that encourages. The young farmer's daughter found in her very innocence a source of mischievous and piquant self-assurance. In an instant she was surrounded, and, as it were, kidnapped by her country admirers. Bénédict followed her about the ball for some little time. Then, being displeased to see her leave her mother and mingle with a swarm of young giddy-pates about whom clouds of swains were hovering, he tried to make her understand by signs and glances that she was abandoning herself too freely to her natural forwardness. Athénaïs did not see, or did not choose to see. Bénédict lost his temper, shrugged his shoulders and left the fête. He found his uncle's man at the inn ; he had come on the little gray mare that Bénédict usually rode. He told him to drive Monsieur Lhéry and his family home in the carriage, and, mounting his horse, rode off alone toward Grangeneuve just at nightfall.

V

Valentine, after thanking Bénédict with a graceful courtesy, left the dance, and, on returning to the countess, she understood from her pallor, the contraction of her lips and the sternness of her expression, that a storm was brewing against her in her mother's revengeful heart. Monsieur de Lansac, who felt that he was re-

sponsible for his fiancée's conduct, desired to spare her
the first stinging reproaches, so he offered her his arm,
and with her followed Madame de Raimbault at a short
distance, while she dragged her mother-in-law away
toward the place where the calèche was waiting. Valentine was trembling ; she was afraid of the wrath that
was gathering over her head. Monsieur de Lansac,
with the dexterous grace characteristic of his ready wit,
sought to divert her thoughts, and, affecting to look upon
what had happened as the merest trifle, undertook to
pacify the countess. Valentine, grateful for the delicate
consideration which seemed always to encompass her,
without a trace of self-conceit or absurdity, felt a perceptible increase of the sincere affection which her future
husband inspired in her.

Meanwhile the countess, enraged at having no one to
quarrel with, attacked her mother-in-law the marchioness.
As she did not find her people at the appointed spot, because they did not expect her so soon, she had to walk
some distance over a dusty, stony road, a painful trial for
feet which had trodden on velvet carpets in the apartments of Joséphine and Marie-Louise. The countess's
wrath waxed hotter ; she almost pushed away the old
marchioness, who stumbled at every step and tried to
lean on her arm.

" This is a lovely fête, a charming pleasure party ! "
said the countess. " It was you who insisted on coming ;
you dragged me here against my will. You love the
canaille, but I detest them. You have had a fine time,
haven't you ? Pray go into ecstasies over the delights
of the country ! Don't you find this heat very agreeable ? "

" Yes, yes," replied the old woman, " I am eighty
years old."

" But I'm not ; I am stifling.   And this dust, and these stones that make holes in the soles of your feet !   It is all most delightful ! "

" But, my love, is it my fault if it's hot, if the roads are bad, if you are out of temper ? "

" Out of temper !   you never are, of course, I can un-derstand that, as you pay no attention to anything and let your family act as God pleases.   So the flowers with which you have strewn your life have borne their fruit—premature fruit, I may say."

" Madame," said the marchioness bitterly, " you are ferocious in your anger, I know."

" I presume, madame, that you call the righteous pride of an insulted mother ferocity ? "

" Who insulted you, in God's name ? "

"Ah !   you ask me that !   You do not think that I was insulted in my daughter's person, when all the *canaille* in the province clapped their hands to see her kissed by a peasant, before my eyes, against my will !   when they will say to-morrow : 'We put a stinging affront on the Comtesse de Raimbault !' "

" What   exaggeration !   what   puritanical   nonsense ! Your daughter dishonored because she was kissed before three thousand people !   A heinous crime indeed !   In my day, madame, and in yours too, I'll wager, although I agree they didn't do just that, they did no better.   Besides, that fellow is no countryman."

" He is much worse, madame ; he's a rich countryman, an *enlightened* clown."

"Don't speak so loud ; if you should be overheard !—"

" Oh !   you are always dreaming of the guillotine, you think that it is walking behind you, ready to seize you at the slightest sign of courage or pride.   But I will speak low, madame; listen to what I have to say : Have

as little to do with Valentine as possible, and don't forget
so soon the results of *the other one's* education."

"Again ! again !" exclaimed the old woman, clasping
her hands in distress.   "You never miss an opportunity
to reawaken that sorrow !   Oh ! let me die in peace, madame ; I am eighty years old."

" Everybody would like to be as old as that, if it would
justify all the vagaries of the heart and the mind.   Although you make yourself out to be old and harmless,
you still have a very great influence over my daughter
and my household.   Make that influence serve the common good ; cease to set before Valentine that deplorable
example, the memory of which is unfortunately alive in
her mind."

" Oh ! there's no danger ! Isn't Valentine on the eve
of being married ? What do you fear after that ? Her
errors, if she makes any, will concern nobody but her
husband ; our task will be accomplished."

" Yes, madame, I know that you reason so ; I won't
waste my time arguing about your principles ; but, I say
again, remove the last trace that still lingers about you of
the life that has left a stain on us all."

" Great God, madame ! have you finished ? She of
whom you speak is my granddaughter, the daughter of
my own son, and Valentine's only sister.   Those are
facts which will make me always deplore her fault instead of cursing it.   Has she not expiated it cruelly ?
Will your implacable hatred pursue her in exile and poverty ? Why this persistence in rasping a wound which
will bleed until I have breathed my last ? "

" Madame, listen to what I say : your *estimable* granddaughter is not so far away as you pretend to believe.   I
am not your dupe, you see."

" Great God !" cried the old woman drawing herself

up, "what do you mean? Explain yourself! my child! my poor child! where is she? Tell me; I ask you on my knees!"

Madame de Raimbault, who had pleaded the false in order to ascertain the truth, was satisfied with the pathetically sincere tone with which the marchioness destroyed her suspicions.

"You shall know, madame," she replied, "but not before I do. I swear that I will soon find out the hiding-place she has chosen in this neighborhood, and will drive her out of it. Wipe away your tears; here are our people."

Valentine entered the calèche, but alighted again after putting on over her clothes a blue merino skirt, which took the place of a riding-habit, the latter being too heavy for the season. Monsieur de Lansac offered his hand to assist her to mount a handsome English horse, and the ladies took their places in the calèche; but as Monsieur de Lansac's horse was being led out of the village stable, he fell and could not get up. Whether as a result of the heat, or of the quantity of water he had been allowed to drink, he had a violent attack of colic, and was absolutely unable to travel. Monsieur de Lansac was compelled to leave the groom at the inn to look after him, and to take a seat in the carriage.

"Well," exclaimed the countess, "is Valentine to ride home alone?"

"Why not?" said the Comte de Lansac, wishing to spare Valentine the discomfort of a drive of two hours in her angry mother's company. "Mademoiselle will not be alone if she rides beside the carriage, and we can talk with her perfectly well. Her horse is so clever that I see no objection to leaving him to her guidance."

"But it is hardly proper," said the countess, over whom Monsieur de Lansac had acquired great influence.

"Everything is proper in this region, where there is no one to decide what is proper and what is not. At the bend in the road we enter the Black Valley, where we shall not meet a cat. Moreover, it will be so dark ten minutes hence that we shall have no reason to fear that she will be seen."

This momentous discussion having terminated in Monsieur de Lansac's favor, the calèche turned into one of the narrow roads of the valley. Valentine followed at a canter, and the darkness deepened.

As they rode farther into the valley the road became narrower. Soon it was impossible for Valentine to ride beside the carriage. For some time she remained behind; but the inequalities of the ground often compelled the coachman to stop his horses abruptly, and Valentine's horse took fright every time that the carriage halted almost against his chest. So she took advantage of a place where the ditch was hardly perceptible, to ride ahead, and thereafter proceeded under much pleasanter circumstances, having no fear of accident, and allowing her strong and spirited horse full liberty of action.

The weather was beautiful; the moon had not risen, so that the road was buried beneath the dark shadows of the trees. From time to time a glow-worm gleamed in the grass, a lizard crawled through the bushes, a hawk-moth buzzed about a moist flower. A warm breeze had sprung up, laden with the odor of vanilla which exhales from fields of beans in flower. Young Valentine, who had been educated by her banished sister, her haughty mother, the nuns at her convent, and her careless and youthful grandmother, one after another, had really received no bringing-up at all. She had made herself what she was, and, for lack of any really sympathetic heart in her family, had acquired a taste for study and

meditation. Her naturally calm mind and her sound
judgment had preserved her from the errors of society
and from those of solitude alike. Absorbed by thoughts
as pure and sweet as her heart, she enjoyed to the full
that tranquil May evening, so full of chaste delights to a
young and poetic soul. Perhaps she thought of her
fiancé too, of the man who had first shown her confidence and respect, sentiments so grateful to a heart
which esteems itself and has never yet been understood. Valentine did not dream of passion; she did not
share the overbearing eagerness of those young brains
which look upon it as an imperious necessity of their
organizations. Valentine, being more modest, did not
believe that she was destined to undergo such energetic
and violent experiences. She accommodated herself
readily to the reserve which society imposed upon her as
a duty; she accepted it as a blessing and not as a law.
She promised herself that she would steer clear of those
ardent fantasies which made other women miserable
before her eyes: the love of luxury, to which her grandmother sacrificed all pretence of dignity; ambition, which
tormented her mother with unfulfilled hopes; love, which
had so cruelly led her sister astray. This last thought
brought tears to her eyes. That was the only important
event in Valentine's life; but it had filled it, it had influenced her character, it had made her at once bold and
timid: timid for herself, bold where her sister was concerned. It is true that she had never been able to prove
to her the self-sacrificing courage of which she was conscious. Her sister's name had never been mentioned by
her mother in her presence; she had never had a single
opportunity to defend her or to be of service to her. Her
desire was the more intense on that account, and this
passionate affection which she cherished for a person

whose image she saw only through the vague memories
of childhood, was really the only romantic affection that
had ever found a place in her heart.

The species of agitation which this repressed attachment had brought into her life had become intensified
during the last few days. A vague rumor was current
in the neighborhood that her sister had been seen in a
town eight leagues away, where she had once lived temporarily for a few months. This time she had passed
only one night there, and had not given her name ; but
the people at the inn declared that they had recognized
her. This report had reached the château of Raimbault
at the other end of the Black Valley. A servant, eager
to ingratiate himself with the countess, had repeated it
to her. Chance willed that Valentine, who was at work
in an adjoining room at that moment, heard her mother
raise her voice and utter a name which made her heart
leap. Thereupon, unable to control her anxiety and her
curiosity, she listened and discovered the secret of the
interview. This incident occurred on the eve of May
first ; and now Valentine, excited and perturbed in mind,
asked if that report was probable, and if it might not be
that the people at the inn were mistaken in thinking that
they recognized a person who had been exiled from the
province for fifteen years.

As she indulged in these reflections, Mademoiselle de
Raimbault, not thinking to slacken the pace of her horse,
had gained a considerable lead on the calèche. When
she remembered it she stopped, and being unable to distinguish anything in the darkness, she leaned forward to
listen ; but, whether because the noise of the wheels
was deadened by the long, damp grass that grew in the
road, or because the loud, hurried breathing of her horse,
impatient at the delay, prevented distant sounds from

reaching her, she could hear nothing at all in the solemn silence of the night. She turned back at once, concluding that she had left the others far behind, and, after galloping for some time without meeting anyone, she stopped again to listen.

This time she heard only the chirp of the cricket, waking as the moon rose, and the distant barking of a dog.

She urged her horse on anew until she came to a fork in the road. She tried to make out which road she had come by, but the darkness made any sort of observation impossible. The wiser course would have been to wait there for the calèche, which must reach that point by one road or the other. But fright began to disturb the young woman's judgment; to stand still in that state of uncertainty seemed to her the worst thing she could do. She fancied that her horse's instinct would lead him toward the horses that were drawing the carriage, and that the sense of smell would guide him if his memory was at fault. The horse, left to his own judgment, took the left hand road. After a fruitless chase, Valentine, whose uncertainty constantly increased, thought that she recognized a large tree which she had noticed in the morning. That circumstance restored her courage to some extent; she even smiled at her cowardice, and urged her horse forward.

But she soon found that the road descended more and more into the depths of the valley. She did not know the country, which she had very seldom visited since she was a child, but it seemed to her that, in the morning, they had not left the higher ground at all. The aspect of the landscape had changed; the moon, rising slowly above the horizon, shone obliquely through the interstices of the branches, and Valentine was able to distinguish objects which she had not noticed before. The road was

wider, more open, more cut up by the feet of cattle and
by cart-wheels; great branchless willows rose on both
sides of the hedge, and, with their strange, mutilated
figures outlined against the sky, seemed like so many
hideous creatures on the point of moving their monstrous
heads and armless bodies.

VI

Suddenly Valentine's ear detected a dull, prolonged
sound like the rumbling of a carriage. She left the road
and took a path which led in the direction of that sound,
which constantly grew louder, but changed its nature.
If Valentine could have looked through the mass of flowering apple trees through which the moonbeams forced
their way, she would have seen at a little distance the
white, silvery line of the river rushing into a mill pond.
But the increasing coolness of the air and a delicious odor
of mint disclosed to her the proximity of the Indre. She
concluded that she had gone considerably astray; but
she decided to descend the stream, hoping soon to find a
mill or a cottage where she could ask her way. She
came at last to an old barn, standing all by itself and
without lights, which she supposed to be inhabited because of the barking of a dog shut up in the yard. She
called in vain, no one stirred. She rode her horse up to
the gate and knocked with the steel knob of her riding-
crop. A plaintive bleating answered her; it was a sheep-
fold. And in that region, as there are no wolves or
thieves, there are no shepherds either. Valentine rode
on.

Her horse, as if he shared the disheartened feeling which had taken possession of her, slackened his pace to a careless walk. From time to time he struck his shoe against a stone, making the sparks fly, or thrust his thirsty mouth toward the tender little shoots of the young elms.

Suddenly, in the silence of that deserted spot, over those fields which had never heard any other melody than the whistle of some idle child, or the hoarse, obscene ditty of a belated miller; suddenly, with the murmuring of the stream and the sighing of the breeze was blended a pure, sweet, fascinating voice, a man's voice, as fresh and strong as the note of a hautboy. It was singing a ballad of the province, very simple and slow and sad, as they all are. But with what feeling it sang! Certainly it could not be a villager who had the art of emitting and modulating his notes in that way. Nor was it a professional singer who paid no heed to aught save purity of rhythm, without regard to system or to ornamentation. It was someone who *felt* music, but did not know it; or, if he did know it, he was the greatest singer on earth, for he seemed not to know it, and his melody, like the voice of the elements, soared heavenward without any other poesy than that of sentiment.

"If," thought Valentine, "in a virgin forest, far from works of art, far from the lamps of the orchestra and reminiscences of Rossini, among those mountain firs where the foot of man has never left its imprint, Manfred's ideal creations should awake to new life, they would sing like that."

She had let her reins fall; her horse was browsing along the edge of the path; Valentine was no longer afraid; she was under the spell of that mysterious music, and her emotion was so pleasant that it did not occur to her to be astonished to hear it in that place and at that hour.

The singing ceased. Valentine thought that she had been dreaming; but it began again not so far away, and each moment brought it more distinctly to the fair amazon's ear; then it ceased again and she could hear nothing but the trot of a horse. By the heavy, lumbering way in which it just grazed the ground, it was easy to determine that it was a peasant's horse.

Valentine felt a thrill of fear at the thought that she was about to find herself, in that solitary spot, face to face with a man who might prove to be a drunken clown; for was it really he who had been singing, or had his approach put the melodious sylph to flight? However, it was better to accost him than to pass the night in the fields. Valentine reflected that, in case of an attempted insult, her horse had better legs than the one approaching her, and, seeking to feign a self-assurance which she did not possess, she rode straight toward him.

"Who goes there?" called a manly voice.

"Valentine de Raimbault," replied the girl, who was not, perhaps, altogether devoid of pride in the possession of the most honored name in the province.

There was nothing ridiculous in that little touch of vanity, since the name owed all the esteem in which it was held to the virtues and gallantry of her father.

"Mademoiselle de Raimbault! all alone in this place!" rejoined the horseman. "Where is Monsieur de Lansac, pray? Has he fallen from his horse? Is he dead?"

"No, thank Heaven!" said Valentine, reassured by that voice, which she thought that she recognized. "But if I am not mistaken, monsieur, your name is Bénédict, and we danced together to-day?"

Bénédict started. It seemed to him that it was not

very modest to refer to so delicate an occurrence, the mere thought of which, at that moment and in that solitude, sent the blood rushing back to his heart. But extreme innocence sometimes resembles effrontery. The fact was that Valentine, absorbed by the agitation due to her nocturnal ride, had completely forgotten the episode of the kiss. She was reminded of it by the tone in which Bénédict replied :

"Yes, mademoiselle, I am Bénédict."

"Very well," said she, "do me the favor to put me in the right road."

And she told him how she had gone astray.

"You are a league from the road you should have taken," he replied, "and to reach it you must pass the farm of Grangeneuve. As I am on my way there, I shall have the honor of serving you as a guide ; perhaps we shall find the calèche waiting for you at the junction of the roads."

"That is not probable," said Valentine ; "my mother saw me ride ahead, and undoubtedly thinks that I shall reach the château before her."

"In that case, mademoiselle, if you will allow me, I will accompany you to your house. My uncle would be a more suitable escort, of course, but he has not returned from the fête, and I don't know when he will return."

Valentine thought sadly of the increased indignation of her mother at such a dénouement ; but, as she was entirely innocent of all the incidents of the day, she accepted Bénédict's offer with a frankness which enforced esteem. Bénédict was touched by her sweet and simple manners. The very thing that had offended him in her at first, the ease which she owed to her consciousness of the social superiority in which she had been reared, won his respect at last. He found that she bore herself nobly

in perfect good faith, without arrogance and without false
humility. She was a sort of mean between her mother
and grandmother ; she knew how to enforce respect
without ever inflicting a wound. Bénédict was surprised
to find that he no longer felt the timidity, the palpitations
which a young man of twenty, brought up away from
the world, always feels when alone with a young and
beautiful woman. His conclusion was that Mademoiselle
de Raimbault, with her placid beauty and her natural
sincerity of character, was worthy to inspire a lasting
attachment. No thought of love entered his mind with
respect to her.

After some questions on both sides concerning the hour,
the road, the qualities of their horses, Valentine asked
Bénédict if it were he who was singing. Bénédict was
aware that he sang exceedingly well, and it was with secret
satisfaction that he remembered that he had lifted up his
voice in the valley. Nevertheless, with the profound
hypocrisy due to self-esteem, he answered carelessly:

"Did you hear anything? It was I, I fancy, or else
the frogs among the reeds."

Valentine said nothing more. She had admired that
voice so heartily that she was afraid of saying too much
or too little. However, after a pause, she artlessly inquired:

"Where did you learn to sing?"

"If I had any talent in that direction, I should be
justified in replying that it cannot be taught ; but such
a reply would be foolish conceit in me. I took a few
lessons in Paris."

"Music is a fine thing!" said Valentine.

And they passed from music to all the other arts.

"I see that you are very musical," said Bénédict, in
reply to a rather learned observation from her.

"I was taught music as I was taught everything else," she replied; "that is to say, superficially; but as I had an instinctive liking for that art, I readily grasped it."

"And doubtless you are a very talented musician?"

"I? I play contra-dances, that is all."

"You have no voice?"

"A little; I used to sing at one time, and was thought to have some talent, but I gave it up."

"What! when you love the art?"

"Yes, I devoted myself to painting, which I cared much less for, and in which I was proficient."

"That is strange!"

"No, in these days we must have a specialty. Our rank and fortune are of no account. In a few years, perhaps, the estate of Raimbault, my patrimony, will again be the property of the State, as it was half a century ago. The education we receive is wretched; they give us the elements of everything, but do not allow us to learn anything thoroughly. They want us to be well educated, but, on the day that we became learned, we should be ridiculous. We are always brought up to be rich, never to be poor. The limited education of our grandmothers was much more valuable; they at least knew how to knit. The Revolution found them women of moderate parts; they spun flax for a living without repugnance. We who have a smattering of English, drawing and music; who make lacquer pictures, water-color screens, velvet flowers and a score of other extravagant trifles of which the sumptuary laws of a republic would forbid the use—what should we do? which of us would stoop without regret to a mechanical trade? For not one in twenty of us knows anything thoroughly. I know but one trade for which we are adapted, and that is the trade of lady's maid. I realized early in life, from the tales of my grandmother and my mother—two such widely different lives: the Emigration and the Empire, Coblentz and Marie-Louise—that I must protect myself against the misfortunes of the first and the prosperity of the other. And, when I was almost at liberty to follow my own ideas, I suppressed those of my talents which could be of no service to me. I devoted myself to a single one, because I have noticed that, whatever the times and the fashions, a person who does a thing very well can always support herself in society."

"Then you think that painting will be less neglected than music in the Spartan régime which you anticipate, since you have deliberately adopted it as against your real vocation ?"

"Perhaps so ; but that is not the question. As a profession, music would not have suited me. It puts a woman too much in evidence ; it draws her onto the stage or into salons ; it makes her an actress, or an upper servant to whom the education of a provincial young lady is entrusted. Painting gives one more liberty ; it allows one to lead a more retired life, and the pleasures it procures become doubly precious in solitude. I think that you will no longer disapprove of my choice.—But let us ride a little faster, I beg ; my mother is probably waiting anxiously for me."

Bénédict, full of approbation and admiration of the young woman's good sense, flattered by the trustful way in which she revealed her thoughts and her character to him, quickened his pace regretfully. But, as the farm-house of Grangeneuve displayed its great white gable in the moonlight, a sudden thought passed through his mind. He halted abruptly, and, engrossed by that agitating thought, mechanically put out his hand to stop Valentine's horse.

"What does this mean?" she said, drawing rein; "isn't this the way?"

Bénédict was profoundly embarrassed. But he suddenly recovered his courage.

"Mademoiselle," he said, "what I have to say to you causes me great anxiety, because I am not at all sure how you will receive it, coming from me. It is the first time in my life that I have ever spoken to you, and heaven is my witness that I shall leave you with the utmost veneration. But this may be the only, the last time that I shall have this good fortune; and if what I have to say offends you, it will be easy for you never to look again on the face of a man who will have had the misfortune to displease you."

This solemn exordium alarmed Valentine no less than it surprised her. At all times Bénédict had a peculiarly remarkable face. His mind had the same tinge of singularity; she had noticed it in the talk they had just had together. That superior musical talent, those features of which it was impossible to grasp the predominant expression, that mind, so cultivated yet sceptical on every subject, combined to make him a strange creature in the eyes of Valentine, who had never before come so closely in contact with a young man of a different class from her own. Thus the species of preface he had delivered terrified her. Although she was an entire stranger to self-conceit, she feared a declaration, and had not sufficient presence of mind to say a single word in reply.

"I see that I frighten you, mademoiselle," Bénédict continued. "It is because, in the delicate position in which chance has placed me, I have not enough wit or familiarity with the ways of society to make myself understood by a hint."

These words increased Valentine's dismay and terror.

"Monsieur," said she, "I do not think that you can have anything to say to me to which I can listen, after the admission you have just made of your embarrassment. As you fear lest you may offend me, I cannot help dreading that I may allow you to commit a *gaucherie*. Let us stop here, I beg; and, as I know my way now, accept my thanks, and do not trouble yourself to go any farther."

"I should have expected this reply," said Bénédict, deeply wounded. "I should at least have counted upon the evidences of sound judgment and sensibility which I observed in Mademoiselle de Raimbault."

Valentine did not deign to reply. She bowed coldly, and, dismayed at the position in which she found herself, lashed her horse and rode away.

Bénédict looked after her in consternation. Suddenly he struck his forehead angrily with his hand.

"I am a stupid animal," he cried; "she doesn't understand me!"

And, jumping his horse across the ditch, he rode diagonally across the enclosure Valentine was skirting. In three minutes he was in front of her, barring her road. Valentine was so frightened that she almost fell backward.

VII

Bénédict threw himself from his horse.

"Mademoiselle," he cried, "I fall at your feet! Do not be afraid of me. You see that I cannot follow you on foot. Deign to listen to me a moment. I am a miserable fool. I offered you a deadly insult, imagining that you did not choose to understand me ; and, as I shall simply heap folly upon folly if I try to prepare you, I will go straight to my goal. Have you not recently heard something of a person who is dear to you ? ”

“Oh ! speak ! ” cried Valentine, with a cry that came from her heart.

“I knew it,” said Bénédict, joyfully. “You love her, you are sorry for her ; we have not been deceived. You want to see her ; you are ready to hold out your arms to her. All that is said of you is true, is it not, mademoiselle ? ”

It did not occur to Valentine to distrust Bénédict's sincerity. He had touched the most sensitive chord of her heart ; prudence would thenceforth have seemed to her rank cowardice ; that is the characteristic of impulsive and generous natures.

“If you know where she is, monsieur,” she cried, clasping her hands, “I bless you, for you will surely tell me.”

“I am about to do a thing that will perhaps be blameworthy in the eyes of society, for I am about to lead you aside from the path of filial obedience. But I shall do it without remorse ; my friendship for that person makes it my duty, and my admiration for you leads me to believe that you will never reproach me for it. This morning she walked four leagues through the dew-laden grass, over the stones in the pastures, wrapped in a peasant's cloak, just to obtain a glimpse of you at your window or in your garden. She returned unsuccessful. Are you willing to compensate her this evening, and to pay her for all the sorrows of her life ? ”

“Take me to her, monsieur ; I ask it in the name of all that you hold dearest on earth.”

"Very well," said Bénédict, "trust yourself to me. You must not be seen at the farm. Although my people are still away, the servants might see you. They would talk, and to-morrow your mother, being informed of your visit, would begin to persecute your sister afresh. Let me hitch your horse with mine under these trees, and follow me."

Valentine sprang lightly to the ground, without waiting for Bénédict to offer her his hand. But she was no sooner on her feet than the instinct of danger, natural to the purest women, awoke in her; she was afraid. Bénédict fastened the horses under a clump of maples. As he walked back toward her, he cried, with evident sincerity:

"Oh! how happy she will be, and how little she expects the joy that is approaching her!"

These words reassured Valentine. She followed her guide along a path, all damp with the evening dew, to the entrance to a hemp field which was enclosed by a ditch. They had to pass over a tottering plank. Bénédict jumped into the ditch and held it while Valentine crossed.

"Here, Perdreau! down, keep quiet!" he said to a great dog which rushed toward them growling, and, on recognizing his master, made as much noise by his caresses as he had made by his demonstrations of distrust.

Bénédict sent him away with a kick, and ushered his trembling companion into the farm garden, which was situated behind the buildings, as in most rustic dwellings. The garden was a dense mass of vegetation. Brambles, rose bushes, fruit trees grew there in confusion, and their sturdy shoots, which the gardener's pruning-hook never touched, were so intertwined over the paths as to make them almost impassable. Valentine caught her long riding-skirt on all the thorns; the profound darkness amid all that untrammeled vegetation increased her embarrassment, and the violent emotion which she naturally felt at such a moment made her almost too weak to walk.

"If you will give me your hand," said her guide, "we can go faster."

Valentine had lost her glove in her excitement; she placed her bare hand in Bénédict's. It was a strange position for a girl brought up as she had been. The young man walked in front of her, drawing her gently toward him, putting the branches aside with his other arm so that they should not strike his lovely companion's face.

"*Mon Dieu!* how you tremble!" he said to her, releasing her hand when they reached an open space.

"Ah! monsieur, I tremble with joy and impatience," Valentine replied.

There remained one more obstacle to surmount. Bénédict had not the key to the garden; in order to get out of it they must climb over a quickset hedge. He proposed to assist her, and she had no choice but to accept. Thereupon the farmer's nephew took the Comte de Lansac's fiancée in his arms. He placed his trembling hands about her slender waist; he breathed her agitated breath. And that condition of affairs lasted some time, for the hedge was broad, bristling with thorny branches; the stone in the banking crumbled, and Bénédict was not wholly self-possessed.

However—so great is the modest reserve of this age!— his imagination fell far short of the reality, and the fear of offending his conscience prevented him from realizing his good fortune.

When they reached the door of the house, Bénédict

noiselessly raised the latch, ushered Valentine into the living-room on the second floor, and felt his way to the hearth. He soon had a candle lighted, and, pointing to a wooden staircase not unlike a ladder, said to Mademoiselle de Raimbault:

"That is the way."

He threw himself into a chair and prepared to do sentry duty, begging her not to remain more than a quarter of an hour with her sister.

Fatigued by her long walk in the morning, Louise had fallen asleep early. The little room which she occupied was one of the worst in the farm-house; but as she was supposed to be a poor relation from Poitou whom the Lhérys had been helping for a long while, she insisted that the farmer should not disabuse his servants of the error into which they had fallen by receiving her with undue honor. She had voluntarily chosen a sort of little loft with a round window looking on a most fascinating landscape of fields and islets, intersected by the innumerable windings of the Indre, and covered with the most beautiful trees. A reasonably good bed had been hastily made up for her on a wretched pallet; peas were drying on a hurdle, bunches of golden onions hung from the ceiling, skeins of double thread slumbered on a disabled reel. Louise, who had been brought up in opulence, found a charm in these accessories of country life. To Madame Lhéry's great surprise, she had insisted upon allowing her little room to retain that rustic air of disorder and crowding which reminded her of the Flemish paintings of Van Ostade and Gerard Dow. But the things she liked best in that modest retreat were an old chintz curtain covered with faded flowers, and two old-fashioned arm-chairs, the woodwork of which had long ago been gilded. By the merest chance in the world

those things had been relieved from duty at the château
about ten years before, and Louise recognized them as
having been familiar to her in her childhood. She wept
and almost embraced them as old friends, as she remembered how many times in those happy days of peace and
ignorance, gone by forever, she had crouched, a laughing, fair-haired girl, between the broad arms of those
old chairs.

That night she had fallen asleep with her eyes fixed
mechanically on the flowers in the curtain ; and, as she
gazed, her memory reviewed her past life to its most trivial details. After a long period of exile, the keen sensation of her former sorrows and her former joys awoke
with great force. She fancied that it was only the day
after the events which she had atoned for and bewailed
during a heart-broken pilgrimage of fifteen years. She
fancied that she could see behind that curtain, which the
wind blew back and forth across the window, the whole
brilliant, fairy-like scene of her younger years, the tower
of the old manor-house, the venerable oaks in the great
park, the white goat she had loved, the field in which she
had plucked corn-flowers. Sometimes the image of her
grandmother, a selfish, easy-going creature, rose before
her with tears in her eyes, as on the day of her banish-
ment. But that heart, which only half knew how to
love, was closed against her, and that consoling apparition vanished with airy indifference.

The only pure and always refreshing image in that
imaginary picture was that of Valentine, the lovely child
of four, with the long golden hair and rosy cheeks,
whom Louise had known. She saw her once more running through the fields of grain taller than herself, like a
partridge in a furrow ; jumping into her arms with the
frank and caressing laughter of childhood which brings

tears to the eyes of the loved one ; passing her plump white hands over her sister's neck, and chattering to her of the thousand artless trifles which make up the life of a child, in that primitive, sensible, sprightly language which always charms and surprises us. From that time Louise had been a mother ; she had loved childhood no longer as a source of entertainment but as a sentiment. That love of long ago for her little sister had awakened, more intense and more motherly than before, with the love she bore her own son. She imagined her just as she was when she left her ; and when she was told that she was a tall and beautiful woman now, stronger and straighter than herself, Louise could not succeed in be-lieving it for more than an instant ; her imagination soon recurred to little Valentine, and she longed to hold her on her knee.

That fresh and smiling apparition played a part in all her dreams since she had passed all her waking hours trying to find a way to see her. Just as Valentine softly ascended the stairs and raised the trap-door which gave access to her chamber, Louise fancied that she saw among the reeds along the Indre her Valentine of four years of age, running after the long blue dragon-flies which skim the water with the tips of their wings. Suddenly the child fell into the river. Louise rushed to rescue her ; but Madame de Raimbault, the haughty countess, her stepmother, her implacable foe, appeared before her, pushed her away, and let the child die.

"Sister !" cried Louise, in a choking voice, struggling with the visions of her troubled slumber.

"Sister !" replied a strange voice, as sweet as that of the angels whose singing we hear in our dreams.

Louise, raising herself on her bolster, lost the silk handkerchief which held her long brown hair in place.

In that dishevelled condition, pale, startled, her face lighted by a moonbeam which stole furtively through the chinks in the curtain, she leaned toward the voice that called her. Two arms are thrown about her, two fresh, warm lips cover her cheeks with holy kisses; Louise, speechless with emotion, feels a shower of tears on her face; Valentine, almost fainting, drops exhausted on her sister's bed. When Louise realized that she was no longer dreaming, that Valentine was in her arms, that she had come to her, that her heart was as full of affection and gladness as her own, she was unable to express what she felt otherwise than by embraces and sobs. At last, when they were able to speak, Louise cried: "Is it really you, you of whom I have dreamed so many years?"

"Is it really you," cried Valentine, "and do you still love me?"

"Why this *you?*"* said Louise; "aren't we sisters?"

"Oh! but you are my mother too!" Valentine replied. "I have forgotten nothing, you see! You are still present in my memory, as if it were yesterday; I should have known you among a thousand. Oh! yes, it is you, it is really you! This is your beautiful brown hair, which I can still see arranged in bands over your forehead; these are your dainty little white hands, and your pale complexion. You are just as I saw you in my dreams."

"Oh! Valentine, my own Valentine! Do put the curtain aside that I can see you too. They told me that you were beautiful, but you are a hundred times more so than words can express. You are still fair, still spotless; the same sweet blue eyes, the same caressing smile! I brought you up, Valentine, do you remember?

* Louise used the familiar *toi*, Valentine *vous*.

It was I who preserved your skin from sunburn and freckles; it was I who took care of your hair and arranged it every day in golden curls. You owe it to me that you are still so lovely, Valentine, for your mother paid little attention to you; I alone watched over you every moment."

"Oh! I know it! I know it! I can still remember the songs with which you used to sing me to sleep. I remember that I always found your face leaning over mine when I woke. Oh! how I cried for you, Louise! how long it was before I was able to do without you! how I spurned the help of other women! My mother has never forgiven me for the species of hatred of her which I exhibited at that time, because my poor nurse had said to me: 'Your sister is going away; your mother has turned her out of the house.'—Oh! Louise! Louise! you are restored to me at last!"

"And we will never part again, will we?" cried Louise; "we will find a way to meet often, to write to each other. You won't allow yourself to be frightened by threats; we will not become strangers again?"

"Have we ever been strangers?" was the reply; "is it in anyone's power to make us strangers? You know me very little, Louise, if you think that it is possible to banish you from my heart, when it was impossible to do it even in my helpless childhood. But never fear; our troubles are at an end. In a month I shall be married. I am to marry a refined, sweet-tempered, sensible man, to whom I have often spoken of you, who approves of my affection for you, and who will allow me to live near you. Then, Louise, you won't be unhappy any more, will you? You will forget your misery by pouring it out on my bosom. You shall bring up my children, if I have the good fortune to be a mother; we will imagine that we live again in them. I will dry all your tears, I will devote my life to making up to you for all the sufferings of yours."

"Sublime child, angelic heart!" cried Louise, weeping with joy; "this day wipes out all the rest. Ah! I will never complain of the lot which affords me such an instant of ineffable happiness. You have already sweetened the memory of my years of exile. See," she continued, taking from under her pillow a small package carefully wrapped in velvet, "do you recognize these four letters? You wrote them to me at different times during our separation. I was in Italy when I received this one; you were not ten years old."

"Oh! I remember very well," said Valentine; "I have yours too. How many times I have read them, and how I have cried over them! This one I wrote to you from the convent. How I trembled; how I quivered with fear and joy when a woman I did not know handed me yours in the parlor! She slipped it into my hand with a significant nod, as she gave me some sweets which she pretended to have brought me from my grandmother. And two years later, when I was in the suburbs of Paris, I saw a woman at the garden gate pretending to ask alms, and, although I had never seen her but once, I instantly recognized her. I said to her: 'Have you a letter for me?'—'Yes,' said she, 'and I'll come for the answer to-morrow.' Then I ran to shut myself up in my room, but someone called me, and I was watched all the rest of the day. At night my governess sat by my bed working until nearly midnight. I had to pretend to be asleep all that time, and when she left me and went to her own room she took the light. With what pains and precautions I finally succeeded in obtaining a match and a candle and writing materials, without making

a noise, without rousing my keeper! However, I succeeded; but I splashed a little ink on my sheet, and the
next day I was questioned and scolded and threatened!
How impudently I lied! how willingly I submitted to the
penance they imposed on me! The old woman returned
and wanted to sell me a little kid. I handed her the
letter and I reared the kid. Although it did not come to
me directly from you, I loved it on your account. O
Louise! I believe that I owe it to you that I haven't an evil
heart. They tried to wither mine early in life; they did
everything imaginable to crush my natural delicacy of
feeling in the germ; but your dear image, your loving
caresses, your goodness to me, had left an ineradicable
impression on my memory. Your letters reawoke in my
heart the sentiment of gratitude you had left there. Those
four letters marked four very distinct epochs in my life;
each of them inspired me with a stronger determination
to be a good woman, to detest intolerance, to despise
prejudices; and I venture to say that each of them
marked a step forward in my moral life. Louise, my
sister, you have really been my teacher to this very
day."

"You are an angel of purity and virtue!" cried
Louise; "I am the one who should be at your feet."

"Come! quickly!" cried Bénédict's voice at the foot
of the stairs; "come away, Mademoiselle de Raimbault!
Monsieur de Lansac is looking for you."

VI

Valentine rushed from the room. Monsieur de Lansac's arrival was an agreeable incident to her. She longed to tell him of her happiness, but, to her great displeasure, Bénédict informed her that he had thrown him off the scent by telling him that he had heard nothing of Mademoiselle de Raimbault since the fête. Bénédict excused himself on the plea that he had no idea what Monsieur de Lansac's feeling might be with regard to Louise. But in the bottom of his heart he had felt an indefinable thrill of malignant joy in sending the unfortunate lover to scour the country in the middle of the night, while he, Bénédict, had his fiancée under his protection.

"The falsehood may have been ill-timed," he said ; "but I told it with the best intentions, and it is too late to retract it. Allow me, mademoiselle, to urge you to return to the château at once. I will attend you as far as the gate of the park, and you can say that you lost your way, and that you chanced to find it again without assistance."

"Of course," replied Valentine, evidently much disturbed, "that is the least compromising thing to do after deceiving Monsieur de Lansac and sending him away. But suppose we meet him ? "

"I will say," replied Bénédict, eagerly, "that I shared his alarm and took my horse to help him to find you ; and that fortune was more kind to me than to him."

Valentine was more than a little troubled by the pos-

sible consequences of this adventure, but she was hardly
given time to think of them. Louise had thrown a cloak
over her shoulders and had gone down into the lower room
with her. She seized the candle which Bénédict had in
his hand, held it near her sister's face in order to see her
plainly, and, having gazed at her with a rapt expression,
she exclaimed enthusiastically, turning to Bénédict:

"Just see how lovely my Valentine is!"

Valentine blushed, and Bénédict blushed even more
than she. Louise was too engrossed by her own joy to
notice their embarrassment. She covered her sister with
kisses, and, when Bénédict tried to part them, she overwhelmed him with reproaches. But, passing abruptly
to a juster appreciation of the state of affairs, she effusively threw her arms about her young friend's neck,
telling him that all her blood would not pay for the happiness he had afforded her.

"For your reward," she added, "I am going to ask
her to do as I do. Will not you too, Valentine, give a
sisterly kiss to this poor Bénédict, who, when he found
himself alone with you, remembered Louise?"

"Why," said Valentine, blushing, "it will be the
second time to-day!"

"And the last time in my life," said Bénédict, bending
his knee before the young countess. "Let this one efface all the suffering which I shared when I obtained the
first against your will."

Lovely Valentine recovered her serenity, but she
raised her eyes toward heaven with an expression of
dignified modesty.

"God is my witness," she said, "that I give you this
token of my truest esteem from the bottom of my
heart."

She leaned toward the young man, and lightly deposited on his forehead a kiss which he dared not return even on her hand.

He rose, filled with an indescribable feeling of respect and pride. He had not known such sweet peace of mind, such delicious emotion since the day when, a credulous and pious young villager, he had taken the first communion, one lovely spring morning, amid the perfume of incense and flowers.

They returned as they had come, and Bénédict felt perfectly calm as he rode by Valentine's side. That kiss had bound them together by a sacred bond of fraternal affection. Mutual confidence was established between them, and, when they parted at the park gate, Bénédict promised to come soon to Raimbault with news of Louise.

"I hardly dare ask you to do it," said Valentine, "and yet I desire it very earnestly. But my mother is so harsh in her prejudices!"

"I shall have no difficulty in submitting to every sort of humiliation in your service," Bénédict replied, "and I flatter myself that I can expose myself to danger without compromising anybody else."

He bowed low and disappeared.

Valentine took the darkest path through the park; but she soon spied, through the leaves, beneath those long galleries of verdure, the gleam of torches moving to and fro. She found the whole household in commotion, and her mother wringing the coachman's hands, abusing the footman, appealing humbly to some, flying into a passion with others, weeping like a mother, issuing orders like a queen, and, probably for the first time in her life, appealing for help to the compassion of others. But as soon as she recognized the step of Valentine's horse, instead of giving way to an outburst of joy, she abandoned herself

to the wrath which had long been held in check by anxiety. Her daughter read in her eyes no feeling save
resentment for having suffered.

"Where have you been ? " she cried in a loud voice,
pulling her from her saddle with a violence which nearly
threw her to the ground. "Do you worry me to death
for amusement ? Do you think this a well-chosen time
to dream by moonlight and forget yourself wandering
over the country? After I have worn myself out to
humor your whims, do you think it's decent to stay away
until this time of night ? Is this all the respect you have
for your mother, even if you don't love her ? "

She dragged her to the salon, overwhelming her thus
with the bitterest reproaches and the most cruel accusa-
tions. Valentine stammered a few words in her own
defence, but had no need of the presence of mind which
she would have been compelled to exert in explanations
which luckily she was not called upon to give. She
found her grandmother in the salon, drinking tea ; the old
lady held out her arms, crying :

"Ah! here you are, my love! Do you know that you
have caused your mother much uneasiness ? For my
part, I knew perfectly well that nothing serious could
have happened to you in this country, where everybody
reveres the name you bear. Come, kiss me, and let's
forget all about it. As you are found again, I can eat
with a better appetite. That ride in the calèche has
made me infernally hungry."

As she spoke, the old marchioness, whose teeth were
still sound, attacked a slice of English *toast,* which her
companion had prepared for her. The painstaking care
with which the woman performed the task proved how
important a matter the proper preparation of that delicacy
was in her mistress's eyes. Meanwhile the countess, in

whom overbearing pride and a violent temper were at all events the vices of an impressionable nature, had yielded to the force of her emotions and fallen half-fainting upon a chair.

Valentine threw herself at her feet, assisted to unlace her, covered her hands with tears and kisses, and sincerely regretted the taste of happiness she had enjoyed, when she saw what suffering it had caused her mother. The marchioness abandoned her supper, taking little pains to dissemble the annoyance she felt, and hustled about her daughter-in-law with her usual alertness and vivacity, assuring her that it would amount to nothing.

When the countess opened her eyes, she pushed Valentine roughly away, and told her that she had too much reason to complain of her to accept her attentions ; and when the poor child expressed her sorrow, and with clasped hands asked her pardon, she was sternly ordered to bed, without the maternal kiss.

The marchioness, who prided herself on being the consoling angel of the family, took her granddaughter's arm to go up to her room, and said to her as they parted, after kissing her on the forehead :

"Come, come, dear girl, don't worry. Your mother's a little out of sorts to-night, but it's nothing. Don't amuse yourself by worrying about it ; you will have blotches on your face to morrow, and that won't suit our good Lansac."

Valentine forced herself to smile, and, when she was alone in her room, threw herself on her bed, utterly worn out with grief, joy, fatigue, fear, hope and a thousand conflicting feelings, which jostled one another in her heart.

About an hour later she heard the sound of Monsieur de Lansac's spurred boots in the corridor.   The marchioness, who never went to bed before midnight, called him into her room, and Valentine, hearing their voices, at once joined them.

"Ah!" said the marchioness, with the malevolent joy of old age, which respects none of the finer feelings of modesty, because it no longer knows what modesty is, "I was very sure that the hussy, instead of going to sleep, was waiting for her fiancé's return, with ear on the alert and throbbing heart! Well, well, my children, I think it's high time you were married."

Nothing could have been less appropriate than that suggestion to Valentine's placid and dignified attachment to Monsieur de Lansac. She flushed with annoyance, but the mild and respectful expression of her fiancé reassured her.

"I could not sleep, it is true," she said, "until I had asked your pardon for all the anxiety I have caused you."

"When a person is dear to us," replied Monsieur de Lansac, with the utmost grace, "we love even the torments of anxiety she causes us."

Valentine retired, confused and agitated. She felt that she had involuntarily treated Monsieur de Lansac very badly, and her conscience was vexed at the thought that she must wait some hours more before confessing it.

If she had had less refinement of sentiment and more knowledge of the world, she would have refrained from making that confession.

Monsieur de Lansac had played the most important part in the evening's adventure, and, however innocent Valentine might be, it might, perhaps, seem a difficult matter to that man of the world to forgive his fiancée fully and freely for the species of conspiracy she had entered into with another man to deceive him. But Valen-

tine was ashamed to be an accessory to a falsehood told
to the man who was to be her husband.

The next morning she went to him in the salon.

"Evariste," she said, going straight to the goal, "I have
a troublesome secret on my mind; I must tell it to you.
If I am blameworthy, you will blame me, but at all events
you shall not reproach me for my lack of loyalty."

"*Mon Dieu!* my dear Valentine, you make me shudder! What can be coming after this solemn preamble?
Think of the position in which we stand! No, no, I do
not choose to listen to anything. This is the day that I
am to leave you, to go to my post and sadly await the
end of the everlasting month which stands between me
and my happiness, and I do not propose to have this day,
which is sad enough already, made sadder by a commu-
nication which will evidently be painful to you. Whatever you may have to say to me, whatever *crime* you
may have committed, I forgive you. I tell you, Valentine, your heart is too noble, your life too pure for me to
have the insolence to presume to confess you."

"What I have to tell you will not sadden you," replied Valentine, recovering all her confidence in Monsieur
de Lansac's judgment. "On the contrary, even if you
should accuse me of acting too precipitately, you will re-
joice with me none the less, I am sure, over an event which
fills my heart with joy. I have found my sister——"

"Hush!" exclaimed Monsieur de Lansac, hastily,
with a comical affectation of alarm. "Don't mention
that name here! Your mother already has suspicions
which are driving her to desperation. What would happen, great God! if she knew how far you had gone!
Take my advice, my dear Valentine, keep this secret
closely guarded in your heart, and don't mention it even
to me. If you do, you will deprive me of the means of

convincing your mother, which my present air of perfect
innocence gives me. And then," he added, with a smile
which took from his words all their harsh significance,
"I am not yet your master—that is to say your protector
—to a sufficient degree to consider myself justified in
sanctioning an overt act of rebellion against the maternal
will. Wait a month. It will seem much less long to you
than to me."

Valentine, who was bent upon unburdening her conscience of the most delicate portion of her secret, tried
in vain to persist. Monsieur de Lansac would listen to
nothing, and finally persuaded her that she ought to tell
him nothing.

The fact was that Monsieur de Lansac was well-born,
that he occupied a desirable post in the diplomatic service, that he was extremely bright, fascinating and
crafty; but he had debts, and not for anything in the
world would he have lost Mademoiselle de Raimbault's
hand and fortune. In the constant dread of alienating
either the mother or the daughter, he dealt secretly with
both. He flattered their sentiments and their opinions,
and, taking little interest in the affair of Louise, he had
determined not to intervene in it until he should be in a
position to put an end to it at his pleasure.

Valentine took his prudent reserve for a tacit author-
ization, and, being reassured in that direction, turned her
whole attention to the storm which threatened to burst
upon her head from her mother's direction.

On the previous evening, the crafty, evil-minded servant, who had already dropped some hints concerning
Louise's appearance in the province, had entered the
countess's apartment on the pretext of carrying her a
glass of lemonade, and had had the following conversation with her.

IX

"Madame ordered me yesterday to inquire about the person——"

"Enough. Never mention her name in my presence. Have you done it?"

"Yes, madame, and I think I am on the track."

"Speak then."

"I do not dare to assure madame that the thing is as certain as I would like to have it. But this is what I know: there has been a woman at the farm-house of Grangeneuve for about three weeks, who passes for Père Lhéry's niece, and who looks to me like the one we're looking for."

"Have you seen her?"

"No, madame. Besides, I don't know her, and no one here is any better off than I am."

"But what do the peasants say?"

"Some of them say that she is really a relation of the Lhérys; the proof of it is, they say, that she doesn't dress like a young lady, and then, too, she occupies a farm hand's room in their house. They think that, if it was mademoiselle, she'd have had a different kind of a reception at the farm. The Lhérys were entirely devoted to her, as madame knows."

"To be sure, Mère Lhéry was her nurse at a time when she was very happy to make a living that way. But what do the others say?—How does it happen that no one hereabout is able to say positively whether this person is or is not the one whom everybody used to know?"

"In the first place, very few people have seen her at Grangeneuve, which is a very solitary place. She almost never goes out, and, when she does, she's always wrapped in a cloak, because she's sick, so they say. Those who have met her have hardly caught a glimpse of her, and they say it's impossible for them to tell whether the rosy-cheeked, buxom girl they used to see fifteen years ago has become the pale-faced, thin woman they see now. It's a very embarrassing thing to straighten out, and requires much shrewdness and perseverance."

"Joseph, I will give you a hundred francs if you will undertake it."

"An order from madame is enough," replied the valet with a hypocritical air. "But if I do not succeed as soon as madame desires, she will do well to remember that the peasants here are crafty and suspicious; that they show a very bad spirit, and are not in the least inclined to regard what used to be their duty; and that they would not be at all sorry to oppose madame's wishes in any respect."

"I know that they don't like me, and I congratulate myself on it. The hatred of these people honors me instead of annoying me. But hasn't the mayor of the commune brought the stranger here to question her?"

"As madame knows, the mayor is a Lhéry, a cousin of her farmer; in that family they are as closely united as the fingers on the hand, and they understand one another like thieves at a fair."

Joseph smiled complacently at his facility in caustic speech. The countess did not condescend to encourage him in that feeling, but she rejoined:

"Oh! it's exceedingly disagreeable to have the mayor's office filled by peasants, who thereby acquire a certain authority over us!"

"I must see about obtaining this fellow's dismissal," she thought, "and my son-in-law must submit to the ennui of taking his place. He can let the deputies do the work."

Then, recurring suddenly to the original subject of conversation, she said, with one of those swift and unerring intuitions which hatred prompts:

"There's one way: that is to send Catherine to the farm and make her talk."

"Mademoiselle's nurse! Oh! she's a slyer creature than madame thinks. It may be that she already knows very well what is up."

"Well, we must find some way," said the countess, angrily.

"If madame will allow me to act——"

"Oh! certainly!"

"In that case, I hope to find out by to-morrow what madame is interested in knowing."

The next morning about six o'clock, just as the *Angelus* was ringing in the valley and the sun lighting up all the roofs round about, Joseph bent his steps toward the most solitary and, at the same time, the most cultivated part of the country. It was a portion of the Raimbault domain, which comprised a large portion of fertile land, sold as national property during the Revolution, and redeemed under the Empire by means of the dowry of Mademoiselle Chignon, daughter of a wealthy manufacturer, whom General Comte de Raimbault had married for his second wife. The Emperor loved to unite ancient names with newly-made fortunes. This marriage was brought about by his supreme influence, and

the new countess's pride soon surpassed that of the old
nobility, whom she detested, but whose honors and titles
she had been none the less determined to obtain at any
price.

Joseph had undoubtedly woven a very cunning fable
to explain his appearance at the farm without frightening
anyone. He had in his bag many Scapin-like tricks to
play upon the simplicity of the natives ; but, unfortunately, the first person he met, about a hundred yards
from the house, was Bénédict, a much more suspicious
and shrewder man than he. The young man instantly
remembered that he had seen him some time before, at
another village fête, where, although he wore his black
coat with apparent ease, although he affected a superior
manner with the farmers who were drinking with him,
he had been ridiculed and humiliated like the lackey he
was. Bénédict realized at once that he must drive that
dangerous witness away from the farm, and, taking possession of him with ironical assiduity, he forced him to
go with him to pay a visit to a vineyard some little distance away. He pretended to believe his statement that
he was the man of business and steward of the family
at the château, and affected a strong inclination to
gossip. Joseph very soon abused the opportunity, and
in ten minutes his plans and his purpose became as clear
as daylight to Bénédict. Thereupon, he stood on his
guard and disabused him of his suspicions concerning
Louise with an air of candor by which Joseph was completely taken in. However, Bénédict realized that that
was not enough, that he must put an end once for all to
that spy's malevolent schemes ; and he suddenly remembered something which seemed to promise a means of
controlling him.

"*Parbleu !* Monsieur Joseph," he said, "I am very

glad that I met you. I have something to say to you
that will interest you deeply."

Joseph opened his great ears, genuine lackey's ears,
deep and restless, quick to hear, careful to retain ; ears
in which nothing is lost, in which everything can always
be found on occasion.

"Monsieur le Chevalier de Trigaud," continued Bénédict, "the country gentleman who lives two or three
leagues from here, and who slaughters hares and par-
tridges in such multitudes that it is impossible to find any
of either where he has been, told me the day before yesterday—we had just killed ten or twelve brace of young
quail in the underbrush, for the excellent chevalier is a
poacher as well as a gamekeeper—as I was saying, he
told me the day before yesterday that he would be very
glad to have such an intelligent fellow as you in his
service."

"Monsieur le Chevalier de Trigaud said that ? " exclaimed his astonished auditor.

"To be sure. He's a rich man, liberal and easy-going,
meddles with nobody's business, cares for nothing but
hunting and the table, is harsh to his dogs but mild to
his servants, hates domestic troubles, has been robbed
ever since he came into the world, and is a subject for
plunder if ever there was one. A man like you, who has
had some education and could keep his accounts, reform
the abuses in his household, and who would keep from
annoying him just after dinner, might easily obtain anything from his easy-going disposition, reign in his house
like a prince, and earn four times as much as in the service of Madame la Comtesse de Raimbault. Now, all
these advantages are at your disposal, Monsieur Joseph,
if you choose to go at once and offer the chevalier your
services."

"I will go as fast as I can !" cried Joseph, who knew all about the place, and that it was a desirable one.

"One moment! " interposed Bénédict. "You must remember that, thanks to my taste for hunting and the well-known moral integrity of my family, the excellent chevalier has a really extraordinary affection for us all, and whoever should be so unfortunate as to offend me or to do any of my people a disservice, *would not be likely to rot* in his employment."

The tone in which these words were uttered made them perfectly intelligible to Joseph. He returned to the château, set the countess's mind at rest, was shrewd enough to obtain the hundred francs as a reward for his zeal and trouble, and saved Valentine from the terrible examination to which her mother had proposed to subject her. A week later he entered the service of the Chevalier de Trigaud, whom he did not rob—he was too bright for that, and his master was so stupid that it was not worth the trouble—but whom he pillaged like a conquered province.

In his desire not to miss such a valuable windfall, he had carried his cunning and his devotion to Bénédict so far as to give the countess false information concerning Louise's place of abode. In three days he invented a story of a journey, which deceived Madame de Raimbault completely. He succeeded in retaining her confidence when he left her service. She had made no objection to his change of masters, and she soon ceased to think of him and his revelations. The marchioness, who loved Louise perhaps more than she had ever loved anyone, questioned Valentine. But she was too well acquainted with her grandmother's weak and fickle character to trust her powerless affection with a secret of such momentous importance. Monsieur de Lansac had gone, and the three women were settled at Raimbault, where the marriage was to take place in a month. Louise, who probably had less confidence than Valentine in Monsieur de Lansac's good intentions, determined to make the most of that time, when her sister was almost free, to see her often ; and, three days after May first, Bénédict appeared at the château with a letter.

In his pride and self-consciousness, he had never been willing to go there on any business for his uncle ; but for Louise, for Valentine, for those two women to whom he did not know what place to assign in his affections, he gloried in the opportunity to brave the countess's disdainful glances and the insolent affability of the marchioness. He took advantage of a hot day, which was likely to keep Valentine in-doors, and, having armed himself with a game-bag well filled with game, he set out in the costume of a village sportsman—blouse, straw hat and gaiters— certain that it would offend the countess's eyes less than a more pretentious exterior would do.

Valentine was writing in her chamber. An indefinable vague anticipation made her hand tremble ; as her pen formed the words addressed to her sister, it seemed to her that the messenger who was to take charge of them could not be far away. The faintest sound out-of-doors, the trot of a horse, the bark of a dog, made her start. She kept rising and running to the window, calling in her heart to Louise and Bénédict ; for in her eyes—at all events so she thought—Bénédict was only a part of her sister, detached and sent to her.

As she was beginning to be exhausted by involuntary emotion, and sought to turn her mind to other things, that beautiful, pure voice, Bénédict's voice, which she had heard at night on the banks of the Indre, charmed her ear once more. The pen fell from her fingers. She

listened, enchanted, to the artless, simple ballad which
had such extraordinary influence over her nerves. Bénédict's voice came from a path which skirted the park on
quite a steep hillside.   The singer, being higher than
the garden, was able to make these lines of his village
ballad distinctly audible within the château ; perhaps
they were intended as a notice to Valentine :

> " Bergère Solange, écoutez,
> " L'alouette aux champs vous appelle."*

Valentine was not unromantic ; she thought that she
was, because her virgin heart had never yet conceived
the idea of love.   But, while she believed that she could
abandon herself unreservedly to a pure and virtuous
sentiment, her youthful brain did not forbear to love
whatever resembled an adventure.   Brought up under
such unbending glances, in an atmosphere of such strait-
laced and repellent customs, she had had so little chance
to enjoy the bloom and poetry of her youth !

Gluing her face to her blind, she soon saw Bénédict
coming down the path.   Bénédict was not handsome,
but his figure was remarkably graceful.   His rustic costume, which he wore with a somewhat theatrical air, his
light, sure step along the edge of the ravine, his great
spotted dog which ran before him, and, above all, his
song, which was melodious and potent enough to take
the place of beauty of feature—that apparition in a
country landscape which, by the intervention of art, that
despoiler of nature, was not unlike the scenery of an
opera, was enough to excite a youthful brain and to add
an indefinable element of coquetry to the value of the
message he bore.

> * Shepherdess Solange, list ye,
>   The lark in the fields is calling.

Valentine was sorely tempted to rush out into the park, open a little gate by which the path ran, and hold out a greedy hand for the letter which she fancied that she could already see in Bénédict's. That would be decidedly imprudent. But a more praiseworthy motive than the danger detained her—the fear of disobeying twice over by going to meet an adventure which she could not avoid.

So she determined to await a second signal before going down, and soon a great uproar of dogs barking savagely at one another awoke all the echoes of the courtyard. Bénédict had set his dog on those belonging to the château, in order to make known his arrival in the noisiest possible way.

Valentine went down at once. Her instinct led her to divine that Bénédict would preferably pay his respects to the marchioness, as being more approachable. So she joined her grandmother, who was accustomed to take her siesta on the couch in the salon, and, having gently awakened her, made some excuse for sitting with her.

A few minutes later, a servant entered and announced that Monsieur Lhéry's nephew desired to present his respects and his game to the marchioness.

"I can do very well without his respects," the marchioness replied, "but his game is welcome. Show him in."

X

At sight of that young man, whose accomplice she knew herself to be, and whom she was about to assist to deliver a secret message to her under her grandmother's eyes, Valentine had a pang of remorse. She felt that she was blushing, and the crimson of her cheeks was reflected on Bénédict's.

"Ah! so it's you, my boy," said the marchioness, displaying her short, plump leg on the sofa, with the charming manners of the time of Louis XV. "Glad to see you. How is everybody at the farm? Good Mère Lhéry, and the pretty little cousin, and everybody?"

Then, paying no heed to the reply, she plunged her hand in the game-bag which Gabriel removed from his shoulder.

"Ah! this is really a fine lot of game! Did you kill it? They say that you let Trigaud poach a little on our land. But this is enough to absolve you."

"This," said Bénédict, taking from his bosom a little live titmouse, "I caught in the net, by chance. As it's a rare species, I thought that mademoiselle, being interested in natural history, might like to add it to her collection."

As he passed the little creature to Valentine, he pretended to have much difficulty in putting it into her fingers without allowing it to escape. He took advantage of that moment to hand her the letter. Valentine went to a window, as if to examine the bird more closely, and hid the paper in her pocket.

"You must be very warm, my dear fellow ? " said the marchioness. "Pray go to the servants' quarters and get something to drink."

Valentine saw the disdainful smile that curled Bénédict's lip.

"Perhaps monsieur would prefer a glass of pomegranate water ? " she said hastily.

And she took up the carafe, which was on a small table behind her grandmother and herself, and poured out the water for her guest. Bénédict thanked her with a glance, and, passing behind the sofa, took it from her overjoyed to be allowed to touch the glass which Valentine's white hand offered him.

The marchioness had a slight attack of coughing, during which he said rapidly to Valentine :

"What answer shall I carry back to the request contained in this letter ? "

"Whatever it may be, the answer is *yes,*" said Valentine, terrified by such audacity.

Bénédict glanced gravely about that sumptuous and spacious salon, at the limpid mirrors, the polished floor, the thousand and one refinements of luxury, even the uses of which were still unknown at the farm. This was not the first time that he had entered the homes of the wealthy, and his heart was very far from being filled with envious longing for all those baubles of fortune, as Athénaïs's would have been. But he could not help noticing one thing which had never before made such a profound impression on him ; that is, that society had placed tremendous obstacles between Mademoiselle de Raimbault and himself.

"Luckily," he thought, "I can take the risk of seeing her without having to suffer for it. I shall never fall in love with her."

"Well, my dear, won't you go to the piano and continue the song you began for me just now ? "

That was an ingenious falsehood on the old marchioness's part, intended as a hint to Bénédict that it was time for him to retire *to the servants' quarters.*

"You know, grandmamma, I hardly ever sing," Valentine replied ; "but as you are so fond of good music, if you want to give yourself a very great pleasure, ask monsieur to sing."

"Do you mean it ?   But what do you know about it, my child ? " queried the marchioness.

"Athénaïs told me," replied Valentine, lowering her eyes.

"Very well, if it's true, my boy, give me that pleasure," said the marchioness.   "Regale me with some little village ballad ; it will give me a rest from Rossini, whom I don't understand in the least."

"I shall accompany you if you wish," said Valentine shyly to the young man.

Bénédict was more than a little perturbed at the thought that his voice might attract the overbearing countess to the salon.   But he was even more moved by Valentine's efforts to detain him and to make him sit down ; for the marchioness, despite her affectation of popular manners, had not been able to make up her mind to offer her farmer's nephew a chair.

The piano was open.   Valentine seated herself at it, after drawing another chair beside her own.   Bénédict, to show that he had not noticed the affront he had received, preferred to sing standing.

At the first notes Valentine flushed, then turned pale, tears came to her eyes ; gradually she became calm, her fingers followed the singing, and her ear drank it in with zest.

The marchioness listened with pleasure at first. Then, as she was always restless, and could not remain in one place, she left the room, returned, and went out again.

"This tune," said Valentine, when she and Bénédict were alone for a moment, "is the one my sister used to like best to sing to me when I was a child and made her sit down on top of the hill to hear the echoes repeat it. I have never forgotten it, and I almost cried just now when you began it."

"I sang it purposely," said Bénédict; "it was as if I were speaking to you in the name of Louise."

The countess entered the room as that name died on Bénédict's lips. At sight of her daughter's tête-à-tête with a strange man, she glared at them with gleaming, wonderstruck eyes. At first she did not recognize Bénédict, at whom she had hardly glanced at the fête, and her surprise petrified her where she stood. Then, when she remembered the impudent rascal who had dared to put his lips to her daughter's cheeks, she stepped forward, pale and trembling, trying to speak, but prevented by a sudden choking sensation in her throat. Luckily, a laughable incident preserved Bénédict from the explosion. The countess's beautiful greyhound had superciliously walked up to Bénédict's hunting dog, who had unceremoniously thrown himself on the floor under the piano, all covered with dust, and panting. Perdreau, a sensible and patient beast, allowed himself to be sniffed at from head to foot, and contented himself by replying to his host's disdainful advances by the silent display of a long row of white teeth. But when the greyhound, domineering and discourteous, became actually insulting, Perdreau, who had never put up with an affront, and who had held his own against three bulldogs a moment before, stood erect, and threw his slender adversary to the floor with a blow of his head. The greyhound took refuge at his mistress's feet, uttering shrill cries. That was an opportunity for Bénédict, who saw that the countess was fairly beside herself, to rush out of the room, making a pretence of taking Perdreau away and whipping him, whereas in his heart he was sincerely grateful to him for his disregard of the proprieties.

As he went out, escorted by the yelping of the greyhound, the growling of his own dog, and the countess's frantic exclamations, he met the marchioness, who, astonished by the uproar, asked him what it meant.

"My dog has strangled madame's," he replied, with a piteous expression, as he hurried away.

He returned to the farm with an abundant store of contempt and hatred for the nobility, and indulging in a titter at the thought of his adventure. But he was ashamed of himself when he remembered how much more bitter affronts he had anticipated, and how he had plumed himself upon his ironical sangfroid when he left Louise a few hours before. Gradually all the absurdity of the scene seemed to centre about the countess, and he arrived at the farm in high spirits. His story made Athénaïs laugh till she cried. Louise wept when she learned how Valentine had received her message and that she had recognized the ballad Bénédict sang. But Bénédict did not talk about his visit to the château before Père Lhéry. His uncle was not the man to be amused by a joke which might cause the loss of three thousand francs profit every year.

"What does all this mean?" queried the marchioness as she entered the salon.

"I trust, madame, that you will explain it to me," repeated the countess. "Weren't you here when that man came in?"

"What *man?*" said the marchioness.

"Monsieur Bénédict," interposed Valentine, sorely embarrassed, but trying to appear self-possessed. "He brought you some game, mamma; grandmamma asked him to sing, and I played the accompaniment."

"So he was singing for you, madame?" said the countess to her mother-in-law. "You were listening to him at a considerable distance, I should say."

"In the first place," retorted the old woman, "it wasn't I who asked him to sing, it was Valentine."

"This is very strange," cried the countess, with a piercing glance at her daughter.

"I will explain it to you, mamma," said Valentine, blushing. "My piano is horribly out of tune, as you know; we have no tuner in the neighborhood. This young man is a musician; he is also a very good piano tuner. I know it from Athénaïs, who has a piano at home, and often has recourse to her cousin's skill."

"Athénaïs has a piano! this young man a musician! What extraordinary story are you telling me?"

"It is perfectly true, madame," interposed the marchioness. "You are never willing to understand that everybody in France receives some education to-day! Those people are rich; they have bought talents for their children. It is as it should be, it's the fashion; there's nothing to be said. The fellow sings very well, on my word! I listened to him from the hall with much pleasure. Well, what's the matter? Do you think that Valentine was in any danger with him when I was within two steps?"

"Oh! madame," said the countess, "you have a way of interpreting my thoughts——"

"Why, that is because you have such strange thoughts! Here you are all in a fright because you found your daugh-

ter at the piano with a man ! Can a man do any harm
when he is busy singing ? You talk as if I had committed a crime in leaving them alone an instant, as if—
Great heaven ! you didn't look at the fellow, did you ?
He's ugly enough to frighten one ! ''

" Madame," rejoined the countess, with great contempt, " it is very easy to see why you put this construction on my displeasure. As it is impossible for us to
agree on certain matters, I address myself to my daughter. I need not tell you, Valentine, that I do not entertain the coarse thoughts which she attributes to me. I
know you well enough, my child, to know that a man
of that sort is not *a man to you,* and that it is not in his
power to compromise you. But I detest any breach of
propriety, and I consider that you are far too heedless in
that respect. Remember that in society nothing is worse
than absurd situations. You are naturally too good-
humored, too condescending to your inferiors. Remember
that they will not be grateful to you for it, that they will
always abuse your good nature, and that those whom
you treat best will be the most ungrateful. Trust your
mother's experience, and watch yourself more closely.
I have already had occasion several times to reprove you
for lack of dignity. You will realize the inconvenience
of it at some time. Those *creatures* do not understand
how far it is permissible for them to go, and that they
must stop at a fixed point. That little Athénaïs is dis-
gustingly familiar in her manner toward you. I put up
with it because, after all, she is a woman. But I should
not be very much flattered to have her fiancé come and
accost you with a free-and-easy air in a public place.
He is a very ill-bred young man, as all the young men
of his class are, and absolutely lacking in tact. Monsieur de Lansac, who is sometimes inclined to play the

liberal a little too much, gave him far too much credit the other day when he spoke of him as a bright fellow. Another man would have left the dance, but he kissed you most cavalierly, my child. I don't blame you for it," added the countess, seeing that Valentine blushed until she lost countenance. "I know that you suffered sufficiently because of that impertinent performance, and I remind you of it only to prove to you how carefully you must keep the lower classes at a distance."

During this discourse the marchioness sat in a corner shrugging her shoulders. Valentine, crushed under the weight of her mother's logic, replied in a faltering voice:

"It was only because of the piano, mamma, that I thought—I didn't think of the impropriety——"

"If we go about it in the right way," said the countess, disarmed by her submission, "there may not be any harm in having him come here. Did you suggest it to him?"

"I was going to do it, when——"

"In that case we must call him back."

The countess rang, and asked for Bénédict, but she was told that he was already far up the hill.

"This will never do," she said, when the servant had left the room; "not on any account must he be allowed to think that he was admitted here on account of his fine voice. I propose that he shall return in a subordinate capacity, and I will undertake to receive him on that footing. Give me my writing-case. I will explain to him what we want of him."

"Do at least express yourself courteously," said the marchioness, in whose mind fear took the place of reason.

"I know what is customary, madame," retorted the countess.

She hastily wrote a few lines and handed them to Valentine.

"Read this," she said, "and send it to the farm."

Valentine glanced at the note. It was in these words:

"Monsieur Bénédict, will you kindly tune my daughter's piano? I shall be obliged to you.

"I have the honor to salute you.

"F. COMTESSE DE RAIMBAULT."

Valentine took the sealing-wax in her hand and pretended to seal it, but she kept it open and left the room. Should she send that arrogant reprimand? must Bénédict be paid in that way for his devotion? must she treat as a menial the man on whose brow she had not feared to imprint a sisterly kiss? Her heart triumphed over her prudence. She took a pencil from her pocket, and, standing between the double doors of the empty reception room, added these words at the foot of her mother's note:

"Forgive me, forgive me, monsieur! I will explain this request. Come! do not refuse to come! In Louise's name, forgive me!"

Then she sealed the missive and gave it to a servant.

XI

She was unable to open Louise's letter until night. It was a long paraphrase of the few words they had had an opportunity to exchange freely in their interview at the farm. That letter, throbbing with joy and hope, was the outpouring of a typical romantic woman's affection, an effusive affection, true sister to love, and overflowing with adorable childish extravagance and platonic outbursts.

It ended with these words:

"I have discovered by chance that your mother is going to pay a visit in the neighborhood to-morrow. She will not go until toward evening because of the heat. Try to avoid going with her, and as soon as it is dark join me at the end of the large field, by the little copse of Vavray. The moon doesn't rise till midnight, and that spot is always deserted."

The next afternoon about six o'clock the countess left the château, urging Valentine to go to bed, and the marchioness to see to it that she took a very hot foot-bath. But the old woman, saying that she had brought up seven children, and that she knew very well what to do for a sick-headache, very soon forgot everything but herself. Faithful to her old-fashioned indolent habits, she took a bath herself in her granddaughter's place, and summoned her companion to read her one of Crébillon's novels. Valentine made her escape as soon as the shadows began to creep down the hill. She put on a dark dress, in order to be less noticeable in the gathering darkness, and, with no other head covering than her lovely fair hair, which blew about about in the warm evening breeze, she walked rapidly across the field.

The field in question was half a league in length; it was intersected by several wide streams bridged by trunks of trees. Valentine came near falling several times in the darkness. Sometimes her dress caught on invisible thorns, sometimes her foot sank in the treacherous mud of the stream. Her light step roused myriads of buzzing moths; the chirping cricket became mute as she drew near, and now and then an owl asleep in the trunk of an old tree flew up and startled her by grazing her cheek with its soft, flexible wing.

It was the first time that Valentin had ever voluntarily ventured away from her own roof alone, at night. Although her intense excitement lent her strength, fear took possession of her at times, and gave her wings to skim over the grass and across the brooks.

At the appointed place she found her sister impatiently awaiting her. After a thousand loving caresses, they sat down on the bank of a ditch and began to talk.

"Tell me all about your life since I lost you," said Valentine.

Louise told the story of her wanderings, her sorrows, her loneliness, her destitution. She was barely sixteen years old when she went into exile in Germany with an old kinswoman of her family, with a paltry allowance too small to make her independent. As that old woman tyrannized over her, she fled to Italy, where, by hard work and economy, she succeeded in existing. At last, having attained her majority, she came into possession of her patrimony, a very modst sum, for the bulk of the family fortune came from the countess; even the estate of Raimbault, having been redeemed by her, was her own property, and the general's aged mother was indebted for a comfortable existence solely to her daughter-in-law's *excellent behavior.* That was why she was careful not to offend her, and so had entirely abandoned Louise, in order not to be cast into indigence.

Small as was the sum which the unfortunate young woman received, it was wealth to her, and was sufficient to gratify certain desires which she had been able to hold in check. Some circumstance, which she did not explain to her sister, having led her to return to Paris, she had been there ten months when she learned of Valentine's impending marriage. Consumed by the longing to see her sister and her native province, she had written to the old nurse, Madame Lhéry, and that kind-hearted, loving soul, who had never ceased to correspond with her from time to time, lost no time in inviting her to come secretly and pass a few weeks at the farm. Louise eagerly accepted, fearing that Valentine's marriage would soon erect a more insurmountable barrier than ever between them.

"God forbid!" said Valentine; "on the contrary, it will be the signal for our reunion. But look you, Louise, in all that you have told me, you have not referred to a matter which is most interesting to me. You have not told me whether——"

And Valentine, confused at the thought of uttering a single word relating to her sister's terrible wrong-doing, which she would gladly have given all her blood to efface, felt that her tongue was paralyzed and her face bathed in burning perspiration.

Louise understood, and, despite the heart-rending remorse of her whole life, no reproach had ever driven such a keen-edged sword into her breast as that confusion and that silence. She let her head fall on her hands, and, being easily embittered after a life of unhappiness, it seemed to her that Valentine alone had wounded her more deeply than all the rest of the world. But she soon returned to her senses, and said to herself that Valentine was suffering from excessive delicacy; she realized what it must have cost that chaste and modest girl to invite her fuller confidence, or even to dare to wish for it.

"Well, Valentine!" she said, putting an arm about her young sister's neck.

Valentine threw herself upon her breast, and they both burst into tears.

Then Valentine wiped her eyes, and succeeded by a supreme effort in laying aside the rigidity of the young virgin and rising to the rôle of the generous and stout-hearted friend.

"Tell me," she cried, "in all this there is a little being whose blessed influence must have made itself felt throughout your whole life; one whom I do not know, whose name I do not know, but whom it has sometimes seemed to me that I love with all the force of my blood and all the fervor of my affection for you."

"And you want me to speak to you of him, my brave sister! I thought that I should never dare to remind you of his existence. But your greatness of heart surpasses my wildest hopes. My son is alive, he has never left me; I have brought him up myself. I did not try to conceal my error by sending him away from me or denying him my name. He has gone with me everywhere—everywhere his presence has revealed my misfortune and my repentance. And will you believe it, Valentine? I have reached the point where I glory in proclaiming that I am his mother, and in all just hearts I have received absolution in acknowledgment of my courage."

"Even if I were not your sister and your daughter as

well, I would be among those just hearts," said Valentine. "But where is he?"

"My Valentin is at school in Paris. I left Italy to take him there, and it was to see you that I parted from him a month ago. My son is a beautiful boy, Valentine. He has a loving heart; he knows you; he longs most ardently to embrace her whose name he bears. And he resembles you. He is fair-haired and placid like you; at fourteen he is almost your height. Tell me, when you are married, would you like me to bring him to see you?"

Valentine replied by a shower of kisses.

Two hours passed away rapidly, not in recalling the past alone, but in laying plans for the future as well. Valentine went about it with all the confidence of her age; Louise was less hopeful, but she did not say so. Suddenly a black form appeared against the dark blue sky above the ditch. Valentine trembled and uttered a cry of alarm. Louise placed her hand on hers and said:

"Don't be afraid, it's a friend; it's Bénédict."

Valentine was annoyed at first at his presence at the rendezvous. It seemed that all the acts of her life tended to bring that young man and herself together against her will. But she was forced to acknowledge to herself that his presence might be useful to two women in that out-of-the-way spot, and that his escort would be especially agreeable to Louise, who was more than a league from her lodging. Nor could she help noticing the respectful delicacy of feeling which led him to keep out of sight during their interview. A man must surely be very self-sacrificing to mount guard thus for two hours. All things considered, it would be ungrateful to welcome him coldly. She explained her mother's note, took all the blame upon herself, and begged him not to come to the

château without a large supply of patience and philosophy. Bénédict laughingly swore that nothing would
disturb him ; and, after escorting her to the other side
of the field with Louise, he returned with the latter to
the farm.

The next day he appeared at the château. By a freak
of chance, of which Bénédict was not disposed to complain, it was the countess's turn to have a sick-headache ;
but hers was not feigned, it compelled her to keep her
bed. So that things turned out better than Bénédict had
hoped. When he learned that the countess would not
rise during the day, he began by taking the piano apart
and removing all the keys ; then he found that he must
put leathers on all the hammers ; a number of rusted
strings had to be renewed ; in short, he made work for
himself for a whole day, for Valentine was there, handing him the scissors, helping him to unroll the wire from
the reel, striking the keynote for him, and paying more
attention to her piano than she had done in her whole
life before. Bénédict, for his part, was much less skilful at the work than Valentine had declared. He broke
more than one string by tightening it ; more than once he
turned one peg instead of another, and often put a whole
octave out of tune in order to tune a single note. Meanwhile the old marchioness went in and out, coughed and
dozed, and paid no attention to them except to put them
even more at their ease. It was a most delightful day
to Bénédict. Valentine was so sweet, her gayety was
so artless, so genuine, her courtesy so engaging, that it
was impossible not to breathe easily in her company.
And then it happened, I know not how, that after an
hour or two all formal courtesy was banished from their
conversation. A childlike and merry sort of good-fellow-
ship sprang up between them. They joked each other on

their mutual awkwardness, their hands met on the keyboard, and, as merriment banished emotion, they disputed like old friends. At last, about five o'clock, the piano being in tune, Valentine invented a pretext for detaining Bénédict. A touch of hypocrisy made its appearance opportunely in that girlish heart, and knowing that her mother would grant any favor to a deferential exterior, she stole into her bedroom.

"Mamma," she said, "Monsieur Bénédict has passed six hours at my piano, and he hasn't finished; but we are going to sit down to dinner. It seemed to me impossible to send the young man to the servants' quarters, for you never send his uncle there, but have wine served to him on your own table. What shall I do? I dared not ask him to dine with us until I had found out from you whether it would be proper."

A similar request, in more direct terms, would have been met with sharp disapprobation. But the countess was always better satisfied to obtain submission to her principles than passive obedience to her wishes. That preference is characteristic of that form of vanity which seeks to impose respect and love of its domination.

"I think it would be perfectly proper," she replied. "As he complied with my request without hesitation and with a good grace, it is no more than fair to show him some consideration. Go, my child, and invite him yourself in my name."

Valentine returned triumphantly to the salon, delighted to be able to do something agreeable in her mother's name; and she ascribed to her all the honor of the invitation. Bénédict was amazed, and hesitated about accepting. Valentine overstepped her orders somewhat by insisting. As they all three went toward the dining-room, the marchioness whispered to Valentine:

"Was this act of courtesy really an idea of your mother's ? It makes me anxious about her health. Can it be that she is seriously ill ? "

Valentine did not allow herself to smile at that bitter jest. Being the depositary of the lamentations and enmities of those two women in turn she was like a rock beaten by two opposite currents.

The repast was short but cheerful. Then they went into the garden for their coffee. The marchioness was always in good humor after eating. In her day many young women, whose frivolity was tolerated by reason of their charms, and perhaps, also, of the entertainment which their improprieties afforded amid the tedium of a dull and blasé society, used to boast of their bad form : the *naughty* look was very becoming to certain faces. Madame de Provence was the centre of a female coterie who *tossed off champagne to admiration.* A century earlier, *Madame,* sister-in-law to Louis XIV., an honest, solemn German who cared for nothing but *sausages with garlic* and *beer soup,* admired the faculty which the ladies of the French court, especially Madame le Duchesse de Berri, possessed of drinking great quantities without showing it, and of carrying wine of Constance and Hungarian maraschino with marvellous success.

The marchioness was very lively at dessert. She told stories with the ease and naturalness characteristic of those who have lived much in society, in whom those qualities take the place of wit. Bénédict listened to her in amazement. She spoke a language which he supposed to be entirely unknown in her class and to her sex. She used words which did not offend the ear, she said them in such a simple and unaffected way. She told her stories too with an extraordinary clearness of memory, and displayed admirable presence of mind in sparing

Valentine's ear the obscene passages. At times Bénédict looked up at her in dismay, and the poor child's
placid expression showed him so plainly that she had not
understood, that he wondered if he had heard aright himself, if his imagination had not carried him beyond the
real meaning of the words. In fact, he was confounded,
bewildered at the combination of such familiarity with the
usages of society and such moral demoralization, of such
contempt for principle and such respect for social conventions. The society which the marchioness depicted was
to him like a dream in which he refused to believe.

They remained a long while in the garden. Then
Bénédict, tried the piano and sang. It was quite late
when he took his leave, greatly surprised by his intimacy with Valentine, deeply moved, with no idea of the
reason, but dwelling ecstatically upon the image of that
sweet and lovely girl, whom it was impossible not to
love.

XII

A few days later, Madame de Raimbault was invited
by the prefect to a brilliant function which was in preparation in the chief town of the department. It was in honor
of the presence of Madame la Duchesse de Berri, who
was beginning or bringing to a close one of her rollick-
ing expeditions ; an amiable and flighty person, who had
succeeded in winning many hearts despite the lowering
atmosphere, and who long won forgiveness for her extravagant performances by a smile.

Madame de Raimbault was to be one of the small and

7

select party of ladies who were to be presented to the
princess and to have seats assigned them at her table.
In her view, therefore, it was impossible for her to decline
to take that little journey, and she would not have shirked
it for anything on earth.

The daughter of a wealthy tradesman, Mademoiselle
de Chignon had aspired to grandeur from her childhood.
She had chafed indignantly to see her beauty, her queen-
ly charms, her spirit of intrigue and ambition, languish
in the bourgeois atmosphere of a vulgar capitalist. After
her marriage to General Comte de Raimbault, she plunged with transports of delight into the eddying whirl of
the grandeurs of the Empire; she was just the sort of
woman fitted to shine there. Vain, narrow-minded, ignorant, but skilful in the art of crawling at the feet of
royalty; beautiful with that cold, imposing beauty for
which the costume of the time seemed to be especially
chosen; quick to learn the canons of etiquette, shrewd in
conforming to them, fond of dress, luxury, pomp and ceremony, she had never been able to appreciate the pleasures of domestic life; her proud and empty heart had
never realized the joys of home. Louise was ten years
old, and well developed for her years, when Madame de
Raimbault became her step-mother and awoke dismayed
to the fact that her husband's daughter would be a formidable rival within five years. So she relegated her with
her grandmother to the château of Raimbault, and made
up her mind that she would never present her in society.
When, on each occasion that she saw her, she noticed
the progress of her beauty, her coldness for the child
changed to aversion. At last, as soon as she had an opportunity to upbraid her for an error for which her own
neglect of Louise offered some excuse, her aversion became implacable hatred, and she turned her out-of-doors

ignominiously. Some people in society declared that
they knew the more proximate cause of this animosity.
Monsieur de Neuville, the man who seduced Louise and
was afterward killed in a duel by the unfortunate creature's father, had been the countess's lover and her
step-daughter's at the same time, they said.

With the Empire, Madame de Raimbault's brilliant existence came abruptly to an end. Honors, fêtes, amuse-
ments, flattery, display, all disappeared like a dream,
and she awoke one morning, deserted and forgotten in
legitimist France. Some others in her position were
more adroit, and, having lost no time in saluting the
new powers, speedily reascended to the summit of grandeur ; but the countess, who had never had any presence
of mind, and in whom first impulses were always exceedingly violent, absolutely lost her head. She allowed
those who were her friends and companions to see all the
bitterness of her regrets, all her contempt for the *pow-
dered heads,* all her lack of reverence for the rehabili-
tated fashion of piety. Her friends greeted her blas-
phemies with horrified cries ; they turned their backs on
her as a heretic, and aired their indignation in the dress-
ing-rooms and secret apartments of the royal family, to
which they had access, and where their votes disposed
of offices and fortunes.

In the allotment of rewards by the crown, the Comtesse de Raimbault was forgotten ; there was not even a
dame d'atours' berth for her. Compelled to abandon the
menial service so dear to the courtier, she retired to her
estates in the country, and became a declared Bonapart-
ist. The Faubourg Saint-Germain, with which she had
been on friendly terms hitherto, broke with her as being
a person with evil opinions. Her equals, the *parvenus,*
remained, and she accepted them for lack of anything

better ; but she had looked down upon them so in her prosperity, that she could form no substantial attachments among them to console her for what she had lost.

At thirty-five she had been forced to open her eyes to the nothingness of human affairs, and that was a little late for a woman who had wasted her youth, unconscious of its passing, in the intoxication of trivial pleasures. She grew old of a sudden. Not having been cured of her illusions one by one by experience, as is ordinarily the case, she knew nothing of the decline of life save regret and ill humor.

From that time her life was a never-ceasing torment; everything became a subject of envy and irritation to her. To no purpose did she seek to avenge herself by sneers at the absurdities of the Restoration ; in vain did she recall a thousand brilliant memories of the past, in order to disparage by the contrast that new simulacrum of royalty ; ennui was devouring that woman whose life had been a constant holiday, and who was now compelled to vegetate in the obscurity of private life.

The household duties which had always been unfamiliar to her became hateful ; her daughter, whom she hardly knew, poured little balm on her wounds. It was necessary to train the child for the future, and Madame de Raimbault could live only in the past. Parisian society, in which such an extraordinary change in manners and morals took place all of a sudden, spoke a new language which she did not understand. Its diversions bored or disgusted her ; its solitude filled her with feverish unrest and dismay. Ill with wrath and chagrin, she languished on her couch, no longer surrounded by a fawning secondary court, a miniature of the great court of the sovereign. Her companions in disgrace came to her to groan over their own grievances, and to insult hers by

belittling them.   Each one of them claimed a monopoly
of the disgrace of the age and the ingratitude of France.
They formed a little coterie of outraged victims who fed
upon one another.

These selfish recriminations augmented Madame de
Raimbault's feverish bitterness.

If, by chance, some more fortunate mortals offered her
a friendly hand, and told her that the favors of Louis the
Eighteenth had effaced from their minds the memories of
the court of Napoléon, she revenged herself for their
prosperity by overwhelming them with reproaches, ac-
cusing them of treachery to the great man—she, who had
not betrayed him in the same way only because she had
not had an opportunity ! At last, to put the finishing touch
to her distress and consternation, the Comtesse de Raimbault discovered, by dint of looking at herself by daylight in her cold, rigid mirrors, sullen and withered,
without fine clothes, without rouge and without jewels,
that her youth and beauty had come to an end with the
Empire.

Now she was fifty years of age, and although her past
beauty was no longer written on her features except in
hieroglyphics, vanity, which never dies in some women's
hearts, caused her more intense suffering than at any
time in her life.   Her daughter, whom she loved with
the instinctive affection which necessity imposes even on
the most perverse natures, was to her a constant source
of longing for the past and hatred of the present.   She
introduced her in society with the utmost repugnance,
and, when she saw that she was admired, her first feeling was maternal pride, her second, despair.

"Her life as a woman is beginning," she said to herself ; "it is all over with mine ! "

So it was that when she found an opportunity to ap-

pear without Valentine, she felt less unhappy. She no
longer noticed the awkwardly complimentary glances
which seemed to say :

"That is the way you used to look long ago. I can
remember you when you were beautiful."

She did not carry her coquetry to the point of shutting
her daughter up when she went into society ; but the
moment that Valentine manifested the slightest inclination to stay at home, the countess, perhaps unconsciously, would accept her excuses, start off alone with a
lighter heart, and breathe more at her ease in the agitated atmosphere of fashionable salons.

Bound fast to that forgetful and pitiless society which
had naught in store for her now but disappointment and
mortification, she still allowed herself to be dragged
about like a dead body at its chariot wheel. Where was
she to live ? How could she kill time during those end-
less days which were turning her hair gray, and which
she regretted as soon as they had passed ? The slaves
of fashion, when they are deprived of the enjoyment of
self-esteem, when every incentive to passion is taken
away, can still take pleasure in the glare of candles and
the bustle and buzzing of the crowd. After all the dreams
of love and ambition have vanished, there still remains
the longing to stir about and make a noise, to keep watch
and say : " I was there yesterday, I shall be there again
to-morrow."—It is a sad spectacle to see those blighted
women concealing their wrinkles with flowers and
crowning their haggard brows with diamonds and feathers. Everything about them is false : figure, complexion, hair, smile ; everything is depressing : costume,
paint, merriment. Like spectres from the saturnalia of
another age, they seat themselves at the banquets of to-
day as if to give the young a sad lesson in philosophy,

as if to say to them: "The same fate awaits you."
They seem to cling to life as it turns its back on them,
and to repel the insults of decrepitude while displaying it
in its nakedness to insulting glances. Women deserving of pity, almost all without families or without hearts,
whom we see on all festive occasions intoxicating themselves with smoke and memories and noise !

The countess, despite the tedium of that empty, profit-
less life, could not cut loose from it. Although she said
that she had abandoned it forever, she never lost an opportunity to plunge into it anew. When she was invited
to that provincial function over which the princess was
to preside, she was overjoyed ; but she concealed her joy
beneath an air of disdainful condescension. She even
flattered herself secretly that she might be taken into
favor again, if she could attract the princess's attention
and show her how superior she was, both in tone and in
familiarity with the ways of good society, to her whole
entourage. Moreover, her daughter was to marry Monsieur de Lansac, one of the pillars of the legitimate cause.
It was high time to take a step toward that aristocracy of
name to which her aristocracy of wealth was about to
impart new lustre. Madame de Raimbault had hated the
nobility only since the nobility had spurned her. Perhaps the time had come when she was to see all those
vain creatures become more affable to her at a sign from
Madame.

So she exhumed from the depths of her wardrobe her
richest dresses, meditating awhile what she would put
upon Valentine to make her seem less tall and well
formed than she really was. But during her scrutiny
it happened that Valentine, desirous to take advantage
of that week of freedom, became more ingenious and
keen-witted than she had been as yet. She began to

comprehend that her mother raised those momentous questions of dress, and created those insoluble difficulties, in order to induce her to remain at the château. A few stinging words from the old marchioness on the inconvenience of having a daughter of nineteen to bring out, completed Valentine's enlightenment. She hastened to condemn fashions, festivities, journeys and prefects. Her mother, amazed beyond measure, agreed with her most heartily, and proposed that they should both abandon the journey. The decision was soon made ; but, an hour later, when Valentine had ceased her preparations and was unpacking her boxes, Madame de Raimbault renewed her preparations, saying that she had reflected ; that it would be a breach of propriety and perhaps dangerous for her not to go and pay her respects to the princess ; that she would sacrifice herself to the necessity of taking that step from pure policy, but that she would excuse Valentine.

Valentine, who had become extraordinarily crafty within a week, dissembled her joy.

The next day, as soon as the wheels of the countess's calèche had left their tracks on the gravel of the avenue, Valentine ran and asked her grandmother's permission to pass the day with Athénaïs at the farm. She pretended to have been invited by her young friend to partake of cakes on the greensward. She had no sooner mentioned the subject of cakes than she shuddered with fright, for the old marchioness was at once sorely tempted to join her ; but the distance and the heat led her to abandon the idea.

Valentine rode to within a short distance of the farm, where she dismounted, sent away her groom and her horse, and flew like a turtle-dove along the flowering hedges which lined the road to Grangeneuve.

XIII

She had found a way, the day before, to warn Louise of her visit; so that the whole farm-house was in order and waiting joyfully to receive her. Athénaïs had put fresh flowers in the blue glass vases. Bénédict had trimmed the trees in the garden, raked the paths and repaired the benches. Madame Lhéry had made with her own hands the finest cake that had been seen since housekeeping was invented. Monsieur Lhéry had shaved, and drawn some of his best wine. There were exclamations of joy and surprise when Valentine entered the living-room quietly and alone. She embraced Mère Lhéry like a madcap, and the old woman bowed to the ground. She shook hands warmly with Bénédict; she frolicked like a child with Athénaïs; she hung about her sister's neck. Valentine had never felt so happy. Out of reach of her mother's eyes and of the frigid constraint which impeded her every step, it seemed to her that she breathed a clearer air, and, for the first time since she was born, lived her whole life. Valentine was naturally amiable and sweet. Heaven had gone astray in sending that simple, unambitious soul to dwell in palaces and breathe the atmosphere of courts. No one could be less adapted for a life of show, for the triumphs of vanity. On the contrary, her pleasures were all modest, all domestic; and the more she was blamed for indulging in them, the more eagerly she aspired to that simple life which in her eyes was the promised land. If she wished to marry, it was that she might have a home and children, and live a retired life. Her heart craved close affections, few in number and without variety. To lead a virtuous life seemed likely to be as easy a matter to her as to any woman on earth.

But the luxury with which she was encompassed, which anticipated her slightest wants, which divined even her caprices, forbade her to perform the most trivial household duties. With twenty servants at her call, it would have seemed absurd, almost parsimonious, for her to take an active part in the management of the household. She was hardly allowed to take care of her aviary, and one could easily divine Valentine's character by the love with which she devoted herself to the welfare of its tiny occupants, even to the smallest details.

When she found herself at the farm, surrounded by hens, hunting-dogs and kids; when she saw Louise spin-ning, Madame Lhéry cooking, and Bénédict mending his nets, it seemed to her that that was the sphere for which she was made. She insisted on having some employ-ment herself, and, to Athénaïs's great surprise, instead of opening the piano or asking for a piece of her em-broidery, she began to knit on a gray stocking which she found on the chair. Athénaïs was amazed at her dexterity, and asked her if she knew for whom she was working so zealously.

"For whom?" said Valentine. "I haven't an idea; it's for some one of you, at all events; for yourself, perhaps."

"Those gray stockings for me!" said Athénaïs, dis-dainfully.

"Are they for you, my dear sister?" Valentine asked Louise.

"I work on them sometimes," said Louise, "but Mamma Lhéry began them. For whom? I know no better than you."

"Suppose they were for Bénédict?" queried Athénaïs, looking at Valentine with a mischievous expression.

Bénédict stopped working, raised his head, and watched the two young women without speaking.

Valentine blushed slightly, but instantly recovered herself.

"Why, if they're for Bénédict," she replied, "it's all right; I will gladly work on them."

She looked up with a smile at her old playmate. Athénaïs was purple with anger. An indefinable feeling of irony and distrust had found its way into her heart.

"Oho!" said honest Valentine, with heedless candor, "that doesn't seem to please you overmuch. In truth, I am doing wrong, Athénaïs; I am poaching on your preserves, usurping privileges which belong to you. Come, come, take the work now, and forgive me for putting my hand to the wedding outfit."

"Mademoiselle Valentine," interposed Bénédict, impelled by a pitiless feeling toward his cousin, "if you do not regret working for the humblest of your vassals, continue, I beg you. My cousin's pretty fingers have never touched such coarse yarn and such heavy needles."

A tear glistened on Athénaïs's black lashes. Louise glanced reprovingly at Bénédict. Valentine looked in amazement from one to another, trying to fathom the mystery.

The thing that hurt the young woman most in her cousin's words was not so much the reproach of frivolity —she was used to that—as the submissive and, at the same time, familiar tone in which he addressed Valentine. She knew in a general way the story of their acquaintance, and hitherto she had not thought of taking alarm at it. But she had no idea of the rapid progress of an intimacy which would never have come about under ordinary circumstances. She was amazed and pained to hear Bénédict, naturally so rebellious and so hostile to the pretensions of the nobility, style himself Mademoiselle de Raimbault's humble vassal. What sort of a revolution had taken place in his ideas ? How had Valentine already acquired such influence over him ?

Louise, observing an expression of gloom on every face, proposed a fishing party in the Indre before dinner. Valentine, who had an instinctive feeling that she had been unfair to Athénaïs, affectionately passed her arm through hers, and started to run with her across the field. Warm-hearted and sincere creature that she was, she succeeded in scattering the clouds that had gathered in the girl's heart. Bénédict, dressed in his blouse and carrying his net, followed them with Louise, and the four soon reached the banks of the river, lined with lotus and soapwort.

Bénédict threw the net. He was strong and dexterous. In bodily exercises he displayed the power, the courage and the rustic grace of the peasant. They were qualities which Athénaïs did not appreciate at their true value, being shared by all the men about her ; but Valentine marvelled at them as at supernatural things, and readily accorded to Bénédict superiority in one respect to all the men whom she knew. She was frightened to see him venture on a rotten willow which overhung the water and crumbled under his feet ; and when she saw him escape, by a vigorous leap, what seemed a certain fall, and coolly and adroitly land on small level spots which it seemed the rushes and grass must hide from him, she felt her heart beat with an indefinable emotion, as al-

ways happens when we see a perilous or difficult undertaking bravely performed.

After catching a few trout, Louise and Valentine
pouncing with childish glee on the dripping net and
seizing the booty with shouts of joy, while Athénaïs,
fearing to soil her fingers, or harboring a grudge against
her cousin, sulkily concealed herself in the shadow of
the alders, Bénédict, exhausted with the heat, sat on a
roughly-hewn ash-tree which was thrown from bank to
bank by way of bridge. Scattered over the bright green
grass by the river, the three women employed themselves in different ways. Athénaïs gathered flowers,
Louise tossed leaves into the stream with a melancholy
air, and Valentine, being less accustomed to the fresh
air and sunshine and walking, dozed gently, concealed
as she supposed by the tall river-grass. Her eyes, after
wandering for a long while over the rippling surface of
the water and a sunbeam that stole through the branches,
fell by chance upon Bénédict, whom she discovered
about ten yards in front of her, seated on the springy
bridge with his legs hanging down.

Bénédict was not absolutely without beauty. His complexion was of a bilious pallor, his long eyes were of no
color, but his forehead was very high and extremely
smooth. By virtue of a power inherent in men endowed
with some mental force, the eye became gradually accustomed to the shortcomings of his face and saw only its
beauties. This is true of some ugly faces, and was no-
ticeably true of Bénédict's. His smooth, sallow skin
gave an impression of tranquillity which inspired a sort
of instinctive respect for that mind whose impulses were
betrayed by no outward alteration of his features. His
eyes, in which the colorless pupils swam in a sea of
white vitreous humor, had a vague and mysterious ex-

pression which could not fail to arouse the curiosity of
every observer. But they would have driven Lavater
to despair with all his learning; they seemed to read
the eyes of others to their lowest depths, and their immo-
bility was positively metallic when they had occasion to
be suspicious of an impertinent examination. A woman,
when she was beautiful, could not endure their gleam ;
an enemy could not detect any sign of weakness in them.
He was a man whom one could look at at any time and
never find him below his own level ; it was a face which
could allow the thoughts to wander without being made
ugly thereby, as so many faces are. No woman could
view him with indifference, and, if the lips sometimes
decried him, the imagination did not readily lose the impression he made upon it ; no one could meet him for the
first time without following him with the eye as long as
possible ; no artist could look at him without admiration
for his singular countenance, and without longing to re-
produce it.

When Valentine looked at him, he was absorbed in
one of those profound reveries which seemed of frequent
occurrence with him. The shadow of the foliage above
him gave a greenish tinge to his broad forehead, his eyes
were fixed intently on the water and seemed to see nothing. The fact is that they did see to perfection Valentine's face reflected in the motionless stream. He took
keen pleasure in that contemplation, the object of which
vanished whenever a faint breeze ruffled the surface of
the mirror; then the charming image gradually took
shape again, uncertain and vague at first, and in due
time became placid and lovely against the crystalline
background. Bénédict was not thinking ; he was gazing,
he was happy, and it was at such moments that he was
handsome.

Valentine had always heard it said that Bénédict was
ugly. According to provincial ideas—in the provinces,
as Monsieur Stendhal has wittily said, a *handsome man*
is always stout and redfaced—Bénédict was the most ill-
favored of youths. Valentine had never looked closely
at him. She had retained in her mind the impression
she had received at their first meeting ; that impression
was unfavorable. Not until the last few moments had
she begun to find that there was something inexpressibly
charming about him. Absorbed herself in a reverie
which had no definite subject, she yielded to that hazardous curiosity which analyzes and compares. She discovered that there was a vast difference between Bénédict
and Monsieur de Lansac. She did not ask herself in
whose favor that difference was ; she simply recognized
its existence. As Monsieur de Lansac was handsome, and
as she was engaged to him, she was not disturbed as to the
result of that imprudent contemplation. It did not occur
to her that her fiancé might come out of it vanquished.

And yet that is what happened. Bénédict, pale, fatigued, pensive, with dishevelled hair ; Bénédict, dressed
in coarse clothes and smeared with mud, with his bare,
sunburned neck ; Bénédict, seated in an unstudied attitude amid that lovely verdure, over that lovely stream ;
Bénédict, who was gazing at Valentine without Valentine's knowledge, and smiling with admiration ; Bénédict
at that moment was a man ; a man of the fields and of
nature, a man whose manly breast could throb with an
intense passion, a man forgetful of himself in the contemplation of the fairest of God's creatures. I know not
what magnetic emanations played in the scorching air
about him ; I know not what mysterious, vague, involuntary emotions suddenly made the young countess's pure
and ignorant heart beat fast.

Monsieur de Lansac was a dandy endowed with beauty
of the conventional type, exceedingly clever, an unex-
celled talker, who always laughed at the right moment,
and never did anything out of season. There was never
a wrinkle on his face any more than in his cravat;
one could see that his costume, even to the smallest details, was to him as important and sacred a matter as the
most momentous diplomatic discussion. He had never
wondered at anything; at all events, he had ceased to
wonder, for he had seen the greatest potentates of Eu-
rope. He had gazed unmoved at the most exalted lead-
ers of society; he had soared aloft in the highest social
spheres; he had discussed the very existence of nations
between dessert and coffee. Valentine had always seen
him in society, in full dress, on his guard, exhaling perfumes and making the most of every fraction of an inch
of his stature. She had never had a glimpse of the man
in him; at morning and at night Monsieur de Lansac was
always the same. He rose a secretary of embassy; he
never mused; he never forgot himself so far before any
person as to commit the impropriety of reflecting; he was
as impenetrable as Bénédict, but with this difference,
that he had nothing to conceal, that he had no will of his
own, and that his brain contained nothing except the
solemn nonsense of diplomacy. In short, Monsieur de
Lansac, a man devoid of generous passion, of mental
vigor, already worn out and withered by years of fashionable society, incapable of appreciating Valentine,
whom he praised incessantly and never admired, had
not, at any time, aroused in her one of those swift, irresistible impulses which transform and enlighten, and lead
one impetuously on to a new life.

Imprudent Valentine! She had so little idea what
love is, that she believed that she loved her fiancé;

not passionately, it is true, but with all her power of loving.

Because that man inspired no passion in her, she fancied that her heart was incapable of passion; she felt the first thrill of love in the shadow of those trees. In that hot, stinging air her blood began to stir; several times, as she looked at Bénédict, she felt a strange flush rise from her heart to her forehead, and the innocent girl did not know what excited her so. She was not alarmed: she was engaged to Monsieur de Lansac, Bénédict was engaged to his cousin. Those were excellent reasons; but Valentine, being accustomed to look upon her duties as easy to perform, did not dream that a sentiment fatal to those duties might be born in her.

XIV

At first, Bénédict gazed at Valentine's image calmly enough; gradually, a painful sensation, more prompt in its action and more keen than that which she experienced, forced him to change his position and to try to turn his mind to something else. He took up his net and made another cast, but he could not catch anything; he was distraught. He could not take his eyes from Valentine's; whether he leaned over the bank or ventured on the loose stones or on the smooth and slippery pebbles in the river-bed, he inevitably met Valentine's glance, watching him, brooding over him, so to speak, with tender solicitude. Valentine did not know how to dissemble; she did not consider that on that occasion there

8

was the slightest occasion for her to do so. Bénédict's heart beat fast beneath that artless and affectionate glance. For the first time he was proud of his strength and his courage. He crossed a dam over which the river was rushing furiously; in three leaps he was on the other bank. He returned; Valentine's face was white; Bénédict's bosom swelled with pride.

And then, as they returned to the farm by a long circuit through the meadows, all three women walking in front of him, he reflected a little. He said to himself that of all the mad things he could possibly do, the most wretched, the most fatal to his future repose would be to fall in love with Mademoiselle de Raimbault. But did he love her?

"No!" said Bénédict, with a shrug, "I am not such a fool; I am not in love with her. I love her to-day, as I loved her yesterday, with a purely brotherly, placid affection."

He closed his eyes to all the rest, and, summoned by a glance from Valentine, quickened his pace and went to her side, resolved to enjoy the charm which she had the art of diffusing all about her, and in which there *could be no danger*.

The heat was so intense that those three delicate women were obliged to sit down to rest. They sat in the shade in a little ravine through which a small brook had once flowed into the river. It had run dry only a little while before, and an abundant crop of osiers and wild flowers was growing in the damp ground. Bénédict, staggering under the weight of his nets, which were weighted with lead, threw himself on the ground a few steps from them. But in a few minutes they were all grouped about him, for all three of them loved him: Louise with fervent gratitude because of Valentine, Val-

entine—at least, so she believed—because of Louise, and
Athénaïs on her own account.

But they were no sooner seated beside him, alleging
that there was more shade there, than Bénédict moved
nearer to Valentine on the pretext that the sun was creep-
ing in on the other side. He had put the fish in his handkerchief, and was wiping his forehead with his cravat.

"That must be pleasant," said Valentine, in a jesting
tone; "a silk cravat! I should as lief wipe my face with
a handful of these holly leaves."

"If you were more humane, you would take pity on
me instead of criticizing me," retorted Bénédict.

"Will you have my fichu?" said Valentine. "I have
nothing else to offer you."

Bénédict held out his hand without speaking. Valentine untied the kerchief she wore about her neck.

"Here, here's my handkerchief," said Athénaïs, hastily, tossing him a tiny square of lawn, embroidered and
trimmed with lace.

"Your handkerchief isn't good for anything," rejoined
Bénédict, seizing Valentine's before she had thought of
taking it back.

He did not deign even to pick up his cousin's, which
fell on the grass beside him. Athénaïs, wounded to the
quick, rose and sullenly walked back toward the farm-
house. Louise, who understood her chagrin, ran after
her to console her, to show her how utterly absurd her
jealousy was; and, meanwhile, Bénédict and Valentine,
who had noticed nothing, were left alone in the ravine,
within two feet of each other, Valentine seated and pretending to play with the wild flowers, Bénédict reclining,
pressing that burning neckerchief to his brow, to his
neck, to his breast, and gazing at Valentine with a look
whose flame she felt but dared not meet.

She sat thus under the spell of that electric current which, at her age and Bénédict's, with hearts so inexperienced, imaginations so timid, and senses whose ardor nothing has blunted, possesses such magical power! They did not speak; they dared not exchange a smile or a word. Valentine was as if fascinated, Bénédict forgot himself in an impetuous flood of happiness; and, when Louise's voice called them, they regretfully left that spot, where their hearts had spoken secretly but forcibly to each other.

Louise came to meet them.

"Athénaïs is angry," she said. "You treat her cruelly, Bénédict; you are not generous. Tell him so, Valentine, darling. Urge him to show more appreciation of his cousin's affection."

Valentine was conscious of a cold sensation about her heart. She could not understand in the least the extraordinary grief that took possession of her at that thought. However, she soon mastered her agitation, and, looking at Bénédict in surprise, said to him in the innocent candor of her heart:

"Have you grieved Athénaïs? I didn't notice it. What did you say to her, pray?"

"Oh! nothing," said Bénédict, with a shrug; "she is foolish!"

"No, she is not foolish," said Louise, severely, "but you are cruel and unjust. Bénédict, my friend, do not ruin this day, such a lovely day to me, by a fresh blunder. Our young friend's grief spoils my happiness and Valentine's."

"That is true," said Valentine, putting her arm through Bénédict's in imitation of Louise, who was dragging him along on the other side. "Let us go and overtake the poor child, and if you have really treated her badly, make up to her for it, so that we may all be happy to-day."

Bénédict started when he felt Valentine's arm slipping under his. He unconsciously pressed it against his breast, and ended by holding it there so fast that she could not take it away without showing that she noticed his agitation. It was so much better to pretend to be insensible to the violent throbs with which the young man's bosom rose and fell. Moreover, Louise was hurrying them along toward Athénaïs, who took a malicious pleasure in quickening her pace to prevent their overtaking her. How little the poor girl suspected her fiancé's frame of mind! Quivering with emotion, drunk with joy between those two sisters, one whom he had loved, the other whom he was in a fair way to love—Louise, who, no longer than the day before, awoke some reminiscences of a love that was hardly dead, and Valentine, who was beginning to intoxicate him with all the fervor of a new passion—Bénédict was not quite sure for which of them his heart yearned, and at times imagined that it was for both—one is so rich in love at twenty! And both were dragging him along so that he might lay at the feet of another woman that pure homage which each of them perhaps regretted that she could not accept. Wretched women! Wretched state of society when the heart can find no real enjoyment except in total forgetfulness of duty and reason!

At a bend in the road, Bénédict halted abruptly, and, their hands in his, looked at them one after the other—at Louise with affectionate regard, then at Valentine with less assurance and greater warmth.

"So you want me to go and soothe that girl's capricious sensibilities, eh?" he said. "Very well, I will go to please you, but you will be grateful to me, I trust!"

"Why is it necessary for us to urge you to do a thing that your conscience should dictate to you?" said Louise.

Bénédict smiled and looked at Valentine.

"Why, yes," she faltered, confused beyond words, "isn't she worthy of your affection? isn't she the woman you are to marry?"

Bénédict's face lighted up. He dropped Louise's hand, but retained Valentine's a moment longer, pressing it imperceptibly; and exclaimed, raising his eyes to the sky, as if to record his oath there in presence of those two witnesses:

"Never!"

His glance seemed to say to Louise: "Never will love for her find its way into a heart where you have reigned!"—and to Valentine: "Never! for you will reign in my heart forever!"

Thereupon he ran after Athénaïs, leaving the two sisters speechless with surprise.

It must be confessed that that word *never* made such an impression on Valentine that it seemed to her that she would fall. Never did such selfish, cruel joy invade by force the sanctuary of a generous heart.

She stood for a moment unable to recover her self-possession; then, leaning on her sister's arm, never thinking, innocent creature, that the trembling of her body could easily be detected, she asked:

"What does this mean?"

But Louise was so engrossed by her own thoughts that Valentine had to repeat the question twice before she heard it. At last she answered that she did not understand it at all.

Bénédict overtook his cousin in three bounds, and said to her, putting his arm around her waist:

"Are you angry?"

"No," the girl replied, in a tone which indicated that she was exceedingly angry.

"You are a child," said Bénédict; "you are constantly doubting my friendship."

"Your friendship?" said Athénaïs, bitterly. "I don't ask you for it."

"Ah! so you spurn it, do you? In that case——"

Bénédict walked a few steps away. Athénaïs, pale as death and hardly able to breathe, dropped on an old willow at the side of the road.

Bénédict at once returned to her. He did not love her enough to care to enter into a discussion with her; he preferred to take advantage of her emotion rather than waste time justifying himself.

"Come, come, cousin," he said in a stern tone which cowed poor Athénaïs completely, "will you stop being sulky with me?"

"Am I the one who is sulky, pray?" she retorted, bursting into tears.

Bénédict stooped and imprinted a kiss on a cool, white neck which the sunshine of the fields had not reddened. The young woman quivered with pleasure and threw herself into her cousin's arms. Bénédict had a painful feeling of discomfort. Athénaïs was unquestionably a very beautiful girl. Moreover, she loved him; and, believing that she was to be his wife, she artlessly manifested her love. It was very hard for Bénédict to avoid a feeling of gratified self-esteem and a sensation of physical pleasure when she caressed him. But his conscience bade him put aside all thought of a union with that young woman, for he felt that his heart was enchained forever elsewhere.

So he rose hastily and led Athénaïs back toward their

two companions, after kissing her. That was the way
that all their quarrels ended. Bénédict, who could not,
who did not choose to tell her his thoughts, avoided anything like an explanation, and always succeeded in soothing the credulous Athénaïs by some slight manifestation
of affection.

When they joined Louise and Valentine, Bénédict's
fiancée threw herself effusively on the neck of the latter.
Her easily moved and kindly heart sincerely abjured all
hard feeling, and Valentine, as she returned her caresses,
was conscious of something like remorse.

Nevertheless, the good humor depicted on Athénaïs's
face infected them all three. They soon arrived at the
house, laughing and frolicking. Dinner not being ready,
Valentine wished to walk about the farm, to visit the
sheepfolds, cowsheds and dovecote. Bénédict paid little
heed to such matters, yet he would have been glad to
have his fiancée display more interest in them. When
he saw Mademoiselle de Raimbault go into the stables,
run after the young lambs and take them in her arms,
fondle all of Madame Lhéry's pets, and even feed with
her white hand the great oxen, who gazed at her with
a dazed expression, he smiled at a flattering and cruel
thought that came into his mind—that Valentine seemed
much better fitted than Athénaïs to be his wife; that
there had been a mistake in the distribution of parts,
and that Valentine as a cheerful and contented farmer's
wife would have made domestic life attractive to him.

"If only she were Madame Lhéry's daughter!" he
said to himself, "then I should never have had the ambition to study; even now I would abandon the empty
dream of playing a part in the world. I would joyfully
turn peasant. I would lead a useful, practical life; with
Valentine, in the heart of this lovely valley, I would be

poet and ploughman at once : poet to admire her, ploughman to serve her. Ah! how readily would I forget the
buzzing crowds in the cities!"

He indulged in these reflections as he followed Valentine through the barns, where she delighted to inhale the
healthy country odor. Suddenly she turned to him and
said :

"I really believe that I was born to be a farmer! Oh!
how dearly I should have loved this simple life and these
placid everyday occupations! I would have done everything myself like Madame Lhéry. I would have raised
the finest flocks in the province; I would have had
beautiful tufted fowls, and goats which I would have
taken out to graze in the bushes. If you knew how
often in salons, in the midst of brilliant festivities, wear-
ied by the noise of the crowd, I have dreamed that I was
a shepherdess sitting under the trees in a field! But the
orchestra would summon me to join the whirl; my dream
was a vain hope!"

Bénédict, leaning against a manger, listened with profound emotion, for she had just answered aloud, as if by
a sympathetic interchange of ideas, the wishes he had
formed under his breath.

They were alone. Bénédict determined to take the
risk of pursuing the dream.

"But suppose that it would have been necessary for
you to marry a peasant?" he said.

"In these days of ours," she replied, "there are no
longer any peasants. Do not almost all classes receive
the same education? Is not Athénaïs more talented than
I am? Is not such a man as you, by reason of his attain-
ments, far superior to a woman like me?"

"Have you none of the prejudices of birth?" queried
Bénédict.

"But I am supposing that I am a farmer's daughter ; in that case I could not have had them."

"That doesn't follow. Athénaïs was born a farmer's daughter, and she is sorry that she wasn't born a countess."

"Oh ! how happy I should be if I were in her place ! " she said earnestly.

And she leaned pensively against the crib, facing Bénédict, with her eyes fixed on the ground, not dreaming that she had just said things to Bénédict which he would gladly have bought with his blood.

Bénédict was intoxicated for a long time by the wild but flattering dreams to which this conversation gave rise. His reason fell asleep in that delicious silence, and all sorts of joyous and deceitful ideas came to the surface. He fancied himself a master farmer and happy spouse in the Black Valley. He fancied that Valentine was his helpmeet, his housekeeper, his fairest possession. He dreamed wide awake, and two or three times the delusion was so complete that he almost took her in his arms. When the sound of voices warned them of the approach of Louise and Athénaïs, he fled in the opposite direction and hid in a dark corner of the barn behind the bundles of grain. There he wept like a child, like a woman, as he never remembered having wept before. He wept for the dream which had taken him away for an instant from the world, and had given him more joy in a few moments of illusion than he had known in a whole lifetime of reality. When he had wiped away his tears, when he saw Valentine, as lovely and serene as ever, questioning his face with mute anxiety, he was happy again. He said to himself that there was more happiness and glory in being loved, in despite of men and of destiny, than in winning a lawful affection without trouble or danger. He plunged up to the neck in that deceitful sea of desires and chimerical fancies ; his dream began anew. At table he took his seat beside Valentine ; he imagined that she was mistress of his house. As she was delighted to assume the whole burden of the service, she carved, distributed the portions, and took pleasure in making herself useful to all. Bénédict looked at her with a dazed, ecstatic expression. He did not pay her a single one of the customary courteous attentions which constantly recall social conventions and distinctions ; and when he wished to be served with anything, he said, as he passed his plate :

"Give me some, *Madame la fermière!*"

Although they drank native wine at the farm, Monsieur Lhéry had some excellent champagne in reserve for great occasions ; but no one indulged in it. The mental intoxication was strong enough. Those healthy young people had no need to excite their nerves and lash their blood. After dinner they played hide-and-seek in the fields. Even Monsieur and Madame Lhéry, relieved at last from the cares of the day, took part in the game. A pretty maid-servant at the farm and the tenant-farmer's children were also admitted. Soon the fields rang with joyous shouts and laughter. It was the last blow to Bénédict's reason. To pursue Valentine, slacken his pace to let her gain on him and force her to go astray in the bushes, then to pounce upon her unexpectedly, laugh at her shrieks and her ruses, to overtake her at last and not dare to touch her, but to see her heaving bosom, her rosy cheeks and her moist eyes, was too much for one day.

Athénaïs, noticing these frequent absences of Bénédict and Valentine, and wishing to make him run after her, proposed that the pursuer should be blindfolded.

She cunningly tied the handkerchief over Bénédict's eyes, thinking that he could no longer select his victim ; but little did Bénédict care for the bandage ! The instinct of love, that powerful, magic spell which enables the lover to recognize the air through which his mistress has passed, guided him as unerringly as his eyes. He always caught Valentine, and was even happier than in the other game, for he could take her in his arms, and, pretending not to recognize her, keep her there a long time. Games of that sort are the most dangerous things in the world.

At last night came, and Valentine spoke of returning home. Bénédict was beside her, and could not conceal his disappointment.

"Already !" he cried in a loud, rough tone, which carried conviction of the true state of affairs to Valentine's heart.

"Already !" she replied, "the day has seemed very short to me."

She kissed her sister, but she was not thinking of Louise when she made that remark.

The carriage was made ready. Bénédict promised himself a few more moments of happiness, but the young women seated themselves in a way to disappoint expectations. Louise sat on the back seat in order not to be seen in the neighborhood of the château. Her sister sat beside her. Athénaïs took her place on the front seat beside her cousin ; he was so angry that he did not speak to her during the whole drive.

At the park gate, Valentine asked him to stop because of Louise, who was afraid of being seen in spite of the darkness. Bénédict leaped to the ground in order to help her to alight. All was dark and silent about that sumptuous abode, which Bénédict would have been glad to see sink into the earth. Valentine kissed her sister and Athénaïs, gave her hand to Bénédict, who ventured to kiss it this time, and hurried away across the park. Through the gate, Bénédict watched the fluttering of her white dress for a few moments as it receded through the trees: he would have forgotten the whole earth had not Athénaïs called him from the carriage and said sharply:

"Well, are you going to leave us to pass the night here?"

XV

At the farm, no one slept during the night which followed that day. Athénaïs complained of feeling ill when they returned; her mother was very anxious, and consented to go to bed only at Louise's earnest entreaty. The latter agreed to pass the night with her young friend, and Bénédict retired to his own room where, torn as he was between joy and remorse, he was unable to obtain an instant's sleep.

As a result of the fatigue caused by a hysterical attack, Athénaïs slept soundly; but soon the troubles which had tormented her during the day entered into her dreams, and she began to weep bitterly. Louise, who was dozing in a chair, woke with a start when she heard her sobbing, and, leaning over affectionately, asked her the cause of her tears. Obtaining no reply, she saw that she was asleep, and hastened to rouse her from that painful state. Louise was the most compassionate creature on earth; she had suffered so much on her own ac-

count, that she could sympathize with all the troubles of
another. She put forth all the gentleness and kindliness
at her command to comfort the girl, but she only threw
her arms about her neck, crying :

"Why do you also try to deceive me ? Why do you try
to prolong an error which must come to an end sooner or
later ? My cousin doesn't love me ; he never will love
me, and you know it very well ! Come, confess that he
has told you so."

Louise was sorely embarrassed to reply. After Bénédict's *never*—a word of which she had no means of estimating the real meaning—she dared not guarantee the
future to her young friend, for fear of becoming a party
to a deception. On the other hand, she would have
been glad to find some excuse for consoling her, for her
grief caused her sincere pain. So she strove to prove to
her that, even if her cousin had no love for her, it certainly was not probable that he loved any other woman,
and she did her utmost to encourage the hope that she
would eventually triumph over his coldness ; but Athénaïs would listen to nothing.

"No, no, my dear young lady," she replied, abruptly
wiping away her tears, "I must make the best of it.
I shall die of grief, perhaps, but I will do my best to cure
myself. It is too humiliating to see one's self despised
thus. I have plenty of other suitors ! If Bénédict thinks
he is the only man in the world who's courting me, he's
mistaken. I know some others who won't think me so
unworthy to be sought after. He will see ! he will see
that I'll have my revenge, that I won't be long unpro-
vided, that I'll marry Georges Simonneau or Pierre
Blutty, or else Blaise Moret. To be sure I can't endure
'em. Oh! yes, I know well enough that I shall hate
the man who marries me instead of Bénédict ! But it

will be his fault; and if I go to the bad, he will be responsible for it before God!"

"All this won't happen, my dear child," replied Louise;
" you won't find among your numerous adorers a man
who can be compared to Bénédict for intellect and refinement and talent, just as he, for his part, will never find
a woman who excels you in beauty and attachment to
him."

"Oh! stop there, my dear Mademoiselle Louise, stop.
I am not blind, nor you either. It's easy enough to see
when one has eyes, and Monsieur Bénédict doesn't take
much pains to avoid ours. Nothing could be clearer to
me than his actions to-day. Ah! if she wasn't your
sister, how I'd hate her!"

" Hate Valentine! your playmate from childhood, who
loves you so dearly and is so far from imagining such a
thing as you suspect! Valentine, who is so affectionate
and kind-hearted, but so reserved because of her modesty! Ah! how she would suffer, Athénaïs, if she could
guess what is going on in your heart!"

"Ah! you are right!" said the girl, weeping afresh;
" I am very unjust, very impertinent to accuse her of
such a thing! I know very well that if such a thought
should occur to her, she would shudder with anger. But
that is what drives me to despair on Bénédict's account;
that is what makes me frantic with his madness: to see
him make himself miserable to no purpose. What does
he hope for, pray? What insane freak draws him on to
his destruction? Why must he fall in love with the
woman who can never be anything to him, while there
is one right at his hand who would bring him youth,
love and wealth? O Bénédict! Bénédict! what sort of
man are you? Yes, and what sort of woman am I, that
I cannot make him love me? You have all deceived me;

you told me that I was pretty, that I had talent, that I was lovable and attractive. You deceived me ; you see well enough that I am not attractive ! ''

Athénaïs ran her hands through her black hair as if she would tear it out ; but her glance fell upon the lemon-wood dressing table beside her bed, and the mirror contradicted her so flatly that she became somewhat reconciled to herself.

"You are very childish !'' said Louise. "How can you believe that Bénédict is already in love with my sister, whom he has seen only three times ? ''

"Only three times ! Oh ! only three times !''

" Call it four or five, what does it matter ? Surely, if he loves her, it must be very recent, for only yesterday he told me that Valentine was the loveliest, the most estimable of women——''

"You see, the loveliest, the most estimable——''

"Wait a moment. He said that she was worthy of the homage of the whole world, and that her husband would be the most fortunate of men. 'And yet,' he added, ' I think that I could live near her for ten years without falling in love with her, her frank trustfulness inspires so much respect, her pure and serene expression diffuses such tranquillity all about her ! ' ''

" He said that yesterday ? ''

"I swear it by my affection for you.''

"Oh, yes ! but that was yesterday ! to-day it is all changed !''

" Do you think, pray, that Valentine has lost the charm that made her so imposing ? ''

" Perhaps she has acquired other charms ; who knows ? love comes so swiftly ! Why, it is hardly a month since I began to love my cousin. I didn't love him before that. I hadn't seen him since he left school, and I was so young

then ! And I remember him as being so tall and awkward and embarrassed by his arms, which were too long
for his sleeves ! But when I found him so elegant and
attractive, carrying himself so well and knowing so many
things, and with that glance of his, just a little stern,
which is so becoming to him, and makes one always a
little afraid of him—why, I loved him from that minute,
and all at once ; between night and morning my heart
was taken by surprise. What was to prevent Valentine
from taking his to-day in the same way ? She is very
beautiful, Valentine is ; she always has the knack of
saying just what's in Bénédict's mind. It seems to me
that she divines what he wants to hear her say, and I do
just the opposite. Where does she get that knack ?
Oh ! it's not because he's disposed to admire what she
says. And, then, even if it were just a fancy, begun this
morning and ended to-night, suppose he should come to
me to-morrow and hold out his hand and say : ' Let's
make up ; ' I see well enough that I haven't really won
him and that I never shall win him. Just think what a
happy life I should lead, married to him, if I should have
to be always weeping with rage or burning up with jealousy ! No, no, it will be much better to invent some
excuse and give it up."

"Well, my dear girl," said Louise, "as you can't put
this suspicion out of your mind, we must find out the
truth. To-morrow I will speak to Bénédict ; I will question him frankly concerning his intentions, and, whatever the truth may be, you shall be informed. Do you
feel that you have the courage to bear it ? "

"Yes," Athénaïs replied, kissing her ; "I prefer to
know my fate rather than live in such torments."

"Make up your mind then to try to rest," said
Louise, "and don't let your emotion be perceptible to-

9

morrow. As you do not think that you can count on
your cousin's attachment, your womanly dignity demands that you put a good face on the matter."

"Yes, you are right," said the girl, burying her face
in the bedclothes. "I will follow your advice. I feel
stronger already since you take my side."

This resolution having tranquillized her to some extent, she fell asleep, and Louise, whose heart was much
more violently disturbed, waited open-eyed until the first
rays of dawn appeared on the horizon. Then she heard
Bénédict, who also had been unable to sleep, softly open
his door and go downstairs. She followed him without
waking anybody, and together, having greeted each
other with more than customary gravity, they turned
into one of the garden paths, where the dew lay heavily.

XVI

Louise was sorely embarrassed at the thought of broach-
ing so delicate a subject, but Bénédict, breaking the silence first, said in a firm tone :

"My friend, I know what you are going to talk about.
Our oak partitions are not so thick, there is not so much
noise around this house at night, and my sleep was not
so sound that I lost a single word of your conversation
with my cousin. So that the confession which I proposed to make to you would be absolutely useless now,
as you are as well informed as myself of the state of my
heart."

Louise halted and looked him in the face to see if he

were not joking, but his expression was so perfectly calm that she was dumbfounded.

"I know that you have a way of jesting with a marvellously sober face," she said, "but I beg you to talk seriously with me. This is not a question of feelings with which you have a right to trifle."

"God forbid!" said Bénédict, vehemently; "it is a question of the most important and most sacred sentiment of my life; Athénaïs told you, and I swear upon my honor it is true, that I love Valentine with all the strength of my heart."

Louise clasped her hands with an expression of dire dismay, and, raising them to heaven, cried:

"What utter madness!"

"Why so?" retorted Bénédict, with that steady gaze whose authoritative expression was so hard to resist.

"Why so?" echoed Louise. "You ask me that question! Why, Bénédict, are you under the influence of a dream, or am I fully awake? You love my sister, you say; what in God's name do you hope from her?"

"What do I hope? This," he replied: "I hope to love her all my life."

"And perhaps you think that she will allow it?"

"Who knows? Perhaps!"

"But surely you know that she is rich—that she is of high birth——"

"She is, like yourself, the daughter of the Comte de Raimbault, and I have presumed to love you! Was it because I was the son of the peasant Lhéry, pray, that you repulsed me?"

"No, certainly not," replied Louise, turning as pale as death; "but Valentine is not twenty years old, and, even assuming that she had none of the prejudices of birth——"

"She hasn't," Bénédict interrupted.

"How do you know?"

"As you know it yourself. Our acquaintance with Valentine dates from about the same time, I believe."

"But you forget that she is dependent on a vain and pitiless mother, and a social circle which is no less vain and pitiless; that she is engaged to Monsieur de Lansac; in a word, that she cannot break the bonds which bind her to her duties without bringing upon herself the maledictions of her family and the contempt of her caste, and without destroying her repose forever."

"How can I fail to know all that?"

"Well, then, what in heaven's name do you expect from her madness or your own?"

"From hers, nothing; from my own, everything."

"Ah! you think that you can conquer destiny solely by the force of your character! Is that it? I have sometimes heard you develop that utopian theory, but be sure, Bénédict, that you would not succeed, even though you were more than man. From this moment I openly oppose your projects; I would rather give up seeing my sister than furnish you with opportunities and means to endanger her future."

"Oh! what fierce opposition!" retorted Bénédict, with a smile which had a most painful effect on Louise. "Be calm, my dear sister. You gave me permission, you almost ordered me to call you so, when we did not know Valentine. If you would have given your consent, I would have claimed the right to call you by a still sweeter name. My restless heart would have been anchored, and Valentine might have passed through my life without making any impression upon it; but you would not have it; you spurned vows which, now that I think of them in cold blood, must have seemed very absurd to you. You pushed me with your foot into this sea of uncertainty and tempests. I attempt to follow a beautiful star which shines upon me. What does it matter to you ? ''

"What does it matter to me, when my sister's welfare is at stake—my sister to whom I am almost a mother ! ''

"Oh! you are very young to be her mother !'' said Bénédict, with a suggestion of irony. " But listen, Louise. I am almost inclined to believe that you manifest all this alarm in order to make fun of me, and in that case you must confess that I have borne the raillery very well for quite a long time.''

"What do you mean ? ''

" It is impossible that you should think that your sister is in any danger from me, when you know so well from your own experience that I am not dangerous at all. Your terror is very strange, and you apparently consider Valentine's common sense very weak, since you are so terrified by the blows I may aim at it. Have no fear, my dear Louise ; you gave me a lesson not long ago for which I am grateful to you, and which I shall be able to profit by, it may be. I shall no longer take the risk of laying at the feet of such a woman as Valentine or Louise the homage of a heart like mine. I shall not again be mad enough to believe that to touch a woman's heart it is enough to love her with all the fervor of a brain of twenty years ; that, to efface in her eyes difference of rank and to hush the outcry of false shame in her heart, it is enough to be devoted to her body and soul, blood and honor. No, no, all that is as nothing in the eyes of a woman. I am a peasant's son ; I am horribly ugly, ridiculous to the last degree. I have no right to expect to be loved. Only a poor affected bourgeoise like Ath-

énais could think of stooping so low as to take me, for
lack of a better man hereabout."

"Bénédict!" cried Louise, hotly, "all this is cruel
mockery, I can see plainly enough. You mean to reproach me bitterly. Oh! you are very unjust. You
refuse to understand my position ; you do not consider
that, if I had listened to you, I should have been guilty
of shameful conduct to your family. You do not give me
credit for the virtuous determination which may have
been necessary on my part in order to make me seem
so cold to you. Oh! you will not understand anything !"

Poor Louise hid her face in her hands, alarmed lest
she had said too much. Bénédict, amazed beyond
measure, scrutinized her closely. Her breast was heaving, a burning flush was visible on her brow despite her
efforts to conceal it. Bénédict realized that she loved him.

He paused, irresolute, trembling, overwhelmed. He put
out his hand to take Louise's. He was afraid of being too
ardent ; he was afraid of being too cold. Louise, Valentine—which of the two should he love ?

When Louise, alarmed by his silence, timidly raised
her head, Bénédict was no longer beside her.

XVII

But no sooner was Bénédict alone than, suddenly freed
from the emotion which had possessed him, he was surprised that it had been so intense, and could explain it
only by attributing it to a feeling of gratified self-esteem.

In truth, that youth, who was ugly enough to frighten one, as the Marquise de Raimbault said, who was so enthusiastic in praise of others and so sceptical of his own merits, found himself in a strange position. Loved by three women at once, the least fair of whom would have filled any other man's heart with pride, he had much difficulty in combating the gusts of vanity which rose within him. It was a severe trial for his good sense, and he realized it. To resist it, he set himself to think of Valentine, that one of the three as to whom he felt the least certainty, and who must necessarily be the first to disabuse him. He knew nothing of her love, except by those sympathetic revelations which rarely deceive lovers. But, even if it had really taken root in the young countess's heart, it would surely be stifled at its birth, as soon as it betrayed its presence to her. Bénédict said all this to himself in order to triumph over the demon of pride; and he did triumph, for which, it may be, he was entitled to some credit at his age.

Thereupon, viewing his situation with a glance as keen as could be expected of a man so deeply in love, he said to himself that he must fix his choice upon one of the three, and cut short the painful suspense of the other two. Athénaïs was the first flower which he cast out from that lovely wreath; he believed that she would soon be consoled. The artless threats of vengeance of which he had been the involuntary confidant during the preceding night led him to hope that Georges Simonneau, Pierre Blutty, or Blaise Moret would take it upon himself to unburden his conscience of any remorse so far as she was concerned.

The most reasonable, perhaps the most generous choice would be to take Louise. To bestow a position in society and a happy future on that unfortunate creature,

who had been so cruelly outraged by her family and by
public opinion, to make up to her for the harsh chastise-
ment which the past had inflicted upon her, to constitute
himself the protector of so unfortunate and so interesting
a woman—there was something chivalrous in the idea,
which had already tempted Bénédict. Perhaps the love
which he had fancied that he felt for Louise had its birth
in the somewhat heroic tendency of his temperament.
He had seen in it an opportunity for self-sacrifice. His
youthful ardor, eager for glory of some sort, challenged
public opinion to single combat, like the adventurous
knights of old, who hurled defiance at the giant who held
a whole country in dread, in their longing to make men
talk of them, even though it were by means of a glorious
death.

Louise's refusal, which had offended Bénédict at first,
now appeared to him in its true light. Loath to accept
so great a sacrifice, and fearing lest she should allow
herself to be outdone in generosity, Louise had sought
to deprive him of all hope, and she had succeeded perhaps beyond her desire. In all virtue there is some
slight hope of reward ; she had no sooner rejected Bénédict than she suffered bitterly on that account. Now
Bénédict realized that, in her rejection of him, there
was more real generosity, more profound and delicate
affection than in his own conduct. Louise raised herself in
his eyes almost above the heroism of which he felt himself to be capable ; that was enough to move him deeply
and launch him upon a new sea of emotion and desire.

If love were a calculating and reasoning sentiment, like
friendship or hatred, Bénédict would have thrown himself at Louise's feet ; but the fact that gives it its vast
superiority to all other sentiments and proves its divine
essence is that it is not born of man's own volition, that

man cannot do with it as he chooses; that he can no more bestow it than take it away by the exertion of his own will; that the human heart surely receives it from on high to be bestowed on the king whom Heaven in its wisdom has chosen; and, when an energetic heart has once received it, in vain do all human considerations raise their voices to destroy it; it subsists alone, by virtue of its inherent force. All the auxiliaries with which it is provided, or which it attracts rather—friendship, trust, sympathy, even esteem—are simply subordinate allies; it calls them into being, it controls them, it survives them.

Bénédict loved Valentine and not Louise. Why Valentine? She was less like him; she had fewer of his faults and of his good qualities; she would undoubtedly understand him and appreciate him less—and yet it was she whom he was destined to love, apparently. He began to love in her the qualities which he did not himself possess; he was restless, dissatisfied, inclined to grumble at destiny; Valentine was placid, easily satisfied, pleased with everything. Very good; was not that in accordance with God's designs? Was not omnipotent Providence, which rules everywhere in spite of all that men can do, responsible for their coming together? One was necessary to the other! Bénédict to Valentine, to teach her to know those emotions without which life is incomplete; Valentine to Bénédict, to bring comfort and repose into a stormy and troubled life. But society stood between them and made their mutual choice absurd, reprehensible, impious. Providence created the admirable order of nature, men have destroyed it; whose is the fault? Must we part with every ray of sunlight in order to assure the solidity of our walls of ice?

When he returned to the bench on which he had left

Louise, he found her with her hands hanging listlessly at her sides, eyes fixed on the ground, and face as pale as death. She started when she heard his clothes rustling against the leaves; but when she had looked at him—when she realized that he had taken refuge in his unassailable impenetrability—she awaited in even more agonizing suspense the result of his reflections.

"We have failed to understand each other, sister," said Bénédict, seating himself beside her. "I will try to explain my meaning more clearly."

That word *sister* dealt Louise a deadly blow; she summoned what strength she could, to conceal her distress and to listen with apparent calmness.

"I am very far from cherishing any grudge against you," Bénédict began; "on the contrary, I admire the sincerity and kindness with which you continue to treat me despite my madness. I feel that your refusal to listen to me has confirmed my respect and affection for you. Rely upon me as upon the most devoted of your friends, and let me speak to you with all the confidence which a brother owes his sister. Yes, I love Valentine—I love her passionately; and, as Athénaïs well said, not until yesterday did I realize the sentiment she inspires in me. But I love her without hope, aimlessly, with no settled plan. I know that Valentine will not renounce her family for my sake, nor her approaching marriage, nor even, assuming that she was free, the conventional duties which the ideas of her caste may have marked out for her. I have considered in cold blood the impossibility of ever being anything more to her than an obscure and submissive friend, secretly esteemed, perhaps, but never dangerous to her peace of mind. Even if such a paltry, imperceptible creature as I could arouse in Valentine one of those passions which equalize ranks and overcome obstacles, I would shun her rather than accept sacrifices of which I feel that I am not worthy. All this, Louise, should reassure you to some extent as to the state of my brain."

"In that case," said Louise, trembling, "you propose to try to destroy this love, which would be the bane of your life?"

"No, Louise, no, I would die first," replied Bénédict, vehemently. "My whole happiness, my whole future, my whole life are bound up in it! Since I have loved Valentine I have been another man; I feel that I exist. The dark veil which shrouded my destiny is torn away on every side. I am no longer alone on earth; I am no longer distressed by my nothingness; I feel myself grow greater every hour with this love. Do you not see on my face an expression of tranquillity which must make it more endurable?"

"I see a self-assurance which terrifies me," Louise replied. "My friend, you are ruining yourself. These chimeras will wreck your destiny. You will waste your energy in fruitless dreams, and, when the time comes for you to be a man, you will regret to find that you have lost the strength to be one."

"What do you mean by being a man, Louise?"

"I mean filling your place in society without being a burden to others."

"Very good; I can be a man to-morrow, lawyer or porter, musician or ploughman; I have more than one string to my bow."

"You cannot be any of those things, Bénédict, for within a week any trade whatsoever——"

"Would be a bore to me, I agree; but I shall still have the resource of knocking my brains out if I get tired of life, or of turning beggar if life is very attractive to me. And, all things considered, I believe I am no longer fit for anything else. The more I have learned, the more disgusted with life I have become. I propose to return now, so far as I can, to my natural state, to the unrefined life of a peasant, his simple ideas and frugality. I have about five hundred francs a year in good land, left by my father, with a thatched-roof cottage. I can live honorably on my own estate, alone, free, contented, idle, without being a burden to anyone."

"Are you speaking seriously?"

"Why not? In the present state of society, the best possible result of the education we receive would be a voluntary return to the brutish state from which we are forced to emerge for twenty years of our life. But listen, Louise. Don't you indulge in any of the same chimerical dreams for me which you blame me for indulging in myself. It is you who urge me to expend my energy in smoke, when you tell me to work in order to be a man like other men; to devote my youth, my vigils, my fairest hours of happiness and poesy to the earning of the wherewithal to die comfortably in old age, with my feet in a fur muff and my head on a down pillow. And yet that is the aim of all those who are called sensible fellows at my age, and practical men at forty. God bless them! Let them put forth all their efforts to reach this supreme goal: to be electors in the *grand college*, or municipal councillors, or secretaries of prefecture. Let them fatten cattle and train race-horses for provincial fairs; let them become courtiers or farmhands,* slaves of a minister or of a flock of sheep, prefects in their gold livery, or dealers in swine with their belts lined with *pistoles;* and after a whole lifetime of sweat and sharp dealing, dullness or vulgarity, they leave

* Valets de cour ou valets de basse-cour.

the fruit of all their toil to a kept mistress, a scheming city wanton, or a redfaced serving-maid from Berry, either by their last will, or through the medium of their heirs, who are in haste *to enjoy life,* Such is the practical existence which I see unfolded about me in all its splendor ! Such is the glorious condition of being *a man,* to which all my schoolmates aspire. Frankly, Louise, do you think that I am turning my back on a very charming and glorious existence ? "

"You know yourself, Bénédict, how easy it would be to demolish that exggerated satire. So I will not take the trouble. I will simply ask you what you expect to do with this ardent activity which is consuming you, and if your conscience does not bid you to employ it in some way useful to society ? "

" My conscience bids me do nothing of the sort. *Society* does not need those who do not need it. I can imagine the power of that imposing word over new peoples, in a newly-discovered country which a small number of men, assembled only yesterday, are striving to fertilize and to make it supply their needs. In such a case, if colonization is voluntary, I despise the man who will go there and grow fat in idleness by the labor of others. I can imagine patriotism in free or virtuous nations, if there are any such. But here on French soil, where, whatever people may say, the soil lacks arms to work it, where every profession is full to overflowing with aspirants, where the human species, crowding in sickening fashion about the palaces of the great, crawls and licks the footprints of the rich man ; where vast sums, heaped up according to all the laws of social wealth in the hands of a few men, are the stakes in the never-ending game between greed, immorality and stupidity, in this land of immodesty and poverty, of vice and desolation ; and you expect me to be a *citizen* in this rotten civilization—rotten to the core ? to sacrifice my desires, my inclination, my caprice to its needs, that I may be its dupe or its victim, and that the coin which I might have tossed to the beggar shall fall into the millionaire's strong-box. Must I expend my energies in doing good in order to increase the sum total of evil, to furnish my contingent to the departments which license spies, gamblers and prostitutes? No, on my life ! I will not do it ! I prefer to be nobody in this fair France, the most enlightened of nations. As I have told you, Louise, I have five hundred francs a year ; any man who has five hundred francs a year can live and live in peace."

"Very well, Bénédict, if you propose to sacrifice every noble ambition to this craving for repose which has so suddenly succeeded your fierce impatience, if you choose to make no use of all your talents and all your estimable qualities, and to live an obscure and placid life in the seclusion of this valley, make sure of the first essential element of that happy existence,—banish from your thoughts this absurd love."

"Absurd, did you say ? No, it shall not be absurd ; I will take my oath to that. It shall be a secret between God and myself. And how could heaven, which inspired it, make sport of it ? No, it shall be my shield against sorrow, my resource against ennui. What else than it suggested to me yesterday the resolution to remain free and to be happy at small expense ? O blessed passion, which, from its very inception, makes itself manifest by brightness and peace ! Celestial truth, which unseals the eyes and sweeps the mind clear of all earthly things ! Sublime power, which takes possession of all the senses and floods them with joys hitherto unknown ! O Louise ! do not try to take my love from me. You could not succeed, and, perhaps, you would become less dear to me; for, I confess, nothing could contend successfully against it. Let me adore Valentine in secret and cherish those illusions which transported me to the skies yesterday. What would reality be compared with them? Let me fill my life with this one chimera, let me live in the heart of this enchanted valley, with my recollections and with the traces which she left here, with the perfume which remained behind in every field in which she placed her foot, with the harmonies which her voice awoke in every breeze, with the sweet, ingenuous words which escaped her in the innocence of her heart, and which I interpreted as my fancy bade me; with that pure and ineffable kiss which she deposited on my brow the first day I saw her. Ah! Louise, that kiss! Do you remember it? It was you who suggested it."

"Oh! yes," said Louise, rising with an air of consternation, "it was I who did all the mischief."

XVIII

Valentine, on returning to the château, had found a letter from Monsieur de Lansac on her mantelpiece. According to the custom in fashionable society, she had corresponded with him since her betrothal. This correspondence between a young man and woman who are engaged, which, it would seem, should afford an opportunity for them to know each other intimately and to become more closely united, is almost always cold and stilted. They talk of love in the language of the salons, they display their wit, their literary style and their handwriting—nothing more.

Valentine wrote so simply that, in the eyes of Monsieur de Lansac and his family, she seemed a person of very small account. Monsieur de Lansac was by no means sorry for it. On the eve of having a considerable fortune at his disposal, it was a part of his plan to hold his wife in complete subjection. And so, although he was not at all in love with her, he exerted himself to write letters which would have been considered epistolary masterpieces according to the ideas of the *beau monde*. He imagined that he simulated thus the warmest attachment that ever entered a diplomat's heart, and that Valentine must necessarily form an exalted opinion of his intellect and his wit. And, in truth, that young woman, who knew absolutely nothing of life and of the passions, had hitherto conceived a great admiration for her fiancé's depth of feeling, and, when she compared his expressions of devotion with her own replies, she accused herself of lagging far behind him by reason of her coldness.

On that evening, fatigued as she was by the intense and joyous emotions of the day, the sight of that superscription, usually so agreeable to her, aroused in her heart a feeling of sadness and remorse. She hesitated some moments before reading it, and at the first words fell into such profound abstraction that she read it with her eyes to the end without understanding a word of it, and without thinking of anything except Louise, Bénédict, the bank of the stream and the osier-beds in the field. She found in this preoccupation a fresh source of self-reproach, and she courageously re-read the letter of the secretary of Embassy. He had written it with the utmost care ; unfortunately, it was more obscure, more vapid and more affected than any of the others. In

spite of herself, Valentine was chilled by the mortal indifference which had dictated that composition. She
consoled herself for this involuntary impression by attributing it to the fatigue she felt. She went to bed,
and, as she was unaccustomed to taking so much exercise, she slept soundly; but she woke the next morning
with burning cheeks and sorely disturbed by the dreams
she had had.

She took the letter, which she had left on her dressing-
table, and read it again with the fervor with which a
pious woman begins her prayers anew when she thinks
that she has said them too lukewarmly. But it was all
in vain! Instead of the admiration with which she had
previously perused his letters, she had now no other
feeling than surprise and something which resembled
ennui. She rose, frightened at herself, and her mental
weariness drove the color from her cheeks.

Then, as she was accustomed to do absolutely as she
chose in her mother's absence, and as it did not occur
to her grandmother to question her concerning her employment of the previous day, she started for the farm,
carrying in a small cedar box all the letters she had received from Monsieur de Lansac during the past year,
and flattering herself that Louise's admiration upon hearing them read would rekindle her own.

It would be rash perhaps to assert that that was the
sole motive of this second visit to the farm; but, if Valentine had any other motive, she certainly was not aware
of it. However that may be, she found Louise alone.
At the request of Athénaïs, who wished to pass a few
days away from her cousin, Madame Lhéry had gone
with her to pay a visit to one of their relations in the
neighborhood; Bénédict was hunting, and Père Lhéry
at work in the fields.

Valentine was alarmed at the change in her sister's face. Louise explained it by saying that she had had to sit up with Athénaïs because of her indisposition. However, her grief was allayed by Valentine's caresses, and they soon began to talk freely of their plans for the future. She gave Valentine an opening to show Monsieur de Lansac's letters.

Louise read a few of them, which seemed to her as cold as death and utterly absurd. She instantly passed judgment on the heart of the writer, and saw plainly enough that his kindly intentions with respect to her were entitled to little confidence. The melancholy which oppressed her was intensified by this discovery, and her sister's future seemed to her as hopeless as her own; but she dared not let Valentine detect her feeling. On the day before, perhaps she would have had the courage to enlighten her; but, after Bénédict's declarations, Louise, who, it may be, suspected Valentine of encouraging him a little, dared not dissuade her from a marriage which would, at all events, remove her from the perils of the existing condition of affairs. So she gave no opinion, but asked Valentine to leave the letters with her, promising to say what she thought of them after reading them carefully.

They were both much depressed by this conversation. Louise had found in it fresh cause for unhappiness, and Valentine, observing her sister's constrained air, had failed to obtain the result which she expected, when Bénédict returned to the farm, singing as he approached, the cavatina *Di piacer mi balza il cor.* Valentine started when she recognized his voice; but Louise's presence caused her an embarrassment which she could not understand, and it was with difficulty that she awaited his appearance with a hypocritical air of indifference.

Bénédict entered the living-room, where the shutters were closed. The sudden transition from the bright sunlight to the darkness of that room prevented his discovering the two women. He hung his gun on the wall, still singing, and Valentine, with beating heart and a smile on her lips, was silently following all his movements, when, as he passed close to her, he discovered her, and uttered a cry of surprise and joy. That cry, from the lowest depths of his heart, expressed more passion and rapture than all of Monsieur de Lansac's letters which were scattered over the table. The instinct of the heart could not deceive Valentine in that respect, and poor Louise realized that her rôle was a pitiful one.

From that moment, Valentine forgot Monsieur de Lansac and the letters and her doubts and her remorse ; she was conscious of nothing save that imperious happiness which stifles every other feeling in the presence of the being whom one loves. She and Bénédict selfishly feasted upon it in the presence of poor Louise, whose situation between them was so false and so painful.

The Comtesse de Raimbault's absence being prolonged several days beyond the time originally fixed for her return, Valentine visited the farm several times. Madame Lhéry and her daughter were still absent, and Bénédict, lying near the path by which Valentine was certain to come, passed many blissful hours awaiting her in the shadow of the hedge. Often he watched her pass, but dared not show himself for fear of betraying his secret by too great earnestness ; but, as soon as she had entered the farm-house, he would hurry after her, and, to Louise's great displeasure, he would not leave them during the day. Louise could not complain, for Bénédict was tactful enough to understand their longing to talk together, and he would follow them at a respectful distance, pretending to beat the bushes with his gun ; but he never lost sight of them. To gaze at Valentine, to intoxicate himself upon the indescribable charm which emanated from her, to pluck lovingly the flowers which her dress had touched, to follow devoutly the path of down-trodden grass which she left behind her, and to notice with rapture that she often turned to see if he were there ; to seize, sometimes to divine her glance at a bend in the path, to feel the summons of a sort of magical attraction when she was really calling him in her heart, to obey the subtle, mysterious, irresistible impressions of which love is composed—all these were to Bénédict pure and never wearisome delights which will not seem puerile to you, if you remember that you were once twenty years old.

Louise could not reproach him, for, having solemnly promised her that he would not try to see Valentine alone for a single instant, he kept his promise religiously. So that there was no apparent danger in their life ; but the arrow buried itself deeper each day in those inexperienced hearts, each day they became more oblivious to the future. Those fleeting moments, cast into their lives like a dream, formed already in their eyes a whole existence, which it seemed to them must last forever. Valentine had determined not to think any more of Monsieur de Lansac, and Bénédict said to himself that such happiness could not be swept away by a breath.

Louise was very unhappy. When she saw of what profound love Bénédict was capable, she learned to know that young man, whom she had hitherto looked upon as being ardent and passionate rather than as capable of deep feeling. This power of loving which she discovered in him made him dearer than ever to her. She realized the magnitude of a sacrifice which she had not understood at all when she made it, and mourned in secret the loss of a happiness which she could have enjoyed more innocently than Valentine. Poor Louise, who was naturally passionate but had learned to conquer her passion after having to undergo its deplorable effects, was contending with bitter and painful emotions. In spite of herself, a consuming jealousy made Valentine's innocent happiness unendurable to her. She could not help deploring the day when she had found her, and their romantic and exalted affection had already lost all its fascination for her ; like most human emotions, it was already stripped of heroism and poesy. Sometimes Louise surprised herself sighing for the time when she had no hope of being reunited to her sister. At such times she had a horror of herself, and prayed to God to put such ignoble feelings away from her. She dwelt upon Valentine's sweet disposition, her purity and her affection, and prostrated herself before her image as before that of a saint whom she was imploring to effect her reconciliation with God. Now and again she formed the enthusiastic but rash project of opening her sister's eyes unreservedly to Monsieur de Lansac's lack of genuine merit, of urging her to break openly with her mother, to yield to her liking for Bénédict, and to make for herself in obscurity a life of love, courage and independence. But this project, although it may be that the self-sacrifice involved in it was not beyond her strength, soon disappeared under the scrutiny of common sense. To lead her sister into the abyss into which she herself had plunged, to deprive her of the fair fame which she herself had lost, to lure her on to the same misery, to sacrifice her to the contagion of her own example—the prospect was of a kind to deter the most fearless unselfishness. Thereupon, Louise persisted in the plan which had seemed the wisest at first sight : to refrain from enlightening Valentine concerning her fiancé, and to cenceal Bénédict's confidences from her with the utmost care. But, although this was, in her opinion, the best possible course to pursue, she was not without remorse for having led Valentine into such perils, and for lacking the strength to rescue her from them on the instant by leaving the neighborhood.

But that was something that she realized that she had not the moral force to do. Bénédict had made her swear that she would remain until Valentine's marriage. He did not ask himself what would become of him after that, but he was determined to be happy until then ; his mind was set upon it with the selfish strength which a hopeless love imparts. He had threatened Louise to do a thousand mad things if she drove him to despair, while he vowed that he would bow blindly to her will if she would allow him to enjoy those few days of life. He had even threatened her with his wrath and his hatred. His tears, his outbreaks of passion, his obstinacy, had so daunted Louise, whose nature was at best weak and irresolute, that she had submitted to that stronger will. Perhaps, too, her weakness was attributable to the love which she secretly nourished for him ; perhaps she flattered herself that she could rekindle his love by her self-sacrifice and generosity, when Valentine's marriage should have ruined his last hope.

Madame de Raimbault's return put an end at last to this dangerous intimacy. Valentine ceased to come to the farm, and Bénédict fell from the sky to the earth.

As he had boasted to Louise of the courage he would show when the time came, he bore this painful trial well enough at first, to all appearance. He would not confess how much he had miscalculated his strength. He contented himself during the first few days with hovering about the château on various pretexts, happy when he caught a glimpse of Valentine in her garden; then he stole into the park at night to watch the light of the lamp in her room. Once, Valentine having ventured to go out to watch the sunrise at the end of the field, where she had first met Louise, she found Bénédict seated on the spot where she had sat; but, as soon as he saw her, he fled, pretending not to see her, for he felt that he had not the self-control to speak to her without betraying his agitation.

Another time, as she was strolling about the park at nightfall, she heard a rustling in the foliage near her several times, and, when she had left the place where she had been thus startled, she saw a man crossing the path in the distance, who had Bénédict's figure and was dressed like him.

He induced Louise to ask for another meeting with her sister. He accompanied her as on the first occasion, and held aloof while they talked together. When Louise called him, he walked toward them in indescribable perturbation.

"Well, my dear Bénédict," said Valentine, who had mustered all her courage for that moment, "this is the last time that we shall meet for a long while, I suppose. Louise has just told me of her approaching departure and yours."

"Mine!" said Bénédict, bitterly. "Why mine, Louise? What do you know about it?"

In the darkness he had kept Valentine's hand in his, and he felt it tremble.

"Haven't you decided not to marry your cousin—at all events this year?" said Louise. "And is it not your purpose now to create an independent position for yourself?"

"It is my intention never to marry anybody," he replied in a harsh and vehement tone. "It is also my intention not to be a burden to anyone; but it doesn't necessarily follow that I intend to leave the province."

Louise made no reply, and swallowed tears which they could not see. Valentine pressed Bénédict's hand slightly in order to release her own, and they parted, more agitated than ever.

Meanwhile, the preparations for Valentine's marriage were going forward at the château. Each day brought new gifts from the prospective bridegroom. He was to arrive in person as soon as the duties of his office would permit, and the ceremony was appointed to take place on the second day thereafter, for Monsieur de Lansac, being a valued member of the diplomatic service, had very little time to waste upon such a trivial matter as marrying Valentine.

One Sunday, Bénédict had driven his aunt and cousin to hear mass in the largest village in the valley. Athénaïs was coquettishly dressed and lovely. Her complexion had recovered all its splendor, her black eyes all their vivacity. A tall youth of five feet six, whom the reader has already met under the name of Pierre Blutty, had accosted the ladies from Grangeneuve, and had taken his seat on the same bench, beside Athénaïs. This was an outspoken manifestation of his intentions with respect to the lass, and Bénédict's heedless attitude, as he leaned against a tree at some distance, was, in the eyes of all observers, an unequivocal indication of a rupture between his cousin and himself. Moret, Simonneau and many others had already entered the lists, but Pierre Blutty had received the warmest welcome.

When the curé entered the pulpit to deliver his sermon, and his cracked and trembling voice summoned all its

strength to pronounce the names of Louise-Valentine
de Raimbault and Norbert-Evariste de Lansac—the second and last publication of their banns having been posted
that same day at the door of the mayor's office—there
was a sensation in the congregation, and Athénaïs exchanged a glance of malicious gratification with her new
adorer ; for Bénédict's absurd passion for Mademoiselle
de Raimbault was no secret to Pierre Blutty ; Athénaïs,
with her usual frivolity, had yielded to the temptation to
speak ill of them with him, in order, perhaps, to encourage herself in her schemes of revenge. She even ventured to turn her head quietly to observe the effect of
this publication on her cousin ; but the flush faded from
her cheeks, and her triumph changed to sorrow when
she saw Bénédict's distorted features.

XIX

Louise, on learning of Monsieur de Lansac's arrival,
wrote a farewell letter to her sister, expressed to her in
the warmest terms her gratitude for the affection she had
shown her, and said that she would await at Paris the
result of Monsieur de Lansac's good intentions with
respect to their future relations. She begged her not to approach the subject hastily, but to wait until her husband's
love should assure the triumph which she might well
expect from it.

After sending this letter to Valentine by Athénaïs, who
was going to inform the young countess of her approaching marriage to Pierre Blutty, Louise prepared for her

journey. Alarmed by Bénédict's gloomy air and almost brutal taciturnity, she dared not seek a final interview with him. But on the morning of the day fixed for her departure he went to her room and, lacking the strength to say a word to her, pressed her to his heart and burst into tears. She did not try to comfort him, and, as they could say nothing to each other to allay their mutual grief, they contented themselves with weeping together, swearing everlasting friendship. This leave-taking relieved Louise's heart to some extent, but Bénédict, as he watched her go away, felt that his last hope of renewing his intercourse with Valentine had vanished.

Thereupon he gave way to despair. Of those women who had recently vied with one another in heaping attentions and affection upon him, not one remained; thenceforth he was alone in the world. His dreams, but now so bright and flattering, became dismal and painful. What would become of him?

He was no longer willing to owe anything to the generosity of his relations; he realized fully that after the affront he had put upon their daughter he could not continue to live at their expense. As he had not enough money to live in Paris, and not enough courage, at so critical a moment, to earn his own living by hard work, there was nothing left for him to do but to retire to his cabin and one field, pending the time when he should recover his self-control sufficiently to decide upon something better.

So he had the interior of his cabin arranged as comfortably as his means permitted; that was a matter of a few days. He hired an old woman to keep house for him, and took up his abode under his own roof, having taken leave of his relations with cordiality. Good Mère Lhéry felt all her resentment fade away, and kissed him with

tears in her eyes. Honest Lhéry lost his temper, and
tried to keep him at the farm by force ; Athénais shut
herself up in her room, where the violence of her emotion
caused another hysterical attack. For Athénais was
sensitive and impulsive. She had turned to Blutty only
from spite and vanity ; in the bottom of her heart she
still loved Bénédict, and would have forgiven him if he
had taken a step toward her.

Bénédict could not tear himself away from the farm
except by giving his word to return after Athénais was
married. When he found himself alone in his silent
house at night, with no companion save Perdreau, who
was dozing between his feet, no sound save that made
by the saucepan containing his supper, which emitted a
shrill and plaintive note in front of the blazing sticks on
the hearth, a feeling of depression and discouragement
took possession of him. Solitude and poverty at twenty-
two, after making the acquaintance of the arts and sciences, of hope and love—a melancholy conclusion in
very truth !

Not that Bénédict was particularly alive to the advantages of wealth. He was at the age when one can
best do without them ; but it is impossible to deny that
the aspect of external objects exercises a direct influence
on our thoughts, and in most cases determines the tinge
of our temper for the moment. Now, the farm-house, with
its disorder and its contrasts, was a paradise compared
with Bénédict's hermitage. The unplastered walls, the
hearse-shaped serge bed, a few cooking utensils of cop-
per and earthenware arranged on shelves, the flooring
of limestone tiles, uneven and broken in a thousand
places, the rough furniture, the faint grayish light which
came in through four panes of glass, stained by sunshine
and rain—all these were not calculated to give birth to

gorgeous dreams. Bénédict fell into gloomy meditation. The landscape which he could see through his partly-open door, although picturesque and bold in outline, was no better adapted to impart a cheerful tinge to his thoughts. A gloomy ravine strewn with furze separated him from the steep winding road which uncoiled itself like a snake on the hillside opposite, and, plunging in among the dark-leaved holly and box, seemed to fall from the clouds, so steep was the pitch.

But, as Bénédict's memory wandered back to the years which he had passed on that spot as a child, he gradually found a melancholy fascination in his retreat. Beneath that humble and insecure roof he had first seen the light; beside that hearth his mother had lulled him to sleep with a rustic ballad, or with the monotonous whirring of her spinning-wheel. At night he had watched his father come down that steep path, a grave and powerful peasant, with his axe over his shoulder and his oldest son behind him. Bénédict had also a vague remembrance of a sister younger than himself, whose cradle he had rocked, of some aged relations and old servants. But they had all crossed the threshold for the last time. They were all dead, and Bénédict hardly remembered the names which had formerly been familiar to his ear.

"O father! O mother!" he said to the ghosts who passed before him in his waking dreams, "this is the very house which you built, the bed in which you slept, the field which your hands tilled. But your most valuable possession you did not hand down to me. Where are the simplicity of heart, the tranquillity of mind, the real fruits of labor? If you wander about your former abode in search of the objects which were dear to you, you will pass me by unrecognized, for I am no longer the happy and pure-minded creature who went forth from your hands, and who should have profited by your exertions. Alas! education has corrupted my mind; vain longings, stupendous dreams have perverted my nature and wrecked my future. Resignation and patience, the cardinal virtues of the poor man—these, too, I have lost. I return to-day, like an outlaw, to live in this hovel of which you were innocently vain. To me this soil, made fruitful by the sweat of your brows, is like a place of exile; this, which was your treasure, is my last resource to-day."

Then, as his thoughts reverted to Valentine, Bénédict asked himself with a bitter pang what he could have done for that girl, brought up in luxury as she had been; what would have become of her if she had consented to come and bury herself with him in that rough and pitiable existence; and he applauded himself for not even having tried to turn her aside from the path of duty.

And yet he said to himself, also, that with the hope of a wife like Valentine to spur him on, he would have developed talent and ambition, and have made a career for himself. She would have stirred to life within him that active principle of energy which, as it was of no use to anyone, had become benumbed and paralyzed in his breast. She would have embellished poverty, or rather she would have banished it, for Bénédict could think of nothing which it was beyond his strength to do for Valentine.

And she had slipped from his grasp forever! Bénédict relapsed into despair.

When he learned that Monsieur de Lansac had arrived at the château, that in three days Valentine would be married, he flew into such a savage fit of passion, that for a moment he believed that he was born to commit the greatest crimes. He had never allowed his mind to

rest on the thought that Valentine might belong to another man than himself. He had become resigned to the
thought of never possessing her, but to see that bliss fall
to the lot of another, that was something which he could
not yet believe to be possible. He had persisted in the
belief that the most evident, the most inevitable, the
most imminent element of his unhappiness would never
come to pass, that Monsieur de Lansac would die, that
Valentine herself would prefer to die when the moment
arrived to contract that hateful tie. Bénédict had not
said anything about it for fear of being taken for a madman ; but he had really counted upon some miracle, and,
when no miracle occurred, he cursed God for suggesting
the hope to him and for abandoning him ; for man attributes everything to God in the great crises of his life.
He always has a craving to believe in Him, whether to
bless Him for his joys, or to accuse Him of responsibility
for his errors.

But his rage became even fiercer when, as he was
prowling about the park one day, he saw Valentine
walking with Monsieur de Lansac. The secretary of
Embassy was attentive, courtly, almost triumphant.
Poor Valentine was pale and downcast, but her face
wore a sweet and resigned expression. She forced herself to smile at her fiancé's honeyed words.

So it was a fact, that man was there ! He was going
to marry Valentine ! Bénédict hid his face in his hands,
and passed twelve hours in a ditch, absorbed by a sort
of stupefied despair.

For her part, the poor girl submitted to her fate with
passive and silent resignation. Her love for Bénédict
had made such swift progress that she had been compelled to admit the truth to herself ; but, between the
consciousness of her sin and the determination to abandon

herself to it, there was a long distance to travel, especially as Bénédict was no longer there to destroy with a glance the whole result of a day of good resolutions. Valentine was pious; she confided herself to God's care, and awaited Monsieur de Lansac with the hope that she should feel once more what she believed that she had previously felt for him.

But, as soon as he appeared, she realized how far removed the blind and indulgent good-will which she had accorded him was from genuine affection. He seemed to her to have lost all the charm with which her imagination had endowed him for an instant. She felt dull and bored in his company. She listened to him with a distraught air, and replied only as a matter of courtesy. He was much disturbed at first, but when he found that the preparations for the marriage went forward none the less briskly, and that Valentine did not seem inclined to make the slightest opposition, he was readily consoled for a caprice which he did not try to fathom, and pretended not to see.

Valentine's repugnance increased from hour to hour, however. She was pious, even devout, by education and conviction. She shut herself up to pray for hours at a time, always hoping to find in meditation and devout fervor the power which she lacked to return to a sense of duty. But these meditations in seclusion fatigued her brain more and more, and intensified the influence which Bénédict possessed over her heart. She came forth more exhausted, more agitated than ever. Her mother was surprised by her depression, became seriously angry with her, and accused her of trying to poison that moment which is always so sweet, she said, to a mother's heart. It is certain that all these annoyances were terribly wearisome to Madame de Raimbault. She had determined, in order to diminish their force, that the nuptials should take place quietly and simply in the country. She was in great haste to have done with them, and to be free to return to society, where Valentine's presence had always been extraordinarily embarrassing to her.

Bénédict conceived a thousand absurd plans. The last, upon which he determined, and which restored his tranquillity to some extent, was to see Valentine once before she went out of his life forever ; for he almost believed that he should no longer love her when she had submitted to Monsieur de Lansac's embraces. He hoped that Valentine would soothe him with kindly and comforting words, or would cure him by prudishly denying his request.

He wrote to her :

" Mademoiselle :

"I am your friend in life and death, as you know. You once called me your brother ; you imprinted on my brow a sacred proof of your esteem and confidence ; you led me to hope, at that moment, that I should find in you an adviser and a support in the difficult crises of my life. I am horribly unhappy. I long to see you for an instant, to ask you, who are so strong and so far above me, for a little courage. It is impossible for you to refuse me this favor. I know your generosity, your contempt for foolish conventionalities and for danger when it is a question of doing good. I saw you with Louise ; I know what you can do. In the name of an affection as pure and holy as hers, I beg you, on my knees, to walk this evening to the end of the field.

" BENÉDICT."

XX

Valentine loved Bénédict; she could not refuse his request. There is so much innocence and purity in a first love that it hardly suspects the dangers which lurk within it. Valentine refused to consider the causes of Bénédict's unhappiness. She saw that he was unhappy, and she would have imagined the most impossible misfortunes rather than admit to herself what it was that overwhelmed him. There are paths so misleading and such a labyrinth of folds in the purest conscience! How could a woman who, having an impressionable heart, was forced into the rough and pitiless path of impossible duties, resist the necessity of compromising with them at every instant? Valentine readily found excuses for believing that Bénédict was the victim of some misfortune of which she knew nothing. Louise had often said of late that the young man distressed her by his melancholy and his heedlessness with respect to the future. She had also told her that it would soon be necessary for him to leave the Lhéry family, and Valentine persuaded herself that, having been cast adrift without means and without friends, he might really need her advice and assistance.

It was quite a difficult matter to escape from the house on the very eve of her wedding, beset as she was by Monsieur de Lansac's courtesies and petty attentions. She succeeded, however, by telling her nurse to say that she had lain down, if anyone should ask for her; and in order to lose no time, and to make it impossible

to reconsider a resolution which was beginning to frighten
her, she walked rapidly across the field. The moon was
then full, and objects could be seen as distinctly as in
broad daylight.

She found Bénédict standing with his arms folded
across his breast, so absolutely motionless that she was
terrified. As he did not step forward to meet her, she
thought for a moment that it was not he, and was on the
point of turning back. Then he came toward her. His
face was so changed, his voice so faint, that Valentine,
overwhelmed by her own sorrows and by those of which
she could see the traces in him, could not restrain her
tears, and was obliged to sit down.

It was all over with Bénédict's resolutions. He had
come to that place, determined to follow religiously the
course he had marked out in his note. He intended to
talk with Valentine of his separation from the Lhérys,
of his uncertainty with respect to the choice of a profession, of his isolation, of all the pretexts farthest removed
from his real purpose. That purpose was to see Valentine, to hear the sound of her voice, to find in her feelings toward him courage to live or to die. He expected
to find her serious and reserved, armed with a full consciousness of her duties. Indeed, he almost expected
not to see her at all.

When he spied her on the farther side of the field,
hastening toward him at the top of her speed ; when she
sank upon the turf, breathless and overwhelmed with
emotion ; when her grief found expression, despite her
efforts, in tears—Bénédict believed that he was dreaming. Oh ! that was not compassion merely, it was love !
A wave of delirious joy swept over him. Once more he
forgot both his own unhappiness and Valentine's, both
yesterday and the morrow, to see naught but Valentine,

who was by his side, alone with him, Valentine who loved him, and who no longer concealed it from him.

He threw himself on his knees before her ; he kissed her feet passionately. It was too severe a trial for Valentine. She felt all her blood congeal in her veins ; a mist passed over her eyes. As the fatigue caused by running made the task of concealing her tears even more painful, she fell, pale as death and almost unconscious, into Bénédict's arms.

Their interview was long and tempestuous. They did not attempt to deceive each other as to the nature of the sentiment they felt ; they did not seek to avoid the danger of yielding to the most ardent emotions. Bénédict covered Valentine's clothes and hands with tears and kisses. Valentine hid her burning face on Bénédict's shoulder. But they were twenty years old ; they were in love for the first time, and Valentine's honor was safe on Bénédict's breast. He dared not even utter the word *love,* which frightens love itself. His lips dared do no more than breathe upon his mistress's lovely hair. First love hardly knows that there exists a greater joy than that of knowing oneself to be loved. Bénédict was the most timid of lovers and the happiest of men.

They parted without making any plans, without deciding upon anything. In those two hours of rapture and oblivion, they had exchanged only a few words concerning their situation, when the clear note of the château clock fell faintly on their ears in the silence of the fields. Valentine counted ten almost inaudible strokes, and suddenly remembered her mother, her fiancé, the morrow. But how could she leave Bénédict ? what could she say to comfort him ? where find the strength of mind to abandon him at such a moment ? The appearance of a woman a short distance away extorted an exclamation of alarm from her. Bénédict slunk hurriedly into the shrubbery, but Valentine almost instantly recognized in the bright moonlight her nurse Catherine, who was anxiously searching for her. It would have been an easy matter to avoid her glances, but she felt that she ought not to do it; so she walked toward her and asked, as she clung trembling to her arm:

"What is the matter?"

"For the love of God, mademoiselle, come home," said the good woman; "madame has asked for you twice already, and, when I told her that you had lain down on your bed, she told me to let her know as soon as you woke. I was worried then; and as I had seen you go out by the small gate, and as I know that you sometimes come to walk here in the evening, I came out to look for you. Oh! mademoiselle, to think of going so far all by yourself! You did wrong; you ought at least to have told me to go with you."

Valentine kissed the old nurse, cast a sad and anxious glance at the bushes, and purposely dropped her handkerchief—the one she had lent to Bénédict on the occasion of their walk over the farm. When she returned to the house, her nurse looked everywhere for it, and observed that she must have lost it during her stroll.

Valentine found that her mother had been waiting for her for some minutes in her room. She expressed some surprise to find her fully dressed after passing two hours on her bed. Valentine replied that as she had had a headache, she had felt the need of fresh air, and that her nurse had given her her arm for a turn in the park.

Thereupon Madame de Raimbault entered upon a serious dissertation concerning matters of business. She informed her that she would leave to her the château

and estate of Raimbault—the bare name having constituted substantially the whole of her father's inheritance
—the value of which, apart from her own fortune,
formed a handsome marriage-portion. She asked her to
do her the justice to acknowledge that she had been a
faithful steward of her fortune, and to bear witness to
all the world, so long as she lived, of her mother's just
treatment of her. She went into financial details which
made of that maternal exhortation a genuine lawyer's
interview, and concluded her harangue by saying that,
now that the law was about to make them *strangers* to
each other, she hoped to find Valentine disposed to be
considerate and attentive to her.

Valentine did not hear one-half of this long harangue.
Her cheeks were pale, her downcast eyes were surrounded by purple rings, and from time to time a shiver ran
through every limb. She kissed her mother's hands
sadly, and was preparing to go to bed, when her grandmother's maid appeared and informed her with great
solemnity of manner that the marchioness wished to see
her in her apartments.

Valentine dragged herself to this additional ceremony.
She found the old lady's bedroom embellished with a
sort of religious decoration. An altar had been made of
a table covered with embroidered linen. Flowers arranged
like church decorations were wound about a crucifix of
guilloched gold. A missal bound in scarlet velvet lay
upon the altar. A cushion awaited the pressure of Valentine's knees, and the marchioness, seated in a theatrical
pose in her great arm-chair, was making ready with childish satisfaction to play her little conventional comedy.

Valentine entered the room in silence, and, because her
piety was genuine, she viewed these absurd preparations
without emotion. The maid opened a door on the oppo-

site side of the room, through which all the female servants of the château entered, with a humble and at the
same time curious air. The marchioness ordered them
to kneel and pray for the happiness of their young mistress; then, having bade Valentine also to kneel, she
rose, turned the pages of the missal, put on her spec-
tacles, read a few verses of one of the Psalms, bleated a
chant with her maid, and ended by laying her hands on
Valentine's head and giving her her blessing. Never
was a simple, patriarchal ceremony more wretchedly
burlesqued by an aged sinner of the time of La Du-
barry.

As she kissed her granddaughter, she took—from the
improvised altar itself—a case containing a pretty set of
cameos, which she presented to her, and, blending devotion with frivolity, said to her almost in the same breath:

"May God give you the virtues of a good mother of
a family, my child!—Here, my girl, is your grandmother's little gift; you can wear them with half-
dress."

Valentine was in a fever all night, and did not sleep
until morning. She was soon awakened by the sound
of bells summoning the whole neighborhood to the
chapel of the château. Catherine came to her room
with a note which an old woman had given her for
Mademoiselle de Raimbault. It contained only these
few words in a trembling hand:

"Valentine, there is still time to say no."

Valentine shuddered and burned the note. She tried
to rise, but several times her strength failed her. She
was seated, half-dressed, on a chair, when her mother
appeared, reproved her for being so late, refused to believe
that she was seriously ill, and informed her that several
people were already awaiting her in the salon. She herself

assisted her to complete her toilet, and when Valentine stood before her in her bridal dress, wonderfully beautiful, but as white as her veil, she insisted upon putting rouge on her cheeks. Valentine reflected that, perhaps, Bénédict would see her as she passed. She preferred that he should see her pallor, and, for the first time in her life, she resisted her mother's wish.

She found in the salon a number of neighbors of secondary rank; for Madame de Raimbault, having determined that the wedding should be unattended by display, had invited only people of *little consequence.* They were to breakfast in the garden, and the peasants were to have their dance at the other end of the park, at the foot of the hill. Monsieur de Lansac soon appeared, dressed in black from head to foot, and with his buttonhole laden with foreign decorations. The wedding-party was taken in three carriages to the mayor's office, which was in the neighboring village. The church ceremony was performed at the château.

Valentine, as she knelt before the altar, emerged for an instant from the species of torpor into which she had fallen. She said to herself that it was too late to withdraw, that men had forced her to make a pledge with God, and that it was no longer possible for her to choose between unhappiness and sacrifice. She prayed fervently, implored heaven to give her strength to keep the oaths which she determined to take with absolute sincerity, and, at the close of the ceremony, exhausted by the superhuman effort she had put forth to remain calm and tranquil, she withdrew to her room to take a little rest. Moved by a secret instinct of discretion and devotion, Catherine seated herself at the foot of her bed and did not leave her.

On the same day the marriage of Athénaïs Lhéry and

Pierre Blutty was celebrated in a small hamlet in the valley, about two leagues from the château. There, too, the young bride was pale and depressed; less so than Valentine, but to a sufficient degree to worry her mother, who was much more affectionate than Madame de Raimbault, and to anger her spouse, who was much more outspoken and less polished than Monsieur de Lansac. It may be that Athénaïs presumed too far on the force of her irritation when she decided so hastily to marry a man whom she did not love. As a result perhaps of the spirit of contradiction commonly attributed to women, her affection for Bénédict reawoke at the very moment when it was too late to change her mind; and, on returning from church, she regaled her husband with a very tiresome paroxysm of weeping. So Pierre Blutty characterized it when he complained of it to his friend Georges Simonneau.

Nevertheless, the wedding at the farm was much more largely attended, noisier and merrier than the one at the château. The Lhérys had at least sixty cousins and second cousins; the Bluttys were no less rich in relations, and the barn was not large enough to hold the guests.

In the afternoon, when the dancing half of the party had feasted sufficiently on fatted calf and game pie, they abandoned the gastronomic arena to the old people, and gathered on the greensward to open the ball. But the heat was extreme; there was little shade in that spot, and there was no very convenient place for dancing near the farm-house. Someone suggested that there was a very large tract of well-shaped level turf near the château, where five hundred people were dancing at that moment. The countryman is as fond of a crowd as the dandy. To enjoy himself thoroughly, he must have a lot of people about, feet stepping on his, elbows elbowing

him, lungs absorbing the air he exhales ; in every country
in the world, in all ranks of society, that is pleasure.

Madame Lhéry welcomed the idea eagerly ; she had
spent enough money on her daughter's dress to wish that
people should see it side by side with Mademoiselle de
Raimbault's, and that the whole province should talk of
its magnificence. She had obtained minute information
concerning Valentine's wedding costume. As it was to
be such an unpretentious occasion, she was to wear only
simple and tasteful ornaments. Madame Lhéry had loaded her daughter with laces and jewels, and, longing to
exhibit her in all her glory, she proposed that they
should join the festivities at the château, to which she
and all her family were invited. Athénaïs remonstrated
a little. She dreaded to see hovering about Valentine
the pale and gloomy face of Bénédict which had distressed her so at the church on the preceding Sunday.
But her mother's obstinacy, the wish of her husband,
who was not exempt from vanity, and perhaps, too, a
little of that same vanity on her own account, overcame
her reluctance. The carriages were made ready ; each
horseman took his sister, his cousin or his fiancée *en
croupe*. Athénaïs sighed profoundly as her new husband
took his place in the wagon, reins in hand, in the seat
which Bénédict had occupied so long and would never
occupy again.

XXI

The dancing in the park at Raimbault was very lively. The peasants, for whose benefit arbors of foliage had been arranged, sang and drank and proclaimed the newly-married couple the handsomest, most fortunate and most honorable in the country. The countess, who was anything but popular, had been very lavish in her preparations for the festival, in order to have done at once, in a single day, with all the affability which another would have distributed throughout a lifetime. She had the most profound contempt for the *canaille,* and declared that, if you only gave them plenty to eat and drink, you could walk on their stomachs without a sign of revolt from them. And the saddest part of it is that Madame de Raimbault was not altogether wrong.

The Marquise de Raimbault was delighted with this opportunity to revive her popularity. She was not very susceptible to the hardships of the poor, but she was no more indifferent in that regard than in regard to the misfortunes of her friends ; and, thanks to her fondness for gossip and her disposition to be familiar, she had acquired that reputation for kindness of heart which the poor award with so little reason, alas ! to those who, although they do no good, at all events do no harm. As the two ladies passed, one after the other, the shrewd minds of the village whispered to one another under the foliage :

"That one despises us, but she entertains us ; the other doesn't entertain us, but she speaks to us."

And they were content with both. The only one who
was really loved was Valentine, because she did not confine herself to a friendly word and smile, to being generous to them and helping them, but shared their sorrows and their joys; they felt that her kindness was not
induced by any selfish interest, or by policy. They had
seen her weep over their misfortunes; they had found
in her heart genuine sympathy; they were more attached than men of coarse mould commonly are to those
of higher station. Many of them knew the story of her
intercourse with her sister at the farm, but they kept
her secret so religiously that they hardly dared mention
Louise's name under their breaths.

Valentine walked from one table to another and strove
to smile in answer to their good wishes, but their merriment vanished when she had passed, for they noticed
that she seemed depressed and ill; they even went so
far as to cast malevolent glances at Monsieur de Lansac.

Athénaïs and her wedding-party dropped into the midst
of the festivities, and there was an instant change in the
aspect of affairs. Her elegant costume and her husband's affable bearing attracted all eyes. The dancing,
which was beginning to flag, became animated once
more. Valentine, having embraced her young friend,
retired again with her nurse. Madame de Raimbault,
being intensely bored, went to her room to rest; Monsieur de Lansac, who always had important letters to
write, even on his wedding-day, went to prepare his
day's mail. The Lhéry party was left in possession of
the field, and the people who had come to see Valentine
dance remained to see Athénaïs dance.

It was growing dark. Athénaïs, fatigued by dancing,
had sat down to take some refreshment. The Chevalier
de Trigaud, Joseph his majordomo, Simonneau, Moret,

and several others who had danced with the bride, had gathered about her at the same table, and were overwhelming her with their attentions. Athénaïs had been so lovely while dancing, her absurdly gorgeous costume was so becoming to her, her husband was gazing at her with such an amorous gleam in his black eye, that she began to be more cheerful and to be reconciled to her wedding-day. The Chevalier de Trigaud, who was moderately drunk, made complimentary remarks in the style of Dorat, which made her laugh and blush at the same time. Little by little the group about her, enlivened by a bottle or two of a light white wine of the province, by the dance, by the bride's lovely eyes, by the occasion and by custom, began to address to her some of those equivocal remarks which are enigmatical at first and end by becoming indecent.

Athénaïs, who realized that she was pretty, saw that she was admired, and did not in the least understand what they said, except that they envied and congratulated her husband, strove to keep upon her lips the smile which enhanced her loveliness, and was even beginning to reply with a sort of coquettish shyness to Pierre Blutty's burning glances, when a person came silently and sat down in the vacant place at her left. Athénaïs, involuntarily stirred by the imperceptible rustling of her dress, turned, stifled a cry of alarm and turned pale : it was Bénédict.

It was Bénédict, even paler than she, but grave, cold and ironical. He had wandered about the woods like a hunted man all day long. When evening came, losing all hope of calming himself by fatigue, he had determined to watch Valentine's wedding festival, to listen to the ribaldry of the peasants, to hear the signal for the newly-married pair to withdraw to the nuptial chamber, and to cure himself by dint of wrath, pity and disgust.

"If my love survives all this," he said to himself, "it must be because there is no remedy for it."

And, to be prepared for any emergency, he had loaded the pistols which he carried in his pocket.

He had not expected to find this other wedding-party there, and this bride. He had been watching Athénaïs for several minutes. Her merriment aroused his most profound contempt, and he determined to place himself in the very centre of the mortifications he had come there to defy, by taking a seat beside her.

Bénédict, who was by nature peevish and cynical, one of those discontented, grumbling creatures who have little patience with the absurdities and caprices of society, always declared—it was one of his paradoxes—that there could be no more monstrous impropriety, no more scandalous custom than the publicity given to the marriage ceremony. He had never seen, without a feeling of pity, a poor girl amid the hurly-burly of the wedding festival, almost always with some shrinking love concealed in her heart, and compelled to run the gauntlet of insolent attentions and impertinent glances in order to reach the arms of her husband, already defiled by the wanton imaginations of all the men in the crowd. He also pitied the poor young man whose love was placarded at the door of the mayor's office and in the church, and who was compelled to abandon his fiancée's spotless robe to the vulgarities of the town and the surrounding country. He considered that love was profaned by taking from it the veil of mystery. He would have liked to encompass the woman with so much respect that no one would know the object of her choice, and that people would be afraid of offending her by naming him to her.

"How," he would say, "do you expect your wives to
have pure morals when you publicly do violence to their
modesty; when you bring them unsullied into the midst
of the multitude, and say to them, calling the multitude
to witness: 'You belong to this man, you are a virgin
no longer?' And the crowd claps its hands, laughing
exultantly, jeers at the blushes of the husband and wife,
and pursues them, even in the seclusion of the nuptial
chamber, with its obscene shouts and songs! The bar-
barians of the new world had more decent marriage rites.
At the festival of the sun, they brought to the temple a
man and a woman—virgins both. The multitude, grave
and silent, prostrated themselves, blessed the god who
created love, and, with all the solemnity of love, physical and divine, the mystery of generation was performed
before the altar. That ingenuous ceremony, which dis-
gusts you, was more chaste than your marriages. You
have so offended modesty, so neglected love, so degraded
woman, that you have fallen to the point of insulting
woman, love and modesty."

When he saw Bénédict seated beside his wife, Pierre
Blutty, who knew of Athénaïs's fondness for her cousin,
cast a threatening glance at them. His friends exchanged
glances of similar import with him. They all hated Bénédict for his superior parts, of which they believed him to
be vain. The merry chatter flagged for an instant, but
the Chevalier de Trigaud, who esteemed him highly,
gave him a cordial greeting, and offered him the bottle
with a trembling hand. Bénédict bore himself with a
calm and indifferent air which led Athénaïs to think that
he had determined to make the best of it; she timidly
offered him some attentions, which he received respectfully and without apparent ill-humor.

Little by little the conversation resumed its free and

indelicate tone, with the manifest intention on the part of Blutty and his friends of giving it a turn that would be offensive to Bénédict. He at once detected that intention, and armed himself with the contemptuous tranquillity which his features seemed naturally to express.

Until his arrival, Valentine's name had not been mentioned; it was the weapon to which Blutty resorted to wound him. He gave the signal to his companions, and they began to draw, in ambiguous terms, a parallel between Pierre Blutty's good fortune and Monsieur de Lansac's, which caused the blood to boil in Bénédict's frozen veins. But he had come there to hear what he was hearing. He put a good face upon it, hoping that the inward rage which was consuming him would soon change to disgust. Moreover, if he had given way to his wrath, he had no right to protect Valentine's name from this besmirching.

But Pierre Blutty did not stop there. He was determined to insult him grievously, and even to make a scene, in order to procure his expulsion from the farm forever. He ventured to say a few words which conveyed the implication that Monsieur de Lansac's good fortune was a bitter blow to the heart of one of the guests. Everyone looked at him in surprise, with a questioning glance, and saw that his eyes were fixed on Bénédict. Thereupon the Morets and the Simonneaus, taking up the ball, fell upon their adversary with more brutality than real force. For a long time he remained impassive; he contented himself with a reproachful glance at poor Athénaïs, who alone could have betrayed his secret. The young woman, in desperation, tried to change the subject, but that was impossible; and she sat there more dead than alive, hoping that her presence would at least restrain her husband to some extent.

"There be some folks," said Georges, affecting to speak in a more countrified fashion than usual, in order to present a more striking contrast to Bénédict's manner, "there be some folks who try to get their feet higher than their legs and break their noses on the ground. That reminds me of the story about Jean Lory, who didn't like neither dark girls nor light ones, and ended, as everyone knows, by thinking himself mighty lucky to marry a red-haired one."

The whole conversation was pitched in this key, and was far from intellectual, as will be seen.

"That isn't right," said Blutty, correcting his friend Georges; "this is Jean Lory's story. He said that he couldn't love anyone but a blonde, but neither blondes nor brunettes would have him; so that the red-haired girl had to take pity on him."

"Oh!" said another, "the women have eyes, I tell you."

"On the other hand," chimed in a third, "there are some men who cannot see beyond the ends of their noses."

"*Manes habunt,*" observed the Chevalier de Trigaud, who, although he did not understand their conversation, was determined to display his learning.

And he continued his quotation, murdering the Latin without pity.

"Ah! monsieur le chevalier," said Père Lhéry, "you are talking to deaf men; we don't know Greek."

"Perhaps Monsieur Bénédict, who has never learned anything else, can translate it for us," sneered Blutty.

"The meaning is," rejoined Bénédict, calmly, "that there are some men like brutes, who have eyes but do not see, and ears but do not hear. That fits in very nicely as you see, with what you were saying just now."

"Oh! as to ears," said a short, stout cousin of the groom, who had not previously spoken, "*pardieu!* we have said nothing about them, for a good reason; we know the consideration one should have for one's friends."

"And then, too," said Blutty, "there are none so deaf as those who won't hear, as the proverb says."

"There is none so deaf," interposed Bénédict in a loud voice, "as the man whose ears are stuffed with contempt."

"Contempt!" cried Blutty, springing to his feet, flushed with wrath, and with gleaming eyes; "contempt!"

"I said contempt," Bénédict replied, without changing his attitude and not deigning to look at him.

He had no sooner repeated the word than Blutty, raising his glass, filled with wine, threw it at his head; but his hand, trembling with rage, proved a worthless auxiliary. The wine covered the bride's lovely dress with indelible stains, and the glass would certainly have wounded her, had not Bénédict, with no less coolness than dexterity, caught it in his hand without sustaining any injury.

Athénaïs, terribly frightened, rose and threw herself into her mother's arms. Bénédict contented himself with glancing at Blutty, and saying to him with perfect tranquillity:

"But for me there would have been an end of your wife's beauty."

With that he set the glass down in the centre of the table, and crushed it with a piece of sandstone which happened to be at hand. He dealt it several blows in order to break it into as many pieces as possible; then said, as he scattered them about the table:

"Messieurs, cousins, kinsmen and friends of Pierre Blutty, who has just insulted me, and you yourself, Pierre Blutty, whom I despise with all my heart, I give each of you a bit of this glass. Each bit is a challenge to give me satisfaction, and a portion of the insult to me, which I call upon you to repair."

"We don't fight with swords, nor sabres, nor pistols," cried Blutty, in a voice of thunder. "We are not popinjays—*black coats* like you. We haven't taken lessons in courage ; we have it in our hearts and at our finger ends. Take off your coat, monsieur, the dispute will soon be settled."

And Blutty, grinding his teeth together, began to remove his flower and ribbon-laden coat and to roll up his sleeves to the elbow. Athénaïs, who had fallen fainting into her mother's arms, suddenly rushed forward and threw herself between them, with piercing shrieks. This proof of interest, which Blutty rightly judged to be wholly in Bénédict's behalf, increased his rage. He pushed her away and rushed at Bénédict.

The latter, who was plainly less powerful, but was active and cool, thrust his foot between his legs and threw him down.

Blutty had not risen again when a swarm of his friends threw themselves on Bénédict. He had barely time to draw his pistols from his pocket and present them at their heads.

"Messieurs," he said, "you are twenty against one ; you are cowards ! If you take a step toward me, four of you will be shot down like dogs."

The sight calmed their valor for an instant ; whereupon Père Lhéry, knowing Bénédict's obstinacy, and fearing a tragic result of the incident, rushed in front of him, and, raising his knotted stick over the heads of the

assailants, pointed to his white hair spattered with the
wine which Blutty had thrown at Bénédict.   Tears of
anger glistened in his eyes.

"Pierre Blutty," he cried, "you have behaved out-
rageously to-day.   If you think that you can obtain
the control of my house by such performances, and drive
my nephew out of it, you are sadly mistaken.   I am
still at liberty to shut the door on you and to keep my
daughter.   The marriage is not consummated yet.   Athénaïs, step behind me."

The old man took his daughter's arm and drew her
roughly toward him.   Athénaïs, anticipating his purpose,
cried with an accent of hatred and alarm :

"Keep me, father, keep me forever.   Defend me from
this madman, who insults you and your family !   No, I
will never be his wife !   I will never leave you !"

And she clung with all her strength to her father's neck.

Pierre Blutty, whose title as his father-in-law's heir
was not assured as yet by any legal document, was
struck by the force of these arguments.   Concealing the
wrath which his wife's conduct aroused, he instantly
changed his tone.

"I admit that I spoke too quickly," he said.   "If I
have failed in my respect to you, father-in law, accept
my apologies."

"Yes, monsieur, you have failed in respect to me, in
the person of my daughter, whose clothes bear the marks
of your brutality ; also, in the person of my nephew,
for whom I shall find a way to enforce respect.   If you
wish your wife and your father-in-law to forget this conduct, offer Bénédict your hand, and let there be an end
of all this."

A large crowd had collected about them, and was
awaiting with interest the conclusion of this scene.

Every eye seemed to say to Blutty that he must not give way; but, although Blutty did not lack a certain brute courage, he had as clear an understanding of his own interests as every countryman has. Moreover, he was really very much in love with his wife, and the threat of separation from her alarmed him more than everything else. So he sacrificed the counsels of empty glory to those of common sense, and said after a moment's hesitation:

"Very well, I will obey you, father-in-law, but it comes hard to me, I admit; and I hope you'll give me credit, Athénaïs, for what I am doing to get you."

"You will never get me, whatever you do," cried the young woman, who had just noticed the numerous stains with which she was covered.

"Daughter," rejoined Père Lhéry, who was well able to assume on occasion the dignity and authority of a father, "in your present situation you must have no other will than your father's. I order you to take your husband's arm and make peace between him and your cousin."

As he spoke, Père Lhéry turned to his nephew, who, during the discussion, had uncocked his pistols and put them out of sight; but, instead of yielding to the friendly push which his uncle attempted to give him, he recoiled from the hand which Pierre Blutty reluctantly offered him.

"Never, uncle!" he replied. "I am sorry that I cannot by obeying you show you my gratitude for the interest you have manifested in me. But it is not in my power to forgive an insult. The most that I can do is to forget it."

Thereupon, he turned his back and disappeared, imperiously forcing his way through the open-mouthed bystanders.

XXII

Bénédict plunged into Raimbault park, and, throwing himself down on the moss in a dark, secluded spot, abandoned himself to the most disheartening reflections. He had just broken the last tie which bound him to life, for he realized fully that, being on such terms with Pierre Blutty, he could no longer maintain direct relations with his kinsman at the farm. That neighborhood, where he had passed so many happy moments, and which was filled to overflowing with reminders of Valentine, he should never see again ; or, if he did come thither at rare intervals, it would be as a stranger, without the right to retrace his memories of her, but yesterday so sweet, to-day so filled with gall. It seemed to him that long years of misery already lay between him and those hours so recently flown, and he blamed himself for not having enjoyed them enough. He regretted the momentary outbursts of temper which he had not held in cheek ; he bewailed the unfortunate disposition of man, who never realizes the value of his joys until he has lost them.

His existence thenceforth was horrible to contemplate. Surrounded by enemies, he would be the laughing-stock of the province ; every day some voice, too humble for him to take the trouble to reply to it, would shout in his ears impudent and stinging mockery ; every day he would have to be reminded of the pitiful dénouement of his love, and to persuade himself that there was no hope.

However, love of self, which imparts so much energy

to a shipwrecked man at the point of death, inspired
Bénédict for a moment with a determination to live on,
in spite of everything. He made superhuman efforts to
devise some aim, some object of ambition, some charm,
no matter what, in life. It was all in vain : his heart
refused to admit any other passion than love. Indeed,
at twenty years of age, what other passion seems worthy
of man ? After that swift and insane existence, which
had lifted him above the earth, everything seemed dull
and colorless ; that which would have been far beyond
his hopes a month earlier seemed now unworthy of his
desires. There was in the world but one happiness, one
love, one woman.

When he had exhausted to no purpose his remaining
strength, he fell into a state of deathly loathing for life,
and resolved to have done with it. He examined his
pistols and walked toward the exit from the park, in
order to carry out his plan without disturbing the nuptial
fête, the lights of which still gleamed through the foliage.

But he determined first to drain his cup of sorrow to
the dregs ; he retraced his steps and glided through the
shrubbery to the foot of the walls within which Valentine was imprisoned. He followed them at random for
some time. All was silence and gloom in that great
mansion ; all the servants were at the fête, and the
guests had long since retired. Bénédict could hear
nothing save the voice of the old marchioness, who
seemed considerably excited. It came through the open
window of a room on the ground floor. Bénédict crept
nearer, and heard certain words which suddenly changed
his plans.

"I assure you, madame," said the marchioness, "that
Valentine is seriously ill, and that Monsieur de Lansac
must be made to listen to reason."

"*Mon Dieu!* madame," replied another voice, which Bénédict thought must be the countess's, "you have a perfect passion for meddling in everything! It seems to me that your intervention or my own at such a time can be nothing less than indelicate."

"Madame," retorted the other voice, "I know no in‑delicacy where my granddaughter's health is concerned."

"If I didn't know what pleasure you take in holding a different opinion from mine, I should find it difficult to explain this attack of consideration for others."

"Sneer as much as you please, madame; I just listened at Valentine's door, not knowing what was going on in‑side, and suspecting something very far from the truth. When I heard the nurse's voice instead of the fond hus‑band's, I went in, and found Valentine in great distress and completely exhausted. I assure you that this is not at all the time——"

"Valentine loves her husband, her husband loves her, and I am quite sure that he will show her all the con‑sideration she demands."

"Can the bride of a day demand anything, pray? Has she any rights? Does anyone pay any attention to them?"

The window was closed at that moment and Bénédict could hear no more. Whatever insane and awful proj‑ects frenzy can inspire passed through his brain in that instant.

"O outrageous violation of the most sacred rights!" he exclaimed inwardly; "shocking tyranny of man over woman! Marriage, society, all existing institutions, I hate you! I hate you to the death! And thou, O God! thou creating Will, who dost cast us upon earth and dost then refuse to interpose to shape our destinies; thou who dost abandon the weak to such despotism and degrada‑

tion—I curse thee! Thou dost fall asleep content with
having created, caring naught to preserve. Thou dost
place within us an intelligent mind, and dost permit misfortune to stifle our faculties! Be thou accursed! accursed be the womb that bore me!"

As he raved thus, the wretched youth cocked his
pistols, tore his breast with his nails, and strode forward
in his excitement, no longer thinking of remaining hidden.
Suddenly his reason, or rather a sort of lucidity in the
midst of his frenzy, cast a light upon his path. There
was a way of rescuing Valentine from a hateful and dis-
honoring tyranny ; there was a way of punishing that
heartless mother who in cold blood condemned her daughter to legitimate degradation, to the vilest degradation
inflicted on woman—to rape.

"Yes, rape!" Bénédict repeated furiously—and we
must not forget that Bénédict was of a most excitable
and wholly exceptional temperament.—" Every day, in
the name of God and of society, some clown or some
dastard obtains the hand of an unfortunate girl, who is
forced by her parents, her good name or her poverty to
stifle in her heart a pure and sanctified love. And before
the eyes of society, which approves and sanctions the
outrage, the modest, trembling woman, who has been
able to resist the transports of her lover, falls dishonored
beneath the kisses of a detested master! And this must
go on!"

And Valentine, the fairest work of creation, the sweet,
chaste, simple-hearted Valentine, was among those reserved for that outrage. Her tears, her pallor, her depression,
must have enlightened her mother's conscience and
alarmed the delicate sensibility of her husband ; but all
in vain! There was nothing that could protect the unfortunate creature from shame—not even the weakness

of disease and the exhaustion of fever! There is one
man on earth vile enough to say: "No matter!" and a
mother so icy-hearted as to close her eyes to this crime!

"No!" he cried," it shall not be! I swear it by my
mother's good name!"

He cocked his pistols again and ran forward at random.
A short, dry cough brought him abruptly to a stand-
still. In his state of nervous irritation, the instinctive
penetration of hatred enabled him to divine from that
slight indication that Monsieur de Lansac was coming
straight toward him.

They were approaching each other along the path of
an English garden, a narrow, winding and densely-shaded
path. Bénédict was hidden by a thick clump of firs. He
crouched under their dark branches, and stood ready to
blow out his enemy's brains.

Monsieur de Lansac was coming from the pavilion in
the park, where he had been quartered hitherto, from
respect for the proprieties. He was walking toward the
château. His clothes exhaled an odor of amber which
Bénédict detested almost as bitterly as he detested the
man; his boots creaked on the gravel. Bénédict's heart
beat far up in his chest; his blood ceased to flow; but his
hand was steady and his eye sure.

But, just as he raised his arm to the level of that detested head, with his finger on the trigger, he heard
other footsteps coming behind him. He trembled with
rage at that infernal mischance. A witness might cause
his enterprise to fail, and prevent him, not from killing
Lansac—he felt that no human power could protect him
from his hate—but from killing himself immediately after.
The thought of the scaffold made him shudder. He remembered that society prescribed infamous penalties for
the heroic crime which his love dictated to him.

Hesitating, irresolute, he waited and overheard this dialogue :

"Well, Franck, what reply did Madame la Comtesse de Raimbault make ? "

"That monsieur le comte may go to her room," a servant answered.

"Very good ; you may go to bed, Franck. Here is the key to my room."

"Will not monsieur come back ? "

"Ah ! he suspects the truth ! " muttered Monsieur de Lansac between his teeth, as if speaking to himself.

"I mean, monsieur le comte, that—madame la marquise—Catherine——"

"I understand ; go to bed."

The two dark figures passed each other under the firs, and Bénédict saw his enemy approaching the house. As soon as he lost sight of him his resolution returned.

"As if I could allow this opportunity to pass ! " he cried ; "as if I could allow his foot to profane the threshold of that house, which contains my Valentine ! "

He began to run, but the count had too great a start ; he failed to overtake him before he had entered the château.

He entered mysteriously, alone, without lights, like a prince in search of adventures. He sprang lightly up the steps, passed through the peristyle, and ascended to the second floor ; for this pretence of going to converse with his mother-in-law was simply a convenient scheme to avoid telling his valet the private reason for his eagerness. He had agreed with the countess that she should send for him as soon as his wife should consent to receive him. Madame de Raimbault, as we have seen, did not consult her daughter ; she did not deem it necessary.

But, when Monsieur de Lansac was almost overtaken

by Bénédict, whose pistol, still cocked, followed him in the shadow, the marchioness's companion glided toward the expectant spouse as lightly as her tightly-corseted body and her sixty years would permit.

"Madame la marquise has a word to say to monsieur," she said.

Thereupon Monsieur de Lansac turned in another direction and followed her. All this took place very quickly and in semi-darkness. Bénédict, after a fruitless search, was unable to discover by what infernal trickery his prey had escaped him once more.

Alone, in that immense house, where all the lights had purposely been extinguished, and the few servants who were not at the fête had been sent away on various pretexts, Bénédict wandered about at random, trying to recall his previous visit and to go toward the room which Valentine probably occupied. His mind was made up; he would rescue her from her fate, either by killing her husband, or by killing herself. He had often gazed at Valentine's window from out-of-doors; he had recognized it at night during the long vigils to which the light of her lamp bore witness; but how could he tell where it lay in that darkness and in his terrible agitation?

He abandoned himself to chance. He knew simply that the room was on the second floor; he passed through a long corridor and paused to listen. At the farther end he spied a ray of light shining through a partly-open door, and it seemed to him that he could hear women's voices whispering. That was the marchioness's room. She had sent for her grandson-in-law to urge him to renounce the idea of enjoying that first night, and Catherine, who had been summoned to testify to her mistress's indisposition, did her best to second Valentine's wishes. But Monsieur de Lansac was not easily persuaded, and considered it most unseemly that all those women should already be interfering in the mysteries of his domestic life with their curiosity and their evil influence. He resisted with due courtesy, and swore upon his honor that he would obey Valentine's verbal command to retire if delivered in person.

Bénédict, having crept noiselessly to the door, overheard the whole discussion, although it was carried on in undertones, for fear of attracting the attention of the countess, who would have wrecked the whole negotiation with a word.

"Will Valentine have the strength to give that command?" Bénédict asked himself. "Oh! I will give her strength to do it!"

And he felt his way along toward another fainter ray of light which shone under a closed door. He put his ear to the crack: that was the room; he knew it by the beating of his heart and by Valentine's faint breathing, which none but such a passionately loving man as he could possibly have detected and recognized.

He leaned against that door, breathless and panting, and imagined that it yielded to his weight; he pushed it, and it opened noiselessly.

"Great God!" thought Bénédict, always ready to imagine anything that could torment him, "can she be expecting him?"

He stepped into the room; the bed was so placed as to conceal the door from a person lying on it. A night lamp was burning in its ground glass globe. Was that really the right room? He stepped forward. The curtains were half-down. Valentine, fully dressed, lay on her bed asleep; her attitude was sufficiently eloquent of her terror. She was half-seated on the edge of the bed, with her feet on the floor; her head, yielding to fatigue, had fallen on the pillow; her face was ghastly pale, and one could count the rapid pulsations of fever in the swollen veins of her neck and temples.

Bénédict had barely time to step behind the back of the bed and squeeze between the curtain and the wall, when he heard De Lansac's steps in the corridor.

He was coming in that direction; in a moment he would enter the room. Bénédict still had his hand on his pistol. In that room his foe could not escape him; he had but to raise his hand to strike him dead before he had even touched the linen of the marriage bed.

Valentine, suddenly awakened by the noise Bénédict made in concealing himself, uttered a faint exclamation and hastily sat erect; but, seeing nothing, she listened and heard her husband's step. Thereupon, she rose to her feet and hurried to the door.

That movement nearly caused Bénédict to lose his head. He half emerged from his hiding-place to blow out that shameless, lying woman's brains; but Valentine had no other purpose than to bolt her door.

Five minutes passed in absolute silence, to the great surprise of both Valentine and Bénédict, who had concealed himself again. Then someone tapped gently at the door. Valentine did not answer, but Bénédict, leaning out from behind the curtains, heard her hurried, uneven breathing. He saw her terror, her pale lips, her hands clutching the protecting bolt. "Courage, Valentine," he was on the point of crying out, "there are two of us to sustain the assault!" when he heard Catherine's voice.

"Open, mademoiselle," she said; "don't be afraid any more; it's I; and I am alone. *Monsieur* has gone; he yielded to madame la marquise's arguments and to the prayer that he would go away, which I addressed to

him in your name. Oh! we made you out much sicker
than you are, I trust," the good woman added, as she
entered the room and took Valentine in her arms. "In
heaven's name don't take it into your head to be as badly
off in reality as we boasted that you were!"

"Oh! I felt as if I were dying just now," replied Valentine, embracing her; "but I am better now; you have
saved me for a few more hours. After that, may God
protect me!"

"Oh! bless my soul, my dear child, what ideas you
have!" said Catherine. "Come, go to sleep. I will
pass the night by your bed."

"No, Catherine, go and get some rest. I have kept
you awake many nights now. Go, I say; I insist upon
it. I am better; I shall sleep well. But lock me in and
take the key, and don't go to bed till the whole house is
locked up."

"Oh! never fear. Hark, they are locking up already;
don't you hear the big door?"

"Yes, it's all right. Good-night, nurse, dear nurse!"

The nurse made some further objection to leaving her
mistress; she was afraid that Valentine might be worse
during the night. She yielded at last, and left the room,
locking the door behind her and taking the key.

"If you want anything," she called from the corridor,
"you must ring for me."

"Yes, never fear; sleep soundly," Valentine replied.

She bolted the door, then threw back her dishevelled
hair and pressed her hands against her forehead, drawing a long breath like a person relieved of a burden; then
she returned to her bed and sank upon it in a sitting
posture, with the rigidity characteristic of illness and discouragement. Bénédict put out his head and was able
to see her face. He could have shown himself to her

without attracting her attention. With her arms hanging at her sides and her eyes fixed on the floor, she was like a lifeless statue. Her faculties seemed exhausted, her heart cold and dead.

XXIII

Bénédict heard all the doors of the house closed and locked one after another. Little by little the footsteps of the servants receded from the ground floor ; the reflection cast on the foliage by a few stray lamps disappeared ; only the sound of the instruments in the distance, and an occasional pistol shot, which it is customary in Berri to fire at weddings and baptisms as a sign of enjoyment, broke the silence at rare intervals. Bénédict was in a most extraordinary situation, of which he would never have dared to dream. That night—that ghastly night which he had expected to pass in the agony of impotent rage—had brought him and Valentine together ! Monsieur de Lansac returned to his quarters alone, and Bénédict, the forsaken, who proposed to blow out his brains in a ditch, was locked into that room alone with Valentine ! He felt a sting of remorse for having denied his God, for having cursed the day of his birth. This unforeseen joy, coming so close upon the heels of thoughts of murder and suicide, took possession of him with such irresistible violence, that it did not occur to him to contemplate its terrible sequel. He did not admit to himself that, if he should be discovered in that place, Valentine was ruined ; he did not ask himself whether that un-hoped-for conquest of an instant of joy would not render the necessity of dying even more hateful. He abandoned himself to the delirious excitement which such a triumph over destiny aroused in him. He pressed both hands against his breast to check its frantic palpitations. But just as he was on the point of betraying himself by his agitation, he paused, mastered by the dread of offending Valentine, by that respectful and chaste shyness which is the principal characteristic of true love.

He stood irresolute, his heart overflowing with agonizing joy and impatience, and was about to take some decisive step, when she rang, and in a moment Catherine appeared.

" Dear nurse," said Valentine, " you didn't give me my potion."

"Ah! your *portion!*" said the good woman. "I thought that you would not need to take it to-day. I will go to prepare it."

" No, that would take too long. Just dissolve a little opium in some orange-flower water."

" But that may do you harm."

" No ; opium can never injure me in the state I am in now."

" I don't know anything about it. You are no doctor ; would you like me to go and ask madame la marquise ? "

"Oh! for heaven's sake, don't do that. Don't you be afraid. Here, give me the bottle ; I know the dose."

"Oh! you put in twice too much."

" No, I tell you ; since I am free to sleep at last, I propose to make the most of it. While I am asleep, I shall not have to think."

Catherine sadly shook her head as she diluted a strong dose of opium, which Valentine took in several swallows while she undressed ; and, when she was wrapped in her *peignoir,* she dismissed her nurse once more and went to bed.

Bénédict, crouching in his hiding-place, had not dared to move hand or foot. But the fear of being discovered by the nurse was much less painful than that which he felt when he was alone with Valentine. After a terrible battle with himself, he ventured to raise the curtain gently. The rustling of the silk did not wake Valentine ; the opium was doing its work already. However, Bénédict fancied that she partly opened her eyes. He was frightened and dropped the curtain, the fringe of which caught on a bronze candlestick which stood on the light stand, and dragged it noisily to the floor. Valentine started, but did not come out of her lethargy. Thereupon, Bénédict stood beside her, with even greater liberty to gaze at her than on the day when he adored her reflection in the water. Alone at her feet in the solemn silence of the night, protected by that artificial slumber which it was not in his power to interrupt, he fancied that he was fulfilling a supernatural destiny. He had naught to fear from her anger. He could drink his fill of the happiness of gazing at her, without being disturbed in his enjoyment ; he could speak to her unheard, tell her of his great love, of his agony, without putting to flight that faint, mysterious smile which played about her half-parted lips. He could put his lips to hers with no fear of being repelled by her. But the certainty of impunity did not embolden him to that point. For Valentine was the object of an almost divine adoration in his heart, and she needed no exterior protection against him. He was her safeguard and defender against himself. He knelt beside her, and contented himself with taking her hand as it hung over the edge of the bed, holding it in his, examining with admiration its whiteness and the fineness of the skin, and putting his trembling lips to it. That hand bore the wedding ring, the first link of a burdensome and indissoluble chain. Bénédict might have taken it off and destroyed it, but his heart had recurred to gentler sentiments. He determined to respect everything about Valentine, even the emblem of her duty.

For in that ecstasy of rapture he speedily forgot everything. He deemed himself as fortunate and as sure of the future as in the happy days at the farm; he imagined that the night would never end, that Valentine would never wake, and that he would live out his eternity of happiness in that room.

For a long time that blissful contemplation was without danger; the very angels are less pure than the heart of a man of twenty when he loves passionately; but he trembled when Valentine, excited by one of those happy dreams to which opium gives birth, leaned gently toward him and feebly pressed his hand, murmuring indistinct words. Bénédict trembled and moved away from the bed, afraid of himself.

"Oh! Bénédict!" said Valentine slowly, in a faint voice, "Bénédict, was it you who married me to-day? I thought that it was somebody else. Tell me that it was really you!"

"Yes, it was I, it was I!" said Bénédict, beside himself with excitement, as he pressed to his wildly beating heart that soft hand which sought his.

Valentine, half awake, sat up in bed, with eyelids parted, and gazed at him with expressionless eyes, wandering uncertainly in the vague land of dreams. There was an expression of something like terror in her features; then she closed her eyes, and smiled as her head fell back on the pillow.

"It was you whom I loved," she said; "but how did they ever allow it?"

She spoke so low and her articulation was so indistinct that her words fell upon Bénédict's ears like the angelic murmur one hears in dreams.

"O my beloved!" he cried, leaning over, "tell me that again, tell me again, and let me die of joy at your feet!"

But Valentine pushed him away.

"Leave me!" she said.

And her words became unintelligible.

Bénédict thought that he could understand that she took him for Monsieur de Lansac. He called himself by name again and again, and Valentine, hovering between reality and illusion, now waking, now falling asleep, innocently revealed all her secrets to him. At one time she fancied that Monsieur de Lansac was pursuing her, with drawn sword; she threw herself on Bénédict's breast, and exclaimed as she put her arms about his neck:

"Let us both die!"

"Oh! you are right," he cried. "Be mine and let us die!"

He placed his pistols on the table and strained Valentine's inert and supple body to his heart. But again she said to him:

"Leave me, my friend; I am dying of fatigue; let me sleep."

She rested her head on Bénédict's shoulder, and he dared not move for fear of disturbing her. It was such great joy to him to see her sleeping in his arms! He had already forgotten that there could be any greater joy.

"Sleep, sleep, my life!" he whispered, touching her

forehead gently with his lips.   " Sleep, my angel !
Doubtless you can see the Virgin in heaven ; and she
smiles upon you, for she protects you.   I promise you
we shall be united there ! "

He could not resist the temptation to unfasten gently
her lace cap, and allow that magnificent fair hair, at
which he had gazed lovingly so many times, to fall in
waves about them both.   How silky and fragrant it was !
How its cool touch kindled fever and delirious excitement
in his veins !   A score of times he bit Valentine's sheets
and his own hands, to cast himself loose from the frenzy
of his joy by the sensation of physical pain.   Seated on
the edge of that bed, whose fine, perfumed linen made
him quiver from head to foot, he suddenly fell on his
knees, seeking to recover his self-control, and confined
himself to gazing at her.   Chastely he drew about her
the embroidered lawn which protected her pure and untroubled bosom ; he even threw the curtain partly over
her face, so that he could no longer see her, and could
thereby muster courage to go away.   But Valentine,
with the longing for air which one feels in sleep, pushed
the curtain away, and, moving nearer to him, seemed to
invite his caresses with an artless and trustful air.   He
raised her thick tresses and filled his mouth with them
to prevent himself from crying out ; he wept with love
and frenzy.   At last, in a moment of indescribable anguish, he bit the round, white shoulder which she uncov-
ered before him.   He bit it cruelly, and she woke, but
with no indication of suffering.   When he saw her sit up
in bed again, gaze at him more closely, and pass her
hand over him to make sure that he was not a ghost,
Bénédict, who was kneeling beside her in a sort of
stupor, thought that he was lost.   His blood, which
was boiling madly in his veins, stood still ; he turned

as pale as death, and said to her, not knowing what
he said :

"Forgive me, Valentine ; I shall die if you do not take
pity on me."

"Pity on you !" she said, in the loud, sharp tone of
the somnambulist ; "what is the matter with you ? Are
you ill ? Come to my arms as you did just now; come.
Weren't you happy ? "

"O Valentine !" cried Bénédict, fairly beside himself,
"do you mean it ? do you recognize me ? do you know
who I am ? "

"Yes," she said, letting her head fall drowsily on his
shoulder ; "my dear nurse ! "

"No ! no ! Bénédict ! Bénédict ! Do you understand ? the man who loves you more than life ! Bénédict ! "

And he shook her to wake her, but that was impossible. He could arouse in her only the ardor born of
dreams. But this time her dream was so vivid that he
was deceived.

"Yes, it is you," she said, raising her head again,
"my husband. I know you, my Bénédict ; I love you
too. Kiss me, but do not look at me. Put out the light ;
let me hide my face on your breast."

As she spoke, she threw her arms about him and drew
him toward her with an astounding feverish strength.
Her cheeks wore a deep flush, her lips glowed with color.
A sudden, fleeting flame shone in her dull eyes. But
how could Bénédict distinguish that unhealthy excitement from the passionate frenzy by which he was himself consumed ? He threw himself upon her in desperation and, on the point of yielding to the violence of his
agonizing desires, he uttered nervous, heart-rending cries.
Instantly he heard footsteps, and the key turned in the

lock. He had barely time to jump behind the bed ; Catherine entered.

She scrutinized Valentine closely ; was evidently surprised by the disordered condition of her bed, and that her sleep should be so agitated. She drew a chair to the bed and sat beside her for about a quarter of an hour. Bénédict supposed that she intended to pass the rest of the night there, and he cursed her a thousand times. But Valentine, no longer excited by her lover's burning breath, relapsed into a state of motionless and peaceful torpor. Catherine, reassured as to her condition, concluded that she herself was dreaming when she thought that she heard shrieks. She rearranged the bed, drew the clothes over Valentine, replaced her hair under her cap, and adjusted the folds of her night-dress over her breast to keep off the night air ; then she left the room on tiptoe and turned the key twice in the lock. Thus it was impossible to make his escape in that way.

When he found himself once more master of Valentine, fully realizing now the danger of his position, he walked away from the bed in dismay and threw himself on a chair at the other end of the room. There he hid his face in his hands, and tried to anticipate the consequences of his night's work.

He no longer had the ferocious courage which would have made it possible for him, a few hours earlier, to kill Valentine. After gazing upon her modest and soul-stirring charms, he felt that he had not the strength to destroy that lovely work of God : Lansac was the one whom he must kill. But Lansac could not die alone ; he himself must follow him to the tomb ; and what would become of Valentine without lover or husband ? How would the death of one benefit her, if the other were not left ? And then, who could say that she would not curse the murderer of the husband whom she did not love ? She was so pure and saintly, by nature so straightforward and honorable, would she appreciate the sublimity of a devotion which manifested itself by such a barbarous deed ? Would not Bénédict's memory be hateful and painful to her, stained with her husband's blood and branded with the terrible name of *assassin?*

"Ah ! since I can never possess her," he said to himself; "I must see to it that she does not hate my memory ! I will die alone, and perhaps she will venture to weep for me in the privacy of her prayers."

He drew a chair to Valentine's desk ; it contained everything necessary for writing. He lighted a candle and drew the bed-curtains so that the sight of her might not deprive him of the courage to bid her adieu forever. He bolted the door to avoid being taken by surprise, and wrote to Valentine as follows :

" It is two o'clock in the morning, and I am alone with you, Valentine, alone in your chamber, and you are more entirely in my power than you will ever be in your husband's, for you have told me that you love me ; you have called me to your heart in the privacy of your dreams ; you have almost returned my caresses ; you have unconsciously made me the happiest and the most miserable of men ; and yet, Valentine, I have respected you, amid the tortures of the most terrible frenzy that ever swallowed up the faculties of man. You are still lying there, pure and unprofaned at my hands, and you can wake without blushing. Oh ! Valentine, I must love you very dearly.

" But, agonizing and incomplete as my happiness has been, I must pay for it with my life. After hours like those which I have just passed at your knees, with my lips glued to your hand, to your hair, to the unsubstantial garment which hardly covers you, I cannot live another day. After such transports I cannot return to commonplace life—to the hateful life which I should lead apart from you. Have no fear, Valentine; the man who possessed you in his thoughts to-night will never again see the sunrise.

"Except for this irrevocable resolution, how could I have found courage to make my way to this room and to dream dreams of happiness? How could I have dared to look at you and speak to you as I have done, even while you slept? All my blood will be too small a price to pay for the fate which has sold me such moments as these.

"You must know all, Valentine. I came here to kill your husband. When I found that he had escaped me, I determined to kill you and myself. Have no fear; when you read this, my heart will have ceased to beat; but to-night, Valentine, at the very moment that you called me to your arms, a loaded pistol was pointed at your head.

"But I had not the courage—I should never have it. If I could kill you and myself with the same shot, it would have been done before this; but I should be compelled to see you suffer, to see your blood flow, your heart fight against death; and, though that sight should last but a second, that second alone would contain more agony than my whole life has known.

"Live, therefore, and let your husband live also. The letting him live is even more painful than the respect for you which tied my hands just now as I stood, dying with desire, at the foot of your bed. It costs me more to renounce the satisfaction of my hatred than it costs me to overcome my love; but it may be that his death would bring dishonor upon you. Thus to exhibit my jealousy to the world would, perhaps, reveal your love as well as my own; for you love me, Valentine, you told me so just now, involuntarily. And last evening, in the field, when you were weeping on my breast, was not that love too? Oh! do not wake; let me carry that belief with me to the tomb.

"My suicide will not compromise you; you alone will know for whom I die. The surgeon's scalpel will not disclose your name written on my heart, but you will know that its last pulsations were for you.

"Adieu, Valentine; adieu, thou first and only love of my life! Many others will love you, as who would not? But you will have been loved once and once only as you deserve to be loved. The heart which you have loved must needs return to God's bosom, in order not to degenerate on earth.

"After I am gone, Valentine, what will your life be? Alas! I do not know. Doubtless you will submit to your lot. My memory will grow dim; you will put up with all that seems hateful to you to-day—indeed you will have to do it. O Valentine, I spare your husband so that you may not curse me, and that God may not shut me out of heaven, where a place is reserved for you. O God, protect me! O Valentine, pray for me!

"Adieu! I have just been to your bedside; you are sleeping quietly. Oh! if you knew how lovely you are! Never, oh! never, can a man's heart contain without bursting all the love which I have for you.

"If the soul is not an empty breath which the wind blows away, mine will live always near you.

"At eve, when you go to the end of the field, think of me if the breeze plays with your hair, and if, amid its cool caresses, you suddenly feel a burning breath; at night, in your dreams, if a mysterious kiss grazes your cheek, remember Bénédict."

He folded the letter and placed it on the table where his pistols lay, which Catherine had almost touched without seeing them. He uncocked them, put them in his pocket, leaned over Valentine, gazed at her with rapture for the first and last time; then he rushed to the window, and, with the courage of a man who has nothing to risk, dropped to the ground at the peril of his life. He might fall thirty feet, or be shot for a thief; but what did it matter to him? Only the fear of compromising Valentine led him to take precautions against waking anyone. Despair gave him superhuman strength; for, to anyone who observes in cold blood the distance between the second floor and ground-floor windows of the château of Raimbault, and the bare face of the wall with no projection or foothold, such an undertaking would seem utterly incredible.

Nevertheless, he reached the ground without arousing anyone, and climbed the wall into the open country.

The first rays of dawn were whitening the horizon.

XXIV

Valentine, more exhausted by such sleep than she would have been by a sleepless night, woke very late. The sun was high and hot in the heavens; myriads of insects buzzed in its rays. Buried for a long time in the indolent torpor which follows one's waking, Valentine did not try at first to collect her thoughts; she listened indifferently to the innumerable noises of the air and the fields. She did not suffer, because she had forgotten many things, and was in ignorance of many more.

She sat up to take a glass of water from the table, and found Bénédict's letter. She turned it over slowly in her fingers, not conscious of what she was doing. At last she looked at it, and, on recognizing the writing, started, and opened it with a convulsive hand. The curtain had fallen; her whole life was laid bare before her eyes.

On hearing her heart-rending shrieks, Catherine hastened to her side. The good woman's face was intensely agitated: Valentine instantly realized the truth.

"Speak!" she cried; "where is Bénédict? what has become of Bénédict?"

And observing the nurse's distress and consternation, she added, clasping her hands:

"O *mon Dieu!* it is really true, it is all over!"

"Alas! mademoiselle, how do you know about it?" said Catherine, sitting down on the bed. "Who could have come into this room? I had the key in my pocket. Did you hear anything? But Mademoiselle Beaujon told me about it in such a low tone, for fear of waking you. I knew that the news would make you unhappy."

"Ah! it is indeed everything to me!" cried Valentine impatiently, springing suddenly to her feet. "Speak, I say! What has become of Bénédict?"

Terrified by her vehemence, the nurse hung her head and dared not reply.

"He is dead, I know it!" said Valentine, falling back on her bed, pale and gasping for breath; "but how long since?"

"Alas!" said the nurse, "no one knows; the unfortunate young man was found on the edge of the field this

morning at daybreak. He was lying in a ditch and covered with blood. The farmers from the Croix-Bleue
found him when they were going to pasture with their
cattle, and they carried him to his house at once. He
had a pistol bullet in his head, and the pistol was still in
his hand. The law people met there right away. Ah!
mon Dieu! what a misfortune! What can have made that
young man so unhappy? Nobody can say that it was
poverty. Monsieur Lhéry loved him like his own son,
and Madame Lhéry, what will she say? It will be a
terrible blow to them."

Valentine was not listening; she had fallen back upon
her bed, cold and stiff. In vain did Catherine try to
rouse her by calling her name and by her caresses; she
was like one dead. The good nurse, trying to open her
clinched hands, found a crumpled letter in them. She
did not know how to read, but she had that instinct
which warns us that the person we love is in danger;
she took the letter from her and concealed it carefully
before calling for help.

Valentine's chamber was soon full of people, but all
their efforts to revive her were fruitless. A physician
who was hastily summoned found a very serious cerebral
congestion, and succeeded, by bleeding her, in restoring
the circulation; but that state of unconsciousness was
succeeded by convulsions, and for a week Valentine
hovered between life and death.

The nurse was careful to say nothing as to the cause
of her mistress's dangerous agitation. She told the
physician alone, under the seal of secrecy. This is how
she was forced to believe that there was, behind all
these distressing events, a liaison which no one must be
allowed to suspect. Finding that Valentine was a little
better after the bloodletting, on the day of the event

which caused her illness, she began to reflect upon the supernatural way in which her young mistress had been informed of that event. The letter she found in her hand reminded her of the note which she had been asked to give her on the previous day, before the wedding, and which had been handed to her by Bénédict's old house-keeper. Happening to go down for a moment to the butler's pantry, she heard the servants discussing the cause of the suicide, and saying to one another, under their breath, that Pierre Blutty and Bénédict had quar-relled the night before on the subject of Mademoiselle de Raimbault. They added that Bénédict was still living, and that the same physician who was attending Valen-tine had dressed his wound in the morning, and had re-fused to give a positive opinion as to his condition. One bullet had entered his forehead and come out above the ear. That wound, although serious, might not prove fatal ; but no one knew how many bullets there were in the pistol. It might be that a second one had lodged in the skull, and in that case the respite which the wounded man was enjoying at that moment might serve simply to prolong his suffering.

Thus it was proved to Catherine's satisfaction that that catastrophe and the painful events immediately pre-ceding it were directly responsible for Valentine's alarm-ing condition. The good creature fancied that a gleam of hope, however feeble it might be, would have more effect upon her mistress's trouble than all the physician's remedies. She hurried to Bénédict's cottage, which was only half a league from the château, and assured herself with her own eyes that the poor fellow was still alive. Many neighbors, drawn thither by curiosity rather than concern, were gathered about the door, but the physician had given orders that only a few should be admitted, and Monsieur Lhéry, who was installed by the dying man's bedside, allowed Catherine to enter only after much resistance. Madame Lhéry was still in ignorance of the sad news; she had gone to Pierre Blutty's farm to pay the wedding visit.

Catherine, after examining the wounded man and asking Lhéry's opinion, turned away, knowing as little as before of the probable results of the wound, but fully enlightened as to the cause of the suicide. Just as she was leaving the house, she happened to glance at a chair on which Bénédict's blood-stained clothes had been placed. She started, and as it always happens, do what we will, that our eyes are attracted by a shocking or disgusting object, Catherine could not remove hers from that chair, and she discovered there a handkerchief of India silk, horribly stained with blood. She instantly recognized the kerchief which she herself had tied about Valentine's neck when she left the house on the evening before the wedding, and which she had lost during her walk in the fields. That was an indisputable ray of light; so she took advantage of a moment when no one was looking at her to possess herself of the handkerchief, which might have compromised Valentine, and thrust it in her pocket.

When she returned to the château, she lost no time in concealing it in her room, and gave no further thought to it. On the rare occasions when she was left alone with Valentine, she tried to make her understand that Bénédict might be saved, but it was all in vain. Valentine's mental faculties seemed to be completely exhausted; she did not raise her eyelids to see who spoke to her. If she had any thought at all in her mind, it was one of satisfaction to see that she was dying.

A week passed in this way. Then there was a per-

ceptible change for the better ; Valentine seemed to recover her memory, and found relief in floods of tears.
But as no one could induce her to divulge the cause of
her grief, they believed that there was still some trouble
with the brain. The nurse alone was on the watch for
a favorable moment to speak, but Monsieur de Lansac,
being on the eve of going away, *made it his duty* not to
leave his wife's apartments.

Monsieur de Lansac had received his appointment as
first secretary of Embassy—hitherto he had been only
second secretary—and, at the same time, orders to join
his chief at once, and to start for Russia, with or without his wife.

Monsieur de Lansac had never really intended to take
his wife abroad with him. In the days when he had
been most fascinating to Valentine, she had asked him
if he would take her to his post of duty, and he, in order
not to fall short of the devotion which he affected, had
answered that it was his most fervent wish never to be
parted from her. But he had secretly determined to use
all his adroitness and, if necessary, his authority, to preserve his wandering life from domestic annoyances.
Thus the coincidence of an illness, which was no longer
desperate, but which threatened to be of long duration,
with the necessity of leaving France immediately, was
favorable to Monsieur de Lansac's interests and desires.
Although Madame de Raimbault was very shrewd in
financial matters, she had allowed herself to be completely circumvented by the far superior skill of her son-
in-law. The marriage contract, after discussions most
revolting as to substance, but most refined as to form,
had been drawn altogether in Monsieur de Lansac's favor.
He had availed himself to the greatest possible extent
of the elasticity of the laws, to make himself master of

his wife's fortune, and he had made the *contracting parties* consent to offer his creditors flattering expectations
based on the estate of Raimbault.   These trifling pecu-
liarities of his conduct had come very near breaking off
the marriage ; but, by dint of flattering all the countess's
pet ambitions, he had succeeded in obtaining a stronger
hold upon her than before.   As for Valentine, she was so
ignorant of business, and had such a distaste for it, that
she agreed, without understanding anything about it, to
whatever was demanded of her.

So it was that Monsieur de Lansac, seeing that his debts
were paid, so to speak, left Raimbault with no great
regret for his wife, and he rubbed his hands as he felici-
tated himself inwardly upon having brought so delicate
and advantageous an affair to a satisfactory conclusion.
His orders to repair to his post arrived most opportunely
to relieve him from the difficult part he had been playing
at Raimbault since his marriage.   Suspecting, perhaps,
that a thwarted fancy was the cause of Valentine's distress and illness, and, at all events, bitterly aggrieved
by the feeling which she manifested for him, he had had
no excuse thus far for showing his irritation.   Under the
eyes of those two mothers, who made a great parade of
their affection and their anxiety, he dared not allow the
ennui and impatience which consumed him to make
themselves manifest.   So that his situation was extremely trying ; whereas, by going away for an indefinite time,
he would avoid, in addition, the disagreeable consequences sure to result from the forced sale of the Raimbault estates ; for his principal creditor was imperatively
demanding the amount of his claim, which was about
five hundred thousand francs ; and before long that
beautiful domain, which Madame de Raimbault had
taken so much pride in improving, would be, to her

unbounded disgust, dismembered and reduced to paltry dimensions.

At the same time, Monsieur de Lansac would escape from the tears and whims of a newly-married wife.

" In my absence," he said to himself, " she will have a chance to accustom herself to the idea of having given up her liberty. Her placid and retiring nature will accommodate itself to the quiet and secluded life to which I leave her ; or, if her repose is disturbed by some romantic love-affair, why, she will have time to cure herself of it or tire of it before I return."

Monsieur de Lansac was a man without prejudices, in whose eyes all sentiment, all argument, all conviction was governed by that omnipotent word which rules the universe : money.

Madame de Raimbault had other estates in various provinces, and law-suits everywhere. Law-suits were the principal business of her life. She declared that they wore her out with fatigue and excitement, but without them she would have been bored to death. Since the loss of her social grandeur they were all that her activity and her love of intrigue had to feed upon. In them, too, she vented all the spleen which the vexations of her position heaped up in her heart. At that moment, she was engaged in a very important suit in Sologne, against the inhabitants of a village who disputed her title to a vast tract of moorland. The case was about to be tried, and the countess was most anxious to be present to spur on her counsel, cajole the judges, threaten her opponents ; in a word, to give free rein to that feverish restlessness which is the gnawing worm of minds long fed upon ambition. But for Valentine's illness, she would have gone, as she intended, on the day following the wedding, to attend personally to that matter ; now, seeing that her daughter was out of danger, and having to be absent but a short time, she decided to go with her son-in-law, who was going to Paris, and who bade her adieu at the seat of the litigation, halfway to the capital.

Valentine was left alone with her grandmother and her nurse, at the château of Raimbault, for several days.

XXV

One night, Bénédict, who had been so crushed hitherto by horrible pain that he had been unable to think, woke feeling somewhat relieved, and made an effort to recall his situation. His head was so swathed in bandages that a part of his face was covered. He raised his hand to remove the obstacle and to recover the power to use the first faculty which comes to life within us—sight, which precedes even thought. Instantly, a light hand removed the pins, lifted a bandage, and enabled him to gratify his longing. He glanced at the pale-faced woman who was leaning over him, and, by the flickering gleam of a night light, distinguished a pure and noble profile which resembled Valentine's. He thought that he was dreaming, and his hand groped for the phantom's. The phantom seized his hand and pressed her lips to it.

"Who are you?" queried Bénédict, with a shudder.

"Can you ask me?" replied the voice of Louise.

The kind-hearted Louise left everything to go to nurse her friend. She was at her post day and night, hardly allowing Madame Lhéry to relieve her for an hour or two in the morning, devoting herself to the depressing duties of a nurse at the bedside of a man at the point of death, with almost no hope of recovery. However, thanks to Louise's wonderful nursing and to his own youthful strength, Bénédict escaped almost certain death, and one day he mustered strength enough to thank her and reproach her in the same breath for saving his life.

"My friend," said Louise, terrified by his mental prostration, "if I have unfeelingly recalled you to a life which my affection has no power to brighten for you, I have done it from consideration for Valentine."

Bénédict started.

"To preserve her life," continued Louise, "which is at this moment in at least as much danger as yours."

"In danger? why?" cried Bénédict.

"When she learned of your madness and your crime, Bénédict, Valentine, who undoubtedly was tenderly attached to you, fell suddenly ill. A gleam of hope might save her, perhaps, but she doesn't know that you are alive and that you may be restored to us."

"Then let her never know it!" cried Bénédict; "and as the harm is done—as the blow is dealt—let her die with me!"

As he spoke, he tore the bandage from his wound, and would have reopened it, but for Louise, who struggled manfully with him, and fell to the floor exhausted by her exertions and crushed with grief, after saving him from himself.

At another time he seemed to emerge from a profound torpor, and said to Louise, grasping her hand convulsively:

"Why are you here? Your sister is dying, and you are taking care of me!"

Carried away by a wave of passion and excitement, Louise, forgetting everything, exclaimed:

"And what if I love you even more dearly than I love
Valentine ? "

" In that case you are cursed," replied Bénédict, pushing her away with a wild look in his eye, " for you prefer chaos to light, the devil to the archangel ! You are
a miserable fool ! Leave this house ! Am I not unhappy
enough, that you must come and tear my heart with your
unhappiness ? "

Louise, utterly overwhelmed, hid her face in the curtains and wrapped them about her head to stifle her sobs.
Bénédict, too, began to weep, and his tears soothed him.

A moment later he called her back.

" I believe I spoke harshly to you just now," he said ;
" you must forgive something to the delirium of fever."

Louise replied by simply kissing the hand he held out
to her. Bénédict needed all of the little mental force he
had recovered to endure without an angry outbreak that
manifestation of love and submission. Let him explain
it who can. Louise's presence, instead of being a comfort to him, was positively disagreeable ; her attentions
irritated him. Gratitude contended in his heart with
impatience and displeasure. To receive from Louise all
those services, all those tokens of devotion, was like a
rebuke—a bitter reproach of his love for another. The
more disastrous that love proved to be to him, the more
he was offended by the efforts which were made to dissuade him from it. He clung to it as one clings to a
desperate undertaking, from a feeling of pride. Moreover, even if his heart had been large enough, in his good
fortune, to feel any interest in Louise or any compassion
for her, it had ceased to be so in his despair. He found
his own misfortunes heavy enough to bear, and this sort
of appeal to his generosity which Louise ventured to
make seemed to him the most selfish and ill-timed of de-

mands. Such injustice was inexcusable, perhaps, and yet is a man's strength always proportioned to his suffering ? That is a comforting promise of the Gospel ; but who is to hold the scales—who shall be the judge ? Does God account to us ? Does he vouchsafe to measure the cup after we have drained it ?

The countess had been absent two days when Bénédict had his most alarming paroxysm of fever. He had to be strapped to his bed. A most cruel tyranny is the tyranny of friendship. It often forces upon us an existence worse than death, and employs arbitrary force to bind us to the pillory of life.

At last Louise, having asked to be left alone with him, pacified him by repeating patiently, and again and again, the name of Valentine.

"Well," said Bénédict, suddenly, struggling violently to rise, and apparently much surprised, "where is she ? "

"Like you, Bénédict, she is at the door of the tomb," she replied. "Do you wish to embitter her last moments by dying like a madman ? "

"She is going to die ! " he said with a ghastly smile. "Ah ! God is good ! We shall be united then ! "

"And suppose she should live ? " said Louise ; "suppose she should order you to live ; suppose that she would give you her friendship again as the price of your obedience ? "

"Her friendship ! " said Bénédict, with a contemptuous laugh ; "what should I do with it ? You have mine, haven't you ? What do you get out of it ? "

"Oh ! you are very cruel, Bénédict ! " cried Louise sorrowfully ; "but what would I not do to save you ? Tell me, then, suppose Valentine loves you, suppose I have seen her, and heard in her delirium confessions which you would never have dared to hope for ? "

"I have received her confession myself!" replied
Bénédict, with the apparent calmness with which he
often concealed his most violent excitement. "I know
that Valentine loves me as I longed to be loved. Now,
will you make sport of me?"

"God forbid!" replied the stupefied Louise.

Louise had stolen into Valentine's room during the
previous night. It had been an easy matter for her to
send word to and win over the nurse, who was devoted
to her, and had rejoiced to see her at her sister's bedside.
They had succeeded then in making the unfortunate creature understand for the first time that Bénédict was not
dead. At first she had manifested her joy by frantically kissing those two to whom she was so dear; then
she had relapsed into a state of complete prostration,
and, at the approach of dawn, Louise had been obliged to
retire without obtaining a glance or a word from her.

The next day she learned that Valentine was better,
and she passed the whole night in attendance on Bénédict, who was worse; but on the following night, having
learned that Valentine had had a relapse, she left Bénédict at the height of his paroxysm and went to her sister.
Dividing her time and attention between her two patients, the melancholy but courageous Louise forgot
herself.

She found the doctor with Valentine. She was quiet,
and was sleeping when her sister entered the room. She
took the doctor aside, deeming it her duty to open her
heart to him, and to entrust to his sense of delicacy the
secrets of the two lovers, so that he might be in a position to try some more efficacious moral treatment.

"You have done exceedingly well," the physician
told her, "to entrust this story to me, but there was no
need of it; I should have guessed it even if you had not

informed me. I fully understand your scruples in the delicate situation in which you are placed by social prejudices and customs; but I, who am deeply interested in obtaining physical results, will undertake to soothe these two excited hearts, and to cure one by the other."

At that moment, Valentine opened her eyes and recognized her sister. After kissing her, she asked under her breath for news of Bénédict. Thereupon the doctor interposed :

"Madame," he said, "I am the one to tell you about him, for I have been attending him, and have had the good fortune to keep him alive thus far. The friend concerning whom you are anxious, and who is entitled to the friendly interest of every noble and generous heart like yours, is now out of danger physically. But his mind is very far from making so rapid a recovery, and you alone can effect its cure."

"O *mon Dieu!*" said the pale-cheeked Valentine, clasping her hands and gazing into the physician's face with the sad and searching gaze characteristic of the sick.

"Yes, madame," he continued, "a command from your lips, an encouraging, strengthening word alone can close that wound. It would have been healed before this but for the patient's ghastly persistence in tearing off the bandages as soon as the healing begins. Our young friend is a prey to profound discouragement, and I have no secrets powerful enough to cure mental pain. I need your assistance; will you give it to me ? "

As he spoke, the kind-hearted old country doctor, an obscure practitioner, who had staunched the flow of blood and tears many a time in his life, took Valentine's hand with an affectionate gentleness which was not without a touch of old-fashioned gallantry, and gravely kissed it after counting the pulse.

Valentine, who was too weak to understand what she heard, looked at him with ingenuous surprise and a sad smile.

"Well, my dear child," said the old man, "will you be my assistant, and come with me and complete his cure?"

Valentine made no other reply than an artlessly eager gesture.

"To-morrow?" he added.

"Oh! instantly!" she replied in a feeble but penetrating voice.

"Instantly, my poor child?" said the doctor, with a smile. "Why, look at these candles! It's two o'clock in the morning; but, if you will promise to be good and sleep soundly, and not have another attack of fever between now and morning, we will go for a drive in Vavray wood during the forenoon. There's a little cottage in that neighborhood to which you will carry hope and life."

Valentine pressed the old doctor's hand, allowed herself to be dosed with childlike docility, put her arms around Louise's neck, and fell asleep peacefully on her breast.

"Can you think of such a thing, Monsieur Faure?" said Louise when she saw that she was dozing. "How do you suppose she will have strength to go out, when she was at death's door only a few hours ago?"

"She will have strength enough, depend upon it," replied Monsieur Faure. "These nervous attacks weaken the body only while the paroxysms last. This one is so evidently due to mental causes that a favorable change in her ideas should lead to a similar change in the disease. Several times since she was first taken sick, I have seen Madame de Lansac pass from an alarming state of pros-

tration to an exhibition of superabundant strength to
which I would have liked to give something to feed upon.
There are symptoms of the same sort in Bénédict's case ;
these two people are necessary to each other."

"Oh ! Monsieur Faure !" said Louise, "aren't we on
the point of doing something very imprudent ? "

"I don't think so. The passions which are dangerous
to the existence of individuals as well as of societies are
the passions which are irritated and inflamed. Have not
I been young ? Have not I been so madly in love that I
lost my wits ? Am I not cured ? Haven't I grown old ?
Time and experience do everything, I tell you. Let these
poor children get well ; after they have recovered
strength to live, they will find strength to part. But
take my advice, and let us hasten the paroxysm of passion. Without our help it may burst out in more alarming fashion ; by giving it the sanction of our presence,
we shall allay it somewhat."

"Oh ! I would make any sacrifice for him or for her ! "
said Louise; "but what will people say about us, Monsieur Faure ? What a blameworthy part we are going to
play ! "

"If your conscience doesn't reproach you for it, what
have you to fear from what men say ? Haven't they
done you all the harm they could do ? Do you owe them
much gratitude for such indulgence and charity as you
have found in the world ? "

The old man's shrewd and affectionate smile made
Louise blush. She undertook to keep Bénédict's house
clear of indiscreet witnesses ; and, on the following morning, Valentine, Monsieur Faure and the nurse, having
driven for an hour or more in the Vavray wood, alighted
at a dark and lonely spot, where they told the driver to
wait for them. Valentine, leaning on her nurse's arm,

turned into one of the winding paths which go down into the ravine, while Monsieur Faure went ahead to make sure that there was no one in the way at Bénédict's house. Louise had sent everybody away on various pretexts; she was alone with her sleeping patient. The doctor had forbidden her to tell him of their visit, fearing that the suspense would be painful to him and increase his nervous irritation.

When Valentine approached the door of the cottage, she began to tremble convulsively, but Monsieur Faure went to her and said:

"Come, madame, this is the time to have courage and give some to those who lack it; remember that my patient's life is in your hands."

Valentine instantly repressed her emotion with that strength of soul which should destroy all the arguments of materialism, and entered the dismal, dimly-lighted room where the wounded man lay between his four green serge curtains.

Louise would have led her sister to Bénédict's bedside, but Monsieur Faure took her hand.

"We are in the way here, my dear inquisitive young lady," he said; "let us go to admire the vegetables in the garden. And do you, Catherine," he said to the nurse, "install yourself on this bench, in the doorway; and if anyone appears on the path, clap your hands to notify us."

He led away Louise, who suffered beyond words during that interview. We cannot assert that an involuntary but stinging jealousy did not count for much in the bitterness of her position and in the reproaches which she heaped upon herself.

XXVI

At the slight noise made by the curtain rings sliding on the rusty pole, Bénédict partly rose, half-awake, and whispered Valentine's name. He had just seen her in his dreams, but, when he saw her standing before him in the flesh, he uttered a cry of joy, which Louise heard in the garden, and which pierced her breast.

"Valentine," he said, "was it your ghost that just now called me? I am ready to follow you."

Valentine sank on a chair.

"I have come to command you to live," she replied, "or to beg you to kill me with you."

"I should prefer that," said Bénédict.

"O my friend," said Valentine, "suicide is a wicked act; but for that, we should be together in the tomb. But God forbids it. He would curse us. He would punish us by an everlasting separation. Let us accept life, whatever it may bring. Have you not a thought in your heart to give you courage?"

"What thought, Valentine? Tell me."

"Is not my friendship——"

"Your friendship? It is much more than I deserve, madame; so that I do not feel worthy to respond to it, and I will not. Ah! Valentine, you ought to sleep all the time, for the purest woman becomes a hypocrite when she wakes. Your friendship!"

"Oh! you are selfish; you care nothing for my remorse!"

"I respect it, madame; that is why I wish to die. Why

did you come here ?   You must throw aside all religion,
all scruples, and come to me and say: 'Live, and I will
love you ;' or else stay at home, forget me and let me die.
Have I asked you for anything ? have I tried to embitter
your life ? have I made a plaything of your happiness—
of your principles ? have I so much as implored your
pity ?   Look you, Valentine, this compassion for me
which you display, this humane sentiment which brings
you here, this friendship which you offer me—they are
all meaningless words, which would have deceived me a
month ago when I was a child and when a glance from
you kept me alive for a whole day.   Now, I have lived too
much, I have learned too much about the passions, to be
blind.   I will not carry on a fruitless, insane struggle
against my fate any longer.   You ought to resist me, I
know; that you will do it, I have no doubt.   You will
toss me now and then a word of encouragement and compassion, to help me suffer, and even that you will reproach
yourself for as a crime, and you will have to have absolution from a priest before you can forgive yourself for
it.   Your life will be made wretched, ruined by me ;
your heart, which has always been serene and untroubled, will be henceforth storm-tossed like mine !
God forbid !   And I, despite these sacrifices, which seem
so great to you, I shall be the most miserable of men.
No, no, Valentine, let us not deceive ourselves.   I must
die.   Being the woman that you are, you cannot love me
without remorse and a tormented conscience ; I do not
desire a happiness which would cost you so dear.   Far
from blaming you, I love you so fervently and so passionately because of your very virtue and your strength of
character.   So remain as you are ; do not descend to a
lower level to be with me.   Live and deserve heaven
hereafter.   For myself, my heart is in hell, and I propose

to go thither. Adieu, Valentine; you came to bid me
adieu, and I thank you."

This harangue, of which Valentine felt the whole force
only too keenly, drove her to despair. She could think
of nothing to reply, and she buried her face in the bed,
weeping bitterly. Valentine's greatest charm was her
frankness in revealing her feelings, seeking to deceive
neither herself nor others.

Her grief produced more effect upon Bénédict than anything she could have said. When he saw that that noble
and upright heart was breaking at the thought of losing
him, he reproached himself bitterly. He seized Valentine's hands; she rested her head on his hands and
drenched them with tears. At that his heart was inun-
dated, as it were, with joy and courage and repentance.

"Forgive me, Valentine," he cried, "I am a coward
and a villain to make you cry like this. No, no, I do not
deserve such regret and such love; but God is my witness that I will make myself worthy of them! Give me
nothing, promise me nothing; simply command and I
will obey. Ah! yes, it is my duty; rather than cost
you one tear, I must live, unhappy though I may be!
But, with the memory of what you have done for me to-
day, I shall not be unhappy, Valentine. I swear that I will
endure everything, that I will never complain, that I will
not seek to force sacrifices and battles upon you. Just
tell me that you will pity me sometimes in the secret
depths of your heart; say that you will love Bénédict in
silence and on God's bosom. But no, say nothing, have
you not told me everything? Can I not see how ungrateful and stupid I am to demand anything more than
these tears and this silence?"

Is not the language of love a strange thing? and, to an
indifferent spectator, what an inexplicable contradiction is

presented by that oath of stoicism and virtue, sealed by
kisses of fire, in the shadow of heavy curtains surrounding a bed of love and pain ? If we could bring to life
the first man to whom God gave a mate, with a bed of
moss and the solitude of the forest, perhaps we should
seek in vain in that primitive heart for the power of
loving. Of how much of grandeur and poesy should we
find him ignorant! And what should we say if we
should discover that he was inferior to the degenerate
man of our civilization ? that that muscular body contained only a passionless, listless heart ?

But no, man has not changed, but his strength is exerted against different obstacles, that is all. Formerly
he subdued bears and tigers ; to-day he contends against
society, with all its errors and its ignorance. Therein lies
his strength, his courage, and, it may be, his glory.
Physical power is succeeded by moral power. As the
muscular system became weaker in successive generations, the human mind increased in vigor and strength.

Valentine's recovery was rapid ; Bénédict's was slower,
but miraculous none the less to those who did not know
the secret of it. Madame de Raimbault, having won her
suit—a triumph of which she claimed all the honor—returned to the château and passed a few days with Valentine. She was no sooner assured of her recovery than
she started for Paris. It seemed to her that she was
twenty years younger when she felt that she was rid of
the duties of maternity. Valentine, thenceforth entirely
free, and sovereign mistress of her château of Raimbault,
was left alone with her grandmother, who was not, as we
know, a troublesome guardian.

Then it was that Valentine determined to be really
united to her sister. It required only Monsieur de Lansac's consent, for the marchioness would certainly be

overjoyed to see her granddaughter. But Monsieur de Lansac had never committed himself definitely enough on the subject to inspire Louise with confidence, and Valentine, too, was beginning to have serious doubts of her husband's sincerity.

Nevertheless, she determined at any risk to offer her a home in her house, and to display her affection openly, as a sort of reparation for all that she had suffered from her family; but Louise positively refused.

"No, dear Valentine," she said, "I will never allow you to run the risk of displeasing your husband for my sake. My pride would be wounded by the thought that I was in a house from which I might be driven out. It is much better that we should live as we are living. We are at liberty now to see each other, and what more do we want? In any event, I could not stay long at Raimbault. My son's education is far from being finished, and I must stay in Paris to superintend it a few years more. There we can meet even more freely; but let our intimacy remain a pleasant mystery between us. The world would certainly blame you for giving me your hand—your mother would almost curse you. Those two are the unjust masters of whom we must stand in awe, and whose laws we could not openly defy with impunity. Let us stay as we are; Bénédict still needs my care. In a month at most I shall have to go away; meanwhile, I will try to see you every day."

They did, in fact, have frequent interviews. There was a pretty little pavilion in the park, which Monsieur de Lansac had occupied during his stay at Raimbault; Valentine had it fitted up as a sort of study. She carried her books thither and her easel; she passed a part of every day there, and in the evening Louise would join her there and talk with her two or three hours. Despite these precautions, Louise's identity was now well understood in the neighborhood, and the report had finally reached the ears of the old marchioness. At first she had felt a thrill of joy as keen as it was possible for her to feel, and had made up her mind to send for her granddaughter and embrace her, for Louise had been for a long time dearer to the marchioness than anything else in the world; but her companion, who was a staid and prudent person and held her mistress in complete subjection, had reminded her that Madame de Raimbault would surely learn sooner or later what she had done, and might wreak vengeance on her for it.

"But what have I to fear from her now?" the marchioness had replied. "Isn't my pension to be paid henceforth by Valentine? Am I not in Valentine's house? and if Valentine sees her sister in secret, as we are told, wouldn't she be delighted to have me share her pleasure?"

"Madame de Lansac," replied the old lady's maid, "is dependent on her husband, and you know very well that you and Monsieur de Lansac do not always get on together. Look out, madame la marquise, that you don't imperil the comfort of your old age by a rash act. Your granddaughter can't be very eager to see you, as she hasn't sent you word of her arrival in the province; Madame de Lansac herself has not thought it best to entrust her secret to you. My advice, therefore, is that you do just as you have done heretofore; that is to say, pretend not to see the danger to which others are exposing themselves, and try to ensure your own tranquillity at any price."

This advice was too powerfully seconded by the marchioness's own nature to be disregarded; so she closed her eyes to everything that was going on about her, and matters remained where they were.

Athénaïs had been very cruel to Pierre Blutty at first, and yet it had afforded her a certain pleasure to observe the obstinacy with which he fought against her disdain. A man like Monsieur de Lansac would have retired offended at the first refusal, but Pierre Blutty had a diplomacy of his own which was no less effective than some others. He saw that his ardent endeavor to earn his wife's forgiveness, the humility with which he implored her, and the somewhat ridiculous account of his martyrdom, with which he regaled some thirty auditors, flattered the young country maiden's vanity. When his friends left him on his wedding-night, although he had not been restored to favor ostensibly, a significant smile which he bestowed upon them gave them to understand that he was not in such a despairing frame of mind as he chose to make it appear. The fact was that he had conceived the scheme of allowing Athénaïs to barricade the door of her bedroom, and then climbing in the window. It would be difficult to avoid being touched by the determination of a man who runs the risk of breaking his neck to obtain you; and, on the following day, when the news of Bénédict's death was brought to the farm in the middle of breakfast, Athénaïs's hand was in her husband's, and every resolute glance from the farmer brought a flush to the lovely cheek of the farmer's wife.

But the story of the catastrophe aroused the expiring tempest anew. Athénaïs gave vent to piercing shrieks, and had to be taken from the room. The next day, as soon as she learned that Bénédict was not dead, she insisted on going to see him. Blutty realized that that was not the moment to thwart her, especially as her father and mother set her the example and hastened to the dying man's cottage. He thought that he would do well to go there himself, and thus show his new family that

he was disposed to defer to their wishes. This mark of
submission could not imperil his pride so far as Bénédict
was concerned, as he was not in a condition to recognize
him.

So he escorted Athénaïs, and, although his interest was
not very sincere, he behaved decently enough to deserve
honorable mention from her. That evening, despite the
remonstrances of her daughter, who wished to pass the
night in attendance on the sick man, Madame Lhéry ordered her to start for home with her husband. Tête-à-
tête in the *carriole,* the husband and wife sulked at first,
and then Pierre Blutty changed his tactics. Instead of
seeming offended by the tears which his wife shed over
her cousin, he began to deplore Bénédict's misfortune
with her and to pronounce the dying man's funeral ora-
tion. Athénaïs, did not expect such generosity; she offered her husband her hand and said, moving closer to him:

"You have a good heart, Pierre; I will try to love
you as you deserve."

When Blutty found that Bénédict did not die, he was
a little more disturbed by his wife's visits to the cottage
in the ravine. However, he gave no sign; but, when
Bénédict was sufficiently recovered to get up and walk,
he was conscious that his hatred of him came to life again,
and he decided that it was time to exert his authority.
He was *in his right,* as the peasants say so slyly when
they can add the support of the laws to that of their con-
sciences. Bénédict no longer needed his cousin's attentions, and the interest in him which she displayed could
not fail to compromise her. When he placed these arguments before his wife, there was in his voice and his
expression a flavor of determination with which she was
not familiar, and which served admirably to convince her
that the time had come to obey.

She was depressed for a few days, then she made the best of it ; for, although Pierre Blutty was beginning to play the husband in certain directions, in all others he had remained the passionate lover ; and his conduct was an excellent example of the difference in the prejudices of different classes of society. A man of quality and a bourgeois would both have considered themselves compromised by their wife's love for another man. The fact being established before marriage, they would not have married her, or public opinion would have branded them ; if they had been betrayed after marriage, they would have been pursued by ridicule. On the other hand, the bold and shrewd manner in which Blutty managed the whole affair was most creditable to him in the eyes of his equals.

"Look at Pierre Blutty," they would say to one another when they wished to cite an example of determination. "He married a very coquettish, very headstrong little woman, who hardly took the trouble to conceal her love for another man, and who, on her wedding-day, kicked up a row in order to have an excuse for leaving him. Well, he wasn't frightened off ; he has succeeded not only in making her obey him, but in making her love him. There's a fellow who knows what he's about. There's no danger of anyone making sport of him."

And, taking pattern by Pierre Blutty, every young fellow in the neighborhood vowed inwardly that he would not take his wife's initial cruelty too seriously.

XXVII

Valentine had paid more than one visit to the cottage in the ravine. At first, her presence had allayed Bénédict's irritation; but as soon as he had recovered his strength, as she then ceased to visit him, his love became bitter and intensely painful to him; his position seemed to him intolerable. Louise was forced to consent to take him to the pavilion in the park now and then, in the evening. Poor, weak-minded Louise, being absolutely under his domination, felt profound remorse, and could invent no excuses to offer Valentine for her imprudence. Valentine, for her part, made no attempt to avoid perils in which she was not sorry to have her sister for a confederate. She allowed herself to be swept along by her destiny, refusing to look forward, and found in Louise's lack of foresight excuses for her own weakness.

Valentine was not naturally passionate, but fate seemed to take pleasure in forcing her into exceptional situations and surrounding her with perils which were beyond her strength. Love has caused many suicides, but it is doubtful whether many women ever saw at their feet the man who had tried to blow out his brains for love of them. If we could bring the dead to life, doubtless feminine generosity would pardon such vehement devotion in many instances; and, while nothing touches a woman's heart more keenly than the suicide of a lover, nothing is more flattering to the secret vanity which finds its place in all human passions. And that was Valentine's situation. Bénédict's forehead, still furrowed by a broad scar, was always before her eyes, like the seal of a terrible oath, the sincerity of which she could not question. Valentine could not use against Bénédict those refusals to believe, that distrustful raillery to which all women resort to avoid the necessity of pitying and comforting us. He had proved his sincerity; his was not one of those indefinite threats by which women are so often imposed upon. Although the broad, deep wound was closed, Bénédict would bear all his life its indelible scar. A score of times during his illness he had tried to reopen it; he had torn away the bandages and parted the edges. That firm determination to die no one but Valentine had been able to shake. It was at her command, in answer to her prayers, that he had abandoned it. But had Valentine herself clearly understood to what extent she had pledged herself to him by demanding that sacrifice?

Bénédict could not shut his eyes to the fact that, when he was apart from her, he formed a thousand audacious schemes; he persisted in grasping at new hopes. He said to himself that Valentine no longer had the right to refuse him anything; but as soon as he found himself once more under the influence of her pure glance, of her dignified and gentle manners, he stopped short, completely subjugated, and deemed himself fortunate to obtain the faintest indications of friendship.

Meanwhile, their situation became constantly more hazardous. To throw their real feelings off the scent, they treated each other like intimate friends; this was an additional imprudence, for even the chaste Valentine could not deceive herself. In order to make their interviews less stormy, Louise, who tortured her brain to devise some means, conceived the idea of music. She was something of an accompanist, and Bénédict sang beautifully. This put the finishing touch to the perils by which they were encompassed. To placid and untroubled minds music may seem a pleasing art, a frivolous and innocent amusement; to impassioned souls it is the source of all poetic feeling, the expression of every strong passion. It was thus that Bénédict understood it. He knew that the human voice, modulated by the heart, is the swiftest, the most forcible instrument of the feelings; that it appeals to the intelligence of others more powerfully than when it is cooled by the developments of ordinary speech. Thought, in the guise of melody, is noble, poetic and beautiful.

Valentine, recently subjected to the trial of a very violent attack of hysteria, was still subject at certain hours to a sort of feverish excitement. Those hours Bénédict passed in her company, and he frequently sang to her. Valentine would shiver from head to foot; all her blood collected in her heart and her brain; she alternated between devouring heat and deadly cold. She pressed her hands against her heart to keep it from bursting through its walls, for it throbbed so fiercely at certain tones from Bénédict's chest and his heart. When he sang, he was handsome, in spite of, or rather because of, the mutilation of his forehead. He loved Valentine passionately, and had proved it beyond question. Was not that enough to embellish him a little in her eyes. And, then, his eyes were marvellously brilliant. When he sat at the piano, in the semi-darkness, she could see them gleaming like two stars. When, in the uncertain glimmer of twilight, she looked upon that broad, white forehead, heightened in effect by the abundant masses of black hair, that flashing eye and that long, pale face, whose features, seen indistinctly in the shadow, appeared in a thousand strange aspects, Valentine was frightened: it seemed to her that she saw in him the bleeding spectre of the man who had loved her; and if he sang in a hollow, melancholy voice some fragment of Zingarelli's *Romeo,* she felt so moved by superstitious fear that she shuddered and drew closer to her sister.

These scenes of silent and restrained passion took place in the pavilion in the park, to which she had sent her piano, and where Louise and Bénédict, after a time, passed every evening with her. During the summer evenings Valentine adopted the custom of having no light, so that Bénédict might not detect the violent emotion which often took possession of her. Bénédict would sing something from memory; then they would walk a little in the park or sit by the window, talking and inhaling the pleasant odor of the wet foliage after a shower, or they would go to look at the moon from the top of the hill. That life would have been delightful if it could have lasted, but Valentine knew full well, from the stings of remorse, that it had already lasted too long.

Louise did not leave them for an instant. This constant watch on Valentine seemed to her a duty, but that duty often became a heavy burden to her; for she realized that it was largely influenced by her own jealousy, and she suffered all the torture of a noble heart at strife with honorable sentiments.

One evening, when Bénédict seemed to her more animated than usual, his ardent glances and the tone of his voice when he spoke of Valentine caused her such pain that she withdrew, discouraged by her suffering and by the rôle she was playing. She went out to meditate alone in the park. Bénédict's heart beat frantically when he saw that he was alone with Valentine. She tried to speak on indifferent subjects, but her voice trembled. Afraid of herself, she was silent for a few moments, then asked him to sing; but his voice produced a still more violent effect on her nerves, and she left the room, leaving him alone at the piano. Bénédict was piqued, and continued to sing. Meanwhile, Valentine had seated herself under the trees on the terrace, a few steps from the open window. Bénédict's voice had a softer, more caressing sound, as it was borne to her ears by the fragrant evening breeze, amid the rustling leaves. All about her was fragrance and melody. She hid her face in her hands, and allowed her tears to flow, yielding to one of the most irresistible fascinations that ever woman faced. Bénédict ceased to sing, and she hardly noticed it, so completely under the spell was she. He walked to the window and saw her.

The salon was on the ground floor; he leaped through the window and sat down at her feet. As she did not speak, he feared that she was ill, and ventured gently to remove her hands. Then he saw her tears, and uttered a cry of surprise and triumph. Valentine, overwhelmed with shame, tried to hide her face against her lover's breast. How happened it that their lips met? Valentine tried to protect herself; Bénédict had not the strength of mind to obey. Before Louise had joined them, they had exchanged twenty oaths of love, twenty fervent kisses. Louise, where were you then?

XXVIII

From that moment the danger became imminent. Bénédict was so happy that he was proud of his happiness, and
began to despise danger. He scoffed at destiny, and said
to himself that with Valentine's love he could overcome
all obstacles. The pride of triumph made him overbold;
he would not listen to Louise's scruples. Moreover, he
was free from the species of dependence upon her to
which her nursing and her devotion had subjected him.
Since he had completely recovered, Louise had been
living at the farm, and at night they went separately to
join Valentine at the pavilion. It happened several times
that Louise arrived considerably later than he; sometimes, too, it happened that Louise could not go at all,
and Bénédict passed long evenings alone with Valentine.
The next day, when Louise questioned her sister, it was
always easy to divine from her confusion the nature of
the interview she had had with her lover; for it was impossible that Valentine's secret could be a secret to Louise
any longer; she was too much interested in detecting it
not to have succeeded long before. Nothing more was
lacking to her unhappiness, and it was intensified by the
feeling that she was incapable of applying any remedy.
Louise felt that her weakness would cause Valentine's
ruin. If she had had no other motive than her interest
in her sister, she would not have hesitated to open her
eyes to the perils of her situation; but, devoured by
jealousy as she was, and retaining none the less all her
pride, she preferred to imperil Valentine's happiness

rather than yield to a feeling which brought the blush of shame to her cheeks. There was some selfishness in her unselfishness.

She determined to return to Paris in order to put an end to the torture she was undergoing, without having fixed upon any plan to save her sister. She simply resolved to inform her of her approaching departure; and one evening, when Bénédict took his leave, instead of going down with him, she told Valentine that she wanted to speak with her a moment. Her words offended Bénédict; he was constantly beset by the idea that Louise, stung by remorse, desired to injure him in Valentine's eyes. That idea served to embitter him still more against that generous and self-sacrificing woman, and made him bear the burden of gratitude to her grudgingly and angrily.

"Sister," said Louise, "the time has come when I must leave you. I cannot stay away from my boy any longer. You do not need me any more, and I am going to-morrow."

"To-morrow!" cried Valentine, in dismay. "You are going to leave me, to leave me all alone, Louise? Why, what will become of me?"

"Aren't you well again? aren't you happy and free, Valentine? What good can your poor Louise do you now?"

"O sister, dear sister!" said Valentine, throwing her arms about her. "You shall not leave me! You have no idea of my unhappiness and the perils by which I am surrounded. If you leave me, I am lost."

Louise sadly held her peace. The idea of listening to Valentine's confession was mortally repugnant to her; and yet she dared not refuse. Valentine, her face flushed with shame, could not make up her mind to speak. Her sister's cold and cruel silence caused her blood to stand

still with fear. At last she overcame her repugnance,
and said in a trembling tone:

"Well, Louise, won't you stay with me, when I tell you
that without you I am lost?"

That word, twice repeated, bore in Louise's ears a
meaning which irritated her in spite of herself.

"Lost!" she retorted bitterly; "you say you are *lost!*
Valentine?"

"O sister!" said Valentine, hurt by the eagerness
with which Louise seized upon the idea; "God has protected me thus far. He is my witness that I have not
voluntarily given way to any sentiment, taken any step
inconsistent with my duty."

This noble pride in herself, which Valentine was still
entitled to feel, put the finishing touch to the bitterness of
her who had once given way too blindly to her passions.
Always easily wounded, because her past life was marred
by an ineffaceable stain, she felt something very like
hatred for Valentine's superior virtue. For an instant,
affection, compassion, generosity, all the nobler sentiments ceased to exist in her heart; she could think of
no better way to avenge herself than to humiliate Valentine.

"What are you talking about then?" she said harshly. "What danger are you exposed to? I don't understand what you mean."

There was a sharp tone in her voice which hurt Valentine; she had never seen her in this mood. She was
silent a moment or two, and gazed at her in surprise.
In the dim light of a candle which was burning on the
piano at the end of the room, she fancied that she saw on
her sister's features an expression which she had never
before seen on them. Her eyebrows were contracted,
her lips bloodless and compressed; her stern, unfeeling

eye was fastened pitilessly on Valentine's face. Valentine, bewildered, involuntarily moved her chair away,
and, trembling from head to foot, tried to find some explanation of the cold contempt with which her sister was
treating her for the first time in her life. But she would
have imagined every conceivable reason rather than the
true one. Meek and pious as she was, she was inspired
at that moment by all the heroism which the true spirit
of religion imparts to women, and, throwing herself at
her sister's feet, she hid her face, streaming with tears,
upon her knee.

"You are right in humiliating me thus," she said; "I
have deserved it, and fifteen years of virtue entitle you
to rebuke my vain and imprudent youth. Scold me,
despise me, but have pity on my repentance and my
fears. Protect me, Louise, save me; you can do it, for
you know all!"

"Hush!" cried Louise, overwhelmed by her sister's
behavior, and yielding instantly to the noble sentiments
which formed the real foundation of her character; "rise,
Valentine, my sister, my child; do not kneel at my feet
like this. I am the one who should be at your feet; I
am the contemptible creature, who should ask you, you
angel from heaven, to make my peace with God! Alas!
Valentine, I know your suffering only too well; but why
confide it to me, miserable wretch that I am, who can
afford you no protection, and who have no right to
advise you?"

"You can advise me and protect me, Louise," replied
Valentine, embracing her effusively. "Haven't you the
experience which gives strength and good sense? That
man must go away from here, or I must go myself. We
must not see each other again, for every day it grows
worse, and the return to God becomes harder and harder.

Ah! just now I was boasting! I feel that my heart is very guilty."

The bitter tears that Valentine shed broke Louise's heart.

"Alas!" she said, pale and dismayed, "then it is really as bad as I feared! You, too, are unhappy forever!"

"Forever?" echoed Valentine, in alarm. "With the determination to be cured, and with God's help——"

"One is never cured!" rejoined Louise, in a gloomy tone, clasping her hands over her sad and desolate heart.

Then she rose and paced the floor excitedly, halting now and then in front of Valentine to speak to her in a broken voice.

"Why ask me for advice—me of all people? Who am I, to comfort and cure? What! you come to me for the heroism which conquers the passions, and the virtues which keep society intact; to me, unhappy wretch, whom passion has withered and whom society has cursed and cast out? Where, pray, should I go for what is not in me, in order to give it to you? Apply to the women whom the world esteems; apply to your mother! She is irreproachable. No one was able to say positively whether my lover was or was not hers at the same time. She was so prudent! And when my father, her husband, killed that man who had betrayed his friendship, she clapped her hands; and the world saw how she triumphed, she had so much strength of character and pride! Those are the women who can overcome a passion or be cured of it!"

Valentine, horrified by what she had heard, tried to interrupt her; but, impelled by a sort of frenzy, she continued:

"Women like me succumb and are ruined forever!

Women like you, Valentine, must pray and fight; they must seek strength in themselves, not ask it of others. Advice! advice! What advice could I give you which you could not perfectly well give yourself? Strength to follow it is what you must find. Do you think that I am stronger than you? No, Valentine, I am not. You know very well what my life has been, with what unconquerable passions I was born; you know to what they led me!"

"Hush, Louise," cried Valentine, throwing her arms about her with a pained expression; "cease to slander yourself so. What woman was ever nobler and stronger than you in her downfall? Are you to be blamed forever for a sin committed at the age of ignorance and weakness? Alas! you were only a child! and since then you have been sublime; you have compelled the esteem of everyone who has a noble heart. You cannot deny that you know what virtue is?"

"In heaven's name, do not learn it at the same cost," rejoined Louise; "abandoned to my own devices from childhood, deprived of the help of religion and of a mother's love and protection, left in charge of our grandmother, who is so frivolous and so utterly devoid of modesty, I was certain to go from bad to worse. Yes, that would have happened but for the terrible heart-rending lessons that I learned from fate. My lover sacrificed by my father; my father himself, overwhelmed by grief and shame because of my sin, seeking and finding death on the battlefield within a few days; and I, banished, ignominiously driven out of my father's house, and reduced to the necessity of dragging my wretchedness from place to place, with my child starving to death in my arms! Ah! Valentine, that is a ghastly fate!"

It was the first time that Louise had ever spoken thus

openly of her misfortunes. Excited by the impending painful crisis, she yielded to the melancholy satisfaction of pitying herself, and she forgot Valentine's sorrows and the help which it was her duty to give her. But her outcries of remorse and despair produced more effect than the most eloquent remonstrances. By placing before Valentine's eyes the picture of the misery to which the passions may lead, she terrified her beyond words. Valentine felt that she was on the brink of the abyss into which her sister had fallen.

"You are right," she cried, "it is a ghastly fate, and to bear it with courage and virtue one must be you ; my soul, being weaker, would be irrevocably lost. But do you help me to be brave, Louise ; help me to send Bénédict away."

As she uttered that name a slight noise behind her caused her to turn her head. They both gave a piercing shriek when they saw Bénédict standing behind them, like a ghost.

"You mentioned my name, madame," he said, with that profound calmness which often led people astray as to his real feelings.

Valentine tried to smile. Louise did not share her error.

"Where were you, pray, that you heard so distinctly ? " she asked.

"I was very near, mademoiselle," he replied, with a mocking glance.

"That is at least very strange," said Valentine, severely. "My sister told you, I believe, that she wished to speak to me in private, and yet you remained near enough to listen, it appears ? "

Bénédict had never seen Valentine angry with him ; he was dazed for a moment, and was on the point of abandoning his bold project. But, as it was a critical and decisive moment for him, he put a bold face upon it, and, maintaining in his expression and his manner that serious firmness which gave him so much power over the minds of others, he said:

"It is quite useless to conceal the truth; I have been sitting behind this curtain, and have not lost a word of your conversation. I might have listened to still more, and have left the room, unseen, by the same window by which I came in. But I was so interested in the subject of your discussion——"

He paused, seeing that Valentine had become paler than her neckerchief, and had sunk into a chair with an air of consternation. He longed to throw himself at her feet, to weep on her hands; but he realized too fully the necessity of overcoming the excitement of the two women by his own self-possession and firmness.

"I was so interested in your discussion," he continued, "that I thought that it was my right to return and take part in it. Whether I did wrong, the future will decide. Meanwhile, let us try to be stronger than our destiny. Louise, you have no reason to blush on account of what you have said in my presence. You cannot forget that you have often accused yourself in similar terms to me, and I am tempted to believe that there is some coquetry in your virtuous humility, you know so well what the effect of it must be on those who, like myself, revere you for the trials you have gone through."

As he spoke, he took Louise's hand as she leaned over her sister with her arms about her; then he led her gently and affectionately toward a chair at some little distance, and, when he had seated her in it, he tenderly put her hand to his lips, then took possession of the chair from which he had ousted her, turned his back, and paid no further attention to her.

"Valentine!" he said in a deep, grave tone.

It was the first time that he had ventured to call her by her name in the presence of a third person. Valentine started, removed her hands with which she had concealed her face, and bestowed a cold and offended glance upon him. But he repeated her name with an authoritative gentleness, and love shone so brightly in his eyes that Valentine hid her face again in order not to see him.

"Valentine," he said, "do not try upon me these puerile pretences which are said to be the main reliance of your sex; we cannot deceive each other any more. Look at this scar! I shall carry it to the grave! It is the seal and the symbol of my love for you. You cannot believe that I will consent to ruin you; that is too silly an error for you to fall into. Do not think of such a thing, Valentine."

He took her hands in his. Cowed by his air of resolution, she allowed him to retain them, and gazed at him with a frightened expression.

"Do not hide your face from me," he said, "and do not be afraid to look at the spectre whom you drew back from the tomb! You would have it so, madame! It is your own fault that I stand before you to-day an object of terror and aversion. But listen, my Valentine, my all-powerful mistress, I love you too well to vex you. Say a word and I return to the shroud from which you drew me forth."

With that he took a pistol from his pocket and showed it her.

"You see," he continued, "it is the same one, the very same. Its gallant service did not injure it; it is a faithful friend and always at your orders. Speak, send me away, it is always ready.—Oh ! don't be afraid," he cried mockingly, as the two women, pale with terror, recoiled shrieking ; " don't be afraid that I will commit the impropriety of killing myself before your eyes ; I know too well how much consideration must be shown to a woman's nerves."

"This is a horrible scene," cried Louise, in the utmost distress ; "you want to kill Valentine."

"You may scold me in a moment, mademoiselle," he replied shortly, with a haughty air ; "I am speaking to Valentine now, and I have not finished."

He uncocked his pistol and put it in his pocket.

"You see, madame," he continued, addressing Valentine, "it is entirely on your account that I am still alive, not for your pleasure, but for my own. My pleasures are and always will be very modest. I ask nothing which you could not grant without remorse to one for whom you felt only the purest friendship. Consult your memory and your conscience ; have you found him very audacious and very dangerous, this Bénédict, who has but one passion in the world. That passion is you. You cannot hope that he will ever have another, for he is already old in heart and in experience. The man who has loved you will never love another woman, for, after all, this Bénédict, whom you propose to spurn, is no brute ! What ! you love me enough to be afraid of me, and you despise me enough to hope to resign me to the idea of losing you ! Oh ! what madness ! No, no ! I will not lose you so long as I have a breath of life, I swear by heaven and by hell ! I will see you ; I will be your friend, your brother, or may God damn me forever if——"

"Hush, for pity's sake," said Valentine, in a choking

voice, pale as death and clasping her hands convulsively.
"I will do whatever you wish; I will destroy my soul
forever, if I must, to save your life."

"No, you will not destroy your soul," he replied, "you
will save us both. Do you think, pray, that I, too, cannot keep an oath and deserve heaven ? Alas! before I
saw you I hardly believed in God; but I have adopted
all your principles, all your beliefs. I am ready to swear
by whatever one of your angels you prefer. Let me live,
Valentine; what does it matter to you ? I do not fear
death; being imposed upon me by you, it would be
sweeter this time than before. But, Valentine, in pity's
name, don't condemn me to nothingness !—You frown at
that word. Why, you know that I believe in heaven with
you; but heaven without you is nothingness. It cannot
be where you are not; I am so certain of it that, if you
condemn me to death, I shall, perhaps, kill you too, in
order not to lose you. I have had that idea before. It
came very near overshadowing all other ideas. But take
my advice; let us live a few more days on earth. Are
we not happy ? Wherein are we guilty, pray? You
will not leave me, will you ? You will not order me to
die; that is impossible, for you love me, and you know
that your honor, your repose and your principles are
sacred to me.—Do you believe me capable of wronging
her, Louise ? " he said, turning abruptly to the older
sister. "You drew just now a ghastly picture of the
evils into which passions lead us. I tell you that I have
faith in myself, and that, if I had been the man who
loved you long ago, I would not have poisoned and
blasted your life. No, Louise, no, Valentine, all men are
not dastards."

Bénédict talked much more, sometimes with vehemence, sometimes with bitter irony, sometimes gently

and affectionately. After terrifying the two women, and subjugating them by fear, he succeeded in conquering them by emotion. He obtained such mastery over their wills that, when he left them, he had wrested from them promises which, an hour earlier, they would have deemed themselves quite incapable of making.

XXIX

This was the result of their agreement:

Louise went to Paris, and returned a fortnight later with her son. She compelled Madame Lhéry to agree upon an amount which she was to pay each month for board. Bénédict and Valentine undertook Valentin's education between them, and continued to see each other almost every day after sunset.

Valentin was fifteen years old, tall, slender and fair. He resembled Valentine; like her, he had an equable and compliant disposition. His great blue eyes had that expression of caressing softness which was so charming in her; his smile had the same frank kindliness. He had no sooner seen her than he became so fond of her that his mother was jealous.

They arranged the employment of his time thus: in the morning he passed two hours with his aunt, who instructed him in social accomplishments; the rest of the day he passed at the cottage in the ravine. Bénédict was sufficiently well educated to be an acceptable substitute for his teachers. He had, so to speak, forced Louise to entrust the child's education to him; he had

felt that he had the courage and firmness of will to undertake it and to devote several years of his life to him.
It was a way of paying his debt to her, and his conscience
embraced the opportunity with ardor. But when he had
seen Valentin, his resemblance to Valentine in features
and disposition—even the similarity of their names—
caused him to feel an affection for the boy of which he
did not believe himself capable. He adopted him in his
heart, and, to spare him the long walk he was obliged
to take every day, he induced his mother to let him live
at the cottage. As a result, he had to consent that Louise
and Valentine should introduce some improvements there,
on the pretext of making it more convenient for the new
occupant. Through their efforts the little house in the
ravine became in a few days a most delightful retreat
for a frugal and poetic man like Bénédict. The damp,
unhealthy ground was covered by a floor raised several
feet above the earth. The walls were covered with a
dark and very cheap material, which was neatly drawn
together like a tent overhead to conceal the timbers of
the roof. Some simple but neat furniture, choice books,
a few engravings, and some dainty pictures painted by
Valentine, were brought from the château, and a delightful study was created, as if by enchantment, beneath
Bénédict's thatched roof. Valentine presented her
nephew with a pretty little pony, on which he went
every morning to breakfast and study with her. The
gardener came from the château to put the little garden
at the cottage in order. He masked the prosaic vegetables behind hedges of vines ; he sowed flowers over
the patch of greensward in front of the door ; he trained
bindweed and hops over the dark thatch of the roof ;
he crowned the doorway with a canopy of honeysuckle
and clematis ; he thinned out the holly and boxwood in

the ravine, and opened several vistas through which one could obtain views of a wild and picturesque beauty. Like a man of intelligence, not brutalized by the science of horticulture, he left untouched the long ferns which clung to the rocks; he cleansed the brook without removing its mossy stones and the purple heather along its banks; in fact, he beautified the place very considerably. Bénédict's liberality and Valentine's kindness prevented any impertinent gossip. Who could help loving Valentine? At the outset, the appearance of Valentin, that living witness of his mother's disgrace, caused a little idle talk in the village and among the servants of the château. However well inclined one may be to bear good-will to all men, one does not readily let slip so favorable an opportunity of blaming and criticizing. Thereafter they watched everything. Bénédict's frequent visits to the château were observed, and the mysterious and retired life led by Madame de Lansac. Some old women, who, by the way, cordially detested Madame de Raimbault, remarked to their neighbors, with a sigh and a compassionate leer, that there had been a great change in the habits of the people at the château since the countess went away, and that she would hardly be pleased with what was going on there, if she could have any suspicion of it. But the gossip was brought abruptly to a close by the appearance of an epidemic in the province. Valentine, Louise and Bénédict spared no efforts, exposed themselves fearlessly to the danger of contagion, contributed generously, anticipated all the wants of the poor, and enlightened the ignorance of the rich. Bénédict had studied medicine a little. He saved many sufferers with a bloodletting and a few simple prescriptions. The gentle nursing of Louise and Valentine soothed the last sufferings of others, or allayed the grief

of the survivors. When the epidemic had passed, no
one remembered the scruples which had arisen concerning the sudden appearance of that handsome boy in the
neighborhood. Whatever Valentine, Louise or Bénédict
did was declared to be beyond criticism ; and if anybody
from a neighboring town had ventured to refer slight-
ingly to them, there was not a peasant within three
leagues who would not have made him pay dear for it.
An idle and inquisitive stranger would have received a
warm welcome if he had asked prying questions concerning anyone of the three in the village wine-shops.

Their security was the greater because Valentine had
not kept in her service any of those servants born in livery, insolent, ungrateful, low-minded fellows who be-
smirch everything they look at, and whom the Comtesse
de Raimbault delighted to have about her, that she might
seem to have slaves to tyrannize over. After her marriage Valentine had made many changes in her household. It now consisted only of those excellent servants, semi-villagers, who make a contract to enter one's
service, and do their work gravely, moderately—*obli-
gingly,* if we may so describe it; who reply: *Certainly,*
or : *I'll see to it,* to your orders, vex you often and drive
you to despair, break your porcelain, never steal a sou,
but by their clumsiness and awkwardness cause terrible
damage in a fine house ; intolerable but most worthy folk,
who recall all the virtues of a patriarchal age ; who, in
their sturdy good sense and their blissful ignorance, have
no idea of the swift and debasing servility of domestic
service as we understand it ; who obey without haste,
but with respect ; invaluable servants, who still believe
in their duty because their duty is the result of a plain
and equitable agreement ; stout fellows who would return
a dandy's blows with his riding-whip; who do nothing

except from affection ; who cannot be prevented either from loving or cursing ; whom you long a hundred times a day to send to the devil, but whom you never make up your mind to discharge.

The old marchioness might have been an obstacle in the way of our three friends' plans, and Valentine was on the point of taking her into her confidence and winning her over to her side. But just at that time she very nearly died of an attack of apoplexy. Her mind and her memory were so seriously affected that they could not hope to make her understand what was taking place. She was no longer strong and active ; she was almost wholly confined to her room, and passed her time with her companion in trivial religious exercises. Religion, of which she had made a plaything all her life, became a necessary amusement to her, and her enfeebled memory had no other exercise than reciting paternosters. Thus there was only one person who had it in her power to injure Valentine ; that was the marchioness's companion. Mademoiselle de Beaujon—that was her name—desired but one thing on earth,—to remain with her mistress and to obtain such influence over her that the old lady would leave her as large a legacy as it was in her power to do. Valentine, although she watched her closely enough to make sure that she never abused her empire over the marchioness's mind, realized that she earned by her zeal and her care all the reward she could obtain, and treated her with a degree of confidence for which she was grateful. Madame de Raimbault, having received a hint from public rumor—for it is impossible to keep anything absolutely secret, try as hard as we may—wrote to her to inquire what she should believe with respect to the different reports that had come to her ears. She had great confidence in this Beaujon, who had never been fond of

Valentine, but, on the other hand, had always been fond of slander. But La Beaujon, in an epistle remarkable for its peculiar style and orthography, hastened to set her mind at rest, and to assure her that she had never heard a word of those strange rumors, which had been invented probably in some of the small towns in the neighborhood. La Beaujon intended to go out of service as soon as the old marchioness was dead; she cared very little for the countess's wrath so long as she succeeded in leaving the château with well-filled pockets.

Monsieur de Lansac wrote very rarely, and manifested no impatience to see his wife—no disposition to give any attention to his affairs of the heart. Thus a number of favorable circumstances combined to shelter the happiness which Louise, Valentine and Bénédict pilfered, so to speak, from the law of conventionalities and prejudices. Valentine caused a fence to be built around that part of the park where the pavilion stood. That little reservation was very thickly planted and very dark. On its borders they planted clumps of climbing plants, ramparts of wild vine and birthwort, and hedges of young cypresses of the sort that are trimmed like a curtain and form a barrier impenetrable to the eye. Amid all this verdure, and behind those trustworthy barriers of shade, the pavilion stood in a delightful situation, near a spring, from which a bubbling stream escaped among the rocks, maintaining an incessant cool murmur about that mysterious and dreamy retreat. No one was admitted save Valentine, Louise and Bénédict, and Athénaïs, when she could elude the watchful eye of her husband, who was not much pleased to see her friendly relations with her cousin. Valentin, who had a key to the pavilion, went thither every morning to wait for Valentine. He watered the flowers, put fresh ones in the salon, tried a tune

or two on the piano, or attended to the aviary. Sometimes he sat on a bench, absorbed in the vague and restless reveries common at his age ; but the instant that he
spied his aunt's slender figure through the trees he would
resume his work.   Valentine loved to observe the similarity of their natures and inclinations.   She was delighted to detect in that boy, despite the difference of
sex, the quiet tastes, the fondness for a domestic, retired
life of which she herself was conscious.   And then she
loved him because of Bénédict, who gave him lessons,
and of whom he brought to her a sort of reflection every
day.

Valentin, although he did not realize the strength of
the bonds which bound him to Valentine and Bénédict,
already loved them with an earnestness and delicacy of
feeling beyond his years.   That child, born in tears, his
mother's greatest scourge and greatest comfort, had given
proof early in life of that delicate sensibility which is
developed much later in ordinary lives.   As soon as he
was old enough to understand what she said, Louise had
told him, without evasion, of her position in society, her
unhappy destiny, the stain upon his birth, the sacrifices
she had made for him, and all that she had had to face
in order to perform those duties which are so easy and
so sweet to other mothers.   Valentin had felt it all profoundly ; his easily moved and loving disposition had
taken on a tinge of melancholy pride.   He had conceived
a passionate gratitude for his mother, and in all her sorrows she had found in him compensation and comfort.

But it must be admitted that Louise, who was capable
of such great courage and of so many sacrifices beyond
the reach of common mortals, was by no means agreeable in ordinary life.   Passionately earnest on every subject, and, in spite of herself, susceptible to all the wounds

of which she should have been able to deaden the sting,
she often caused the bitterness of her heart to rebound
upon the sweet and impressionable nature of her son.
Thus, by dint of irritating those youthful faculties, she
had already dulled them a little. There was something
like the stamp of old age on that brow of fifteen years,
and that child, his petals scarcely opened to life, already
felt fatigued with living, and loved to find rest in a calm
and stormless existence. Like a lovely flower born on
the cliff in the morning, and beaten down by the wind
before blooming, he hung his pale face on his breast, and
his smile had a touch of languor unsuited to his years.
So it was that his intimate relation with the serene and
loving Valentine, and the prudent and unflagging devotion
of Bénédict began a new era for him. He felt his petals
open in that atmosphere, which was so much more favorable to his nature. His frail and slender body grew more
rapidly, and the dull whiteness of his cheeks was softly
tinged with red. Athénaïs, who thought more of physical
beauty than of anything else in the world, declared that
she had never seen such an enchanting face as that lovely
boy's, with its frame of pale fair hair, like Valentine's,
falling in great curls on a neck as white and smooth as
that of the statue of Antinoüs. The giddy creature lost
no opportunity to remark that he was a child and of no
consequence, so that she might have the right to kiss
from time to time that pure, smooth brow, and to pass
her fingers through that soft hair, which she compared
to the raw silk of the golden cocoons.

Thus the pavilion was a place of rest and pleasure to
all at the close of day. Valentine admitted no profane
interloper to the sanctuary, and allowed no communica-
tion with the people of the château. Catherine alone
was allowed to enter, to take care of the place. It was

Valentine's Elysium, the world of her poetic fancy, her golden life. At the château all was ennui, slavery, depression ; her invalid grandmother, unwelcome visitors, painful reflections, and her oratory with its remorse-laden atmosphere ; at the pavilion, happiness, friends, pleasant reveries, fears forgotten, and the pure delights of a chaste love. It was like an enchanted island in the midst of real life, like an oasis in the desert.

At the pavilion, Valentine forgot her secret vexations, her repressed emotions, her hidden love. Bénédict, overjoyed at Valentine's unresisting trust in his good faith, seemed to have changed his nature. He had laid aside his uneven temper, his injustice, his cruel outbursts of wrath. He was almost as attentive to Louise as to her sister ; he walked with her under the lindens in the park, with her arm in his. He talked to her of Valentin, extolled his good qualities, his intelligence, his rapid progress ; he thanked her for giving him a friend and a son. Poor Louise wept as she listened, and strove to look upon Bénédict's friendship as more flattering and sweeter than his love would have been.

Athénaïs, frolicsome and merry, recovered all the heed-lessness of her age at the pavilion. She forgot there her domestic troubles, the stormy affection and jealous distrust of Pierre Blutty. She still loved Bénédict, but not in the same way as before ; she no longer saw in him anything more than a sincere friend. He called her his sister, like Louise and Valentine, but he preferred to call her his little sister. Athénaïs had not enough poetic feeling to persist in keeping alive a hopeless passion. She was young enough and lovely enough to aspire to a reciprocated love, and thus far Pierre Blutty had done nothing to wound her wifely vanity. She spoke of him with esteem, with a blush on her cheeks and a smile on her lips; and then, at the slightest mischievous remark from Louise, she would run away down one of the paths in the park, playful and light of foot, dragging after her the shy Valentin, whom she treated as a schoolboy, but who was barely a year younger than she.

But it would be impossible to describe the silent and reserved affection of Bénédict and Valentine, that exquisite sentiment of modesty and self-sacrifice which held in check in both of them the ardent passion which was always ready to overflow. There were in that never-ending conflict a thousand pangs and a thousand joys, and it may be that Bénédict delighted equally in both. Valentine might often still fear lest she were offending God, and suffer because of her religious scruples; but he, having a less clear conception of a wife's duties, congratulated himself upon not having lured Valentine into sin and given her any cause for repentance. He gladly sacrificed to her the ardent aspirations which consumed him. He was proud of his ability to suffer and to triumph: secretly his imagination was often excited by desires and dreams innumerable; but aloud he blessed Valentine for her most trifling favors. To breathe upon her hair, to inhale the perfumes that emanated from her, to lie on the grass at her feet, his head resting on a corner of her silk apron, to take from Valentin's forehead the kiss which she had just placed there, to carry away stealthily at night the flowers which had withered at her waist—these were the momentous incidents and the great joys of that life of privation, love and happiness.

XXX

Fifteen months passed thus; fifteen months of tranquillity and happiness in the lives of five persons is almost supernatural. Yet so it was. The only thing that caused Bénédict to grieve was that Valentine was sometimes pale and meditative. At such times he made haste to ascertain the reason, and he always found that it was connected with something that had alarmed her pious and fearful soul. He always succeeded in dispelling these light clouds, for Valentine could no longer doubt his strength and his perfect submission. Monsieur de Lansac's conduct contributed to her sense of security. She had deemed it best to write to him that Louise was settled at the farm with her son, and that Monsieur Lhéry—Bénédict—was attending to the young man's education, without a word as to the intimate terms upon which she was living with those three persons. She had explained her relations with Louise to this extent, affecting to consider Monsieur de Lansac bound by a previous promise to allow her to see her sister. The whole story had impressed Monsieur de Lansac as peculiar and absurd. If he had not divined the whole truth, he was, at all events, on the track. He had reflected, with a shrug, upon the wretched taste and wretched form of an intrigue between his wife and a provincial bumpkin.

But, taking everything into consideration, he was better pleased that it should be so than not. He had married with the firm determination not to be embarrassed by Madame de Lansac, and for the moment he was maintaining relations with a *première danseuse* at St. Petersburg, which caused him to take a very philosophical view of life. So that he considered it eminently fair that his wife, on her side, should form ties which would enable her to bear his absence without reproaches or murmurs. All that he desired was that she should be prudent, and that she should not, by her dissolute behavior, subject him to the foolish and unjust ridicule which is visited upon betrayed husbands. Now, he had sufficient confidence in Valentine's character to sleep in peace in that respect; and, as the deserted young wife must necessarily have what he called some occupation for her heart, he much preferred that she should seek it in the mystery of a secluded life, rather than amid the clamor and publicity of fashionable salons. So he was careful not to criticize or blame her mode of life, and his letters expressed, in most affectionate and respectful terms, the very profound indifference with which he had determined to accept whatever Valentine might do.

Her husband's confidence, which she ascribed to a much nobler motive, tormented Valentine secretly for a long while. Gradually, however, the susceptibility of her rigidly upright mind became drowsy and fell asleep on Bénédict's breast. Such respect, stoicism, unselfishness, a love so pure and so brave, touched her deeply. A time came when she said to herself that, far from being a dangerous sentiment, it was a priceless and heroic virtue, that God and the laws of honor sanctioned their bonds, that her heart was purified and strengthened in that sacred fire. All the sublime utopias suggested by courageous and patient love dazzled her vision. She ventured to thank heaven for having given her for her savior and her support in the perils of life that powerful and generous confederate who protected her and

shielded her against herself.   Hitherto, religion had been
to her like a code of consecrated principles, based upon
sound reasoning, and solemnly repeated every day for
the better defence of her morals; now it changed its
nature in her mind, and became a poetic and enthusiastic passion, a source of ardent but ascetic dreams,
which, far from serving as a breastwork of her heart,
laid it open on all sides to the attacks of passion.   This
new conception of religion seemed to her preferable to
the old.   As she felt that it was more intense and more
fruitful of keen emotions, of ardent aspirations toward
heaven, she welcomed it imprudently, and took pleasure
in thinking that Bénédict's love had kindled it.

" Just as fire refines gold," she said to herself, "virtuous love elevates the soul and guides its flight toward
God, the source of all love."

But alas! Valentine did not see that that faith, tem-
pered in the flame of human passions, often compromised with the duties imposed upon it by its celestial
origin and descended to terrestrial alliances.   She allowed the moral force which twenty years of tranquillity and ignorance had stored up within her to be scattered to the winds; she allowed that faith to invade and
change her convictions, formerly so clearly defined and
unbending, and to cover with its deceitful flowers the
narrow, stony path of duty.   Her prayers increased in
length.   Bénédict's name and image were constantly
blended with them, and she no longer repelled them;
she evoked them in order that she might pray more
fervently.   It was an infallible means, but a hazardous
one.   Valentine would come out from her oratory intensely excited, with her nerves on edge and the blood
flowing hotly through her veins.   At such times Bénédict's glances and words laid waste her heart like a

stream of molten lava. If he had been hypocritical or adroit enough to present adultery to her in a mystic light, Valentine would have been ruined with a prayer on her lips.

But the one thing that was likely to be their safeguard for a long time was the perfect sincerity of the young man, who had a genuinely upright mind. He fancied that, at the slightest attempt to shake Valentine's virtue, he would certainly forfeit her esteem and confidence, which he had found it so difficult to acquire. He did not know that, when once started down the steep incline of passion, one does not often retrace one's steps. He was not conscious of his power; had he been, perhaps he would not have used it, that young and inexperienced heart was still so loyal and honorable.

You should have heard the noble fatuity, the sublime paradoxes with which they sanctioned their imprudent love.

"How could I urge you to be false to your principles," Bénédict would say, "I who adore you for the manly strength with which you resist me? I who prefer your virtue to your beauty, your mind to your body? I who would kill both you and myself, if I could be sure of possessing you instantly in heaven, as the angels possess God?"

"No, you cannot lie," Valentine would reply, "you whom God sent to me to teach me to know Him and love Him, through whom I first formed a true conception of His power, and who first showed me the marvels of creation. Alas! I thought that I was so insignificant and so limited! But you have magnified the meaning of the prophecies; you have given me the key to the sacred poems; you have revealed to me the existence of a vast universe of which pure love is the connecting bond and

the essence. I know now that we were created for each
other, and that the non-material alliance we have formed
is preferable to all earthly ties."

One evening they were all assembled in the small
salon of the pavilion. Valentin, who had a fresh and
agreeable voice, was trying a song; his mother was
playing the accompaniment. Athénaïs, with one elbow
resting on the piano, was watching her young favorite
closely, and refused to see how uncomfortable she made
him. Bénédict and Valentine sat near the window, intoxicating themselves with the evening perfumes, the perfect calm, pure air, melody and love. Never had Valentine had such a sense of absolute security. Enthusiasm
stole farther and farther into her heart, and beneath the
veil of just admiration for her lover's virtue, increased
her intense and swiftly-moving passion. By the dim
light of the stars they could hardly see each other. To
replace the chaste but perilous pleasure which the meeting of the eye affords, they allowed their fingers to become entwined. Gradually the clasp became more
ardent, more eager; their chairs insensibly drew nearer;
their hair touched, and the electric spark passed from
one to the other; their breaths mingled, and the evening
breeze grew stifling about them. Bénédict, overwhelmed
by the weight of the subtle, penetrating happiness born
of a love which is both spurned and shared, leaned over
the window-sill and rested his forehead on Valentine's
hand, which he still held in his. Drunken and trembling
with joy, he dared not move for fear of alarming her
other hand, which had fallen upon his head and was
moving among his coarse black locks as soft and light
as the breath of a will-o'-the-wisp. His emotion burst
the walls of his breast and sent all his blood rushing to
his heart. He thought that he was dying, but he would

have died rather than reveal his emotion, so afraid was he of arousing Valentine's suspicions and remorse. If she had known what torrents of bliss she was pouring into his heart she would have gone away. To enjoy that unrestraint, those soft caresses, that heart-breaking rapture, he must seem insensible to it. Bénédict held his breath and restrained the frenzy of his fever. His silence embarrassed Valentine at last; she spoke to him in a low tone, to divert her own thoughts from the too intense emotion which was beginning to distress her as well.

"Are we not happy?" she said, perhaps to give him, or herself, to understand that they must not desire to be more so.

"Oh!" said Bénédict, doing his utmost to make his voice steady, "we ought to die like this!"

A rapid step crossing the lawn toward the pavilion was distinctly audible during the silence. An indefinable presentiment terrified Bénédict. He pressed Valentine's hand convulsively, and held it against his heart, which was beating as loudly in his breast as the disturbing sound of those unexpected footsteps. Valentine felt her own heart stand still under the spell of an ill-defined but terrible fear; she suddenly withdrew her hand and walked toward the door. But it was opened before she reached it, and Catherine, panting for breath, appeared in the doorway.

"Madame," she said, with a hurried, terrified air, "Monsieur de Lansac is at the château!"

The words produced upon all who heard them the same effect as a stone cast into the clear and motionless water of a lake; the sky, the trees, the lovely landscape which are reflected therein, are thrown into confusion and disappear; a pebble has sufficed to reduce an

enchanting scene to chaos. In like manner was the delightful harmony destroyed which had reigned in that
room a moment before. The pleasant dream of happiness in which that little family were blissfully existing
was shattered. Scattered suddenly, like the leaves
which the wind whirls about in eddying heaps, they
parted full of anxiety and fear. Valentine embraced
Louise and her son.

"I am yours forever!" she said as she left them.
"We will meet again soon, I trust; perhaps to-morrow."

Valentin sadly shook his head; he had an indefinable
thrill of pride and hatred at the name of Monsieur de
Lansac. He had often thought that that nobleman
might drive him from his house; that thought had sometimes poisoned the happiness he enjoyed there.

"That man will do well to make you happy," he said
to his aunt, with a bellicose air which made her smile
with emotion; "if he doesn't, he will have to deal with
me!"

"What can you fear with such a knight?" Athénaïs
asked Madame de Lansac, striving to seem cheerful, and
giving the young man's flushed cheek a gentle tap with
her soft, plump hand.

"Are you coming, Bénédict?" asked Louise, as she
walked toward the gate of the park leading into the
fields.

"In a moment," he replied.

He followed Valentine toward the other exit, and,
while Catherine hastily put out the candles and closed
the pavilion, he said to her in a hollow and violently
agitated voice:

"Valentine!"

He could say no more. Indeed, how could he venture
to mention the subject of his dread and his frenzy.

Valentine understood him. She gave him her hand with a determined air, and said, with a smile of love and pride :

"Never fear."

The expression of her voice and her glance exerted so powerful an influence on Bénédict that he went away in docile obedience to her wish and with his mind almost at rest.

XXXI

Monsieur de Lansac, in travelling costume, and feigning great fatigue, was reclining in a nonchalant pose on the couch in the large salon. He went to meet Valentine with a great show of courteous ardor, as soon as he caught sight of her. Valentine trembled and felt as if she were about to faint. Her pallor and her evident consternation did not escape the count; he pretended not to notice them, and complimented her on the brightness of her eyes and the fresh bloom of her complexion. Then he began to chat with the ease of manner which the habit of dissembling imparts ; and the tone in which he spoke of his journey, the joy which he expressed to be with his wife once more, the affectionate questions he asked concerning her health, and concerning her sources of amusement in her seclusion, assisted her to recover from her emotion, and to appear calm and gracious and courteous, like him.

Not until then did she notice in a corner of the salon a short, thickset man with a rough, unrefined face. Monsieur de Lansac introduced him as *a friend of his*. There was evident constraint in Monsieur de Lansac's manner as he pronounced that phrase. The man's dull and forbidding expression, and the stiff, awkward bow which he bestowed upon her, aroused in Valentine an irresistible feeling of repulsion for that unattractive person, who seemed to feel out of his element in her presence, and strove by a display of impudence to disguise the discomfort of his situation.

Having supped at the same table with and opposite to this stranger whose external aspect was so repellent, Valentine was requested by Monsieur de Lansac to order one of the best rooms in the château to be prepared for his *dear Monsieur Grapp.* Valentine obeyed, and a few moments later Monsieur Grapp retired, after exchanging a few words in an undertone with Monsieur de Lansac, and saluting his wife with the same embarrassment and the same insolently servile glance as before.

When the husband and wife were left alone, Valentine was seized with a deadly terror. With pale face and downcast eyes she was trying in vain to make up her mind to renew the conversation, when Monsieur de Lansac broke the silence by asking her permission to retire, on the ground that he was completely tired out.

"I have come from St. Petersburg in a fortnight," he said with a sort of affectation. "I stopped in Paris only twenty-four hours ; and I think—yes, I certainly am feverish."

"Oh ! of course, you have—you must be feverish," echoed Valentine, with ill-advised eagerness.

A contemptuous smile played about the diplomat's wary lips.

"You act like Rosine in the *Barbier !*" he said in a half-jesting, half-sneering tone ; *"Buona sera, Don Basilio !*—Ah !" he added, dragging himself toward the door, as if utterly exhausted, "I really must have some sleep! One more night on the road, and I should have been ill. It is enough to make one ill, isn't it, my dear Valentine?"

"Yes, yes, indeed," she replied, "you need rest; I have had prepared——"

"The room in the pavilion, I suppose, my love? I can sleep better there. I am very fond of that pavilion; it will remind me of the happy time when I saw you every day."

"The pavilion?" said Valentine, with an expression of dismay which did not escape her husband, and served him as a starting-point for the investigations he proposed to make very shortly.

"You haven't disposed of the pavilion, have you?" he said, with an absolutely artless and indifferent air.

"I have made it into a sort of study," she replied with some embarrassment, for she did not know how to lie. "The bed has been taken away; it couldn't be put back again to-night. But my mother's rooms on the ground-floor are all ready for you—if they will be satisfactory to you."

"I shall, perhaps, ask for other quarters to-morrow," said Monsieur de Lansac, with savagely vindictive meaning and a smile of mawkish affection; "meanwhile, I will put up with those you give me."

He kissed her hand. His lips seemed as cold as ice to Valentine. She rubbed that hand with the other, when she was alone, to restore the circulation. Despite Monsieur de Lansac's compliance with her wishes, she was so far from understanding his real purpose, that, at first, fear overshadowed all the pain at her heart. She locked herself in her room, and, as the confused memory of that night of torpor which she had passed there with

Bénédict recurred to her mind, she rose and paced the floor with an agitated step, to banish the painful and deceptive ideas aroused by the thought of the events of that night. About three o'clock, being unable to sleep or to breathe freely, she opened her window. Her eyes rested for a long while on a motionless object, the nature of which she could not definitely determine, for it was so blended with the tree-trunks that it seemed to be one of them. All at once she saw it move and approach the house, and she recognized Bénédict. Terrified to see him show himself openly thus in front of Monsieur de Lansac's windows, which were directly beneath hers, she leaned out to impress upon him, by signs, the danger to which he was exposed. But Bénédict, instead of being alarmed by it, felt a thrill of keen delight when he learned that his rival occupied that apartment. He clasped his hands, raised them toward the sky in his gratitude, and disappeared. Unluckily, Monsieur de Lansac, who was also prevented from sleeping by the feverish excitement caused by this long journey, had watched this scene from behind a curtain which concealed him from Bénédict.

The next forenoon Monsieur de Lansac and Monsieur Grapp walked out together.

"Well," said the vulgar little man, "have you spoken to your *spouse?*"*

"How fast you go, my dear fellow! For heaven's sake give me time to breathe."

"I have no time for that myself, monsieur. This matter must be settled within a week. You know that I can't wait any longer."

* *Epouse.* It is a vulgarism, in French, to speak, in ordinary conversation, of a man's wife as his *épouse; femme* is the proper word. The distinction can only be indicated, not expressed, by the use of the English word *spouse.*

"Oh! be patient!" said the count, testily.

"Patient!" retorted the creditor, in a surly tone. "I have been patient for ten years now, monsieur, and I tell you that my patience is at an end. You were to pay up when you married, and here it is two years already that you——"

"But what in the devil are you afraid of? This estate is worth five hundred thousand francs, and there is no incumbrance on it."

"I don't say that I run any risk," rejoined the intractable creditor; "but I say that I want to collect what is owing me, get my money together, and without delay. That was understood, monsieur, and I trust that you don't mean to do again as you have done before."

"God forbid! I took this infernal journey for the express purpose of getting rid of you forever—of your claim, I mean—and I long to be free from worry at last. Within a week you shall be paid."

"I don't feel so easy about it as you do," retorted the other, in the same persistent, uncompromising tone; "your wife—that is to say, your *spouse*—may ruin all your plans; she may refuse to sign."

"She won't refuse."

"*Hein!* perhaps you will say that I go too far, but after all I have a right to understand your family affairs. It seemed to me that you two weren't so overjoyed to meet as you led me to expect."

"What do you say?" exclaimed the count, turning pale with wrath at the fellow's insolence.

"No, no!" rejoined the usurer, tranquilly. "Madame la comtesse seemed to be only moderately pleased. I know what I am talking about."

"Monsieur!" said the count, in a thundering tone.

"Monsieur!" said the usurer, in a still more threatening tone, and fixing his little wild boar's eyes on his debtor; "listen to me; frankness is essential in business, and you haven't been frank in this matter. Listen, I say, listen; this is no time to fly into a rage. I know that with a single word Madame de Lansac can prolong my time of waiting indefinitely; and, then, what can I get out of you? Even if I should have you shut up at Sainte-Pélagie, I should have to pay for your keep there; and it isn't at all certain that, in the present state of your wife's affection, she would care to release you very soon."

"Tell me explicitly what you mean, monsieur?" cried the count, in a rage; "upon what do you base——"

"I mean, monsieur, that I, too, have a pretty young wife. What can't one get with money? Very good; when I have been away for no more than a fortnight, although my house is as big as yours, my wife—I mean my *spouse*—doesn't sleep on the first floor and I on the ground-floor. Whereas here, monsieur—I know very well that the old nobility have kept to the old customs and sleep apart from their wives; but *mordieu!* monsieur, you have been away from yours two years."

The count angrily stripped the leaves from a branch which he had picked up to keep himself in countenance.

"Enough of this, monsieur!" he exclaimed, choking with wrath. "You have no right to meddle in my affairs to this extent; to-morrow you shall have the guaranty you require, and then I will convince you that you have gone too far."

The tone in which he said this had very little effect on Monsieur Grapp. The usurer was inured to threats, and there was one thing which he dreaded more than a caning —namely, the insolvency of his debtors.

The day was passed inspecting the estate. Monsieur Grapp had sent for a clerk from the land registry office in the morning. He visited the woods, the fields, the meadows, estimating the value of everything, haggling over a furrow or a felled tree, decrying everything, taking notes, tormenting the count and driving him frantic, so that he was tempted twenty times to throw him into the river. The family at Grangeneuve were much surprised at the arrival of the noble count in person, attended by his acolyte, who scrutinized everything, and seemed to be on the point of drawing up an inventory of the cattle and the farming outfit. Monsieur and Madame Lhéry fancied that they could detect, in this step of their new landlord, a manifestation of distrust and a purpose to cancel their lease. They asked nothing better. A wealthy iron-master, a kinsman and friend of the family, had recently died childless, and had left by his will two hundred thousand francs to *his dear and estimable god-daughter,* Athénaïs Lhéry, Madame Blutty. So Père Lhéry suggested to Monsieur de Lansac that the lease should be cancelled, and Monsieur Grapp undertook to see to it that the parties should come to an understanding in that respect within three days.

Valentine had sought in vain an opportunity to talk with her husband alone, and to broach the subject of Louise. After dinner, Monsieur de Lansac suggested to Grapp that they inspect the park. They went out together, and Valentine followed them, dreading, not without reason, any examination of her little reservation. Monsieur de Lansac offered her his arm, and ostentatiously chatted with her in a perfectly friendly and unembarrassed tone.

She was beginning to recover her courage, and had ventured to ask him a few questions, when the peculiar barrier with which she had surrounded her *reservation* attracted Monsieur de Lansac's attention.

" May I ask you, my dear, what this partition means ? "
he inquired in a perfectly natural tone. "One would
say that it was a game preserve. Have you taken up
the royal sport of hunting, pray ? "

Valentine, struggling to assume a heedless tone, explained that she had fixed upon that spot for her private
retreat, and that she came there to be alone, so that she
could work more freely.

" Bless my soul ! " said Monsieur de Lansac, "what
profound and conscientious work can you be engaged
upon that demands such precautions ? What ! pali-
sades, barred gates, impenetrable shrubbery ! Why, you
must have transformed the pavilion into a fairy palace !
And to think that I imagined that the solitude at the
château was so hard for you ! But you despise anything
so trivial ! Here is the secrecy of the cloister ! Here is
the mystery which your dark meditations demand ! Tell
me, are you in search of the philosopher's stone, or the
most perfect form of government ? I see that we are
wasting time out in the world cudgelling our brains over
the destiny of empires ; it is all pondered and arranged
and unravelled in the pavilion in your park."

Valentine, overwhelmed and terrified by this jesting,
in which it seemed to her that there was less merriment
than malice, would have been glad, for many reasons,
to turn Monsieur de Lansac's mind away from that subject ; but he insisted that she should do the honors of
her retreat, and she had no choice but to submit. She
had hoped to tell him of her daily meetings with her
sister and her son before he started on his walk. Consequently she had not told Catherine to remove such
traces of their daily presence as her friends might have
left there. Poetry written on the walls by Bénédict, in
praise of the pleasures of friendship and of the repose of

country life ; Valentin's name, which, like a true schoolboy, he had written everywhere ; pieces of music belonging to Bénédict, and marked with his initials ; a
pretty little fowling-piece with which Valentin sometimes
hunted rabbits in the park,—all were minutely scrutinized by Monsieur de Lansac, and furnished him with a
theme for divers half-bitter, half-jesting remarks.   At
last he picked up from an easy-chair a dainty velvet cap
belonging to Valentin, and said with a forced laugh,
calling Valentine's attention to it :

"Is this the cap of the invisible alchemist whom you
invoke in this retreat ? "

He tried it on, satisfied himself that it was too small
for a man, and coolly tossed it on the piano ; then, turning to Grapp, as if a paroxysm of vindictive wrath
against his wife had caused him to forget the consideration he owed to her position, he demanded sharply.

"What do you value this pavilion at ? "

"Almost nothing," was the reply.   "These luxuries and
fancy buildings are worth nothing on a country estate.
The Black Band* wouldn't give five hundred francs for
it.   In a city it's different.   But when there's a field of
barley around this building, or an artificial meadow,
we'll say, what will it be good for ?   Just to tear down
for the stone and lumber that are in it."

The serious tone in which Grapp made this reply sent
an involuntary chill through Valentine's veins.   Who
was this man with the repulsive face, whose forbidding
glance seemed to be making an inventory of her property, whose voice called down destruction on the dwelling of her fathers, whose imagination drove a plough

* The Black Band—*Bande Noire*—was an association of specu-
lators, who made a business of buying large estates in order to sell
them in small lots.

through those gardens, but now the secret hiding-place of pure and modest happiness ?

She glanced trembling at Monsieur de Lansac, whose placid, nonchalant air was impenetrable.

About ten o'clock in the evening, as Grapp was preparing to go to his room, he led the count out on the stoop.

"Look you," he said angrily, "here's a whole day wasted ; try to arrange some settlement of my matters to-night, or I'll have an understanding with Madame de Lansac to-morrow. If she refuses to pay your debts, I shall at least know where I stand. I see clearly enough that she doesn't like my face. I don't want to annoy her, but I do not propose to be fooled with. Besides, I have no time to amuse myself with country life. Tell me, monsieur, will you have an interview with your *spouse* to-night ? "

"*Morbleu!* monsieur," cried Lansac, testily, grasping the gilded railing, "you are a perfect butcher ! "

"Possibly," retorted Grapp, eager to avenge himself by insult for the hatred and contempt he inspired ; "but take my advice and move your pillow up one flight."

He withdrew, mumbling some vile insinuation. The count was refined in manner, if not in heart. He could not at that moment avoid the reflection that the chaste and sanctified institution of marriage had been shockingly debased in its progress through the avaricious centuries of our civilization.

But other thoughts, bearing more directly upon his present position, soon took possession of his keen and calculating mind.

XXXII

Monsieur de Lansac was in one of the most delicate situations which are likely to present themselves in the life of a man of the world. There are several varieties of honor in France : the honor of the peasant is different from that of the noble ; that of the noble is different from that of the bourgeois. There is a kind of honor for every rank, and, it may be, for every individual. One thing is certain, that Monsieur de Lansac was a man of honor after his fashion. A philosopher in some respects, he had the prejudices of his caste in many others. In these days of enlightenment, of bold conceptions and general renovation, the old ideas of right and wrong must necessarily change to some extent, and individual opinions hover uncertainly about innumerable quarrels as to the dividing line.

Monsieur de Lansac was quite willing to be betrayed, but not to be deceived. In that respect he was quite right. Considering the doubts which certain discoveries had aroused in his mind relative to his wife's fidelity, it may be imagined that he was not disposed to bring about a more intimate union, and to shield her by his voluntary act from the consequences of a presumed misstep. The ugliest feature of his position was this, that vile pecuniary considerations fettered the exercise of his dignity and compelled him to take a crooked course toward his goal.

He was immersed in these reflections when, about midnight, it seemed to him that he heard a faint voice in the house, where everything had been peaceful and silent for an hour.

A glass door opened into the garden from the salon, on the same floor as the count's apartments, but at the other end of the building ; it seemed to him that somebody was cautiously opening that door. Instantly, the recollection of what he had seen the preceding night, added to his eager desire to obtain proofs which would place his wife in his power, roused him to action. He hastily put on a dressing-gown and slippers, and, walking in the darkness with all the precautions of a man accustomed to be prudent in everything, he went out through the door of the salon, which was still ajar, and followed Valentine into the park.

Although she had locked the gate in the fence behind her, he had no difficulty in entering her reservation a few minutes after her, by scaling the fence itself.

Guided by instinct and by faint sounds, he reached the pavilion, and, crouching out of sight among the tall dahlias which grew in front of the principal window, he could hear everything that was said.

Valentine, oppressed by the conflicting emotions which such a step caused her, had sunk without speaking on the sofa in the salon. Bénédict, standing beside her, and no less moved than she, also remained silent for several moments ; then he made an effort to put an end to that painful situation.

"I was very anxious," he said ; "I was afraid that you didn't receive my note."

"Ah ! Bénédict," replied Valentine, sadly, " that note was written by a madman, and I must be mad myself to comply with such a reckless and wicked summons. Oh ! I was very near not coming, but I had not the strength to resist. May God forgive me ! "

"On my soul, madame," said Bénédict, in a passion which he could not control, "you did well not to have the strength to resist, for I should have gone in search of you, at the peril of your life and my own, even if——."

"Do not finish, my poor fellow! Now you are re-assured, aren't you? You have seen me; you are perfectly sure that I am free; let me leave you."

"Do you think that you are in danger here, and not at the château?"

"That is all very wrong and absurd, Bénédict. Luckily, God seems to have inspired Monsieur de Lansac with the purpose not to force me to culpable rebellion."

"I am not afraid of your weakness, madame, but of your principles."

"Can you dare to combat them now?"

"I do not know what I would not dare to do now, madame. Spare me, for I am beside myself, as you see."

"Oh! *mon Dieu!*" said Valentine, bitterly; "what in heaven's name has happened to you in so short a time? Could I expect to find you in such a state as this, when you were so calm and strong twenty-four hours ago?"

"In twenty-four hours," he replied, "I have lived a whole lifetime of agony; I have fought with all the demons of hell! No, no, indeed I am not what I was twenty-four hours ago. A diabolical jealousy, an inextinguishable hatred have sprung up in my heart. Ah! Valentine, twenty-four hours ago I could be virtuous, but now it is all different."

"You are not well, my dear," said Valentine, in dismay. "Let us part; this interview aggravates your suffering. Remember, too—Great heaven! Didn't I see a shadow pass the window?"

"What does it matter?" said Bénédict, walking calmly to the window; "wouldn't it be a hundred times better to see you lying dead in my arms than to know that you were living in the arms of another man? But you need have no fear; everything is quiet, the garden is deserted. —Listen, Valentine," he continued, in a calm but spiritless tone, "I am very unhappy. You insisted that I should live; you condemned me to bear a heavy burden!"

"Alas!" she said, "reproaches! Have we not been happy for fifteen months, ungrateful boy?"

"Yes, madame, we have been happy, but we shall not be again."

"Why these gloomy presages? What calamity can threaten us?"

"Your husband may take you away; he may separate us forever; and it is impossible that he should not intend to do it."

"But I tell you, on the contrary, that his intentions thus far seem most pacific. If he had proposed to attach me to his career, would he not have done it before this? I have a suspicion that he is in a great hurry to settle some business matter or other."

"I can guess the nature of the business. Allow me to tell you what it is, madame, as I have the opportunity. Do not spurn the advice of a devoted friend, who pays little heed to worldly interests and calculations, but whose indifference disappears when you are concerned. Monsieur de Lansac has debts, as you probably know."

"I do know it, Bénédict; but it seems to me most improper to discuss his conduct with you and in this place."

"Nothing is less *proper* than my passion for you, Valentine; but, as you have submitted to it thus far from compassion for me, you must also submit in your own interest to the advice that I give you. The conclusion which I am forced to draw from your husband's conduct is that he is by no means eager and, consequently, by no means worthy to possess you. You would, perhaps, forward his secret purposes by creating for yourself at once a life distinct from his."

"I understand you, Bénédict. You suggest a separation, a sort of divorce ; you advise me to commit a crime——"

"Oh! no, madame. Even according to the ideas on the subject of conjugal submission which you cherish so piously, nothing can be more strictly moral, if Monsieur de Lansac desires it, than a separation without publicity or scandal. If I were in your place, I would request it, and would seek no other security than the honor of the two persons interested. But, by an agreement of this sort, entered into with good feeling and a sense of loyalty on both sides, you would at least protect your future against the assaults of his creditors ; whereas I fear——"

"I love to hear you talk so, Bénédict," she replied. "Such advice proves your sincerity ; but I have heard my mother talk about business so much that I know a little more about it than you do. I know that no promise can bind a man who is devoid of honor to keep his hands off his wife's property ; and, if I had the misfortune to be married to such a man, I should have no other safeguard than my strength of will—no other guide than my conscience. But never fear, Bénédict, Monsieur de Lansac has an honorable and generous heart. I have no fear of anything of the sort from him, and, besides, I know that he cannot dispose of any of my property without consulting me."

"And I know that you would not refuse to sign any-

thing for him ; for I know your obliging disposition—
your contempt for wealth."

"You are mistaken, Bénédict. I should have courage,
if it were necessary. It is true that, for my own part,
I would be content with this pavilion and a few acres of
land ; if I were cut down to twelve hundred francs a
year, I should still consider myself rich. But this property of which my sister was defrauded, this, at all events,
I propose to bequeath to her son after my death : Valentin will be my heir. I propose that he shall be Comte
de Raimbault some day. That is the object of my life.—
Why did you shudder so, Bénédict ? "

"You ask me why ? " cried Bénédict, suddenly roused
from the calmness induced by the turn their conversation had taken. "Alas ! how little you know of life !
how placid and over-confident you are ! You talk of
dying without children, as if—Merciful Heaven ! All my
blood rises at the thought ! But, by my soul, if you do
not speak the truth, madame——"

He rose and paced the floor excitedly. From time to
time he hid his face in his hands, and his loud breathing
betrayed his mental agony.

"My friend," said Valentine, gently, "you have no
strength of will, no reasoning power to-day. The subject of our conversation is of too delicate a nature ! Take
my advice ; let us stop here, for I am much to blame for
coming here at such an hour at the call of a reckless
child. These stormy thoughts which torment you I cannot banish by my silence ; but you should know how to
interpret it without insisting that I make promises that I
must not make.—But," she added, in a trembling voice,
as she saw that Bénédict became more and more excited
as she spoke, "if it is absolutely necessary, to reassure
you and restrain you, that I fail in all my duties and

disregard all my scruples, why, be satisfied : I swear to you by your affection and my own—I dare not swear by heaven—that I will die rather than belong to any man."

"At last," rejoined Bénédict hurriedly, as he drew nearer to her, "you deign to toss me a word of encouragement! I thought that you were going to send me away devoured by anxiety and jealousy ; I thought that you would never sacrifice to me a single one of your narrow ideas. Do you really promise that ? Why, madame, this is heroic ! "

"You are very bitter, Bénédict. It is a long time since I have seen you like this. Every sort of sorrow must needs come upon me at once ! "

"Ah ! it is because I love you madly," said Bénédict, grasping her arm in an outburst of frenzy. "I would sell my soul to save your life ; I would sell my chance of heaven to spare your heart the slightest pang ; I would commit any crime in the calendar to please you, and you would not make the most trivial misstep to make me happy."

"Oh ! don't talk so," she replied in a disheartened tone. "I have been accustomed to trust you for so long a time ; now I must begin again to fear you and struggle against you ! perhaps I shall have to fly from you."

"Let us not play upon words ! " cried Bénédict, fiercely, dropping with a violent gesture the arm which he held. "You talk about flying from me ! Condemn me to death ; that will be a quicker way. I did not think, madame, that you would go back to such threats. Do you imagine, pray, that these fifteen months have changed me ? Well, you are right; they have made me love you more madly than ever; they have given me the power to live, whereas my former love gave me only strength to die. Now, Valentine, it is too late to stop. I love you to the exclusion of all else ; I have no one but you on earth ; I love Louise and her son only for your sake. You are my future, my goal, my only passion, my only thought. What do you suppose will become of me if you throw me over ? I have no ambition, no friends, no trade ; I shall never have any of the things that make up the lives of other men. You have often told me that when I am older I shall be eager for the same things as the rest of mankind. I don't know whether you will ever prove to be right in that respect ; but this much is certain, that I am still very far from the age when the noble passions die out, and I shall never care to reach that age if you abandon me. No, Valentine, you will not drive me away from you ; it is impossible. Have pity on me, for my courage is exhausted.''

Bénédict burst into tears. It requires such intense mental excitement to reduce an agitated, passionate man to tears and to the weakness of a child, that the least impressionable woman can rarely resist such sudden outbursts of overpowering emotion. Valentine threw herself weeping into the arms of the man she loved, and the consuming ardor of the kiss in which their lips met proved to her at last how closely akin to madness is the mental exaltation of virtue. But they had little time to reflect upon it, for they had no sooner exchanged the fervid effusion of their hearts than a short, dry cough, and the humming of an operatic air under the window with the most perfect tranquillity, almost paralyzed Valentine with terror. She tore herself from Bénédict's embrace, and grasping his arm with one cold, trembling hand, covered his mouth with the other.

"We are lost,'' she whispered ; "it is he !''

"Valentine, my dear, aren't you here ?'' said Monsieur de Lansac, approaching the steps without a trace of excitement.

"Hide!" said Valentine, pushing Bénédict behind a tall mirror which stood in a corner of the room.

And she darted to meet Monsieur de Lansac, armed with that skill in dissimulation which necessity, as if by a miracle, places at the service of the most inexperienced woman.

"I was very sure that I saw you go toward the pavilion a quarter of an hour ago," said Lansac as he entered; "and, as I did not wish to disturb your solitary walk, I went in another direction for my own; but the instinct of the heart or the magic force of your presence leads me involuntarily to the place where you are. I am not impertinent, am I, to interrupt your meditations thus? Will you deign to admit me to your sanctuary?"

"I came here to get a book which I want to finish tonight," said Valentine in a loud, hurried tone, very different from her ordinary voice.

"Allow me to tell you, my dear Valentine, that you are leading a very strange sort of life, and that it makes me very anxious for your health. You pass your nights walking about and reading; that is neither sensible nor prudent."

"But I assure you that you are mistaken," said Valentine, trying to edge him toward the door. "It was by the merest chance that I came out for a breath of fresh air in the park to-night, being unable to sleep. I feel quite calm now, and I will go in."

"But the book that you came for,—you haven't it, have you?"

"Oh! that is true!" said Valentine, in confusion.

And she pretended to look for a book on the piano.

By an unlucky chance there was not a single book in the room.

"How do you expect to find it in this darkness ? " said Monsieur de Lansac. "Let me light a candle."

"Oh! that would be impossible!" exclaimed Valentine in dismay. "No, no, don't light one ; I don't need the book ; I haven't any desire to read now."

"But why give it up when it's so easy to procure a light ? I noticed a very pretty box of phosphorus on the mantel-piece yesterday. I will wager I can put my hand on it."

As he spoke, he took the box and thrust in a match, which blazed up and cast a bright light about the room, then changed to a faint blue flame, and seemed to die while taking fire ; that brief gleam sufficed to allow Monsieur de Lansac to catch the terrified glance which his wife cast at the mirror. When the candle was lighted, he adopted a still calmer and more artless tone : he knew where Bénédict was.

"As we happen to be together, my dear," he said, seating himself on the sofa, to Valentine's intense disgust, "I am resolved to talk to you of a matter of some importance which is annoying me. Here we are quite sure not to be overheard or interrupted. Will you be kind enough to give me your attention for a few moments ? "

Valentine, paler than a ghost, sank into a chair.

"Please come nearer, my dear," said Monsieur de Lansac, drawing toward him a small table on which he placed the candle.

He rested his chin on his hand, and began the conversation with the self-possession of a man accustomed to propose peace or war to monarchs in the same tone of voice.

XXXIII

"I presume, my dear love, that you desire to know something of my plans, in order to make yours conform to them," he began, fixing his eyes upon her with a piercing gaze which held her, like one fascinated, where she sat. "Let me tell you, therefore, that I cannot leave my post, as I had hoped, for several years to come. My fortune has suffered a considerable diminution, which it is necessary for me to make up by my labors. Shall I take you with me, or shall I not take you? *That is the question*, as Hamlet says. Do you wish to go with me? Do you wish to stay here? So far as it is in my power, I will comply with your wishes; but give me a definite answer, for, in this respect, your letters have been marked by a too modest restraint. I am your husband after all, and I have some claim to your confidence."

Valentine moved her lips, but could not utter a word. Between her jocose lord and master and her jealous lover, she was in a horrible position.

She tried to raise her eyes to Lansac's face; his hawk-like gaze was still fixed upon her. She lost countenance altogether, stammered and made no reply.

"Since you are so bashful," he continued, raising his voice a little, "I augur well for your submission to my wishes, and it is time that I should speak to you of the duties we have contracted toward each other. We used to be friends once, Valentine, and this subject of conversation did not frighten you so. To-day you treat me with a reserve which I cannot understand. I fear lest you have been too much in the company of persons unfavorably disposed toward me, during my absence. I fear—shall I tell you everything ?—that your confidence in me may have been somewhat weakened by some too intimate friendships."

Valentine turned red and white by turns; then she mustered courage to look her husband in the face, in order to grasp his meaning. She fancied that she could see an expression of ill-will beneath his air of calm kindliness, and she assumed a watchful attitude.

"Go on, monsieur," she said, with more courage than she herself expected to command; "I am waiting until you say all that you have to say before replying."

"People who are on friendly terms with each other should understand each other before a word is said," rejoined Lansac; "but, since such is your wish, Valentine, I will speak. I desire," he added with terrifying significance, "that my words may not be thrown away. I mentioned just now our reciprocal duties; mine are to assist and protect you."

"Yes, monsieur, to protect me !" echoed Valentine in consternation, but with some bitterness.

"I understand you perfectly," he rejoined; "you consider that my protection thus far has been a little too much like God's. I confess that it has been a little distant, a little reserved; but, if you wish," he added ironically, "it shall be made more apparent."

A sudden movement behind the mirror caused Valentine to turn as cold as a marble statue. She glanced at her husband with a startled expression, but he seemed not to have noticed the sound that had caused her alarm, and he continued :

"We will speak of that at another time, my love; I am too much a man of the world to annoy with mani-

festations of my affection a person who would spurn it.
So that my duty toward you in the way of regard and
protection shall be fulfilled in accordance with your desires, and never beyond them ; for in these days husbands make themselves especially unendurable by
being too faithful to their duties. What do you think
about it ? ''

" I have not had experience enough to answer."

"Very well answered. Now, my dear love, I am
going to speak of your duties toward me. That will
not be very gallant ; and, as I have a horror of anything
resembling pedagogy, it will be the first and last time in
my life that I shall do it. I am convinced that the meaning of the precepts I shall lay down will always remain
in your memory. Why, how you tremble ! what childish folly ! Do you take me for one of those antediluvian
clowns who have nothing pleasanter to hold up before
the eyes of their wives than the yoke of marital fidelity ?
Do you think that I am going to preach to you like an old
monk, and bury in your heart the daggers of the Inqui-
sition, in order to compel a confession of your secret
thoughts ?—No, Valentine, no," he continued, after a
pause, during which he gazed at her coldly ; " I know
very well what I must say to you in order not to disturb
you. I will demand of you only what I can obtain without thwarting your inclinations and making your heart
bleed. Don't faint, I beg you ; I shall soon have said
all I have to say. I have no objection whatever to your
living on intimate terms with a select circle of your own
which often assembles here, and whose recent presence
is proved by various indications."

He took from the table a sketch-book on which Bénédict's name was written, and turned the leaves with an
air of indifference.

"But," he added, pushing the volume away with a resolute and commanding gesture, "I expect that your good sense will see to it that no stranger presumes to offer his advice in our private affairs, or attempts to interpose any obstacle to the management of our common property. I expect this much from your conscience, and I demand it in the name of the rights which your position gives me.—Well, why don't you answer ? What are you looking at in that mirror ? "

"I was not looking at it, monsieur," replied the terror-stricken Valentine.

"On the other hand, I thought that you were looking at it very intently. Come, Valentine, answer me ; or, if your attention is still distracted, I will remove the mirror to another part of the room, where it will no longer attract your eyes."

"Do nothing of the sort, monsieur ! " cried Valentine, beside herself with dread. "What do you want me to answer ? what do you demand of me ? what do you order me to do ? "

"I order you to do nothing," he replied, resuming his usual nonchalant manner ; "I entreat you to be compliant to-morrow. There will be a long and tedious matter of business to be adjusted ; you will be called upon to consent to some necessary arrangements, and I hope that no outside influence will prevail upon you to disappoint me, not even the advice of your mirror, that adviser which women consult on every subject."

"Monsieur," said Valentine in a tone of entreaty, "I agree beforehand to whatever you choose to impose upon me, but let us go back to the château, I beg. I am very tired."

"So I see," observed Monsieur de Lansac.

He retained his seat for several minutes, however,

watching Valentine, who stood, candle in hand, awaiting in mortal dread, the end of the scene.

It occurred to him to carry his vengeance even farther than he had done ; but, as he recalled the profession of faith he had heard Bénédict make a short time before, he very wisely concluded that that young madman was quite capable of murdering him ; so he rose at last and left the pavilion with Valentine. She, with useless dissimulation, ostentatiously locked the door of the pavilion with great care.

"That is a very wise precaution," remarked Monsieur de Lansac, caustically, "especially as the windows are so arranged as to enable anyone who finds the door locked to go in and out with perfect ease."

This last observation convinced Valentine at last of her real situation with respect to her husband.

XXXIV

The next day, she had hardly risen when the count and Monsieur Grapp sought admission to her apartments. They brought a bundle of papers.

"Read them, madame," said Monsieur de Lansac, as he saw that she took up the pen mechanically to sign them.

She glanced up at him, and the color left her cheeks ; his expression was so imperious, his smile so scornful, that she signed them all hastily, and said as she handed them back to him :

"You see, monsieur, that I have confidence in you,

and do not look to see whether appearances are against you."

"I understand, madame," rejoined Lansac, handing the papers to Monsieur Grapp.

At that moment he was so happy and light-hearted at being rid of that debt, to which he owed ten years of annoyance and persecution, that he had a feeling of something like gratitude for his wife, and kissed her hand, saying with an almost sincere air:

"One good turn deserves another, madame."

That same evening he informed her that he was obliged to leave for Paris with Monsieur Grapp on the following day, but that he should not return to his post without saying good-bye to her and consulting her as to her own plans, which, he said, he should never oppose.

He went to bed, overjoyed to be rid of his debt and his wife.

Valentine, when she was left alone at night, reflected calmly on the events of those three days. Until then, terror had made her incapable of considering her situation; now that everything was amicably arranged, she was able to view it understandingly. But the irreparable step she had taken in signing those papers did not occupy her thoughts for an instant; she could find in her heart no other feeling than profound consternation at the thought that she was ruined forever in the estimation of her husband. That humiliation was so painful to her that it absorbed every other feeling.

Hoping to find a little peace of mind in prayer, she shut herself up in her oratory; but even then, accustomed as she was to mingle thoughts of Bénédict with all her aspirations toward heaven, she was horrified to find his image no longer so pure in her mind. The memory of the preceding night, of that tempestuous interview, every word of which, overheard doubtless by Monsieur de Lansac, brought the flush of shame to Valentine's cheek, the sensation of that kiss, which still burned on her lips, her terror, her remorse, her agitation as she recalled even the most trivial details of that scene, all admonished her that it was time to turn back if she did not wish to fall into an abyss. Thus far her overweening trust in his strength had sustained her; but a moment sufficed to show her how weak the human will is. Fifteen months of unrestraint and confidence had not made Bénédict such a stoic that a single moment had not swept away the fruit of painfully acquired, slowly gathered, rashly vaunted virtue. Valentine could not close her eyes to the fact that the love she inspired was not the love of the angels for the Lord, but an earthly, passionate, violent love, a tempest likely to carry everything before it.

She had no sooner descended thus into the recesses of her conscience, than her former piety, stern and terrifying, tormented her with repentance and dread. She passed the whole night in torture; she tried in vain to sleep. At last, toward daybreak, intensely excited by her suffering, she determined upon a sublime and romantic project, which has tempted more than one wife at the moment of committing her first error : she determined to see her husband and implore his assistance.

Terrified at what she was about to do, she was no sooner dressed and ready to leave her room than she renounced the idea, recurred to it, shrank from it again, and, after a quarter of an hour of hesitation and anguish, she summoned courage to go down to the salon and send for Monsieur de Lansac.

It was just five o'clock; the count had hoped to leave the château before his wife was awake. He flattered himself that he should in that way avoid the annoyance of more farewells and more dissimulation. So that the thought of the interview she requested vexed him beyond measure; but he could not in decency avoid it. He joined her in the salon, somewhat disturbed because he could not divine her object in wishing to see him.

The care with which Valentine closed the doors so that they might not be heard, and the agitation of her features and her voice, put the finishing touch to Monsieur de Lansac's impatience, for he felt that he had no time for a sentimental scene. His mobile eyebrows involuntarily contracted, and, when Valentine attempted to speak, she found such a cold and repellent expression on his face that she stood before him crushed and tongue-tied.

A few polite words from her husband gave her to understand that he was tired of waiting; whereupon she made a violent effort to speak, but could not express her sorrow and her shame otherwise than by sobs.

"Come, come, my dear Valentine," he said, forcing himself to assume an open and affectionate manner, "enough of this nonsense! Come, what have you to say to me? I thought that we were perfectly agreed on every point. Let us not waste time, I beg you; Grapp is waiting for me, and Grapp is pitiless."

"Very good, monsieur," said Valentine, summoning all her courage, "I will make my appeal to you in four words: take me with you."

As she spoke, she almost kneeled before the count, who fell back.

"Take you with me! you! Do you mean it, madame?"

"I know that you despise me," cried Valentine, with the resolution of despair; "but I know that you have no right to. I swear to you, monsieur, that I am still worthy to be the wife of an honest man."

"Will you oblige me by informing me," retorted the count, speaking slowly and with ironical emphasis, "how many times you have walked *alone* at night—as you did last night, for instance—to the pavilion in the park, in the two years more or less that we have been separated?"

Valentine, realizing that she was innocent, felt that her courage increased.

"I swear to you, by God and by my honor," she said, "that last night was the first time."

"God is indulgent and a woman's honor is fragile. Try to swear by something else."

"But, monsieur," cried Valentine, grasping her husband's arm with a commanding gesture, "you heard our conversation last night; I am sure of it, I know it. And I appeal to your conscience to say if it did not prove that my madness was involuntary. Didn't you understand that, although I was guilty and hateful in my own eyes, my conduct was not defiled by the stain which a man could not forgive. Oh! you know, you know, that if it were otherwise, I should not have the effrontery to claim your protection. Oh! Evariste, do not refuse it! There is still time to save me. Do not let me succumb to my destiny; rescue me from the seduction that environs me and presses me close. See! I fly from it, I abhor it, I try to push it away; but I am a poor, weak woman, left alone, abandoned by everybody; help me! It is not too late, I tell you; I can still look you in the face. Do I blush? does my face lie? You are shrewd and penetrating; I could not deceive you so grossly. Should I dare to do it? Great God! you do not believe me! Oh! this doubt is a terrible punishment!"

As she spoke, poor Valentine, hopeless of overcoming the insulting coldness of that marble heart, fell on her knees, clasped her hands and held them up toward heaven, as if to call God to witness.

"Really," said Monsieur de Lansac, after a savage silence, "you are very lovely and very dramatic ! One must be very cruel to refuse what you ask so eloquently; but how can you expect me to expose you to the necessity of perjuring yourself anew ? Didn't you swear to your lover last night that you would never belong to any man ? "

At that crushing retort Valentine rose indignantly, and, gazing at her husband with all the lofty scorn of outraged pride, she said :

"What do you think that I came here to demand, I pray to know ? You are laboring under a strange error ; monsieur, but you certainly do not think that I knelt to you to solicit a place in your bed ? "

Monsieur de Lansac, mortally offended by the haughty aversion of that woman who was so humble a moment before, bit his bloodless lip and walked toward the door. Valentine detained him.

"So you spurn me," she said ; "you deny me the protection of your house and the safeguard of your presence ! If you could deprive me of your name, doubtless you would do so ! Oh ! this is abominable, monsieur. You talked to me yesterday about our respective duties ; how do you fulfil yours ? You see that I am on the point of rolling over a precipice from which I shrink in horror, and, when I implore you to give me your hand, you push me over with your foot. Very good ! may my sins recoil on your head ! "

"Yes, Valentine, you are right," he retorted in a sneering tone ; "your sins will recoil on my head."

He left the room, delighted with that witty retort. She still clung to him, and at that critical moment she resort-

ed to every form of entreaty, humble, touching, pa-
thetic, that a woman can devise. She was so eloquent
and so sincere that Monsieur de Lansac, surprised by her
powers of pleading, looked at her for a moment with an
expression which aroused the hope that she had moved
him. But he gently freed himself from her grasp, saying:

"All this is sublime, my dear, but it is absolutely ridiculous. You are very wrong; take a friend's advice: a
woman should never take her husband for her confessor;
that is asking of him more virtue than is consistent with
his profession. For my own part, I consider you charming; but my own life is too busy for me to undertake to
cure you of a great passion. Indeed, I could never be so
conceited as to hope to succeed. I have done enough for
you, it seems to me, by closing my eyes; you have
opened them by force. That being so, I must run
away, for my position in relation to you here is intolerable, and we could not look at each other without
laughing."

"Without laughing, monsieur! laughing!" she exclaimed with justifiable wrath.

"Adieu, Valentine," he continued; "I have had too
much experience, I confess, to blow my brains out for
an infidelity, but I have too much sense to care to serve
as chaperon to such an excitable brain as yours. For the
same reason I am none too anxious to have you break
this *liaison,* which has to you all the romantic beauty
of a first love. The second would be more rapid, the
third——"

"You insult me," said Valentine, with a disheartened
air; "but God will protect me. Adieu, monsieur. I
thank you for this harsh lesson; I will try to profit by
it."

They bowed to each other, and a quarter of an hour later, as Bénédict and Valentin were walking along the highroad, they saw the post-chaise pass which bore the nobleman and the usurer Parisward.

XXXV

Valentine, terrified and at the same time mortally offended by her husband's insulting prophecies, went to her room to devour her tears and her shame. More than ever alarmed by the consequences of an error which society punishes with such scorn, Valentine, being accustomed to regard public opinion with religious respect, looked with horror upon her mistakes and imprudence. Her mind dwelt constantly upon the plan of flying from the perils of her situation. She sought means of resistance from without, for she no longer found any such in herself, and the dread of yielding took away her last remaining strength. She complained bitterly of her destiny for depriving her of all help, all protection.

"Alas!" she said, "my husband spurns me, my mother cannot understand me, my sister dares not do anything; who will stop me on this slope which is so steep that I cannot stop myself?"

Brought up to shine in society, and according to its principles, Valentine could not find anywhere in society the support which she was entitled to expect from it in return for her sacrifices. If she had not possessed the inestimable treasure of faith, she would undoubtedly, in her despair, have trampled on all the precepts of her youth. But her religious belief sustained and encouraged all her other beliefs.

She did not feel strong enough to see Bénédict that evening; so she did not advise him of her husband's departure, and flattered herself that he would not know of it. She wrote a note to Louise, asking her to come to the pavilion at the usual time.

But they had hardly exchanged greetings when Mademoiselle Beaujon sent Catherine to the small park, to inform Valentine that her grandmother was seriously ill, and was asking for her.

The old marchioness had taken a cup of chocolate in the morning; her weakened organs refused to digest it, and she was suffering from a violent attack of indigestion and fever. The old doctor, Monsieur Faure, considered her situation very dangerous.

Valentine was attending to her wants with affectionate zeal when the marchioness suddenly sat up in bed, and, with a distinctness of speech and expression which she had not shown for a long time, requested to be left alone with her granddaughter. All who were in the room at once withdrew, with the exception of La Beaujon, who could not believe that the dismissal extended to her. But the old marchioness, suddenly recovering, by virtue of a miraculous revolution wrought by the fever, her keenness of perception and freedom of will, imperiously ordered her to leave the room.

"Valentine," she said to her granddaughter when they were alone, "I have a favor to ask of you. I have been imploring La Beaujon to do it for a long time, but she confuses my mind by her replies; you will do it, I am sure."

"O grandmamma!" cried Valentine, kneeling beside her bed, "tell me what it is—command me."

"Well, my child," said the marchioness, leaning toward her and lowering her voice, "I don't want to die without seeing your sister."

Valentine sprang eagerly to her feet and ran to a bell.

"Oh! that can be soon arranged," she said joyfully; "she isn't far away. How happy she will be, dear grandma! Her kisses will restore you to life and health!"

Valentine bade Catherine go to fetch Louise, who was still at the pavilion.

"That is not all," said the marchioness; "I would like to see her son too."

Valentin had just arrived at the small park when Catherine appeared. He had been sent by Bénédict, who was anxious about Valentine, and dared not appear in her presence without orders from her. In a few moments, Louise and her son were ushered into their grandmother's chamber.

Louise, abandoned by that woman long ago with unfeeling selfishness, had succeeded in forgetting her; but when she saw her on her deathbed, haggard and decrepit; when she saw the features of her whose indulgent affection had kept watch, whether well or ill, over her early years of innocence and happiness, she was conscious of a reawakening of that inextinguishable sentiment of respect and love which is a part of the first affections of life. She threw herself into her grandmother's arms, and her tears, the source of which she believed to be dry, flowed freely on the breast of her who had rocked her to sleep in infancy.

The old woman likewise was very deeply moved at the sight of Louise, once so full of life and so rich in youth, health and passion, now so fragile and melancholy. She expressed her feelings with a fervor which

was as it were the last gleam of that ineffable love with
which heaven has endowed woman in her rôle of mother.
She asked forgiveness for her neglect with a warmth
which called forth sobs of gratitude from her grand-
daughters; then she embraced Valentin in her lean
arms, and went into ecstasies over his beauty, his grace,
his resemblance to Valentine. They both resembled the
Comte de Raimbault, the marchioness's youngest son.
She also discovered in them some of the features of her
husband. How can the sacred ties of family be shattered and forgotten on earth ? What has more power over
the human heart than a type of beauty handed down as an
heirloom by several generations of loved children ? What
a bond of affection is that which epitomizes memory and
hope ! What an imperious influence is that of one whose
glance revives a whole past of love and regret, a life
which you thought extinct, but whose intense emotions
you find renewed in a child's smile !

But soon the marchioness's emotion seemed to fade
away, whether because it had hastened the exhaustion of
her faculties, or because her natural fickleness needed to
reassert itself. She bade Louise sit on her bed, Valentine at the foot and Valentin by her pillow. She talked
to them wittily and cheerfully, and with as much ease of
manner as if she had parted from them the day before.
She asked Valentin many questions concerning his
studies, his tastes, his dreams of the future.

In vain did her granddaughter urge that she would tire
herself by talking so long. They noticed that her ideas
gradually became confused. Her memory failed her; the
extraordinary intelligence which she had temporarily recovered gave way to vague and effusive reminiscences,
to confused thoughts; her cheeks, burning with fever,
turned purple; her speech became thick. The doctor

was sent for and administered a sedative. It was no longer needed; they saw that she was rapidly sinking.

Suddenly she raised her head on her pillow, called Valentine again, and motioned to the others to retire to the end of the room.

"Here is an idea that has just occurred to me," she whispered. "I knew that I had forgotten something, and I did not want to die without telling you of it. I know many secrets which I pretend not to know. There is one which you haven't confided to me, Valentine, but I guessed it a long while ago: you are in love, my child."

Valentine shuddered from head to foot. Completely mastered by the mental exaltation produced by the crowding of all these events into a few days, she believed that a voice from on high was speaking to her through her dying grandmother's mouth.

"Yes, it is true," she replied, resting her burning cheek on the marchioness's icy hands; "I am very guilty. Do not curse me, but say something to encourage and save me."

"Ah! my child!" said the marchioness, trying to smile, "it isn't easy to save a young creature like you from the passions! Oh! in my last hour I can afford to be sincere. Why should I play the hypocrite with you? Could I do it for an instant before God? No, I say. It is not possible to keep from that disease while you are young. So love on, my child; that is the only good thing in life. But listen to your grandmother's last advice, and don't forget it: never take a lover who is not of your own rank."

At this point the marchioness lost the power of speech.

A few drops of her potion restored her to life for a few moments more. She bestowed a wan smile on those who stood about her, and murmured a prayer with her lips. Then she turned to Valentine.

"Tell your mother that I thank her for her kindness, and forgive her for her unkindness. For a woman of no birth she has behaved well enough toward me, after all. I didn't expect so much, I confess, from Mademoiselle Chignon."

She uttered that name with an affectation of scorn. They were the last words she spoke; and, to her mind, the most satisfying vengeance at her command, amid the sufferings of old age, was to denounce Madame de Raimbault's plebeian extraction as her greatest vice.

The loss of her grandmother, although it touched Valentine's heart, could not cause her real unhappiness. Nevertheless, in her then frame of mind, she looked upon it as a fresh blow of her fatal destiny, and took pleasure in saying to herself that all her natural protectors were taken from her, as if designedly, at the time when they were most necessary to her.

Losing heart more and more over her plight, Valentine determined to write to her mother and beg her to come to her rescue, and resolved that she would not see Bénédict again until she had consummated that sacrifice. And so, after performing the last duties for the marchioness, she went to her own room, locked the door, saying that she was ill and did not wish to see anyone, and wrote to the Comtesse de Raimbault.

Although Monsieur de Lansac's harshness might well have sickened her of pouring out her grief into an insensible heart, she confessed herself humbly before that arrogant woman who had made her tremble all her life. But Valentine, exasperated by suffering, had the courage, born of despair, to undertake anything. She no longer used her reason; one dread overshadowed every other.

To escape her love she would have walked upon the sea. Moreover, when everything failed her at once, an additional pang was less terrifying to her than at ordinary times. She felt that she could be strong and pitiless toward herself, provided that she had not to struggle with Bénédict; the maledictions of the whole world had less terror for her than the idea of facing her lover's grief.

So she confessed to her mother that she loved *another man than her husband.* That was all the information she gave her with respect to Bénédict; but she painted with glowing colors the state of her mind and her need of some one to lean upon. She implored her to write for her to join her; for the countess always exacted such absolute submission from her dependents that Valentine would not have dared to join her without her permission.

In default of affection, Madame de Raimbault might, perhaps, have received her daughter's confidence with a thrill of vanity; perhaps she would have granted her request, had not the same mail brought her another letter from the château of Raimbault, which she read first; it was a formal denunciation from Mademoiselle Beaujon.

That old maid, consumed by jealousy to see the marchioness surrounded by a new family in her last moments, was particularly enraged by the gift of certain antique jewels to Louise by her grandmother as a pledge of renewed affection. She considered herself defrauded by that gift, and, having no legal ground of complaint, she determined at all events to be revenged; so she wrote at once to the countess, on the pretext of informing her of her mother-in-law's death, and took advantage of the opportunity to disclose Valentine's intimacy with Louise, the *scandalous* installation of Valentin in the neighborhood, Madame de Lansac's share in his education, and all that she was pleased to call the *mysteries of the pavilion ;* for she did not confine herself to betraying the friendship of the sisters ; she cast aspersions upon their relations with the farmer's nephew, *BénédictLhéry the peasant;* she described Louise as a scheming creature who shamelessly countenanced that clodhopper's guilty union with her sister ; she added that it was very late, doubtless, to remedy all this, for the *commerce* had been going on for fifteen long months. She ended by declaring that Monsieur de Lansac had certainly made some unpleasant discoveries in that direction, for he had gone away after three days, without having any relations with his wife.

Having thus given vent to her hatred, La Beaujon left Raimbault, rich by reason of the liberality of the family, and revenged for Valentine's kindness to her.

These two letters threw the countess into a terrible rage. She would have had less confidence in the duenna's disclosures had not her daughter's confession, arriving at the same time, seemed a sufficient confirmation of them. Thus Valentine lost all the merit of that naïve confession. Madame de Raimbault saw in her simply a miserable creature whose honor was irretrievably stained, and who implored her mother's assistance because she was threatened by her husband's vengeance. This opinion was only too fully confirmed by the rumors which reached her ears from the province every day. The pure happiness of two lovers can never take shelter in rural silence and obscurity without arousing the jealousy and hatred of all who vegetate stupidly in small provincial towns. The spectacle of another person's happiness consumes and withers the provincial. The only thing which enables him to endure his narrow,

wretched life, is the pleasure of stripping his neighbor's
life of all love and poetry.

Moreover, Madame de Raimbault, who had been surprised at Monsieur de Lansac's return to Paris, saw him,
questioned him, and, although she could obtain no response, understood clearly enough, from his skilfully
managed silence and the dignity of his evasive manner,
that all ties of affection and confidence between his wife
and himself were broken.

Thereupon she wrote Valentine a crushing reply: ad-
vised her to seek shelter thenceforth in the protection of
that sister whose character was as black as her own, declared that she abandoned her to her degradation, and
ended by almost cursing her.

It was true enough that Madame de Raimbault was
distressed to see her daughter's life ruined forever; but
there was more wounded pride than maternal affection
in her grief. That this was so was proved by the fact
that anger triumphed over pity, and she started for Eng-
land, with the object, she said, of forgetting her griefs,
but really to indulge freely in dissipation without running
the risk of meeting people who knew of her domestic
troubles, and might be disposed to criticize her conduct
on that occasion.

Such was the result of the unhappy Valentine's last
efforts. Her mother's reply caused her such bitter pain
that it overshadowed all her thoughts. She knelt in her
oratory, and her affliction found vent in heart-breaking sobs. Then, in the midst of that terrible bitterness
of spirit, she felt the need of that trust and hope which
are the sustenance of pious souls; she felt, above all, the
craving for affection which consumes the youthful heart.
Hated, misunderstood, spurned on all sides, there still
remained one place of refuge: Bénédict's heart. Was

that calumniated love so culpable after all ?   Into what crime had it led her ?

"O my God!" she cried fervently; "Thou who alone seest the purity of my desires, who alone knowest the innocence of my conduct—wilt not Thou protect me? Wilt Thou also turn Thy face from me ?   Is this love of mine so blameworthy ? "

As she leaned over her *prie-Dieu,* she noticed an object which she had placed upon it as the votive offering of a lover's superstition ; it was the blood-stained handkerchief which Catherine had brought from the house in the ravine on the day of Bénédict's suicide, and which Valentine had at once claimed on learning of the incident. At that crisis the sight of the blood shed for her sake was like a triumphant declaration of love and self-sacrificing devotion, in reply to the insults which she had received from all sides.   She seized the handkerchief, put it to her lips, and, plunged in a sea of anguish and rapture, she knelt for a long while, motionless and wrapt in meditation, opening her heart to her trust in Bénédict, and feeling the ardent life which had consumed her being a few days before begin to flow again in her veins.

XXXVI

Bénédict had been very unhappy for a week past. That alleged sickness, of which Louise could give him no details, caused him the keenest anxiety.   Such is the selfishness of love that he chose rather to believe that Valentine was ill than to suspect her of a purpose to avoid him. On that evening, impelled by a vague hope, he prowled about the park for a long time. At last, having obtained possession of a key which was usually in Valentine's keeping, he determined to go to the pavilion. All was silence and solitude in that retreat, lately so filled with joy and confidence and affection. His heart sank ; he went out and ventured into the garden of the château. Since the old marchioness's death, Valentine had dispensed with several servants. So that there were few people in the château. Bénédict met no one as he approached.

Valentine's oratory was in a small tower in the most deserted part of the building. A small spiral staircase, a relic of the old buildings on whose ruins the new manor-house had been built, led down from her bedroom to the oratory, and from the oratory to the garden. The window, which was arched at the top and surmounted by ornamentation in the Italian Renaissance style, overlooked a clump of trees whose tops were at that moment reddened by the rays of the setting sun. The day had been extremely hot ; the lightning flashed silently on the violet horizon ; the atmosphere was rare, and seemed charged with electricity. It was one of those summer evenings when one finds difficulty in breathing, when one's nerves are in a state of extraordinary tension, when one suffers from a nameless pain which one longs to be able to relieve by tears.

When he reached the foot of the clump of trees in front of the tower, Valentine glanced uneasily at the window of the oratory. The stained glass blazed in the sunlight. Bénédict had been trying for a long time to discover something behind that gleaming mirror, when it was suddenly opened by a woman's hand, and a face appeared and disappeared.

Bénédict climbed an old yew, and hidden by its droop-
ing black branches, reached a sufficient height from the
ground to look through the window. He distinctly saw
Valentine on her knees, with her fair hair half-loosened,
falling carelessly over her shoulders and gilded by the last
beams of the sun. Her cheeks were flushed, her uncon-
strained attitude was instinct with grace and innocence.
She was pressing against her heart and kissing passionately the blood-stained handkerchief for which Bénédict
had searched so anxiously after his suicide, and which
he recognized at once in her hands.

Thereupon, Bénédict, after a fearful glance about the
deserted garden, having but to put out his hand to reach
the window, could not resist the temptation. He grasped
the carved balustrade, and swung himself off, at the risk
of his life, from the branch on which he sat.

Valentine shrieked at the sight of a dark figure against
the brilliant sky; but, when she recognized him, her
terror changed its character.

"O heaven!" she exclaimed, "do you dare to pursue
me even here?"

"Do you turn me away?" rejoined Bénédict. "Look!
I am only twenty feet from the ground; tell me to let
go the balustrade, and I obey."

"Great God!" cried Valentine, terrified beyond words
when she realized his position, "come in, come in!
you frighten me to death."

He jumped into the oratory, and Valentine, who had
seized his coat lest he should fall, embraced him in an
involuntary outburst of joy when she saw that he was
safe.

At that moment everything was forgotten, both the
resistance which Valentine had meditated so long, and
the reproaches which Bénédict had resolved to heap upon

her. That week of separation, under such melancholy conditions, had seemed to them like a century. The young man yielded to his frantic joy, straining Valentine to his heart, for he had feared to find her dying, and he found her lovelier and more loving than ever.

At last he remembered all that he had suffered during their separation; he accused her of being false and cruel.

"Listen," said Valentine, excitedly, leading him before her Madonna. "I took an oath never to see you again, because I imagined that I could not do it without crime. Now, swear to me that you will help me to be true to my duty; swear it before God—before this image, the emblem of purity; reassure me, give me back the confidence I have lost. Bénédict, you are loyal at heart, you would not do a sacrilegious thing. Tell me, do you feel stronger than I am ? "

Bénédict turned pale, and recoiled from her in dismay. He had a truly chivalrous sense of honor, and he preferred the misery of losing Valentine to the crime of betraying her.

"Why, you are calling upon me to make a vow, Valentine ! " he cried. "Do you think that I have the heroism to make it or to keep it, unprepared as I am ? "

"What ! have you not been prepared for fifteen months ? Those solemn promises you made one evening in my sister's presence, and which you have kept so loyally thus far——"

"Yes, Valentine, I have had the courage to do it, and, perhaps, I shall have the courage to renew those promises. But do not ask me to do anything to-day; I am too excited; my oaths would be worth nothing. All that has happened lately has banished the calmness which my heart owed to you. And then, Valentine, imprudent creature ! you tell me that you are afraid ! Why do you tell me that? I should not have had the presumption to think it. You were strong when I thought you were strong; why ask of me now the strength which you have not? Where shall I seek it? Adieu; I will go to prepare myself to obey you. But swear to me that you will not avoid me any more, for you see the effect of such treatment on me; it kills me; it does away with all the results of my past virtue."

"Very well, Bénédict, I swear it, for it is impossible for me not to trust you when I see you and hear your voice. Good-night; to-morrow we will all meet at the pavilion."

She offered him her hand; Bénédict hesitated to touch it. He trembled convulsively. He had barely touched his lips to it when a sort of frenzy swept him off his feet. He strained Valentine to his heart, then pushed her away. At last the violent restraint which he imposed upon his fiery nature having exhausted his strength, he wrung his hands frantically and dropped almost lifeless on the steps of the prie-Dieu.

"Have pity on me," he cried in anguish, "Thou who didst create Valentine. Recall my soul to Thee; extinguish this consuming breath which scorches my breast and makes life a torture; grant me the blessed boon of death."

He was so pale, such a world of suffering was written in his dull eyes, that Valentine believed that he was really at the point of death. She threw herself on her knees beside him, embraced him frantically, covered him with kisses and tears, and fell exhausted in his arms with stifled cries, when she saw him sink to the floor and throw back his pallid, lifeless face.

At last she recalled him to consciousness, but he was so weak, so prostrated, that she could not send him away in that condition. Recovering all her energy with the necessity of reviving him, she lifted him and dragged him to her bedroom, where she hastened to brew some tea.

At that moment, the kind-hearted and gentle Valentine became the active, efficient housewife, whose life was devoted to the welfare of others. The panic terror of a passionately loving woman gave place to the solicitude of devoted affection. She forgot where she had taken Bénédict, and what must be taking place in his mind, to think only of attending to his physical needs. The imprudent girl paid no heed to the wild and sombre expression with which he looked about that room which he had entered but once before, at that bed where he had watched her sleeping one whole night, at all that furniture which recalled the most tempestuous crisis and the most profound emotion of his life. Sitting in an easy-chair, with contracted eyebrows and arms hanging at his side, he watched her as she hovered about him mechanically, with no definite idea what she was doing.

When she brought him the calming beverage which she had prepared for him, he rose abruptly and glared at her with such a strange, wild expression that she dropped the cup and stepped back in alarm.

Bénédict threw his arms about her and prevented her from running away.

"Let me go," she cried; "the tea has burned me horribly."

She did, in fact, limp as she walked away. He threw himself on his knees and kissed her tiny foot, which was slightly reddened, through the transparent stocking; then almost swooned again; and Valentine, vanquished by pity, by love, and, above all, by fear, did not again tear herself from his arms when he returned to life.

It was a fatal moment, sure to come sooner or later. It is most presumptuous to hope to overcome a passion, when two people see each other every day, and are only twenty years old.

For the first few days, Valentine, swept far beyond and away from her customary field of reflection, did not think of repentance; but the inevitable moment came, and it was unspeakably terrible.

Then Bénédict bitterly deplored a happiness for which he must pay so dear. His sin received the severest punishment that could have been inflicted upon it; he saw Valentine weep and pine away with grief.

As they were both too virtuous to fall asleep unheeding in joys which they had reprobated and fought against so long, their life became a painful burden. Valentine was not capable of bargaining with her conscience. Bénédict loved her too passionately to enjoy a happiness which Valentine no longer shared. Both were too weak, too devoted to each other, too completely under the domination of the impetuous sensations of youth, to force themselves to renounce those remorse-laden joys. They parted with despair at their hearts; they met again with delirious joy. Their life was a perpetual combat, a storm constantly renewed, a bliss without bounds, and a hell from which there was no issue.

Bénédict accused Valentine of loving him too little—not enough to prefer him to her honor, to her self-esteem; of being incapable of perfect self-sacrifice; and when these reproaches had driven Valentine to a new display of weakness, when he saw her weeping with despair and yielding to ghastly terrors, he abhorred the happiness he had enjoyed; he would have given all his blood to wash away the memory of it. At such times he would offer to fly from her; he would swear that he would endure life in exile ; but she no longer had the strength to send him away.

"Then I should be left alone, given over to my grief!" she would say. "No, do not leave me so, it would kill me ; I cannot live now except by forgetting. As soon as I return to myself, I feel that I am lost; my wits wander, and I should be quite capable of crowning my crimes by suicide. Your presence gives me, at all events, strength to live in forgetfulness of my duties. Let us wait a little longer, and hope and pray. When I am alone, I cannot pray any more ; but with you, hope returns. I imagine that some day I shall find enough courage in my heart to love you without crime. Perhaps you will give me that courage, for you are stronger than I ; I am the one who is forever sending you away and calling you back."

And then would come a wave of overwhelming passion, when hell and its terrors simply made Valentine smile. At such times she was not merely an unbeliever—she was fanatical in her impiety.

"Come," she would say, "let us defy everything. What does it matter if I destroy my soul? Let us be happy on earth. Will an eternity of torment be too high a price to pay for the joy of being yours? I wish I had something more to sacrifice to you. Tell me, don't you know of something I can do to pay my debt to you?"

"Oh! if you were always like this!" Bénédict would exclaim.

Thus Valentine, naturally calm and reserved, had become passionate to the point of delirium as the result of a combination of pitiless misfortunes and seductions which had developed within her unsuspected powers of resisting and of loving. The longer and more resolute her resistance, the more violent her fall. The more strength she had mustered to combat passion, the more elements of force and duration did passion find in her.

An event which Valentine had, so to speak, forgotten to anticipate, turned her mind for a moment to other concerns. Monsieur Grapp made his appearance, armed with documents according to whose tenor the château and domain of Raimbault belonged to him, with the exception of a parcel worth about twenty thousand francs, which constituted Madame de Lansac's entire fortune. The estates were immediately offered for sale to the highest bidder, and Valentine was notified to vacate Monsieur Grapp's house within twenty-four hours.

This was a thunderbolt to those who loved her. Never had a heaven-sent disaster caused such consternation in the province. But Valentine felt her misfortune less keenly than she would have done under other circumstances. She reflected in her secret heart that, as Monsieur de Lansac was base enough to make her pay for her dishonor with money, she was out of his debt, so to speak. She regretted only the pavilion, the scene of a happiness that was gone forever ; and, having removed the few articles of furniture which she was allowed to take, she accepted temporarily the hospitality of the farm of Grangeneuve, which the Lhérys, by virtue of an arrangement with Grapp, were soon to leave.

XXXVII

Amid the excitement caused by this reversal of her
fortunes, Valentine passed several days without seeing
Bénédict. The courage with which she endured the blow
of financial ruin emboldened her to some extent, and she
found herself sufficiently tranquil in mind to renew her
efforts to be free.

She wrote to Bénédict :

"I beg you not to try to see me during the next fortnight, which I am to pass with the Lhérys. As you have
not been to the farm since Athénaïs was married, you
could not appear there now without advertising our relations. However earnestly Madame Lhéry may urge you,
regretting as she still does your apparent drifting apart, refuse, unless you wish to make me very unhappy. Adieu ;
I do not know what I am going to do ; I have a fortnight
to consider. When I have decided upon my future course,
I will let you know, and you will help me to follow it,
whatever it may be.

"V."

This note alarmed Bénédict beyond words. He fancied
that he could read between the lines the same dread
decision which he had made Valentine abandon so many
times, but which might, perhaps, become inevitable, as
the result of so much anguish of mind. Prostrated,
crushed beneath the weight of so tempestuous a life and
so dismal a future, he gave way to discouragement. He

no longer had even the prospect of suicide to sustain him.
In his conscience he was under a binding obligation to
Louise's son ; moreover, Valentine was too unhappy for
him to think of dealing her that terrible blow on top of
all those that fate had dealt her.   Now that she was ruined, abandoned, heart-broken with grief and remorse,
it was his duty to live, to compel himself to be useful to
her, and to watch over her, whether she would or not.

Louise had conquered at last the foolish passion which
had tormented her so long.   Her connection with Bénédict, strengthened and purified by her son's presence,
had become tranquil and venerable.   Her violent disposition had become softened as the result of that great
inward victory.   It is true that she was entirely ignorant
of the calamity of Bénédict's too great happiness with
Valentine.   She strove to console her sister for her loss
of fortune, not knowing that she had met with an irreparable loss—that of her own esteem.   So she passed
all her time with her, and did not know what fresh anx-
ieties were weighing upon Bénédict.

The youthful and sprightly Athénaïs had suffered personally on account of these recent events ; in the first
place, because she was sincerely attached to Valentine ;
and, also, because the closing of the pavilion, with the
consequent interruption of their pleasant meetings in the
evening, and the sale of the park, oppressed her heart
with an indefinable sense of deprivation.   She was surprised to find that she could not think of them without a
sigh ; she was distressed by the length of the days and
the tedium of the evenings.

Evidently something of importance was missing from
her life, and Athénaïs, who had just entered her eighteenth year, questioned herself ingenuously on that subject, but dared not answer her own questions.   In all

her dreams, however, the noble blond head of young
Valentin appeared amid the flower-laden shrubs. She
imagined that he chased her over the fields; she saw
him, tall and slender and agile as a chamois, jump the
hedges to overtake her; she frolicked with him; she
joined in his fresh, joyous laughter; then she would
blush herself as she saw the blood rise to that innocent
brow, as she felt that smooth white hand burn when it
touched hers, as she surprised a sigh and melancholy
glance from that child whom she could not distrust. Unconsciously she felt all the shy tremors of a dawning
love. And when she woke, when she found Pierre
Blutty beside her, that boorish peasant, so brutal in love,
so utterly without refinement and charm, she felt her
heart sink within her, and the tears trembled on her eyelids. Athénaïs had always loved the aristocracy; ele-
vated language, even when it was beyond the scope of
her intelligence, seemed to her the most irresistible form
of seduction. When Bénédict talked of the arts or the
sciences, she listened to him with admiration, because
she did not understand him. It was his superiority in
that respect to which he owed the fascination he had for
a long time had for her. Since she had made up her mind
to give him up, young Valentin, with his gentleness, his
self-restraint, the feudal dignity of his handsome profile,
his aptitude in grasping abstract branches of knowledge,
had become in her eyes the type of charming and perfect manhood. She had long been in the habit of ex-
pressing openly her predilection for him, but she was beginning to have some hesitation in doing so, for Valentin
was growing in most alarming fashion; his glance was
becoming as penetrating as flame, and the young farmer's wife felt that the blood rushed to her face whenever
she mentioned his name.

Thus the deserted pavilion was a subject of involuntary longing and regret. To be sure, Valentin came sometimes to see his mother and aunt; but the house in the ravine was so far from the farm-house that he could not make that expedition often without considerable interference with his studies, and the first week seemed mortally long to Madame Blutty.

The future was very uncertain. Louise talked of returning to Paris with her son and Valentine. At other times the sisters formed the plan of buying a peasant's small cottage and living in it alone. Blutty, who was still jealous of Bénédict, although he had little reason to be, talked of taking his wife to La Marche, where he owned some property. It was necessary to separate Athénaïs and Valentin by some means or other; she could no longer think of him without regrets which cast a bright light into the recesses of her heart.

One day, the pleasure which she took in walking led her to a meadow a long distance away, which, like a thrifty farmer's wife, she wished to inspect. This meadow adjoined Vavray wood, and the ravine was not far away, on the edge of the wood. Now, it happened that Bénédict and Valentin were walking in that neighborhood; that the younger man detected the lithe and well-proportioned figure of Madame Blutty against the dark green; and that he climbed the hedge to join her without consulting his mentor. Bénédict joined them, and they talked together for some time.

Thereupon Athénaïs, who still felt for her cousin a remnant of that deep interest which makes a woman's friendship so considerate and so grateful, noticed the ravages which mental distress had wrought in him, especially within the last few days. The alteration of his features alarmed her, and, putting her arm through his, she insisted upon his telling her frankly the cause of his distress and the state of his health. As she had some suspicion of the truth, she had the delicacy to send Valentin for her umbrella which she had left under a tree.

Bénédict had been forcing himself for so long a time to conceal his suffering from all eyes, that his cousin's affectionate manner was very sweet to him. He could not resist the longing to pour out his heart, and he told her of his attachment to Valentine, his unhappiness in being separated from her, and ended by confessing that he was driven to despair by the fear of losing her forever.

Athénaïs, in her innocence, did not choose to see, in that passion of which she had long been aware, the dubious side, which would have caused a more prudent person to recoil. In the sincerity of her heart, she did not deem Valentine capable of forgetting her principles, and she believed that love to be as pure as her own for Valentin. So she yielded to her sympathetic impulses, and promised that she would urge Valentine to adopt a less harsh course of action than she contemplated.

"I do not know whether I shall succeed," she said to him with that ingenuous frankness which made her attractive despite her faults; "but I promise you that I will work as hard for your happiness as for my own. I hope that I may be able to prove to you that I have never ceased to be your friend!"

Bénédict was touched by this outburst of whole-souled affection, and kissed her hand gratefully. Valentin, who was just returning with the umbrella, saw that kiss, and turned so red and so pale in quick succession that Athénaïs noticed it, and was herself confused; but she tried to assume a serious and self-important manner, and said to Bénédict:

"We must meet again to settle this momentous affair. As I am frivolous and awkward, I shall need your guidance. I will come here to walk to-morrow and tell you how I have succeeded. Then we will consider the best way to obtain more. Until to-morrow!"

And she walked rapidly away with a friendly nod to her cousin; but she was not looking at him when she said the last words.

The next day they had another conference. While Valentin walked on ahead along the wooded path, Athénaïs told her cousin of the failure of her efforts. She had found Valentine absolutely impenetrable. However, she was not discouraged, and for a whole week she tried with all her power to bring the lovers together.

The negotiations did not advance very rapidly. Perhaps the young ambassadress was not sorry to multiply the conferences in the meadow. During the pauses in her conversation with Bénédict, Valentin would join them and find consolation for his exclusion from the secret in a smile and glance which were worth more than a thousand words. And then, when the cousins had said all that they had to say, Valentin would chase butterflies with Athénaïs, and, as they romped together, would succeed in touching her hand, or brushing against her hair, or stealing a ribbon or a flower. At seventeen, one is still at an age to enjoy Dorat's poetry.

Bénédict, even although his cousin brought him no good news, was happy to hear her talk of Valentine. He questioned Athénaïs as to her most trivial acts; he made her repeat their conversations word for word. In short, he yielded to the pleasure of being comforted and encouraged, having no presentiment of the deplorable consequences which his innocent relations with his cousin were destined to have.

Meanwhile, Pierre Blutty had gone to La Marche to look after some private business. At the end of the week he returned by way of a village where a fair was being held, and where he stopped for twenty-four hours. There he met his friend Simonneau.

By an unlucky accident, Simonneau had recently become enamored of a buxom herder of geese, whose cottage was on a sunken road within a few steps of the meadow where Bénédict and Athénaïs met. He went there every day, and, from the little round window of a grain-loft, which served as the temple of his rustic amours, he saw Athénaïs and Bénédict strolling back and forth along the path, arm-in-arm. He did not fail to ascribe a criminal purpose to those meetings. He remembered Mademoiselle Lhéry's former love for her cousin; he knew how jealous Pierre Blutty was, and it never occurred to him that a woman could meet a man and talk confidentially with him, unless impelled by sentiments and purposes at odds with marital fidelity.

With his sturdy good sense he determined to warn Pierre Blutty, and he did not fail to do so. The farmer flew into a terrible rage, and would have set off at once to murder his wife and his rival. Simonneau pacified him to some extent by reminding him that perhaps the wrong done him was not so great at it might be.

"On the word of Simonneau," he said, "I have hardly seen them without Mademoiselle Louise's boy—thirty or forty yards away. He could see them, so I didn't think they could do any great harm, but they could say what they wanted to; for when he went near them they took pains to send him away. Your wife would pat him gently on the cheek, and tell him to run off, so that they could talk at their ease, I suppose."

"See the impudence of the hussy!" cried Blutty,

gnawing his nails. "Ah! I might have known it would
end like this. That popinjay! he gulls all the women
with his soft talk. He paid court to Mademoiselle Louise
and my wife at the same time, before we were married.
Since then, everybody knows that he's had the cheek to
court Madame de Lansac. But she's an honest and re-
spectable woman. She refused to see him, and swore
that he should never set foot in the farm-house while
she was there. I know that for a fact! I heard her
tell her sister so the day she came to live at our house.
And now, for lack of something better, my gentleman
condescends to come back to my wife! For that matter,
who can tell me that they haven't had an understanding
for a long while? Why was she so set on going to the
château every evening these last few months, against
my will? It was because she saw him there. And
there's a damned park there where they walked together
all they wanted to. Twenty thousand devils! I'll have
my revenge! Now that the park's closed, they meet in
the woods; that's clear enough! Do I know what goes
on at night? But damnation! here I am; we'll see
whether Satan will protect his skin this time. I will
show them that Pierre Blutty isn't to be insulted with
impunity."

"If you want anybody to help you, you know I'm
your man," rejoined Simonneau.

The two friends shook hands and walked in the direction of the farm together.

Meanwhile, Athénaïs had pleaded so warmly for Bénédict; she had urged the cause of love with such ingenuous zeal; above all, she had depicted so eloquently his
melancholy, his broken health, his pallor, his wearing
anxiety; she had described him as so submissive and so
fearful of offending her, that poor, weak Valentine had

allowed her resolution to be shaken. Indeed, in her
secret heart, she had been very glad to have him solicit
his recall, for to her, likewise, the days seemed very long
and her resolution very cruel.

Ere long the only subject of discussion was the difficulty of meeting.

"I am compelled," said Valentine, "to hide from this
love as from a crime! Some enemy, whom I do not
know, but who is evidently watching me very closely,
has succeeded in making trouble between my mother
and me. I am trying now to obtain her forgiveness,
for who else is left for me to lean upon? And if I compromise myself by some fresh imprudence, she will learn
of it, and I can no longer hope to move her. So that I
cannot go to the meadow with you."

"No, of course not," said Athénaïs; "but he might
come here."

"Can you think of such a thing?" said Valentine.
"Not only has your husband often expressed himself in
very hostile terms in regard to Bénédict's coming here,
so that his presence at the farm might cause a quarrel
in your family, but nothing could be more certain to compromise me than such a step on his part after two years
have passed since he came here. His visit would be noticed and discussed as an important event, and no one
could doubt that I was the cause of it."

"That is all very well," said Athénaïs, "but what is
to prevent his coming after dark, when he won't be seen?
It is late in the autumn and the days are short. It is
pitch dark at eight o'clock; at nine everybody is abed;
my husband, who doesn't sleep quite so soundly as the
others, is away. If Bénédict should be at the orchard
door at half-past nine, say—if I should let him in, if you
and he should talk together in the lower room an hour

or two, and then he should go home about eleven, before moonrise—just tell me what there would be so difficult and dangerous about it ? "

Valentine raised many objections. Athénaïs persisted, implored, even shed tears, and declared that her refusal would kill Bénédict. She carried the day at last. The next day, she ran off to the meadow in triumph, and carried the good news.

That same evening Bénédict, armed with his protectress's instructions, and being perfectly familiar with the premises, was admitted to the room where Valentine was, and passed two hours with her. He succeeded, during that interview, in re-establishing his empire over her. He set her mind at rest concerning the future, swore to renounce every pleasure that would cause her a pang of regret, wept with love and joy at her feet and left her, happy to see that she was calmer and more confident, after obtaining a second appointment for the next night.

But, during the next day, Blutty and Simonneau arrived at the farm. Blutty artfully concealed his rage, and watched his wife closely. She did not go to the meadow; it was no longer necessary; and, besides, she was afraid of being followed.

Blutty reconnoitred his position with all the adroitness of which he was capable ; and it is true enough that the peasant does not lack adroitness, when one of the dense chords of his organ of sensibility is set in motion. While assuming a well-feigned air of indifference, he kept his eyes and ears on the alert all day. First he heard a ploughman say to his comrade that Charmette, the great yellow watch-dog at the farm, had barked incessantly from half-past nine till midnight. Then he walked in the orchard and saw that the loose stones on top of the

wall had been disturbed in one place. But a surer indication was afforded by several marks of boot-heels in the
smooth clay of the ditch. Now, no one at the farm wore
boots; the only kinds of footwear known there were
wooden clogs and hobnailed shoes with three rows of
nails.

Thereupon, Blutty's last doubts vanished. In order to
make sure of seizing his enemy, he had to restrain his wrath
and his grief; and, toward nightfall, he kissed his wife
with much warmth, and told her he was going to pass
the night at a farm of Simonneau's half a league away.
The grape harvest was just finished; Simonneau, who
was one of the last to get in his crop, needed help that
night to watch and hold in check the fermentation in his
vats. This fable did not arouse suspicion in any mind;
Athénaïs was too conscious of her innocence to be alarmed
by her husband's plans.

So he left the farm for his friend's house, and, bran-
dishing fiercely one of the heavy iron forks used in the
country to load the hay on the wagons, he waited for
night with agonizing impatience. To give him courage
and presence of mind, Simonneau plied him with drink.

XXXVIII

The clock struck seven. It was a cold, gloomy evening. The wind howled through the thatched roof of the
cottage, and the brook, swollen by the rains of the preceding days, filled the ravine with its monotonous plaintive murmur. Bénédict was preparing to leave his young

friend, and was beginning, as on the night before, to invent a fable concerning the necessity of his going out at such an hour, when Valentin interrupted him.

"Why do you deceive me?" he said suddenly, tossing upon the table with an air of decision the book which he held in his hand. "You are going to the farm."

Bénédict, petrified with surprise, could think of nothing to reply.

"Well, my friend," said the young man, with concentrated bitterness, "go and be happy; you deserve it better than I. If anything can lessen my suffering, it is having you for a rival."

Bénédict fell from the clouds. Men have little perspicacity in making discoveries of this sort; and then, too, his own sorrow had engrossed him so entirely for a long time past that he could not well notice the irruption of love into the heart of that child whose guardian he was. Bewildered by what he had heard, he imagined that Valentin was in love with his aunt, and his blood stood still with amazement and grief.

"My friend," said Valentin, throwing himself into a chair with an air of hopeless discouragement, "I wound you, I irritate you, I grieve you, perhaps! I love you so dearly, and yet I am obliged to fight against the hatred which I feel for you sometimes! Beware of me, Bénédict; there are days when I am tempted to murder you!"

"Unhappy child!" cried Bénédict, seizing his arm roughly; "you dare to cherish such a sentiment for her whom you should respect as your mother!"

"As my mother!" he rejoined with a sad smile; "she would be a very young mother!"

"Great God!" exclaimed Bénédict in great dismay, "what will Valentine say?"

"Valentine! What does it matter to her? Indeed, why didn't she foresee what would happen? Why did she allow us to be together every evening before her eyes? and you yourself, why do you take me for a confidant and witness of your love? For you do love her; I am sure of it now. Last night I followed you; you went to the farm, and I don't imagine that you went there with so much secrecy to see my mother or my aunt. Why should you hide if you went to see them?"

"Great heaven! what do you mean?" cried Bénédict, relieved of a terrible weight. "Do you think that I am in love with my cousin?"

"Who wouldn't be?" replied the young man, with ingenuous enthusiasm.

"Come here, my boy," said Bénédict, embracing him warmly. "Can you believe a friend's word? Very good; I swear to you, on my honor, that I have never loved Athénaïs and never shall love her. Are you satisfied now?"

"Can it be true?" cried Valentin, kissing him rapturously; "but, if it is true, why are you going to the farm?"

"To attend to some business of great importance to Madame de Lansac's future," replied Bénédict, sorely embarrassed. "As I am obliged to keep out of sight to avoid meeting Blutty, with whom I am on bad terms, and who would have good reason to be offended by my presence in his house, I have to take some precautions about going to see your aunt. Her interests require all my care. It is a matter of money which you would hardly understand. Indeed, what difference does it make to you? I will tell you about it some time. Now I must go."

"It's all right," said Valentin, "I have no questions

to ask you. Your motives cannot be other than noble and generous. But let me go with you, Bénédict."

"To be sure, part of the way," he replied.

They left the house together.

"Why that gun ?" said Bénédict, seeing that Valentin had a gun on his shoulder.

"I don't know. I want to go all the way to the farm with you. That Pierre Blutty hates you, I know. If he should meet you, he would do you a bad turn. He is a cowardly brute ; let me escort you. Last night I couldn't go to sleep till you came home. I had horrible dreams ; and now that my heart is relieved of that terrible jealousy—now that I might be happy, I feel more depressed than I ever did in my life."

"I have often told you, Valentin, that you have nerves like a woman's. Poor boy! Your friendship is very sweet to me. I believe that it would make life endurable if everything else should fail me."

They walked for some time in silence ; then they resumed their conversation, which was interrupted every moment. Bénédict felt his heart swell with joy as the moment approached which was to unite him with Valentine. His young companion, whose nature was more clinging and impressionable, struggled under the weight of some indefinable presentiment. Bénédict attempted to point out to him the folly of his love for Athénaïs, and to urge him to combat that hazardous inclination. He drew a gloomy picture of the evils of the passion, and all the while his heart was beating with ardent, joyful throbs which gave the lie to his words.

"Perhaps you are right ! " said Valentin. "I believe I am destined to be unhappy. At all events, I believe it tonight ; I feel so blue and oppressed. Come home early, do you hear ? or let me go with you to the orchard."

"No, my boy, no," said Bénédict, halting beneath an old willow which stood at a bend in the road. "Go back; I will soon be with you and continue my sermon. Well, what is it?"

"You must take my gun."

"What nonsense!"

"Listen; what's that?"

It was a hoarse, funereal cry above their heads.

"It's a goatsucker," replied Bénédict. "He's hiding in the rotten trunk of this tree. Do you want a shot at him? I'll start him up."

He kicked the tree. The bird flew away in silence. Valentin took aim, but it was too dark to hit him. He disappeared, repeating his sinister cry.

"Bird of evil omen," exclaimed the boy, "I missed you! Isn't that the bird the peasants call the *bird of death?*"

"Yes," said Bénédict, indifferently; "they claim that he sings over a man's head an hour before his death. Look out! we were under the tree when he sang!"

Valentin shrugged his shoulders as if he were ashamed of his childish fears. However, he pressed his friend's hand more warmly than usual.

"Come home soon," he said.

And they parted.

Bénédict entered the orchard noiselessly, and found Valentine at the door of the house.

"I have great news for you," she said; "but let us not stay in this room; anybody who comes in may take us by surprise. Athénaïs has let me have her chamber for an hour. Come with me."

After Blutty's marriage, a pretty chamber on the first floor had been set aside and newly furnished for the newly-married pair. Athénaïs had offered it to her friend, and had gone to the room of the latter on the floor above to wait until the end of the interview.

Valentine led Bénédict to Athénaïs's room.

At about the same time, Pierre Blutty and Simonneau left the farm-house where they had passed the early evening. They followed, without speaking, a sunken road near the shore of the Indre.

"*Sacrebleu!* Pierre, you are not a man," said Simonneau at last, stopping suddenly. "One would say that you were going to commit a crime. You don't say a word ; you have been as pale and limp as a shroud all day long, and you can hardly walk straight. The deuce! do you let a woman throw you off the track this way?"

"It's not so much my love for the woman now," rejoined Pierre, in a hollow voice, "as it is my hate for the man. That thickens the blood round my heart ; and when you say that I'm going to commit a crime, I don't think you're far out of the way."

"Bah! you're joking, ain't you?" said Georges. "I went in with you just for a thrashing."

"A thrashing till death follows," rejoined the other with the utmost seriousness. "His face has driven me crazy long enough. One of us two must stand aside for the other to-night."

"The devil! it's more serious than I thought. What is it you've got there for a club? It's so dark! Do you still persist in carrying about that infernal pitchfork?"

"Perhaps!"

"But, look here, ain't we going to get into a scrape that will land us at the assizes? That wouldn't amuse me, and I with a wife and children!"

"If you're afraid, don't come!"

"I'll come, to prevent your getting into a bad scrape."

They walked on.

"Listen," said Valentine, taking from her breast a letter with a black seal; "I am utterly upset, and what I feel within me fills me with horror of myself. Read; but, if your heart is as guilty as mine, do not speak, for I am afraid that the earth will open and swallow us."

Bénédict, alarmed by her manner, opened the letter. It was from Franck, Monsieur de Lansac's valet. Monsieur de Lansac had been killed in a duel.

A wave of cruel and overpowering joy took possession of all Bénédict's faculties. He began to pace the floor in his agitation, to conceal from Valentine an emotion which she condemned, but which she herself could not escape. His efforts were fruitless. He rushed to her, fell at her feet, and embraced her in an outburst of frantic passion.

"What is the use of feigning a hypocritical solemnity?" he cried. "Can I deceive you, or God? Does not God guide our destinies? Is it not He who sets you free from the shameful chain of that marriage? Is it not He who has purged the earth of that false, unfeeling man?"

"Hush!" said Valentine, putting her hand over his mouth. "Do you want to call down the vengeance of heaven on our heads? Did we not wrong that man enough in his lifetime? Must we continue to insult him even after his death? Oh! hush! this is sacrilege. Perhaps God has permitted him to die, only to punish us and make us more wretched than ever."

"Foolish, fearful Valentine! What can happen to us now, in God's name? Aren't you free? Is not the future ours? Very good; we will not insult the dead; I agree to that. On the contrary, let us bless that man's memory for having taken it upon himself to level the barriers of rank and fortune between us. Bless him for making you the poor, deserted creature that you are!

for, if it had not been for him, I could never have aspired to you. Your wealth, your rank would have been
obstacles which my pride would not have sought to overcome. Now you belong to me; you cannot, you must
not escape me, Valentine. I am your husband; I have
a claim to you. Your conscience, your religion, order
you to take me for your staff and your avenger. Oh!
let them come and insult you in my arms, if they dare!
I shall know what my duty is; I shall not underrate the
value of the treasure entrusted to my care. I will not
leave you; I will watch over you with a loving heart!
How happy we shall be! See how kind God is! how,
after all these cruel trials, he sends us the blessings we
craved! Do you remember that one day you regretted
that you were not a farmer's daughter, that you could
not escape the slavery of a life of opulence, to live like a
simple village maiden beneath a thatched roof? Well,
now your longing is gratified. You shall be queen in
the cottage in the ravine; you shall run about among
the trees with your white goat; you shall raise your
own flowers, and sleep without fear or anxiety on a
peasant's breast. Dear Valentine! how lovely you will
be in the haymaker's straw hat! how you will be adored
and obeyed in your new home! You will have but one
servant and one slave—myself; but I alone will be more
zealous in your service than a whole liveried household.
All the hard work will be my business; you will have
no other care than to make my life beautiful and sleep
among the flowers at my side. And we shall be rich too.
I have already doubled the value of my property; I have
a thousand francs a year! And you will have almost
as much when you have sold what you have left. We
will add to our estate. Oh! it will be a magnificent
domain! We will have your dear Catherine for our fac-

totum. We will have a cow and calf, and I don't know what else. Come, cheer up; help me to make plans!"

"Alas! I am depressed beyond words," said Valentine, "but I haven't the strength to contradict your dreams. Oh! talk to me! Tell me some more about our happiness; tell me that it cannot escape us. I would like to believe in it."

"And why, in heaven's name, should you refuse to believe in it?"

"I don't know," she said, putting her hand to her breast; "I feel a weight here which suffocates me. Remorse! oh! yes, it is remorse! I have not deserved to be happy; I ought not to be. I have been very guilty; I have broken my oaths; I have forgotten God; God owes me punishment, not rewards."

"Banish these black thoughts, Valentine. Poor Valentine, why allow yourself to be tortured and distracted thus by grief? Wherein have you been so guilty? Did you not resist long enough? Am not I the only culprit? Have you not atoned for your sin by your sorrow?"

"Ah! yes, my tears ought to have washed me clean! But alas! each day buried me deeper in the abyss, and who can say that I should not have grovelled there all my life? What merit shall I have now? How shall I make good the past? Will you yourself be able to love me always? Will you have confidence in a woman who broke her past oaths?"

"But, Valentine, think of all that you had to excuse you. Think of your false and miserable position. Remember the husband who deliberately drove you to your destruction, the mother who refused to open her arms to you in time of danger, the old woman who could think of nothing better to say to you on her deathbed than these pious words: 'My dear, take a lover of your own rank.'"

"Ah ! yes, it is true," said Valentine, reflecting bitterly on the past ; "they all treated my virtue with incredible levity. I alone, whom they all accused of guilt, had a true conception of the grandeur of my duties, and I tried to make our marriage a sacred, mutual obligation. But they sneered at my simplicity ; one talked of money, another of dignity, a third of the proprieties. Ambition or pleasure was the sole incentive of all their acts, the sole meaning of all their precepts. They urged me to sin, and exhorted me only to make a show of virtue. If, instead of being a peasant's son, you had been a duke and peer, Bénédict, they would have borne me in triumph ! "

"You may be sure of it ; so do not mistake the threats of their folly and malignity for reproaches of your conscience."

When the cuckoo clock at the farm struck eleven, Bénédict and Valentine prepared to separate. He had succeeded in pacifying her, in intoxicating her with hope, in making her smile ; but, at the moment that he strained her to his heart to bid her adieu, she was seized with a strange terror.

"Suppose I should lose you ! " she said, turning pale. "We have foreseen everything except that ! Before all our dreams of happiness are realized, you may die, Bénédict ! "

"Die ! " he said, covering her face with kisses ; "as if one could die when he loves as I do ! "

She noiselessly opened the orchard door and kissed him again in the doorway.

"Do you remember," he whispered, "that it was here that you gave me your first kiss on the forehead ? "

"Until to-morrow ! " she replied.

She had hardly reached her room when a terrible, piercing shriek rang out in the orchard. It was the only sound, but it was blood-curdling, and the whole household heard it.

As he approached the farm, Pierre Blutty had seen a light in his wife's bedroom, which he did not know to be occupied by Valentine. He had distinctly seen two shadows pass across the curtain, a man's shadow and a woman's. All doubt was at an end. In vain did Simonneau try to pacify him. Despairing of success, and afraid of being involved in a criminal prosecution, he decided to go away. Blutty saw the door open, and, in the ray of light which shone through the opening, he recognized Bénédict. A woman stood beside him ; he could not see her face, because Bénédict concealed it by kissing her ; but it could be no other than Athénaïs. Thereupon the jealous wretch raised his iron pitchfork, just as Bénédict climbed the wall of loose stones at the same place which still bore the marks of his passage on the preceding night. He leaped down on the other side, and threw himself on the sharp weapon ; the two points sank deep into his breast, and he fell to the ground bathed in blood.

On that same spot, two years before, he had supported Valentine in his arms the first time that she came to the farm secretly to see her sister.

A panic-stricken clamor arose in the house at sight of the crime. Blutty rushed from the spot and placed himself at the disposal of the prosecuting attorney. He told him the story without reservation : the man was his rival ; he had been murdered in the murderer's own garden. The latter could defend his act on the plea that he had taken him for a thief. In the eyes of the law he was likely to be acquitted ; in the eyes of the magistrate, to whom he frankly admitted the passion under the influence of which he had acted and the remorse by which he was consumed, he found mercy. A trial would have resulted in a shocking scandal for the whole Lhéry family, the most numerous and most highly esteemed family in the department. Pierre Blutty was not prosecuted.

The body was taken into the living-room.

Valentine received one last smile, one word of love, one upward glance. He died on her breast.

Then she was led to her room by Lhéry, while Madame Lhéry carried away the unconscious Athénaïs.

Louise, pale and cold, and in full possession of her senses, of all her powers of suffering, was left alone with the dead body.

After an hour Lhéry joined her.

"Your sister is in a very bad way," said the terror-stricken old man. "You must go to attend to her. I will undertake the melancholy duty of remaining here."

Louise made no reply, but entered Valentine's room.

Lhéry had laid her on her bed. Her face was of a greenish pallor; her red eyes glowed like burning coals, but shed no tears. Her hands were clasped rigidly about her neck; her breath came with a sort of convulsive rattle.

Louise, also pale but apparently calm, took a candle and leaned over her sister.

When the eyes of those two women met, it was as if a ghastly sort of magnetism drew them together. Louise's face wore an expression of savage contempt, of pitiless hate; Valentine's, distorted by terror, strove in vain to avoid that awful scrutiny, that avenging apparition.

"And so," said Louise, running her hand fiercely through Valentine's dishevelled locks, as if she would have liked to tear them out, "so you have killed him!"

"Yes, it was I! I! I!" stammered Valentine, with a dazed air.

"That was sure to come," said Louise. "He would have it so; he involved himself in your destiny, and you have destroyed him! Very well, complete your work—take my life too; for my life was his, and I will not survive him! Do you know that you have dealt a twofold blow? No, you did not flatter yourself that you had done so much harm! Well, triumph! You supplanted me; you have tortured my heart all the days of your life, and now you have plunged the knife into it. It is well! You have consummated the work of your family, Valentine. It was written that I should owe all imaginable suffering to your family. You have been your mother's own daughter; yes, and your father's, who also was expert in shedding blood. It was you who drew me back to this neighborhood, which I ought never to have seen again; you who fascinated me like a basilisk, and bound me fast in order to feast upon my entrails at your ease! Ah! you have no conception how unhappy you have made me! You have succeeded beyond your expectations. You do not know how I loved him, this man who is dead! But you cast a spell on him and he could no longer see clearly. Oh! I would have made him happy! I wouldn't have tortured him as you did! I would have sacrificed empty glory and supercilious principles to him. I would not have made his life a daily torment. His noble, lovely youth would not have been blighted by my selfish caresses! I would not have condemned him to pine away consumed by disappointment and vain longings. And I would not then have lured him into a trap to betray him to a murderer. No! he would be full of life and hope to-day, if he had chosen to love me! Curse you, who prevented him from doing it!"

As she hurled these imprecations at her sister, poor Louise grew weaker and weaker, and, finally, fell in a swoon at Valentine's feet.

When she recovered consciousness, she had forgotten all that she had said. She nursed Valentine with devoted affection ; she covered her with kisses and tears. But she could not do away with the horrible impression which her involuntary avowal had produced. In the paroxysms of her fever, Valentine would throw herself into her arms and implore her forgiveness with all the ghastly terror of madness.

She died a week later. Religion afforded her some consolation in her last moments, and Louise's love smoothed that painful journey from earth to heaven.

Louise had suffered so much that her faculties, broken to the yoke of sorrow, hardened in the fire of consuming passions, had acquired supernatural strength. She survived that crushing blow, and lived for her son's sake.

Pierre Blutty never recovered from the effect of his mistake. Despite the unsusceptibility of his nature, remorse and grief devoured him secretly. He became moody, quarrelsome, irritable. Anything resembling a reproach angered him, because he inwardly reproached himself much more bitterly. He had little intercourse with his family during the year which followed his crime. Athénaïs made fruitless efforts to conceal the horror and repugnance which she felt at sight of him. Madame Lhéry hid to avoid seeing him, and Louise left the farm-house on the days when he was likely to come there. He sought consolation for his troubles in wine, and succeeded in diverting his thoughts by getting tipsy every day. One night he went out and jumped into the river which he mistook for a sandy road in the white moonlight. The peasants observed, as an instance of the justice of Heaven in meting out punishment, that his death occurred just a year after Bénédict's, day for day and hour for hour.

Several years later there were many noticeable changes in the neighborhood. Athénaïs, having come into possession of the two hundred thousand francs bequeathed to her by her godfather the iron-master, purchased the château of Raimbault and the surrounding estates. Monsieur Lhéry, spurred on by his wife to that display of vanity, sold his property, or rather exchanged it—at a loss, the malicious gossips said—for the remaining estates of the former domain of Raimbault. So the worthy farmer-folk were installed in the splendid abode of their former lords, and the young widow was able to gratify those luxurious tastes which she had been taught in her childhood.

XXXIX

Louise, who had returned to Paris to complete her son's education, was urged to come and settle down near her faithful friend. Valentin had received his degree in medicine. They urged him to settle in the province, where Monsieur Faure, who was getting too old to practise, would gladly turn over his patients to him.

So Louise and her son returned, and received a most sincere and affectionate welcome at the hands of that excellent family. During their long absence, young Valentin had became a man. His beauty, his learning, his modesty, his many noble qualities, won for him the esteem and affection of those who were most uncompro-

mising on the subject of birth. However, he was law-
fully entitled to bear the name of Raimbault. Madame
Lhéry did not forget it, and said to her husband, under
her breath, that it was worth but little to be a land-
owner if one were not a noble; which signified, in other
words, that their daughter lacked nothing except the
name and title of their former masters. Monsieur Lhéry
considered the young physician very young.

"What of that?" said Mère Lhéry; "our Athénaïs
is very young too. Aren't you and I the same age?
Have we been any the less happy for that?"

Père Lhéry was more practical than his wife. He said
that *money attracts money;* that his daughter was a good
enough match to aspire not only to a noble, but to a rich
land-owner. But he had to surrender, for Madame
Blutty's former inclination reawoke with fresh intensity
when she found her young schoolboy so tall and so accomplished. Louise hesitated; Valentin, torn between
love and pride, allowed himself to be convinced by the
fair widow's burning glances. Athénaïs became his
wife.

She could not resist the longing to be announced in
the aristocratic salons of the neighborhood by the title of
Comtesse de Raimbault. The neighbors turned up their
noses, some in contempt, others from envy. The real
Comtesse de Raimbault brought suit against her for her
presumption; but she died, and no one else thought of
making trouble. Athénaïs was a good soul, and she was
happy. Her husband, who was blessed with Valentine's
excellent disposition and good judgment, easily con-
trolled her, and corrected many of her failings by gentle
means. Those which she still retains add to her charm,
and make her as popular as estimable qualities would do,
for she acknowledges them so frankly.

The Lhéry family is laughed at in the neighborhood for its vanities and its absurdities ; but no poor man is turned away from the door of the château ; no neighbor seeks a favor there in vain ; the mockery is born of jealousy rather than of pity. If some one of Lhéry's old companions happens to indulge in some labored witticism touching the change in his fortunes, the old man finds consolation in the fact that the slightest advance on his part is welcomed with pride and gratitude.

Louise has found rest with her new family from the fatigues of her sad career. The age of passion has vanished behind her ; her daily thoughts are tinged with religious melancholy. Her greatest delight is to superintend the education of her fair-haired little granddaughter, who perpetuates the beloved name of Valentine, and who constantly reminds her very youthful grandmother of that cherished sister's early years. The traveller, as he passes the village cemetery, frequently sees the lovely child playing at Louise's feet, and plucking the cowslips that grow on the double grave of Valentine and Bénédict.